UNSCRIPTED

The Woodstone Falls Series
Book 3

ANNA JERR

Content Warnings

While this story is a work of fiction, it addresses some heavy subject matters that you should be aware of before diving in. Some material in this novel may not be suitable for all.

You can find a list of trigger warnings after the acknowledgements section. These are not meant to be spoilers, but rather a precaution in case you find certain content upsetting.

Please skip this page if you do not wish to see these warnings.

Unscripted Playlist

Teenager in Love - Madison Beer
Cop Car - Sam Hunt
Wildest Dreams - Taylor Swift
Ocean Eyes - Billie Eilish
Angels Like You - Miley Cyrus
King Of My Heart - Taylor Swift
Constellations - Jade LeMac
2 hands - Tate McRae
SOMEONE TO YOU - Matt Hansen
One Last Time - Ariana Grande
Getaway Car - Taylor Swift
Make You Miss Me - Sam Hunt
So High School - Taylor Swift
Hallelujah - Pentatonix
Strawberry Wine - Noah Kahan
Sue Me - Sabrina Carpenter
The Only Exception - Paramore
Dusk Till Dawn (feat. Sia) - ZAYN, Sia
Better Me For You (Brown Eyes) - Max McNown
From Eden - Hozier
Before You Leave Me - Alex Warren
Waves - Dean Lewis
End Game - Taylor Swift

Prologue

THE WOODSTONE FALLS TRIBUNE

FOUR-YEAR-OLD BOY AND FATHER DEAD IN TRAGIC HOUSEHOLD ACCIDENT

A DEVASTATING ACCIDENT ON MAPLEWOOD LANE NEAR SHADOW RIDGE ON MONDAY NIGHT CLAIMED THE LIVES OF A FOUR-YEAR-OLD BOY AND HIS FATHER.

POLICE RESPONDED SHORTLY BEFORE MIDNIGHT AFTER RECEIVING A 911 CALL REPORTING AN EMERGENCY AT THE HUTCHINSON RESIDENCE. UPON ARRIVAL, OFFICERS FOUND THIRTY-TWO-YEAR-OLD PATRICK HUTCHINSON, SON OF CONGRESSMAN DAVID HUTCHINSON, SUFFERING FROM A GUNSHOT WOUND. DESPITE EFFORTS TO SAVE HIM, HUTCHINSON WAS PRONOUNCED DEAD AT THE SCENE. THE BOY WAS RUSHED TO A NEARBY HOSPITAL BUT LATER SUCCUMBED TO HIS INJURIES.

PRELIMINARY INVESTIGATIONS SUGGEST THE FOUR-YEAR-OLD MAY HAVE ACCIDENTALLY DISCHARGED A

FIREARM INSIDE THE HOME, RESULTING IN THE TRAGIC DEATHS.

POLICE CHIEF ROGERS EXPRESSED HIS CONDOLENCES TUESDAY MORNING. "THIS HEARTBREAKING TRAGEDY IS DEEPLY FELT BY OUR COMMUNITY. OUR DEPARTMENT IS CONDUCTING AN INVESTIGATION, BUT AT THIS TIME, ALL SIGNS POINT TO THIS BEING A TRAGIC ACCIDENT."

NEIGHBORS REMEMBER HUTCHINSON AS A DEVOTED FATHER. THE COMMUNITY IS MOURNING THE LOSS, AND A CANDLELIGHT VIGIL IS SCHEDULED FOR THURSDAY EVENING TO HONOR THEM.

ONE

Sawyer

WHEN I WOKE UP THIS MORNING, I THOUGHT THE PLAN WAS simple: check out a house I might move into after the season, politely nod at some crown molding, and catch a flight tonight for tomorrow's game.

What I didn't expect? Maybe for the body camera footage of me kissing Ellie Miles to be blowing up my phone while I stood in a musty living room.

Yeah. *That* Ellie Miles, the pop star with more number one hits than I could count, who got caught in some absolute shit show when a psycho decided to take her and my brother hostage. And somehow, I was the idiot who thought kissing her would help save them.

I'd had a pathetic crush on her for years. Nothing serious—background noise in my brain, really. I was sure she didn't even know I existed, let alone know my name, so kissing her? Yeah, not exactly how I pictured making a first impression.

But there I was, watching as the video played on a loop, trailing behind my realtor, Suzanne. She was seventy-something with pure white hair, sweet as hell, and probably guarding a banana pudding recipe so good, it could bring world peace. Around us, the place smelled like mothballs, the wallpaper barely hanging on, the bathroom a shrine to mint-green tile horror—but all I could focus on was Ellie on that damn screen.

In the footage, I guided her behind me and stepped forward like some half assed bodyguard.

And then, I kissed her. I still don't know if it was tactical genius or pure idiocy. All I know is, it worked. The guy froze, caught off guard, and they finally got him.

In my head, it had been this desperate move—kiss the girl, distract the serial killer, save my brother. But on camera? She'd gone completely still for a heartbeat, and then her hands had fisted in my shirt. When her eyes fluttered shut, it wasn't the look of someone just playing along.

Was she just following my lead to sell the distraction? Or had she kissed me back? Like—*really* kissed me back?

I couldn't decide. So, what did I do? I watched it again. And again. And a-fucking-gain.

"Mr. James?"

I jerked my head up and dropped my phone to my side.

Suzanne stood in the living room, looking at me like I'd lost my damn mind. "What do you think of the fireplace? Beautiful, right?"

"Sorry." I stuffed my phone in my pocket and stepped farther inside. "Yeah. It's…great."

And it was. It wasn't shiny or new; it was worn-in, real, as if it had seen a hell of a lot and wasn't about to pretend otherwise. There was dust thick enough to write my name in it, but underneath all that, this place had character and a hell of a lot of charm.

I wasn't exactly looking for a fixer-upper, but if I found

one, I could call in the Dotty cavalry. My sister would eat this kind of project for breakfast—lining up contractors, micromanaging tile samples while I finished out the season. Easy enough.

I took a few more steps, and a loose floorboard shifted under my boot with a loud clack. "What the hell?"

"Old house." Suzanne shrugged. "Needs a little work."

No kidding.

I crouched, tugging at the board. It creaked as it moved, revealing a hollow pocket beneath. When I peered in, something caught my eye—a small, worn, leather-bound book. I pulled it out and brushed off the dust. It had no title, just a single letter pressed into the cover.

L.

I flipped it open, just a page or two. The handwriting was tight, fast, and something about it hit me low in the gut.

"L?" I asked. "Any idea who that is?"

Suzanne leaned in a bit. "Could've been someone who lived here."

I nodded but didn't ask anything else. I just closed the book quickly and tucked it right back where I found it, pressing the board back into place.

No bad juju for me.

This house had history—not the kind you read in the listings, but the kind whispered about in town for years, the exact reason it sat empty for so long.

Somehow, that didn't scare me. If anything, it made me feel...protective. This place didn't need to be gutted and flipped. It deserved someone to love it.

I stood slowly, glancing around. The carpet was hideous. The windows needed replacing. Overall, it was a mess.

But still, it felt like mine.

"I'll take it," I said before my brain had a chance to catch up.

Suzanne blinked. "I'm sorry?"

"I'll take it. Don't need to see any others."

She stared at me a beat too long, probably doing commission math in her head. "Well, alright. We can head back to the office and start the paperwork."

My phone vibrated in my pocket, and I opened it to find dozens of texts, alerts, mentions, and ESPN notifications flooding my screen. Here it was, early December, and instead of talking about who was fighting for a playoff spot, everyone was replaying a damn GIF of me kissing Ellie.

Just like that, I was back in it: the adrenaline, the chaos, and the damn consequences of my own actions.

I was going to need a drink—a strong one.

Probably a call to my agent.

And definitely a plan.

"What the hell are we supposed to do about this?" Coach groaned, dragging a hand through his salt-and-pepper hair as he stared at the flat screen behind the desk in his office.

I shifted in my seat. "I mean…at least I look like the good guy, right?"

He narrowed his eyes. "Yeah, well, the good guy just kissed Ellie Miles on body cam footage that's been picked up by every major media outlet in the country." He dropped into his chair with a sigh.

"Sorry, Coach."

He rubbed his temples and muttered something under his breath. We both turned back to the screen.

"Yeah, I don't know if I can fix it, but I'm damn sure gonna try."

"That's the dumbest fucking line I've ever heard," Coach said flatly.

"Hey, you try coming up with something better when there's a crazy serial killer with a gun. It wasn't a real kiss. It was just a distraction."

"Real or not, the world thinks that—" he pointed to the screen where Ellie and I were still very much kissing— "is real, and coming off her breakup with that shitty actor? The headlines are already insane. The story still ends with you tangled up with a serial killer and making out with a pop star mid-standoff. This is the NFL, James. We want clean storylines. No drama."

"Technically, I didn't even know the guy."

"I don't care," he snapped. "Right now, the media's making you look good. Keep it that way. Don't let this swing the other direction. I heard she'll be at the game tonight. Use that."

Coach was right. Over the last twenty-four hours, I'd scrolled through every post, comment, and headline. They all said the same thing—that I was brave. As if I'd done something heroic and hadn't reacted on impulse, unsure of what the hell I was doing.

I didn't feel brave. In that moment, all I'd felt was fear. Well, and something else I didn't want to name.

A knock came at the door.

"Come in," Coach said.

West stuck his head in. "We've got twenty, James."

Coach nodded. "You know what to do."

"Yes, sir." I shut the door behind me

West's brow furrowed. "What the hell was that about?"

West was one of the few people I considered a real friend. I got along with almost everyone, but when it came to close friends, I kept my circle tight. Funny enough, he actually grew up in Shadow Ridge—just outside Wood-stone—and was a few years older than me. We never crossed paths until we ended up on the San Francisco Rebels together.

"I might've gotten myself into a little…pickle," I said.

"A pickle? What the fuck does that mean?"

"You remember what happened a couple of months ago?" I asked. "When my brother's girlfriend's ex tried to kidnap him and Ellie Miles?"

He tugged at his shoulder pads as his brown hair fell messily over his forehead with that same arrogant grin he always had. "Kind of hard to forget."

"Well…during all of that, I kind of…kissed Ellie?" I winced. "As a distraction, and now, the body cam footage is out for everyone and anyone's viewing pleasure."

He blinked. "Hold up. You kissed Ellie Miles?"

"Uh…" I scratched the back of my neck. "Yeah. I did."

"Holy shit, dude. Nice. She's hot."

I punched him in the shoulder. "Don't talk about her like that."

"Oh, big SJ kissed his crush, huh?"

"Shut the fuck up."

I didn't know what it was. Her voice, her goddamn eyes, her kindness to the world. Whatever it was, it had me in a chokehold for years.

"So, the world's shipping you two now…or did she slap you after?" He pulled out his phone. "Wait, don't tell me. I wanna see for myself. How have I not heard about this until now?"

I snatched the phone from his hand, but he quickly stole it back.

"She's gonna be here tonight," I said.

"Oh, hell yeah. You should blow her a kiss or something. Really get 'em going. You know how many fans we'll pull if you get the Ellie Miles crowd behind us? Those fans go hard. I wouldn't mind seeing a few of them in the stands." He winked.

"You're an asshole."

"Hey, at least I'm not going around kissing pop stars for funsies."

I glanced down to see his phone playing *that* moment.

Great.

"It was to save—you know what? Never mind. Let's just get out there and play a good game."

West grinned and gave me a fake salute. "Yes, sir."

The crowd roared to life—shouts, stomps, something that might've been a kazoo as West called out the count, but none of it was louder than my heartbeat pounding in my ears.

It was always like this. Not nerves, exactly. More like adrenaline coursing through my veins at the chance to play the game I loved for a living.

We were up by seven points with only a few minutes left and possession of the ball. Things were looking good, but I never wanted to get too comfortable.

I chanted the same mantra I'd carried in my head for two decades.

Show up. Play hard. Don't screw it up.

My job was simple: protect West and give him the time to work his magic. And I was damn good at it.

"Set—hike!"

I exploded forward, slamming into the opposing team's defensive end with a solid blow to his chest. My hands locked in place, and I pushed him back with every bit of strength I could—which was quite a lot, considering my size.

Everything about the play was standard. Same formation. Same footwork. Same muscle memory firing in rhythm. I had the guy locked up—hands solid on his chest, knees bent, weight balanced perfectly over the balls of my feet.

But then suddenly, a helmet slammed straight into my side.

Motherfucker.

My breath vanished. One second, I was upright; the next, I was falling straight down. My helmet hit the turf with a thud that rattled through my spine.

Voices rose around me—whistles and someone yelling my name—but it was like I was hearing everything from yards away. The world tilted sideways, and darkness crept in at the edges of my vision. I tried to move, just enough to prove I was fine, but my body refused to cooperate. My head felt nailed to the turf.

My thoughts tumbled and scattered. No order, no sense, just broken pieces drifting too far out of reach for me to comprehend.

I didn't know how long I stayed down—flat on my back, drifting in and out—when someone knelt next to me.

"Stay down. We've got you." The words came from a trainer's voice, one I recognized.

Everything in me wanted to get up, shake it off, and get back in the damn game.

But I knew I couldn't.

The next few minutes were a blur of medics swarming and assessing me. I think the crowd cheered when I finally made it to my feet, a man braced on each side, helping me to the sidelines.

When I looked up at the big screen, it was showing

Ellie in one of the suites. Her hands were pressed over her mouth, her eyes wide.

God, she was fucking beautiful, even with her expression all adorably scared. She was a dream in a sea of jerseys and stadium lights.

I couldn't leave her looking like that, worrying about little ol' me.

So, I summoned whatever scraps of bravado I had left and did exactly what West said to.

I blew her a kiss.

Followed it with a wink that probably looked a little more like a twitch, considering I could still barely stand with the pounding in my head.

The crowd lost it, cheering as if I'd scored the winning touchdown instead of getting my ass knocked into next week.

TWO

Ellie

THE STADIUM WAS LOUD, THE KIND OF LOUD THAT RATTLED your hands and made your ears feel like they were vibrating. But inside my head?

Silence.

Everything had gone weirdly quiet. My brain hit pause while the rest of the world kept blaring. Rachel was saying something beside me, but nothing registered.

My eyes stayed locked on the Jumbotron.

There he was: Sawyer James. A six-foot-something wrecking ball with a grin that could melt the coldest of hearts, and he'd just blown me a kiss. Not just any kiss—a smirky, smug, too-charming-for-his-own-good kiss. To me. On national television. After getting knocked senseless.

Rachel's voice finally broke through the static in my head as the screen shifted back to the game highlights. "Was that what I think it was?"

I didn't answer, mostly because I didn't trust my voice not to come out as a squeak. I could practically feel the dozen cameras zooming in on my face, so I pasted on my brightest smile, even though internally, I was definitely having a full deer-in-headlights moment.

"That's right, folks!" the commentator said. "Sawyer James, offensive lineman for the San Francisco Rebels, just blew Ellie Miles a kiss from the field!"

Rachel smirked and pushed her auburn hair over her shoulder. "Okay, so that definitely *was* what I thought."

I pressed two fingers to my temple and sat down. "I'm hallucinating, right? That was just some sort of weird, mass hallucination."

"Nope. Very real and *very* viral."

"Oh, God." I dropped my head into my hands. "This is going to be everywhere."

"Most definitely." She sat down and kicked her boots up like we were at a sleepover instead of a professional football game. "But it's not all bad."

"I got kissed during an armed standoff," I said slowly, because I still couldn't quite believe it. "And now, he's blowing kisses on the jumbotron."

Rachel shrugged. "Well, if you ask me, that's some pretty impressive dedication on his part."

"You're impossible."

"I'm strategic." She pulled out her phone and started typing—classic Rachel, unable to turn off publicist mode for even one day.

"Wait." I narrowed my eyes. "Was your whole '*come on, El. Let's go to the game. You need a break before your tour picks back up,*' just code for '*I'm trying to set you up with Sawyer James?*'"

She gave me a guilty little smile and lifted a finger. "Okay, hear me out."

"I'm scared."

"We let the narrative run. We steer it. Ellie Miles, America's pop princess, finally moves on from emotionally constipated C-list actor Harold Douche-Face with a hot NFL player who may or may not secretly be a cinnamon roll. Boom." She paused, then waved her hands in a dramatic rainbow arc. "Media gold."

"You already pitched this to my agent, didn't you?"

"After the footage dropped, we may have exchanged a few texts. I was waiting to talk to you after the game, but now seems like as good of time as any."

"I haven't even talked to Sawyer since that night."

"Like I said, now seems like as good a time as any."

"The last time I talked to him, I was bleeding and in shock, and he was..." I waved my arms around. "I don't even know. Very large. Very protective. Very...unhelpfully charming."

"And now, he's your new PR opportunity."

"I can't date someone just because he saved me and looks great in tight pants."

"But you *can* pretend to date him. I mean, you already kissed him."

"He kissed me as a distraction!"

She pointed at me. "But you kissed him back."

I fought off a smile. "That doesn't mean anything."

"Doesn't it, though?" She tilted her head. "Have you seen the video? I mean, the sparks were undeniable."

"There were no sparks," I falsely denied.

"There were definitely sparks."

"There were trauma-induced coping mechanisms while I was shot!"

She shrugged. "Tomato, tomato. Come on, be honest with me. Didn't you feel something?" She pinched her fingers together and squinted. "Even for a teeny tiny little second?"

I opened my mouth and then closed it. That kiss came out of nowhere in the middle of pure chaos, and it had been electric in the worst possible way, the kind of moment that flips your stomach and hijacks your brain.

Still, every time I closed my eyes, I could feel the press of his mouth against mine. The taste of it, the shock of it, all in a moment. I hadn't known how to process then and still didn't now.

"This is crazy," I muttered instead. "The footage. The kiss. The press. And now this?" I gestured toward the field. "He fucking winked at me!"

"It was a really good wink."

"But I don't want good winks from ridiculously handsome men right now." Still, I couldn't help the smile tugging at my lips. "Even if they are really, really good winks."

After everything with my ex, Harold, I was finally starting to feel like myself again. This was supposed to be my fresh start, time to focus on me, show my parents everything they'd given up for me was worth it, not accidentally stumble into some ridiculous fake romance story with a football player.

"Or," Rachel said, her amber eyes bright, "we lean into it."

"I don't want my life to be a stunt."

"Girl, it's too late for that. You're famous."

I slumped against the seat and let out a long sigh. "Yeah, but I didn't exactly want to be this kind of famous."

"No one does. It just happens. The only choice you get is what you do with it."

She was right. Ugh, I hated that she was right. Dating a football player would actually solve the headline problem —no more speculation about me crawling back to Harold or whoever else I could possibly be dating next. Maybe there was a bright side to this mess after all. I didn't love the idea of playing the game, but at this point, I wasn't sure I had a better alternative.

I stared at the big screen, now replaying the body cam footage of him stepping in front of me and then the kiss that lasted a little too long.

"He's not my type," I said, attempting to deflect.

"Really? Because six-and-a-half feet of golden retriever energy, ridiculous muscles, and a too-perfect smile sounds suspiciously like your type."

And once again, she wasn't wrong. He was stupidly, distractingly handsome. That rough-edged, pretty-boy charm worked in ways it shouldn't, from the strong jaw and trimmed beard to those sparkling eyes that always seemed like they were in on the joke.

That smile, the goofy way he didn't even seem to know he was that pretty? It was enough to send my brain into hyperdrive.

But that was entirely beside the point.

"He has a huge family," I muttered.

Rachel paused. "What?"

"I think he has a lot of siblings, and they're all...close. Like aggressively supportive."

Rachel tilted her head. "What does that have to do with anything?"

"Families like that make me nervous." I crossed my arms. "I don't know how to be around so many people at once."

She gave me a look. "Ellie, your parents are the most wholesome humans I've ever met, and you're around thousands of people when you perform."

"Yeah, but that's different," I said.

"You're projecting."

"Obviously."

"Well, while you sort that out, I'm doing my job and

setting you up with the NFL's hottest distraction." Rachel was already in work mode, her thumbs flying across the screen like a woman possessed. She gave me a cheeky smile. "Texted his agent. I'll let you know when we hear back. Love you," she sing-songed.

"Am I going to regret this?" I muttered.

She smiled without looking up. "Only if you fall in love with him."

I tossed a napkin at her, and she caught it one-handed like a smug little ninja.

I leaned forward, elbows on my knees, eyes on the tunnel where Sawyer had disappeared.

What was he thinking? Was he thinking at all? Maybe it really was slightly unhinged football player logic that said, *Hey, national television seems like a great place to flirt.*

For all I knew, this could implode any second or fade out in a week, dropping me right back into the status quo. But with the whole world watching, it didn't matter how it played out. Either way, they weren't letting it go.

THREE

Sawyer

THE TEAM DOCTOR RAISED AN EYEBROW, CLIPBOARD IN HAND. "Just a concussion. How many have you had?"

"Not a number you want to hear." I forced a smile.

He nodded. "You need to rest for the next couple of weeks. Let your brain heal."

This could've been worse, but not by much. I didn't need a season-ending injury to knock me sideways. This was already damn close. When your job depended on you being fast and game-ready, being benched was hell, especially when the one thing people loved you for was what you did under the lights, not who you were off the field.

I'd already made peace with this year. One last season, one last run before I hung up my helmet for good. Mid-thirties in the league? That's borderline ancient. Every morning reminded me of it—stiff knees, a back that creaked with every movement, and bruises that lingered longer than they used to. I wasn't bitter about it, not really. I had to let go of the game sooner or later, but damn if I didn't want to finish strong on the field, not watching from the sidelines.

"When can I get back in the game?" I asked, my voice rougher than intended.

The doctor didn't hesitate. "We'll reassess in two weeks. For now, no screens, no workouts. Just rest. Ice, over-the-counter meds, and plenty of sleep. Let your body catch up to everything it's been through."

I nodded slowly, my mind racing. "Yes, sir."

He clapped me on the shoulder and gave me a knowing look. "You've earned a little rest, James. Take it."

"Thanks, Doc."

He stepped toward the door, and just as he grabbed the handle, it swung open. West and Bronx strolled in, still in their uniforms and sweaty from the game.

"How are you holding up?" Bronx asked, dropping into the chair beside the bed. His brown eyes were tired, but his grin was wide.

"Out for two weeks," I muttered, running my hand over my face and rubbing the back of my neck.

"Shit," West muttered under his breath, flopping into the chair across from me. "Right when the season's getting real good."

"Tell me about it." I exhaled, leaning back against the wall. My body sagged with the weight of it all.

My phone buzzed in my pocket, pulling me out of my spiral. Unknown number. I squinted at it, raising an eyebrow.

"Spam?" Bronx asked, running a hand through his dark hair.

"Probably." I was about to ignore it when West's eyes lit up with a mischievous spark.

"Let me answer it. I live for messing with telemarketers. Bronx, pull up that fake car crash sound for me, will ya?"

"I'm not doing that," Bronx muttered.

I handed the phone over, figuring he'd get a kick out of it.

"Mr. Sawyer James' phone," West said, his voice dripping with mock professionalism. "How may I direct your call?"

He paused, and I heard a faint rustling on the other end.

West's smirk vanished, and he covered the phone's mic. "I think you'll wanna take this."

"Why?" I asked.

"Uh…so, I think…Ellie is calling you?"

I shot upright, which was a bad fucking idea. The whole damn room spun sideways, and I grabbed the edge of the wall before I tipped right over.

"Easy, man," Bronx said, steadying me with a hand.

"Ellie who?" I mumbled, still half-stuck in a haze.

West gave me a look like I'd asked him to solve a calculus problem. "Ellie Miles, dumbass."

He held out my phone to me.

My stomach went haywire—dropped, maybe. Or twisted. Or both. I didn't even know.

Why was she calling? The body cam? The kiss I stupidly blew her?

Again, I didn't know.

West kept holding the phone out, wide-eyed, as if it was going to explode. I wiped my sweaty palms on my pants and grabbed it. I cleared my throat. Twice.

"This is Sawyer," I said, aiming for casual. It wasn't casual. My voice cracked halfway through like I was thirteen again.

"Hi, Sawyer. It's…um…it's Ellie."

Bronx and West both froze, watching me like I was about to pull a bunny out of a fucking hat. My pulse hammered so hard, I could barely think straight.

"Hey, Ellie." I swallowed. "How's it going?"

"I'm good, but I think the more important question is… how are you? You took one hell of a hit tonight."

There it was—that familiar tug in her voice. The same one that got me every time I heard her voice, except now, it was aimed at me.

I ran a hand over my face. "Eh, I'm good. Concussion. Have to take a couple of weeks off, but I'll live."

"Well, you sure didn't go unnoticed." An adorable little laugh slipped through.

My stomach flipped again. Fuck.

"I'm guessing you saw the body cam footage too, then."

"Oh, I saw it," she said, definitely laughing now.

Double fuck.

"Yeah…about that." I scrubbed a hand over the back of my neck, heat crawling up my ears. "That wasn't exactly planned. It just…happened. I had no idea they were going to release it to the public. Then I panicked and blew you a kiss tonight to top it all off."

"Panicked, huh?"

I knew she didn't buy it for a second.

I had no clue what to do with the way she said that. So, I laughed, all stupidly rough and awkward like a dumbass. "Guess I owe you an apology."

"Mmm, I think you get a pass this time. But actually… that's not why I called."

"Oh?"

"I wanted to ask if you'd maybe want to grab coffee sometime."

A full-body flush hit me almost as hard as the damn hit did. My heart straight-up stalled.

She asked me out. Ellie Miles just asked me out. I had no words. None.

I'd been in this league for more than ten years. I'd handled press, playoff pressure, and stadiums packed with screaming fans. Nothing, and I mean nothing, could have prepared me for this.

"Yeah, I'd like that," I said, somehow sounding halfway normal. "I have to lay low for a few days, but…next week?"

"Next week works," she said, sounding relieved. "I'll text you some times that work. We'll figure it out once you're feeling better."

"Sounds good." My mouth was weirdly dry.

"Okay. I'll text you then." She paused. "Feel better, Sawyer."

"Thanks."

The call ended, and I lowered the phone, staring at the screen as if it might crack right there in my hand.

Holy. Shit.

Is this the concussion talking? Am I dreaming?

How the hell was I supposed to have a normal conversation with a woman I'd been lowkey obsessed with for years? What was I supposed to say?

Hey Ellie, did you know I can recite every lyric to 'Pretty When You Lied,' and I listen to 'The Window Stays Open' on repeat when I can't sleep?

Yeah. I'm fucked.

West waved a hand in front of my face. "Dude. You still breathing?"

I snapped back into reality. "Huh?"

"What the hell just happened?" Bronx asked.

I shook my head, trying to make sense of everything. "Ellie Miles…just asked me out?"

"Dude," West said. "You said yes, right?"

"Bro, he literally said yes while you were standing there," Bronx said.

"Oh, right. Damn, I need to sit down." West dropped into a chair like he was the one who got a concussion.

"I—yeah," I muttered. "I said yes."

"Shit, man."

Yeah. I was in trouble.

Big, big trouble.

FOUR

Ellie

"SEE? THAT WASN'T SO BAD," RACHEL CHIRPED, BUMPING MY shoulder as we stepped into the stadium hallway. She was grinning like she hadn't just made me call a man I barely knew and ask him out.

"Someone answered the phone and asked to direct the call." I slipped my phone back into my pocket as we started walking toward the elevator.

"Okay, so…maybe a little bad."

I shook my head. "I panicked and almost hung up. For a solid three seconds, I think I forgot my own name." I glanced at her, and the familiar sting of embarrassment crawled up my neck. "I should've just texted. I was a mess."

"You actually sounded pretty chill," Rachel said, clearly amused. "Give yourself a break. You're a normal human living on this silly floating rock."

I hummed in response.

"Coffee might not be the worst idea for a first date, but coffee with your security team? That sounds…fun."

"Shit." I bit the inside of my cheek. "I just

thought...normal people go for coffee, right? It's casual. Not date level. Just caffeine-level."

After what happened that night of the body camera footage, we hadn't just updated venue security—we were rebuilding my entire team. I had new personnel, stricter protocols, and every show was planned down to the minute. My new head of security was set to start right before my first show.

Rachel laughed, nudging me. "You do realize the idea is to actually go on a date with him, right?"

"Yeah..."

The elevator opened, and we stepped inside, my temporary security team flanking us. Their eyes scanned every corner like it was second nature until the doors slid shut.

She raised an eyebrow. "So, are you planning to drink your feelings through the entire fake dating experience?"

"That depends. Do they make extra-sweet lattes in IV drip form?"

She snorted. "You're so dramatic."

I gave her a look. "You're the one orchestrating a pretend relationship between me and a man I kissed while bleeding from a gunshot wound."

"I'm not saying it's traditional." She lifted her chin. "I'm just saying it's got potential."

I watched the floor numbers tick down inside the elevator and pulled out my phone to see that Sawyer blowing me a kiss was already all over the internet. I let out a deep breath.

"What's with that look?" Rachel asked.

I kept my eyes on the screen. "It's just...the second anything looks like a story, I stop being a person. All anyone cares about is the next tour or who I might be dating." The words tumbled out before I could stop them.

"That's not true."

I looked up at her and shook my head. "No one's rooting for me, Rach. They're only rooting for the version of me that makes a good headline."

She nudged me with her elbow. "I'm always rooting for you, no matter what."

I let out a dry laugh. "That's your pep talk?"

"Hey, I'm working with what I've got."

The elevator dinged, opening onto a quieter hallway—a VIP exit that kept us away from prying eyes and flashing cameras, for which I was very thankful, especially tonight. My boots echoed on the concrete as we walked, and my security team was a few paces ahead, clearing the way.

"You ready for the tour to start back up again?" Rachel asked.

"Yup," I answered a little too quickly, earning a narrowed look from her.

"You don't have to go full speed the second the curtain lifts. No meet-and-greets, no spontaneous dance numbers, no crowd dives. And we'll figure out the whole football player thing as we go."

"I've never once crowd dived."

"If anyone could get carried off by a group of emotionally unhinged fans, it's you. Your fans love you."

I managed a small smile. "Yeah. That used to feel like the best part."

Rachel tilted her head. "Used to?"

"I used to love the screaming fans, the crowds, the way a new city always felt like a fresh start." I sighed. "Now, I'm just not sure what I want anymore."

I could hit the high notes, charm my way through interviews, go through all the motions—but the pop star the world knew me as felt like a stranger now.

"Do you want to take a longer break?" Rachel asked.

"No. If I walk away now…it would feel like it was all for nothing."

"None of this was for nothing. You don't have to have all the answers right now. If you need some more time, just say the word."

I gave her a weak smile. "Thanks."

"I'm proud of you, you know."

"For being physically able to sit upright and make a phone call asking a stranger out?"

"For trying. Even when it's terrifying. *Especially* when it's terrifying."

FIVE

Sawyer

It'd been a week since I got clocked, and I was doing everything possible to keep my brain from turning to mush.

Five books down. Three audiobooks. Enough podcasts to make a grown man dizzy, and I may or may not have binged Ellie's latest album a few times in my weaker moments.

Okay, probably more than a few.

When you're stuck cooped up in a condo with nothing to do except stare at the same damn four walls, you start to go a little crazy. And doctor's orders? Lie low. No screens. Blue light's the enemy or some shit.

Except lying low had gotten real fucking old real fast. Thank fuck I only had one more week until I'd be back to full clearance.

West and Bronx had come by to keep me company here and there, but they both had their own lives, and I didn't want them to feel like they had to entertain me every moment of the day. I had thought about heading home to

Woodstone Falls to recover, but traveling with a concussion? Not an option, apparently.

Until today, when I got the green light.

As much as I tried to keep myself distracted, my brain kept circling back to Ellie. I tried to shove the whole *Ellie Miles is drop-dead gorgeous and the exact kind of person who could ruin a man* thing into a locked drawer labeled: *danger, do not open.*

The damn box popped open anyway.

Usually, when something got too heavy, I'd reroute. Make a joke. Play it easy and keep it light. That was what I'd always done, especially after my mom died. I did back then what a lot of kids did when life stopped making sense —I leaned into the laughter. Doubled down on it, really.

I'd always been the family goofball. I was the one pulling faces in photos, pranking my siblings, and cracking jokes when things got too quiet. After my mom died, that role became a lifeline. If I could make people laugh, maybe it would ease the weight of everything. Maybe it would help them forget how heavy life felt, if just for a little while.

With my older brother, Colt, locked into his default setting of grump, and the twins, Dotty and Dorian, copying him as if it were a competitive sport, someone had to carry the lightness and be the ridiculous one. That became me.

I carried that same survival tactic into dating, never getting too close. Close meant vulnerable. It meant letting someone see behind the jokes.

That's why my years-long crush on Ellie felt oddly safe. She was so far out of my league that it never occurred to me she would be interested, let alone call and ask me out for coffee. But now that she had, I was afraid I wouldn't be able to pull back. Or worse—I wouldn't want to.

I didn't even know the girl. What kind of coffee did she like? Did she take it black? Or was she one of those tea people? Maybe she liked it extra sweet, just like her.

I told her to give me a few days to recover before I was ready to get out of the house, but a week had passed, and nothing.

Maybe she forgot or changed her mind. Hell, maybe I should text her. I wasn't even sure what the hell to say.

Before I could stop myself, my fingers were typing.

ME

So, do you like your coffee sweet, or are you more of a black coffee and nothing else kind of person? Or are you a tea girl?

ELLIE

Um, hi Sawyer, lol. I'm a sweet coffee person. You couldn't pay me to drink black coffee. What about you? 😊

I start typing…
Same. Fill me with sugar and cream.
Yeah, I backspaced that real fast.

Same. Gimme all the cream and sugar.

Sorry, I haven't texted you. I've been so busy prepping to go back on tour soon.

How's the concussion recovery going?

It's all good. A little boring. I'm on the mend. I'm taking it easy, but I'm ready to get back on the field.

I'm glad you're doing better. When are you free for coffee?

Right now?

Like… right now? It's ten at night…

No, I'm joking. I mean, yes, I could. I literally have no plans, so whenever you're free really.

How about tomorrow? 11? You still in San Francisco, right?

Yeah. 11 works ☺

She hearted my message, but I wasn't done, so I sent another text.

What's one thing you can't live without?

Lol. Well, probably music. I'm sure that's an obvious answer, but it's true. I can't go a day without it. I swear, sometimes it's the only thing that keeps me sane. You?

Would it be lame if I said football?

Not at all.

Well, no, it's not actually football. I think I'm gonna hang up my helmet after this year. Really, the only thing I couldn't live without is my family. I would be lost without them.

That sounds nice.

What are you doing right now?

Not much. I've been chilling on the couch trying to decide if I want to read or watch tv. You?

Can I call you?

She didn't respond.

She just called.

Holy shit. Holy shit. She's calling me. Oh fuck, what do I do? What do I say? Fuck, it keeps ringing. I need to answer. Deep breath. Okay, okay. I got this.

"Hey," I answered, trying to act casual.

"What's up? You okay?"

"Yeah, yeah. I just… I would rather talk to you than text." I ran a hand through my hair.

"Oh."

"Is that okay?"

"Yeah." She let out a little giggle. "It's okay."

"Did you pick?" I asked.

"Pick what?"

"TV or book."

She hummed. "I was leaning toward reading. I've got this book that's been sitting on my nightstand for weeks. I haven't had time."

I grinned. "What's your most read genre?"

"Thrillers or murder mysteries, probably, but I read some fantasy and romance too. Do you like to read?"

"Not typically, but I've been reading a lot this week to keep busy."

"Oh, nice. What do you like?"

"A little bit of everything. This week, I've read a non-fiction, a romance, a sci-fi, a memoir, and a horror." I found myself smiling at the phone, imagining the way she might look right now, maybe curled up somewhere cozy. "What do you like about thrillers?"

She laughed this sweet snort-laugh, and I swear, my heart clutched its metaphorical pearls and fainted like an old lady in a soap opera.

"I like trying to figure out the twist before it hits, even if everything falls apart first."

"That's fair. Life tends to fall apart a lot."

"Yeah, like when your first kiss with a stranger while being held at gunpoint by a crazy man goes viral." I could hear the smile in her voice and even picture her biting her lip.

"First kiss?" I asked. "Does that mean there's gonna be a second?"

"Oh my gosh." She let out a breathless giggle that made me grip the phone tighter.

"But you didn't say no," I murmured.

"I didn't say yes either."

"*Yet*," I said. "You didn't say yes *yet*." I leaned against the couch as my thumb rubbed absent circles on the back of my phone.

"I'm glad you texted me," she said, her voice softer. "You're easier to talk to than I expected."

I chuckled. "I'm not sure if I should be offended or not."

"Don't be. You're not exactly what I pictured, that's all."

"Well, I'm always here to talk."

And somehow, we just...kept talking for hours. It never felt forced; it was just easy and comfortable in that weird way where neither of us had anything to prove. The conversation jumped everywhere—music, favorite foods, embarrassing stories we swore we'd never repeat. She was funny in this dry, low-key way that snuck up on me. Every time she laughed, it pulled something loose in my chest. I kept catching myself smiling like an idiot, not even caring if she heard it in my voice.

After a while, I asked, "So do you have friends you

keep in touch with? I mean, I figure it's gotta be tough with your schedule and, you know...being famous."

"I do, but most of my friends are just as crazy busy, so we barely see each other. My best friend is actually my publicist. She's amazing, but sometimes, I wonder if she'd still like me if I weren't signing her checks. I mean, she's been with me forever, but…"

"That's gotta be tough, but I'm sure she likes you for you. You seem like the kind of person who's hard to hate."

There was a pause and then this soft, almost disbelieving laugh. "You don't really know me, though."

"Not yet, but I trust my instincts."

"What about you? You seem like the type who probably has fifty friends and some group chat that never sleeps."

I smiled. "You'd think, right? But nah, I keep my circle pretty small. Mostly family. A couple of teammates I'm close with, but honestly, my siblings and brother-in-law are my best friends. Though our family group chat does get a little crazy sometimes."

"That's so weird to me," she said. "Probably 'cause it's just me. No siblings."

"Really?" Something in her tone made me pay closer attention.

"Yeah…" She trailed off. "My parents, though—they're incredible. They've always been my biggest supporters."

"That's awesome. So they were on board with the whole music thing from the start?"

"Oh yeah. From the second I showed any talent and said I wanted this, they were all in." Her words were warm, but there was something underneath—as if the love came with a weight. "They believed in me and backed me every step of the way."

"That sounds amazing," I said carefully, "but also maybe...a lot of pressure?"

"Yeah…" She was silent for a beat. "I think when someone believes in you that much, you start living up to their vision. Not because they force it, but because you can't stand the thought of disappointing them."

"So you did this for them?"

"No," she said quickly. "I love music. I wanted this. At least…I thought I did. But lately, I've been wondering if I fell in love with the idea more than the reality, you know? It all seemed so glamorous when I was younger. Maybe I never actually stopped to think about what success would look like if it was just mine." She exhaled softly. "Sorry, that was total word vomit. You probably don't want to hear me ramble."

I found myself smiling. "Don't apologize. Keep going."

I could listen to you talk for hours.

"I mean, I didn't chase this for them. I chose it. But now…now, I just want to prove everything they sacrificed was worth it."

I let her words hang there. The Ellie everyone else saw —polished, untouchable, larger than life—wasn't who I was talking to. It felt like I was talking to the girl behind all that.

And honestly? I liked this one way more than the fantasy I'd been chasing since college.

"That is a lot of pressure," I said finally. "Like you made it to the top of the mountain, but the view isn't what you expected."

"Exactly," she said, barely above a whisper. "Don't get me wrong—I'm grateful. I love what I do. But some days, it just feels…heavy."

I wanted to say something perfect, something that would fix it all, but all I had was the truth.

"Well, for what It's worth, you're crushing it. And if you ever need someone outside all that craziness—

someone who doesn't give a shit about charts or PR—I'm here."

She sighed into the phone. "Thank you, but speaking of PR..."

"Hmm?" I asked, cautiously.

"Well, that's kind of why I asked you to coffee."

"For PR?"

"Yeah. My publicist thinks..." She exhaled. "She thinks we should enter a...mutually beneficial pretend dating arrangement. One in which you'd be my...boyfriend."

My jaw dropped.

I didn't say anything, mostly because I was too busy trying to remember how to breathe. She kept going, words spilling out fast, as if she was trying to outrun them.

"I was going to wait and bring it up tomorrow, but I figured it'd be easier now. Less chance of anyone overhearing, you know..."

I blinked. Nodded. Said nothing. My brain was still stuck on a pretend dating arrangement.

Fake dating.

Fake dating Ellie Miles.

It wasn't a bad plan. Coach would love it. The media would eat it up. Fans would stop losing their minds over the body cam footage and start losing it over real footage of us instead.

Plus, fake felt safe—or at least safer than admitting my heart had tried to stage a full-blown jailbreak the second she said *you* and *boyfriend* in the same sentence.

I mean, the girl I've been low-key crushing on since college just asked me to play her boyfriend? I'd been rehearsing for that role for years in my dreams.

She called it pretend. She could've asked me to pretend to be a pet iguana, and I'd have said yes.

"Oh," was all I managed to say.

"Oh?"

"Yeah. I mean—yeah. Sorry, just didn't expect that. But...I'm in."

"You're in? Don't you want to talk about it first?"

"What's there to discuss?" I asked.

"Well, it's obviously helpful to me. My PR's been a mess since my breakup." She hesitated. "But what do you want out of this?"

I scratched the back of my neck, chuckling. "Actually... my coach kind of asked me to keep the positive media going. This would help me out, too. That's kind of why I blew you the kiss."

"Oh, so it wasn't genuine?"

"I mean, it definitely still was."

"But seriously, you don't have any other terms?"

"No."

"Really? Nothing?"

"Well..." I smiled.

"Name it."

"You come home with me sometimes. My family would see right through me if I said I was dating someone and didn't bring her around. Plus, my niece is obsessed with you. I might retain the favorite uncle spot if I brought you to a family dinner or two."

"Gracie, right?"

I blinked. "Yeah, you remember?"

"Unfortunately, I remember everything from that night. Kind of hard to forget."

"Yeah. How are you doing, really? You healed up okay?"

"Yeah. The bullet only grazed me, so it didn't take long to recover. I took some time off tour, but my first concert back is in a couple of weeks."

"Can I come to a show?" I asked, almost without

thinking.

"Um…sure? If you want to."

"Want to? I'd love to. I'm gonna go check for tickets right now." I placed my phone on speaker and Googled her tour dates.

"Don't. I'll get you some tickets."

"Really?"

"Yeah, of course," she replied. "Just let me know which show."

"Well…thanks. That'd be nice. My last experience was a little tainted. I'd love a second go." A yawn escaped me that I couldn't stop.

"I should probably go to bed, and it sounds like you should too. I'll text you where to meet me tomorrow?"

"Yeah. Sounds good. I'll see ya at eleven."

"Goodnight, Sawyer."

"Goodnight, Ellie."

The line went dead.

But for the first time in a while, I felt alive.

SIX

Ellie

I STOOD IN FRONT OF MY CLOSET, STARING AT THE MESS OF clothes I'd already tried on and discarded. This shouldn't be that freaking complicated. It was just coffee, nothing more.

Except my treacherous mind had other plans. That ridiculous, infuriating, completely unplanned kiss played on repeat in my head, no matter how hard I tried to scrub it out. My brain had gone fully rogue, conjuring up his voice saying things that had nothing to do with coffee orders, replaying the feel of his hands, the way he'd looked at me right before—

Stop.

I tore off the too-tight jeans I'd planned to wear and let out a frustrated sigh. This was insane. In a decision that definitely sounded smarter in theory, I was inviting Sawyer James into my life for PR. For optics. For…whatever people say when they're making objectively terrible decisions and pretending they're strategic.

Because this wasn't even a real date—not even a fake date yet. It was just two people, mutually faking normalcy in a public place with overpriced caffeine and the looming threat of paparazzi. It wasn't like we'd had some sweeping, romantic meet-cute—unless kissing as a distraction while a gun-wielding psychopath glared at us counted as cute. Not exactly the kind of story you'd want to tell your grandkids.

So why was I obsessing over this?

Red flags lit up my brain even just thinking about any kind of relationship, fake or otherwise. I'd been here before. People didn't fall for me—not the whole, messy, tired version. They liked the idea of Ellie Miles. Harold had loved it—right up until he realized I came with inconvenient things like needs and opinions.

I walked back to my closet and spotted a sundress, all bright and cheerful. Because logic had clearly left the building, some traitorous part of my brain went *oh, pretty*— even though it was fifty degrees outside. I put it on, took one look in the mirror, and immediately started wrestling my way back out of it while cursing my entire existence.

After a few more rounds of self-inflicted torture, I finally landed on dark, not-too-tight jeans, an oversized wool coat, and a messy bun that looked like I hadn't tried too hard—even though I absolutely had.

It was fine. Totally fine.

An hour later, I stepped out of my San Francisco home, and instantly, the cameras started clicking like damn buzzing insects.

Flash. Flash. Flash.

"Ellie, over here!"

"Ellie! Are you dating Sawyer James?"

"Ellie, how's the arm? Are you ready for the show coming up?"

I kept my head down, sunglasses on, my smile practiced and polite. My security team moved in instinctively, a quiet, steady shield.

"Let's keep moving," one of my security guards said.

The SUV door opened, and I slid in.

"Coffee shop's prepped. Swept this morning. Owner's good with it. Private booth in the back. No press allowed inside."

I nodded. "Perfect. Thank you."

It was ridiculous, really, but this was my life now. Fame came with security and a media playbook. If I wanted a moment to breathe? That came with a team of two and a blacked-out SUV.

For some reason, I didn't mind it all today. Something stupid and a little hopeful stirred in me that had nothing to do with the cameras.

We pulled up behind the coffee shop, a tucked-away spot nestled between a row of designer boutiques—the kind of place that sold overpriced lavender lattes and had leather armchairs no one actually sat in.

It was supposed to be a private entrance, but somehow, a few paparazzi had still found it. The second I stepped out, the flashing started again.

"Ellie! Who are you meeting? Is it Harold?"

"Ellie, how are you healing after the injury?"

"Are the rumors true?"

I darted inside and let out a breath. When I glanced up, I immediately spotted him leaning against the counter, wearing a flannel over a faded tee and a backwards hat. Sawyer glanced up and grinned like he'd been waiting his whole life for this exact moment.

And just like that, the outside world faded away.

He pushed off the counter, holding five cups.

"Didn't know what you wanted, so I got all their sweetest stuff," he said, lifting the drink carrier like a human coffee menu. "All with enough sugar to bring back the dead. If you don't like them, I can get you something else."

I let out a laugh that surprised even me—a real one. Rachel always said the right guy would make me laugh when I least expected it. I always figured she meant after some time into a healthy relationship, not ten seconds into a fake one, but this guy was always surprising me, apparently.

A staff member appeared and led us past a curtain near the back to a private booth. It was small and circular, with plush cushions and enough privacy so no one could easily eavesdrop or snap a photo for this initial conversation.

Sawyer slid in first, and I sat across from him.

"Pick your poison." He slid the cups toward me.

When our fingers brushed for half a second, my stomach decided to perform a little pirouette.

"This one has whipped cream and what I'm pretty sure is edible glitter," he said, squinting at it. "I didn't even know coffee could sparkle."

I raised an eyebrow. "You got me glitter coffee?"

"I mean, I figured you deserved options…and glitter, obviously."

I picked it up and took a sip. It was sweet, indulgent, and ridiculous. "Okay…why is this actually really good?"

He grinned and just stared at me for a moment before speaking.

"I feel like I should say something smooth right now," he said, leaning forward, "but all I can think about is how your coat makes you look like a very fashionable detective, like you're about to solve a mystery and drop an album all in the same day." His eyes went wide, and he ran a hand down his face. "That was stupid. Let's pretend I didn't say that."

I bit back a smile. "I'll have you know, this detective has excellent taste."

"Oh, no doubt." He gave me a shy smirk. "I mean, you asked to have coffee with me. Clearly impeccable judgment, if I do say so myself."

I rolled my eyes and stirred my drink. "Are you always this charming?"

He tilted his head. "Define *always*."

"Like, is this an everyday thing? Or is it reserved for pop stars you pretend date on Sunday mornings?"

He grinned. "Only for you, Miles."

"So…fake dating…"

Sawyer rolled his bottom lip between his teeth and watched me with annoyingly readable eyes. "I'm still in if you are."

I dropped my voice, glancing toward the counter, even though I knew no one could hear us. "You really don't have any other stipulations?"

"Nope. I'm a delight. No crazy terms."

I narrowed my eyes. "Seriously."

"I am serious," he said, grinning like he wasn't. "But fine. You want rules?"

"Maybe just one. An end date?"

He cocked his head. "Sure, if that makes you feel better."

"Well, I don't want to take over your whole life."

"You don't have to worry about me. I'll survive, but I get it. Having a finish line makes it less…complicated."

"Exactly."

"So, how long does this media charade need to live to feel convincing but not, you know, spiral into joint holiday cards and matching dog sweaters?"

"Aww, you've thought about our future dogs?" I teased.

He tugged at his shirt. "Don't judge. I look great in plaid."

I tried not to smile and failed. "Okay, well, you've got football, obviously."

He stretched one arm across the back of the booth. "Yeah. If we make it deep, I'm booked through late January, maybe early February. You?"

"Tour ends around the same time." I tapped my nails against the cup. "We'll both be on the go until then."

"So the media blitz will be going on while we are both busy. We'll need to be seen together when we can manage, or people will think we're faking it."

I arched a brow.

He grinned. "Well, more than we already are."

I laughed under my breath. "Okay, so we start laying it on thick soon. Then what? Run the course until the Super Bowl?"

He hesitated for a moment. "Let's say end of March? Gives us time to be in love and then gracefully implode before allergy season makes me all miserable and puffy."

"Wow. You've really got the whole heartbreak arc mapped out. Okay. End of March."

"Should we write this down?" he asked. "For legal purposes, of course."

I blinked. "Like a contract?"

"Exactly." He reached for a napkin. "Time to make it binding."

"Do you need a pen?"

He patted down his pockets and held up two empty hands. "I have charm and a wild imagination. Sadly, no ink."

"Here." I chuckled, pulling a pen from my bag and handing it to him. "This is insane."

"Absolutely, and yet, I've never taken a napkin contract more seriously."

After a moment, he pushed it toward me.

Across the top, in all caps: *OFFICIAL CONTRACT* with a doodle of a broken heart and a dramatic underline.

> *I, Sawyer Eugene James, solemnly and enthusiastically agree to enter this entirely legally binding, fake dating arrangement with the stunning Ellie Miles, until the mutually agreed-upon date of March 31st.*
>
> *Signed,*
>
> *Sawyer James*

"Eugene?" I chuckled.

"Hey, it was my grandpa's name. Don't judge."

I laughed and took the pen, signing underneath his name and sliding it back. He carefully folded it and then tucked it into his wallet.

He met my gaze. "Well…guess we're official."

I nodded. "Yep. Signed and even napkin sealed."

"So," he rested his arms on the table, "how have you been?"

I looked down, fingers toying with my coffee. "I'm good."

"Not your go-to media answer. Give me the real one."

I peered up at him and hesitated—not because I didn't want to talk, but because most people didn't ask for the real answer. Something about the way he said it, with no pressure, no angle, made it feel safe. The same steady warmth I'd heard in his voice last night was written all over his face now. Somehow, that made it easier to talk to him.

"Honestly?"

He nodded.

"I'm tired, burnt out, and guilty, even though I know I shouldn't be."

"Guilty?"

"For taking a break. For needing one. For getting shot and not bouncing back overnight like I'm supposed to."

He frowned. "Ellie…"

"I know," I blurted out. "I know it's not rational, but this job doesn't leave much room for recovery. I didn't even get a full week off before people started speculating if I'd gone off the rails. So…I'm a little exhausted lately."

He nodded slowly. "I'm sorry. That's a lot to carry."

I shrugged. "Part of the gig."

"Still, it sucks. Being tired all the time from doing something you're supposed to love. I get it."

"Yeah?"

"Yeah. Football's been my whole life, but lately, it's taken more than it gives. This is my last year, and I keep wondering who I'll be when it's over."

My heart pulled a little. "I think you'd still be you."

"Thanks," he said with a sheepish smile. "You excited for your tour to be ending in a few months?"

"Yeah, it'll be nice. I'm always running and traveling, so it will be good to relax a little."

"Any plans after?" There was something careful in his voice, as if he wasn't sure he should ask.

"I've got another album I'm working on, so I'll probably finish that up."

"Do you sleep, or do you just dream in chord progressions?"

I laughed. "I can't help it if I'm brushing my teeth or something and suddenly, there are some lyrics in my head that won't leave me alone."

"Do you think you'll ever want to slow down?"

I ran my finger along the rim of my coffee cup, trying to line my thoughts up in the right order. I used to think I'd know when I'd made it, like there would be some moment where the Grammy, the chart spots, all the big wins would finally feel like enough. Truthfully, I didn't know what I was chasing anymore.

"I want to slow down," I whispered, "but I'm not sure I'm ready to be done."

"What do you see for yourself when you settle down?"

"God, I don't even know anymore."

"Did you ever think about it? You know, before everything changed?"

"Yeah, I used to."

He cocked his head. "Do tell."

I let out a breathy laugh. "Okay, this is going to sound kind of silly, but when I was little, I used to dream about living on a bunch of land. Like, a big open field with wildflowers and maybe a few dogs. I'd be lying in the grass with my guitar, writing songs while a baby napped next to me. And my husband, who would obviously be very cute and very obsessed with me, would bring me lemonade." I shrugged, still smiling. "I don't know if that's still in the cards for me anymore, but little me was committed to the vision."

"You don't want that now?"

"I don't know." I sighed. "Things are different now. What about you? What does next year look like for you?"

"Ah, good deflection." He shook his head and smiled. "I could retire comfortably and never work another day if I wanted. Perks of the NFL and having a good financial advisor when I was young. Now, I don't know. I want to relax for a bit, rest my body. Who knows? Maybe I'll finally use my degree for something."

"What's your degree in?"

"Education."

"Really?"

"Yup, I always liked kids and teaching. I figured it'd be an easy thing to fall back on. Plus, summers off. Big bonus there."

"Definitely a plus."

Sawyer cleared his throat and tapped his fingers on the table. "I like this. Getting to know you. I mean, we should probably be friends if we're gonna be pretending to date each other."

"You mean we can't just wing it and hope our fake love story magically makes sense?"

"I'm charming, not magical."

"That's debatable," I muttered, hiding a smile.

He leaned back, watching me. "Seriously, though. I think we should actually talk. Call each other when we're on the road. Share the boring stuff—what we had for breakfast, annoying publicist emails, weird dreams…"

"So, like… long distance besties with a fake dating clause?"

"See, you get it." He winked. "I mean, if we show up together and can't name each other's families or favorite foods, we're screwed."

I nodded. "Okay. That makes sense. I like it."

"Plus," he said, a little softer, "I want to be your friend. This would feel kind of hollow if we weren't."

"Okay, then I'll be yours too."

A slow smile tugged at the corner of his mouth. "Good. I'm excellent friend material."

"Oh yeah? What all do I get with that package?"

"Middle of the night pep talks. Bodyguard duties. And I'm not saying I bake when I'm stressed, but…"

I laughed. "You're a stress baker?"

"Don't spread it around. I've got a reputation."

I smiled, warm all over. "Alright, Sawyer. Friends?"

"Friends." He lifted his coffee in a toast. "To the weirdest, most public fake relationship friendship of all time."

I tapped my cup against his. "Cheers to that."

We lapsed into a quiet moment. Not awkward, just… reflective. Then he ruined it in the best possible way.

"So, tell me something random about you. Something someone wouldn't know from the media. Something about just Ellie, not Ellie Miles. No pressure, but make it interesting. Like… totally obscure and random. Do you make your assistant separate your M&Ms by color?"

I chuckled. "No, but maybe I should start."

He gasped. "Missed opportunity. I would totally do that if I were you."

"Okay, fine." I tapped my chin. "Something random… Okay, I'm obsessed with crime documentaries. Probably a little too much. I like to fall asleep to them playing."

"Murder helps you sleep?"

"Yep," I said with a smile.

"Too late to take back the friends thing?" he teased. "I might be a little scared of you now."

I shrugged. "You should be. With everything I've learned, I could totally get away with murder."

He leaned back dramatically, pressing a hand to his chest. "And yet, here I am, willingly. What a beautiful, reckless man I am."

He grinned at me, a slow, crooked smile that took over my entire brain. My gaze dropped to his mouth before I could stop it, and…what were we talking about? I couldn't remember, which was a problem, considering I was supposed to be the one in control of this arrangement, not sitting here staring at my fake boyfriend's lips.

"Okay, big true crime girl," he said, breaking the moment. "What else?"

I exhaled slowly, trying to steady myself. "Uh, I check my horoscope every day. I'm not sure I believe in it all, but it's fun and often pretty spot on."

"You'd like my brother's girlfriend. She's into that kind of stuff too."

"Noah?"

"Yeah." He glanced down for a second.

"How are they doing?"

"They're good, all things considered." He smiled a little and glanced back up. "I think my brother's gonna ask her to marry him soon."

"That's sweet. Makes me happy to hear," I said. "What about you? Tell me something random about yourself."

He tapped his chin. "Okay, this might sound weird, but I can't fall asleep without white noise."

I tilted my head. "Seriously?"

"Yeah. When my niece was a baby, she spent some time in the NICU. My brother, Dorian, is a single dad, so I helped when I could. I read that white noise could help her sleep, so I bought a machine. Turns out, it helped me sleep too. Now, I'm basically useless without it."

"That's actually...really sweet."

"That's just my family. We always show up for each other...but if you ever need someone to give you the best white noise recs, I've got you. Ocean waves are a scam. It's box fan or nothing."

We both laughed again, and for the first time in forever, I wasn't thinking about press, timelines, or damage control. I didn't feel like Ellie Miles, The Brand. I just felt...

like me. The girl who used to play tiny gigs in coffee shops and eat diner pie at midnight with her guitar on her back.

And sitting across from this dorky, too-handsome football player who made napkin contracts and flirted like it was his full-time job?

It was nice. Really nice.

SEVEN

Sawyer

"So, we got the end date down," Ellie said. "Is there anything we didn't cover?"

She had that little smile—the one that could short-circuit brain cells and make you forget your own damn name. Social security number? Gone. The fact that I was supposed to be fake dating her? Whoops.

She was cute.

Pretty.

Fucking stunning.

I mean, I knew she was. I'd always known, but it hit different this time—like my body forgot how to breathe for a second. Because holy hell, she was something else.

She was tall, graceful in that way that made it look effortless—like she had no idea every single person in the room would stare whether she was famous or not. Her collarbones looked like they'd been sketched by an angel with a great eye for detail. And her hair. God, her hair was swept up in one of those messy knots women did, and somehow, it made her look like she belonged in a shampoo commercial.

Her eyes. Fuck me. Those ocean-blue eyes saw everything and yet gave away nothing, as if she were cataloging the whole world while staying just out of reach. Her skin practically glowed under the café lights, and her mouth—don't get me started. It was made for pop songs and trouble.

She was the kind of beautiful that made breathing feel optional.

Surprise, it's not.

Every time she looked at me, my face betrayed me. Full grin. No control. I was a professional athlete. I trained for a living and worked to keep every muscle in top form.

Except apparently, I'd been skipping the cheek workout.

Because being around Ellie Miles? It was an Olympic-level facial exercise.

"Sawyer?" She arched a brow. "You alright?"

"Yeah, I'm great. Why?"

"You just…zoned out. I asked you a question, and you just…stared at me."

"Sorry," I said, leaning in a little. "You're just really pretty. I got distracted. Ask me again, slower this time."

She scoffed, but her smile betrayed her. "I said we have the end date. Is there anything else we need to cover?"

"Oh. Right." I cleared my throat but still couldn't help my eyes drifting down to her mouth. "What do you mean?"

"Well, how do you want to do this? We obviously need to be seen together, make it believable."

She was all business—which, if I was being honest, only made her more attractive.

"I have zero concerns about believability." I threw in a wink because self-control was for lesser men.

She laughed and playfully shoved my shoulder from across the table. "Stop. I'm being serious."

"Okay, okay." I held my hands up. "We hit some public spots. Dinner. Events. Maybe a red carpet or two if you're feeling dramatic. You obviously need to come to the Super Bowl if I make it there. And come to Woodstone with me sometimes. Small town, but if you want believable, that's where I'm usually at when I can be. Everyone there knows I don't bring just anyone home."

She tilted her head. "When are you going next?"

"Tonight. Wanna come?"

Her eyebrows shot up. "*Tonight*?"

"Why not?"

"I mean, we haven't even announced we're dating yet, and meeting your family? That feels…big."

I gave her a look, one brow raised. "You've technically already met half of them, remember?"

She narrowed her eyes, but I caught the corner of her mouth twitching. "That doesn't count."

"I'm staying at my brother-in-law's extra place. It's empty. Plenty of space. You could have a room too."

Her gaze sharpened. "You're inviting me to crash at your family's extra house?"

"More like extending a very generous offer," I smirked. "Think of it as neutral ground. No pressure. Just proximity."

Her phone rang. She glanced down, then ignored it.

"I don't know," she murmured. "When are you headed there again after today?"

"Haven't planned it yet, but I go whenever I can. It's home."

Her phone rang again, and she sighed.

"You can grab that if you need to. I don't mind."

She gave me this look. It was soft and a little sad. Then she nodded and answered. "Hey, Rach. What's up?" A long pause, and then her eyes widened. "Please tell me you're not serious. You're joking, right?" Another pause. "Oh no, no, no, no."

"Everything okay?" I leaned in.

And I shouldn't have, because she smelled like flowers and whatever heaven was supposed to smell like—sweet, soft, and completely wrecking my focus.

She mouthed *one sec* and turned away slightly.

"Yeah, well…what do we do now?" she said into the phone. "Okay… No, not really, but if we don't have much of a choice, then… Let me check. I'll text you. Love you. Bye."

She hung up and stared at the table like it had personally betrayed her.

"You okay?" I murmured.

"Yes and no." She gave me a tight smile. "It's kind of a long story."

"I've got time."

She exhaled slowly. "Long story short, it's another mess. My ex leaked some private texts—twisted things I said to make me look like I don't care about anyone. Called me cold, selfish, and fake. It's everywhere now. Rachel says the headlines are a mess."

"Shit. I'm so sorry. That's awful. Is there anything I can do?"

She hesitated, then glanced up at me through her lashes. "Are you still okay with the story about us…dating going live? It would help shift the focus. I try not to care about bad press, but with everything else going on, I don't want him thinking he still has any kind of power over me."

I didn't even blink. "Of course. I told you, I'm in."

Ellie huffed out a breath, brushing her hair off her face as if she needed a second to reboot. "You really don't have to do this. I don't want you to think I'm using you."

"I know I don't have to." I leaned forward, resting my forearms on the table. "And this is mutually beneficial, remember?"

She watched me, blue eyes glassy with something I couldn't quite read. Doubt, maybe. The kind that made me want to reach across and smooth it away with my thumb.

"Okay," she said slowly. "Let's say we do this. The story goes live, we're officially a couple, the internet explodes. Then what?"

I grinned. "Then we go to Woodstone. You come to dinner with my family. My niece will probably cry, and my sister will flip out, but it will still be a good time. My dad might even try to gift you a cow to get in your good graces."

She blinked. "I'm sorry—a cow?"

"It's a small town. People show affection with livestock. Accept it and move on."

She laughed, head tipping back as the tension slipped from her shoulders.

That sound. I'd bottle it if I could. I'd take it, hide it, keep it somewhere only I could find it, bring it out on the days I needed it most, and take my own personal hit of Ellie.

"You make this sound so easy," she whispered. Her smile melted into something softer.

"That's because I don't care about the media. I care about you."

She peered down at the table, running her finger along the rim of her water glass. "Don't be crazy. You barely know me."

"True," I said gently. "But I'd definitely like to get to know you more."

Her eyes flicked up to mine, and something cracked open between us—small, but real. Then, she nodded once. "Okay. Let's do it."

My heart kicked like I'd just scored in overtime.

"Yeah?" I asked, just to be sure.

"Yeah. Let's go to Woodstone."

"Hell yeah." I pushed my chair back. "I'd recommend packing a flannel. It's kind of the town uniform. I'll get you on my flight."

"I'll see if we can get my jet ready by tonight."

"Oh, a private jet. Very fancy."

Ellie rolled her eyes. "You're ridiculous."

"True." I grinned. "But now I'm *your* ridiculous, Miles."

Her smile widened. "You're enjoying this way too much."

"Ellie Miles pretending to be in love with me?" I whispered, leaning in. "Yeah, I'm living the dream."

She gave me a mock glare. "Just remember, this is fake."

"Totally fake." I nodded solemnly. "So fake. Can't wait to fake hold your hand and fake kiss you in front of everyone I know."

She shook her head, but she was laughing again.

Later that evening, Ellie had one foot propped up on the dashboard, watching out the window as the stars passed us by.

"I didn't realize how dark it gets out here," she said.

"Welcome to the land of zero streetlights and questionable cell service."

able cell service."

She glanced over. "A good place to murder people under some questionable circumstances. Sounds like a true crime documentary waiting to happen."

"Don't get any ideas. You're the one who said yes to the rental car. That's traceable."

She snorted and reached up to retwist her hair into a messy bun with a scrunchie. I loved seeing her like this—relaxed and a little undone in the best way. After a few beats of silence, she caught me sneaking another glance. Those pretty blues narrowed, sharp and knowing.

"I'm not nervous," she said, arching a brow. "If that's what you're wondering."

"Wasn't wondering. But now that you mentioned it…"

She gave me a pointed look. "You think I can't handle your family?"

"Oh, I know you can. Just saying, they're loud, nosy, and at least three of them are already obsessed with you. So maybe…brace for impact."

That earned another real laugh, and I was the lucky son of a gun who got to hear it.

"Did you tell them I'm coming with you?" she asked.

I winced. "Not…exactly."

"Sawyer!"

"I figured I'd just let it be a fun surprise."

"You didn't even warn them?"

"No. I figured I would just let them know when we get there."

She let out a yawn and tried to hide it behind her sleeve.

"Want to grab a coffee before we head to my dad's?" I asked.

"No," she said, stifling another yawn. "I'm okay."

"Ellie." I gave her a look. "We have time. Do you want coffee? There's a good spot on the way."

She sighed, her lips twitching. "Fine. Twist my arm."

I flipped on my blinker and turned toward Woodstone Perks. "You know this counts as a second date, right?"

"It definitely doesn't."

"Let me have my moment, okay?"

She rolled her eyes. "If that's what gets you through the day."

EIGHT

Ellie

SAWYER HELD THE DOOR TO WOODSTONE PERKS OPEN, AND I stepped inside. God, the smell alone brought a smile to my lips—rich espresso mixed with something that reminded me of my late grandmother's kitchen. The murmurs of conversation and the soft clink of ceramic felt like the first real breath I'd taken in months.

I took in the exposed brick walls, the mismatched furniture that actually looked lived-in instead of staged, and shelves packed with well-worn books. "This place is—"

"Ellie Miles."

The voice came from behind the counter, and I turned to see a man watching me with an easy smile. He had warm brown skin and a smile that made you want to immediately trust him with your secrets.

"Thomas," Sawyer said, grinning. "Try not to scare her off in the first thirty seconds."

"I'm not scary!" Thomas immediately proved himself wrong by practically bouncing on his toes. "Oh my God, you're actually here. In our coffee shop. Aiden's going to lose his mind."

As if summoned, another man emerged from behind the espresso machine—tall, pale, with sharp blue eyes. He took one look at me, blinked hard, and looked again. "You've got to be kidding me."

"Aiden," Thomas said in a singsong voice, "it's Ellie Miles."

"I can see that." Aiden wiped his hands on his apron, shaking his head. "Someone please tell me this is actually happening."

I couldn't help but laugh. "Hi, I'm Ellie."

"Nice to meet you. This is Aiden, and I'm Thomas—the better half, obviously." Thomas pointed to himself with both thumbs. "At your service."

"Hey." Aiden scoffed. "I make the coffee. You just look pretty and take people's money."

"And I'm very good at both, thank you."

Thomas turned back to Sawyer, his eyes narrowing. "Wait. How exactly do you know Ellie Miles? Last I checked, your idea of entertainment was arguing about whether pineapple belongs on pizza."

"It absolutely doesn't," Sawyer said.

"See?" Thomas gestured at him like he'd proved his point.

Sawyer glanced at me, a question in his eyes.

When I nodded, he broke into that slow smile that had been doing dangerous things to my pulse all day. "Well, funny story. She's my girlfriend."

The silence that followed was so complete that I could hear the espresso machine hissing in the background.

"I'm sorry," Aiden said slowly, "did you just say—"

"Girlfriend." Sawyer slid his arm around my waist with an ease that shouldn't have felt as natural as it did. "Story's probably breaking as we speak."

Thomas grabbed Aiden's arm. "Are you seeing this? Am I having a stroke?"

"We're both having a stroke," Aiden said.

I buried my face in my hands, laughing despite myself.

Thomas slapped the counter. "Okay, first of all, congratulations. Second of all, how? When? Why didn't you lead with this information?"

"Because," Sawyer said, steering me toward the counter, "we'd like coffee before the interrogation begins."

"Fair point." Thomas was already moving. "The usual for you, and what can I get for the literal pop star dating our favorite customer?"

"Anything extra sweet," I said.

After we ordered, we found a table in the back corner. My shoulders immediately relaxed for the first time all day.

"So," Sawyer said, settling into the chair across from me, "how are we doing? Scale of one to 'I'm booking the first flight to hide out somewhere tropical.'"

"Somewhere around a two?" I took a sip of my latte and sighed. "This is really good coffee."

"The owner will be so pleased. He takes it as a personal insult when people don't appreciate his foam art."

I glanced down and realized he'd made a little heart.

"It's perfect." I tilted my head. "So...what's the story we're gonna tell your family?"

He leaned back in his chair. "Honestly? My family's known I've had a thing for you for a minute now. Not exactly a secret around here. So, when we say we started talking after... Well, they'll probably just ask how I pulled that off."

I caught the blush creeping up his neck and smirked. "Oh, really?"

"Can you blame me? Turns out, you're pretty damn

easy to like off-screen too. So maybe we say we started talking after the night everything went down, took it slow, and well—now we're dating."

"Alright, I can work with that."

The bell above the door chimed, interrupting our conversation.

Sawyer smiled and raised his hand in greeting at the sandy-haired officer who strolled in. "Henry."

"Sawyer James," Henry said, genuine warmth in his voice. "Good to see you back in town, even if it's just for a visit."

"Good to be back." Sawyer stood to shake his hand. "Henry, meet Ellie. Ellie, this is Henry Reynolds. We grew up together."

Henry gave me a polite nod. His expression was calm and unreadable, as if he either didn't recognize me or didn't see the need to, which was a nice change of pace.

"Nice to meet you," he said, extending his hand.

"You too." I smiled and shook his hand.

"This is my partner, Matt Rogers." Henry gestured to the slightly older officer with gray hair. "He just transferred from Shadow Ridge."

Matt nodded hello, and I could see him trying to place me, but he was polite enough not to say anything.

"So," Henry said to Sawyer, "heard you bought the old place on Maplewood."

Sawyer grinned. "You heard right. Time to put down roots."

"That house has some history," Henry said carefully.

"Yeah, well, I'm not superstitious." Sawyer shrugged. "It's got good bones, and the price was right."

Henry chuckled. "Fair enough. Well, welcome back to town."

After they moved to the counter to order, I turned to Sawyer. "They seem nice."

"Henry's good people. We played football together in high school." Sawyer's expression darkened slightly. "His brother, on the other hand... Well, that's a story for another day."

I wanted to ask about that, but my phone chose that moment to explode with notifications. Alert after alert flooded my screen, and my stomach dropped as I read the headlines.

NFL Star Sawyer James and Singer Ellie Miles: Officially Dating!

Ellie Miles Breaks Silence on New Relationship with Sawyer James.

Pop Star Ellie Miles and NFL Star Sawyer James Officially a Couple—Fans React!

"Sawyer," I said, turning my phone so he could see.

He pulled out his own phone and whistled low. "Well, that didn't take long."

"This is happening so fast." I stared at the screen, feeling slightly dizzy, and I lifted my cup to take another sip.

"You've got a little..." Sawyer vaguely gestured at his own mouth.

I reached up to wipe it away, but he was already leaning across the small table, close enough that I caught the scent of his cologne mixed with the coffee. His thumb brushed across my lip, and suddenly, the coffee shop felt about ten degrees warmer.

"There," he whispered.

He didn't pull his hand away. His thumb traced along my lower lip now, and I found myself holding my breath, hyperaware of everything—the way his eyes had gone darker, the little crease between his brows, and the fact that we were supposed to be fake dating.

"Hey." His voice was gentle, his thumb still resting against my cheek. "We've got this, okay? You and me. We'll figure it out as we go."

"Yeah, no going back now."

"Good." He stood and offered me his hand. "Now, let's get out of here before my family murders me."

NINE

Ellie

I STARED OUT THE WINDOW AS THE CAR ROLLED INTO THE neighborhood, my fingers tapping a slow rhythm against the strap of my bag.

I'd stood in front of sold-out crowds and smiled through interviews with strangers who wanted the gossip more than the music. I'd answered questions about my ex, my image, my body, my music, and I'd done it all with a practiced ease I'd been perfecting since the extensive press training I did at seventeen.

But this? This was different.

No cameras. No stage. Just a ranch house full of my fake boyfriend's family. That was scarier than the headlines.

It was also the first time in months I'd been somewhere without my security team. They'd pushed back, of course, until Sawyer stepped in—calm and confident, claiming he was already fulfilling those bodyguard duties he promised.

"Well, here we are."

Rather than rushing, he turned off the engine and

leaned back in his seat, as if the place held more than memories—like it held a piece of him too.

The ranch-style home sat against a backdrop of open sky. A wraparound porch, mismatched rocking chairs, Christmas lights draped in a way that didn't try too hard—it looked...warm and lived in. Something out of a life I didn't know how to imagine until now.

"This is where you grew up?" I asked.

"Yup." He stretched, one hand behind his head. "Still crash here whenever I'm home. Well, not anymore, technically, since I just bought a place."

He glanced at me shyly. "You wanna see it tomorrow? Before we head out?"

"I'd like that. Sounds like a good way to end the trip."

He bumped my elbow with his. "Just warning you, it's not glamorous. It's been sitting empty for years. Needs a lot of work."

I gave him a look. "I'm not here for the granite countertops."

He grinned. "Good, because there are definitely none of those right now." The smile lingered between us for a moment before he finally popped his door open. "Ready?"

No. "Yeah."

I reached for the handle, but he touched my arm gently. "Hold up."

Before I could ask why, he hopped out. My brows knitted together as he jogged around the front of the car and opened my door, holding out a hand.

For some silly reason, my heart fluttered.

Harold never opened a door for me. Not once. Not even ironically. I used to joke he was allergic to chivalry. But this? This was sweet.

"What a gentleman." I stepped out and took his hand. My skin tingled where our hands met as I held his gaze.

He winked. "For you, I try," he said, winking. He had no business looking that good in a flannel and jeans.

He pulled me in like it wasn't up for debate, his arm sliding around my waist. It was confident and easy, as if this was just something he got to do now. His fingers found the small of my back and traced lazy circles—subtle, comforting. Wildly distracting.

We walked towards the ranch house side by side. A chill ran down my spine, and I was unsure if it was the sharp December air or if it was him.

We stepped inside, and it was like being wrapped in a scrapbook of memories. Wood-paneled walls were covered in framed photos: Sawyer as a little boy in a football uniform, another of him with a missing tooth holding a puppy, and one where he stood with his siblings, all wearing matching Christmas pajamas.

Suddenly, all conversations stopped. Every head turned.

It was as if someone had hit pause on a family sitcom. Sawyer didn't miss a beat. He just smiled, as if he walked into rooms full of judgment every day and enjoyed it.

Gracie, the little girl I'd met at the concert, made a beeline for us. "Uncle Sawyer! You're dating Ellie Miles?"

Her dad, Dorian, stood on the other side of the room, on crutches, and I pushed down the anxiety that longed to bubble up. I knew exactly how he had been injured back in San Francisco.

Sawyer peered down at her, then up at me. "Surprise!"

"Are you kidding me?" a woman I vaguely recognized blurted.

Sawyer shrugged, all innocent charm. "What can I say? Go big or go home."

A man I didn't recognize stepped forward. He wasn't

as tall as Sawyer, and his long, brown hair was pulled into a loose bun. "I think you did both, buddy."

And just like that, we were in it. No going back. Just me, a fake boyfriend, a house full of his family.

I pasted on a smile like I'd done a thousand times before.

But this time, it wasn't for the cameras.

TEN

Sawyer

ELLIE SETTLED IN AS IF SHE'D ALWAYS BELONGED HERE—EVEN though she was a damn celebrity half the people in this house worshipped, me included.

My sister Dotty tossed her blonde hair over her shoulder and laughed with Ellie on the couch. Across the room, my older brother Colt stood a few feet back, eyes fixed on the redhead he brought tonight and her son, like the rest of the world had disappeared. I sure as hell was glad I wasn't the only brother who'd brought a surprise.

I turned, cocking my head in silent question toward Colt. *Let's talk.* He narrowed his eyes at me like I was already pissing him off.

"Hey, you okay here for a second?" I asked Ellie.

She glanced from Lilah to me then smiled. "Yeah, I'm good. Go."

I motioned for him to follow. He groaned like it physically hurt him to do so, but he headed for the back hallway of the ranch house anyway.

"What do you want?" he grumbled as soon as we were out of earshot.

"I mean…I'd like to know what's going on between you and the pretty little redhead over there, but I've got a feeling you're not gonna tell me."

"Don't call her that," he snapped.

"Well, that answers my question."

"Nothing is going on," he muttered, but he was smiling.

Smiling.

My brother. Mr. Grumpy, who only loved our sister and his niece, was full-on, stupid boy in love, smiling.

"Holy shit," I whisper-shouted. "Something did happen."

"She's going through a tough time right now. I invited her to be around good people, but I'm starting to question my decision."

"You aren't going to tell me what happened then?"

My brother-in-law rounded the corner and frowned at us. "Wait, what'd I miss?" Trent asked.

"Nothing," Colt barked.

Trent pointed between the two of us, then looked to Colt. "Look, I know I'm not technically your brother, but brother-in-law's got to count for something. That gives me the right to ask if you're sleeping with that gingersnap back there."

Before I could process what was happening, Colt had Trent slammed against the wall with his fist twisted in his shirt.

"First of all," he said in a deadly quiet voice, "call her that again, and I'll fucking kill you."

Trent wheezed against the wall, still trapped in Colt's grip. "And second?"

Even with Trent having a few inches on him, I'd have put my money on Colt in any fight. The way his muscles coiled, the controlled fury in his stance—Trent was outmatched.

Colt shoved him away with enough force to rattle the wall.

"Second, it's none of your goddamn business. Why aren't you more worried about him and the celebrity sitting in our living room?"

"Hey," I said, hands up. "Leave me out of this."

Trent rolled his shoulders and tugged his sleeves back down. "Well, I'm clearly not going to get anything out of him. So yeah, what the hell *is* going on there?"

"We're dating. That's what."

Trent blinked. "And how the fuck did that happen?"

I sighed and rubbed my face, knowing damn well I wasn't about to admit we were fake dating. That didn't mean I had to lie either. So, I gave them the version Ellie and I agreed on—and the one that kept running through my head.

The words tumbled out before I could stop them. "We're dating. We started talking recently. I like her. She's smart, gorgeous, and she smells like heaven. She makes me laugh when I shouldn't even be smiling, and I think I might be going a little bit crazy."

Especially considering we only just had our first real conversation this morning. They didn't need to know that.

Colt looked at me like I'd told him I wrote poetry in my free time. "Oh, you're cooked."

"Welcome to the club." Trent clapped me on the back and turned to Colt. "You too—"

Colt pinned him with a death stare.

"You know what? Never mind."

"I'm done here," Colt muttered, already walking away.

Trent waited a beat and turned back to me. "For real though. You like her?"

"Yeah." Way more than I should, considering it was all

supposed to be fake. I exhaled, leaning back against the wall. "I try not to think about you and my sister together too often. You're welcome, by the way—but seriously, man, this is a lot. How do you do it?"

"It's like you can't breathe around her, right?"

I thought about it for a second—yup, that was exactly it.

"I swear, all I want to do is be near Ellie, touch her, make her laugh…and I'm pretty sure she only tolerates me."

Because that was the truth—this whole thing was an act with a built-in expiration date.

Trent gave a crooked smile. "She's here, isn't she? She must like you a little bit."

"Not helpful."

His smile softened. "Look, you know me. I talk shit, I joke around, but your sister? She's everything. She's brilliant, and beautiful, and somehow both fierce and gentle at the same time. Yeah, it's hard to breathe around her, because every time I look at her, I can't quite believe she chose me. But I wake up every damn day determined to be the man she deserves. I don't ever want her to doubt how much I want her, how much I love her. The truth is, I'd rather lose my breath a thousand times than live a single day without her."

"You know, if she didn't fall in love with you, I might've from that alone. Damn."

"Dinner's ready," Gracie yelled from the other room.

"I have a feeling you'll be fine if you keep up that James family charm," Trent said as we turned back into the living room.

"Alright, let's eat," my dad said.

We all settled around the table, and Ellie squeezed in next to me.

"So, Sawyer," Dotty said. "I got to hear from Ellie a little, but I'd love to hear from you exactly how this all happened. And why didn't you tell me until now?"

Her words might have been cordial, but I knew her better than that.

I cleared my throat, suddenly nervous. "We connected after…" I hesitated, searching for the right words. "Everything happened."

Trent spoke up. "You mean that time Dorian and Ellie were shot by Noah's ex-boyfriend?"

"Trent!" Dorian shot him a sharp glare from across the table.

Noah placed a hand on Dorian's arm. "It's okay. It's the truth. Go on, Sawyer," she said.

I let out a breath. "Yeah, well…after that, we started talking, and we hit it off. So, we decided to give it a shot."

Ellie didn't even have a second to respond before Gracie lit up. "Ellie Miles! Do you know Uncle Sawyer has the biggest crush on you? He told me so himself."

I exhaled through my nose. "Smooth, G."

Even if she wasn't wrong.

"But you do," Gracie insisted. "You don't have to be embarrassed. It's okay to have big feelings."

"Lots of big revelations tonight," my dad chimed in, shaking his head. "First, we get the grump walking in with a plus two, and now, we've got the big, tough football star dating the one woman who could make half the people at this table lose their damn minds."

Colt scoffed. "And I get scolded for my language when you say shit like that?"

Dotty leaned forward, eyes narrowed. "What exactly was your opening line, Sawyer?" She mocked my low voice. "*Hi, I'm huge, concussed, and emotionally unavailable.*

Sorry I kissed you while under duress. Wanna grab dinner sometime?"

Lilah choked on her water, and Caleb giggled.

Ellie smirked, patting my arm. "Something like that."

"Oh, come on. I'm not emotionally unavailable," I groaned, glaring at Dotty. "And I got more game than that."

Dorian chuckled. "Maybe on the field."

"Well, technically," Ellie said, "I asked him out first."

"No freaking way," my dad said.

"Yup. I called and asked him to go for coffee. He was so shocked, he could barely speak, but it was adorable."

I leaned toward her, lowering my voice so only she could hear. "Keep calling me adorable in front of my family, and I might have to show you what else I'm good at, Ellie baby."

She went still for a heartbeat, her fingers tightening almost imperceptibly around her glass, before she turned back to the conversation.

Dotty made a dramatic gagging noise. "I'm gonna need a bucket."

Dorian pointed his fork. "You're the one who asked how it started. As if you and Trent are any better."

"I don't want to hear it from you, Mr. Fell in Love with My Best Friend."

Dorian pointed to Trent. "Says the girl who fell in love with my best friend first."

I looked around the table, then to Ellie. "This is exactly why I never bring people home. They're vultures. Loving, nosy vultures."

My dad raised a brow. "Better to be nosy than unaware. I had to find out my son was dating a celebrity from a news article."

"Sorry about that," Ellie said. "We were hoping to beat the media."

I look across the table to see Colt smiling. Again. This time, Lilah was whispering something in his ear.

The dinner was loud, chaotic, and exactly what you'd expect from a James family gathering—which made it all the more insane how easily Ellie fit in. It was as if she'd been doing this for years instead of a single night.

After dinner, she teamed up with Gracie in a board game and even teased my dad.

I caught Ellie's gaze across the room and gave her a nod, letting her know I was stepping out for a sec.

I needed air, even if that air was cold enough to freeze the freckles off my face.

The wind slapped me the second I stepped onto the porch. I sucked in a deep breath anyway, letting the chill settle in my lungs, and dropped into the old rocking chair that had been here since I was a kid, groaning as it creaked under my weight.

It was all so strange. A small-town boy with big dreams somehow made them all come true. The kid in a pee-wee football league who once dreamed of making it to the NFL was now a man about to retire, a pop star sitting in his childhood home.

Maybe I manifested this shit. Back in college, I used to have her poster taped to my dorm wall right next to my San Francisco Rebels one, as if they belonged in the same universe. Now, she was here—real, grounded, and good in a way that couldn't be faked.

I'd seen firsthand how the spotlight could wreck someone, how it could turn decent people into ego-fueled, power-hungry monsters. But Ellie? Fame hadn't touched her like it did most people. She stood firmly for what mattered, using her voice and generosity to help where it was needed most. She had become a powerful role model —especially for girls like Gracie, who looked up to her as if she were the center of her universe.

She didn't act like the world owed her anything. She was just…Ellie.

Tonight, that same Ellie was letting my niece destroy her in Monopoly while my dad cheered her on—no ego in sight. No complaints. I just sat there, watching her like an idiot. An idiot who was definitely catching feelings in a situation that was supposed to be fake.

I wasn't sure what the hell I was supposed to do. A fake relationship was definitely not on my bucket list, but hey, I wasn't complaining either.

The front door creaked open, and I didn't have to look to know who it was. Colt stepped out like the damn Grim Reaper and dropped into the rocking chair beside me with a heavy sigh. He didn't say a word.

I rocked slowly. "Out here to enjoy the breeze?"

He ran a hand down his face, then let it drop with a thud into his lap. "Needed air."

"Same. Lots going on tonight."

He grunted in agreement. "Does anyone else know you and Ellie are faking it?"

I nearly choked on the air I breathed. "Jesus, man. What the fuck?"

"You heard me." He turned his head and met my eyes. Unbothered and annoyingly fucking perceptive.

I paused. "Is it that obvious?"

"Not really. I had my suspicions. You just confirmed them."

"Sneaky bastard."

He gave the barest smirk. "Detective, remember?"

"Right, right." I leaned back. "Forgot you moonlight as a bloodhound. You think anyone else has picked up on it?"

"I don't think so. Dotty might, but she won't say anything unless she's sure."

I blew out a breath. "It started as a PR thing. You know, damage control. The body cam footage being released made it look like more than it was, and Ellie's got a whole mess of bad press from her ex. It helps keep my coach happy. Seemed like a good idea."

"But you like her." It wasn't a question.

I hesitated, then nodded. "Yeah. I do."

He didn't respond right away. "Good luck with that."

"Thanks," I muttered. "You gonna tell me what's going on with Lilah now?"

"No."

"C'mon, pretty please?" I batted my lashes like an idiot. "You know, if you'd just open up more—"

"She's getting divorced." His tone dropped. "Bad situation, worse guy. I never liked him." He shrugged. "I just want to be there. Make sure she's okay."

I was silent for a second. "So basically, you're as cooked as I am."

"You could say that."

We sat there in silence for a beat, the cold biting at our skin. Somehow, I felt better knowing I wasn't the only idiot sitting outside in freezing temps because he didn't know what to do with his feelings.

"Well," I finally said, "at least we'll freeze to death in good company."

Colt huffed out a laugh. "You talk too much."

"Love you too, brother."

He didn't reply, but I swear, the corner of his mouth twitched.

ELEVEN

Sawyer

My heart was pounding in my chest. I was about to walk a household name celebrity into my little fixer-upper like it was no big deal. She was probably used to mansions with wine cellars and staff who ironed your pillowcases. Meanwhile, this place still had drywall patches and a suspicious creak in the hallway.

But she didn't bat an eye as we pulled up.

The house sat right between Woodstone and the next town over, Shadow Ridge, tucked into a quiet stretch of road. It looked like it had been lifted straight off some cozy countryside Pinterest board—one of the ones I'd never admit to scrolling through at two in the morning. It had white clapboard siding, a deep porch with wide stairs, and one of those old school metal roofs that made rainstorms sound like home.

The flower boxes under the windows were still empty, and a massive willow tree stood off to the side, near the clearing. Just beyond that, a pond shimmered in the morning sun. It was quiet, the type of place that made even a chaos-brained guy like me want to kick off his shoes and stay a while.

I didn't give a damn about the house's history. Sure, I'd heard the stories everyone in Woodstone loved to tell. The place had been sitting vacant for years, ever since that tragedy with the young boy and his father. I was just starting out in my career when it happened, but I still remembered how the whole town became obsessed with every detail. Half the people called it a freak accident; the other half couldn't resist spinning darker theories. For months, you couldn't walk into The Lodge or the post office without someone bringing it up, dissecting every rumor.

No one wanted the place after that. Said it was cursed. Haunted. Touched by something you couldn't scrub out with bleach and paint, but I didn't care. I didn't believe in ghosts or small-town legends. Noah told me I should sage the place before I moved in. I told her I'd consider it, mostly to keep my brother's girlfriend from showing up to do it herself.

This house was mine now, bad stories, ghosts, secrets, and all.

I rounded the car and opened Ellie's door. She slipped her hand into mine as she stood, and for a moment, neither of us moved to drop it.

She smiled shyly and glanced at the house. "It's beautiful."

"Needs a little work, but the bones are there. Want to go inside?"

"I'd love to."

I led her up the front steps. The key stuck in the lock, and I jiggled it until the door creaked open. The inside smelled like cedar as sunlight filtered through gauzy curtains that had probably been white once.

"Wow," she whispered. "You're right. It's got great bones."

She stepped farther into the house, and I followed behind her. The floorboards creaked as we moved through the front room, past a stone fireplace and walls that bore the faded outlines of what once hung there.

I hadn't changed much to make it mine yet, only cleaned it up some. For now, it was quiet until the contractors were set to start in a few days.

"You can almost hear the stories in the walls," she whispered.

I gave a soft laugh. "Yeah, well…hopefully not literally."

She shot me a grin over her shoulder, and that alone made the whole damn room brighter.

We kept walking past the living room, down the hall, through the little kitchen that looked like it hadn't seen a proper meal in years. The counters were chipped, the cabinets a faded yellow that might've once been cheerful, and the sink was deep enough to bathe a puppy—or a baby.

Ellie stepped back into the living room with worn wood floors and windows overlooking the willow tree and pond.

Her foot landed on a floorboard near the center of the room. It shifted with a loud clack then see-sawed back into place.

She froze. "What the hell?"

Oh, shit.

She crouched, tugging at the board. It gave with a soft creak, revealing a shallow hollow beneath. Ellie peered up at me, eyes wide with a glint of curiosity.

She reached inside.

"Careful!"

"Why?" She laughed, halfway into the floor already.

"There might be... I don't know. Spiders. Or, like, a raccoon's nest."

Or a journal best left untouched.

"I'm not scared of spiders," she said, grinning.

"Well, I am."

She pulled out the leather-bound book from inside the hole. "Have you ever seen this before?"

I shook my head. "Yeah, I found it when I was checking out the place. Gave me the heebie jeebies, so I put it right back."

Her fingers brushed the edge of the book. The leather cover was cracked. No title., just a single initial pressed into the front.

"L?" she said. "Who's L?"

"No clue." I scratched the back of my neck.

She opened it. Pages full of looping handwriting filled the inside.

"Who used to live here?" she muttered.

"Uh…funny story."

She glanced up. "Why do I feel like you're about to say something horrifying but try to make it sound chill?"

"Well…this place sat empty for years. No one wanted to buy it because…a boy and his dad died here."

"What?" she said, her voice squeaking. "Here?"

"Yeah. Out there, I think," I gestured to the willow tree. "There was some kind of accident. Kid got a hold of a gun, and well…you can guess the rest."

Her brows pinched, and she covered her mouth with her hand. "The boy? Oh no."

"Yeah. The whole town went nuts about it for a while, but in the end, they called it a tragedy. Said it was an accident. Case closed."

She held out the journal. "Look at this."

I sat beside her, trying not to think about how close she

was and about the way she smelled like flowers and sunlight. Or how pretty she looked when she thought hard about something.

She handed me the book. "Here. Read this."

I fought against the pull to study her face and glanced down at the book.

I can't remember the last time this house felt like a home. Some days, it's just a place I keep clean enough for people to stop asking questions. Other days, it's a cage.

They said I was lucky. Nineteen and already taken care of. Our families had been tied together for decades, the kind of ties people whisper about but never question. They all nodded, smiled, and said he was solid, a man who'd build a good life for me. They forgot to ask what I wanted.

Except he doesn't care about me. I'm something he owns. A body, a name, a quiet life he can control. A late meal, a slammed door, a fist hitting the table because I spoke out of turn. Because I laughed too loud. Because I paused too long.

His words cut before he raises a hand, and sometimes, they cut after. It's always a warning, always a reminder I don't belong to myself here.

Even the people who hover at the edges of our lives— people who open doors and never meet my eyes—remind me he's untouchable. His reach stretches farther than these walls, and I know better than to believe anyone would step in.

I watch his hands, I measure my words, I keep my head down. I know the moment I falter, I'll pay for it. Even in the silence, even when he's gone, I can feel the weight of what's coming. Every day is survival.

I think about leaving more than I say out loud. Not

because I have somewhere to go, but because I want to know if there's a world past these walls.

"What the hell?" I muttered, glancing up.

Ellie watched me with her brows knitted. "When did this all happen?"

"Six, maybe seven years ago. Why?"

"Because this doesn't sound like an accident. This sounds like a woman who was terrified for her life."

"They did a full investigation." I shrugged.

"But how does a little boy get hold of a gun? It doesn't make sense."

"I don't know. I try not to think about it. Bad juju and all."

"What if there's more going on here?"

"Maybe, but maybe it's just one perspective. People say a lot of things when they're scared."

She flipped to the next page, but I snatched the book from her hands.

"Hey!" She glared. "Sawyer, give it back."

I narrowed my eyes at her. "No, little miss true crime."

"You're not even a little curious?"

"Nope, but I like that you are. It's…cute."

Her cheeks flushed a pretty shade of pink that made me think about what else I could do to put that color there. She schooled her expression and scoffed. "Don't distract me with flattery."

"Is it working?"

Her breath hitched slightly, and the space between us felt smaller than it should have. I could see it in her eyes— the way the corner of her mouth twitched, like she wanted to say something but held back instead.

She reached for the journal again, and I pulled it away.

My mind reeled thinking of ways to get her to come back to Woodstone. She looked like she belonged here, and I selfishly wanted to keep her.

"Let's make a deal," I said.

She crossed her arms. "A deal?"

"Mhm."

"Like our fake dating deal?" She cocked her head.

"Sort of, but this one's different. We only read a journal entry when we're together, here, in this house."

She blinked. "Why?"

"Because if we read them all at once, we'll jump to conclusions. We'll miss something. This way, we take our time. Look at things objectively."

Yeah, that sounds legit, right?

"You don't believe that."

"No, I really don't. I just want to see you more often."

She chuckled. "So this is your master plan? Lure me back to Woodstone?"

"Exactly."

"I have one condition," she said.

"Lay it on me."

"Let me read one more. Just this once. Then, we do one entry each time."

"Fine. One more, and then we put it back."

"And if it turns out this is something bigger?" she asked. "If this journal points to something more than a tragedy, what do we do?"

"I'll talk to my brother."

"The detective?"

"Yeah, and he hates digging up old cases."

"Well then, we'd better make this worth it."

I held out my hand to help her up, already craving the contact before it happened. The moment her fingers closed around mine, my heart went absolutely feral. It was dainty, soft, warm, and fucking electric. Every nerve ending suddenly remembered what it meant to be alive.

For a moment, we just stood there. No words, just looking at each other. Her lips parted slightly, as if she was about to speak but forgot how. My thumb traced across her knuckles without permission.

She let go and wiped her hand on her jeans like nothing happened, as if she hadn't set my entire world tilting sideways.

"We got a deal, Miles?" I held it out again, my voice rougher than intended.

Not because I wanted to touch her again, and definitely not because I was already addicted to her pulse fluttering against my palm.

She hesitated for a heartbeat—long enough for me to wonder if she felt it too, this magnetic pull that made breathing feel more difficult. Then, she slid her hand into mine, and we shook on it. Something flickered in my chest —stupid, soft, and way too real for what this was supposed to be. I wanted to memorize the weight of her hand in mine.

"We've got a deal," she said, her voice a little breathless.

I reluctantly let go, my fingers trailing against hers longer than necessary, and moved to the couch, dropping down onto the worn cushions we probably shouldn't be sitting on. She followed, settling beside me.

Close, but not quite close enough. Never fucking close enough.

The inches between us felt like miles. I wanted to pull her into my lap and wrap her up as if it was normal, but that felt borderline insane. So, I leaned enough to nudge her knee with mine, savoring even that small contact, and inched closer so I could see.

She peered down at the journal and back up at me. The

look in her eyes made my chest tight. "Do you want to read it aloud?"

"You go for it."

What I really wanted was to watch her mouth form the words, to study the way her lashes cast shadows on her cheeks when she looked down.

She opened to the first page and started reading.

I almost left today.

I stood at the sink, staring at the road beyond the willow tree, thinking I could finally do it. Pack a bag, grab the cash I've hidden, take the car, and drive. The thought felt real this time, like I might actually have the courage.

Then, I heard the door and his voice, with that tight, sharp edge, like he knew what I'd been thinking.

I folded the dish towel. Sat back down. Pretended the thought never crossed my mind.

I stay because I have to. Because of the boy asleep down the hall, the one who carries the features of the man I wish had chosen me. The man who says he needs time, who whispers promises in the dark that might just be words to pass the time.

I tell myself it's temporary. That there will be a day when the pieces fall in my favor, when those whispered promises become real. But the longer I wait, the more I wonder if that day will ever come.

When Patrick looks at him…it's not the way a father should look at his child. It's like he's looking through him. Like he knows the truth I've kept buried.

And if he knows…

I won't let anything happen to him.

I'm trapped. I watch his hands, I measure my words, I keep my head down. I know the moment I falter, I'll pay for it. Even in the silence, even when he's gone, I can feel the weight of what's coming. Every day is survival.

"So she had an affair," Ellie whispered, peering over at me.

I nodded slowly. "Yeah, sounds like it."

"But she stayed." Ellie flipped back a few pages, scanning with her fingertip. "Look at this." She pointed at the page. "She mentions feeling trapped."

"She was scared."

Ellie's voice dropped, but there was an edge to it now. "You know what's classic? The way abusers isolate their victims right before they try to leave. She had cash hidden, had a plan. He probably knew it, but then he comes home mad, and, suddenly, she's staying. That's textbook intimidation."

She looked up at me. "The way she wrote about him…"

I let out a heavy breath and leaned forward, placing my elbows on my knees. "That line about him looking through the kid…"

"Exactly. That's not normal parental behavior." Ellie shifted, tucking her legs under her. "She says the boy wasn't his. That would explain the sudden behavioral shift if he suspected it. The paranoia. She knew the truth could make things worse."

"Like a kid finding a gun worse?"

"Yup. She says, *the boy asleep down the hall, the one who carries the features of the man I wish had chosen me.* Okay, so we have four players here—the kid, the husband, the wife, and this mystery person who is the real father."

"Sounds like it."

"What if he threatened the kid?" Ellie flipped back to the previous page. "What if that's why she stayed quiet—

not just fear for herself, but knowing he'd take it out on the boy if she said anything?

I tilted my head and smirked. "You do love true crime, huh?"

Ellie rolled her eyes, but she was smiling. "I'm serious. There's more to this, Sawyer. What if someone else came to that house that night of the incident? The real father? Or what if he knows what really happened? Maybe she was too afraid to say anything. Whoever the real dad is, I bet he knows something."

I probably should've told her to let it go, that it wasn't our business, but she looked so damn alive sitting there, digging into this like it mattered. Maybe that should've been my cue to be the responsible one. Instead, I stayed quiet. If chasing this thing kept her here a little longer, I wasn't about to get in the way.

I leaned back on the couch and stretched an arm behind her. "This is heavy shit, El."

She glanced up at me, her expression soft but steady. "Oh, I know, but I love this stuff. It relaxes me, remember?" She glanced at the journal again, fingertips resting on the edge of the page. "She wrote this as some silent plea for help."

"You're not gonna let this go, are you?"

"Not a chance."

My fingers brushed against hers as I lifted the journal from her lap. The leather binding was warm from where it had rested against her legs, and my thumb traced along her knuckle once again.

"Well, too bad." I closed it slowly, still not moving my hand. "You shook on it. Deal's a deal. We wait till next time."

She leaned forward. "You're seriously going to leave me hanging?"

"Absolutely. Builds character."

"You're annoying." Her voice was barely above a whisper.

"I've been called worse."

Ellie laughed, soft and breathy, but it caught in her throat when our eyes met. Her gaze dropped to my mouth and stayed there while my breathing slowed to almost nothing. She leaned closer, her lips parting slightly, and I could feel the warmth of her breath. She bit her lower lip, and I nearly—

She pulled back.

"Next time then," she whispered.

Yeah, next time.

I didn't believe in ghosts or cursed houses, didn't believe in chasing down old tragedies as if they owed us something.

But I believed in Ellie. So, if a dusty old journal kept her coming back here—kept her coming back to me?

Yeah. I'd read every word.

TWELVE

Ellie

I STEPPED INTO MY DRESSING ROOM AND FINALLY LET MYSELF breathe, a real breath for the first time in hours.

After a month-long hiatus, my first show back went off without a hitch—no forgotten lyrics and no wardrobe malfunctions. The lights, the music, the roar of the crowd, it all hit me at once, overwhelming and exhilarating. Ben, my new head of security, dove into the chaos at full speed, keeping everything under control. By the end, I was completely drained.

My body ached from head to toe, but it wasn't the physical kind. It was the pain of holding it all together and pretending to be the version of myself everyone expected —the bright, sparkly, endlessly resilient Ellie Miles.

Putting on that face was like slipping into a familiar costume, one that no longer quite fit. This life was a privilege, and I knew that. Being Ellie Miles meant something to people, which still blew my mind. But it didn't make it any less exhausting.

The last month had been about recovery, both body and mind, the latter more wrecked in a way I didn't want to admit, especially after Harold. I'd made a promise—to myself, to my fans—and after postponing more shows than I wanted to count. I owed it to them to show up.

And they did. Loud and wild, feeding me adrenaline until my bones forgot how tired they were—the energy in that stadium was electric, like a welcome home party with thousands of strangers.

The high was already fading. The adrenaline was wearing off and the crash was coming. It always did.

The last couple of weeks between rehearsals, travel, Sawyer, and that journal…I hadn't had room to unravel.

I'd been chasing shadows ever since we left that house, reading and re-reading the same five articles, as if they might say something new if I stared long enough. It felt like chasing the last thread of a true crime case—one where the podcast cuts off before the last episode, and you're left digging through forums like some armchair detective who can't let go.

I couldn't let go.

If I were being honest, it was more than the mystery pulling me back to Woodstone. It was Sawyer too.

Which made no fucking sense. This thing we were doing, whatever the hell it was, was supposed to be fake—a publicity stunt to get the media off my back about my ex and everything bad that happened in San Francisco. Keep the focus on something new, positive, and fun, especially with Harold trying to come in and spin the narrative wherever he could.

After only a few times together and all the texts and calls, I was craving him in ways that had nothing to do with cameras or headlines.

I didn't expect that, not from someone who admitted he used to crush on me from the outside looking in—drawn to a face on a magazine cover, a voice on the radio. I figured he'd be like the rest: curious, infatuated, and a little starstruck. I figured it would fade the second he saw the real me.

So far, that hadn't happened. If anything, I found myself memorizing the way his hands moved when he talked and wondering what they'd feel like on me. When he laughed at something I said, I caught myself staring at his mouth longer than I should have. When he'd catch me looking, instead of glancing away embarrassed, he'd hold my gaze until I was the one who had to break first—flustered and craving things I had no business wanting from a fake relationship.

A knock broke on my dressing room door, tearing through my thoughts.

"Come in," I called.

Rachel pushed the door open, smiling. "Another amazing show in the books. You crushed it."

I offered a tired smile. "Thanks."

"You ready for next week? Two shows in three days, some time off for the holidays, then back at it for a month."

"Yeah. I think it'll be fun."

I even wondered if I could convince Sawyer to come back to Woodstone for a few days over our two-week break.

"I'll let you get in your comfy clothes. Just wanted to say you killed it. When you're ready, we can go back to the hotel and get some room service?"

"Sounds like a dream. Thanks."

She gave me a smile and then stepped out, closing the door behind her. I pulled out my phone to check the final score from Sawyer's game. I hadn't caught the end, since I was getting zipped into a glitter jumpsuit and given last-minute reminders about choreography.

20–17.

They'd won. A grin tugged at my lips, and I tapped out a quick message.

> Congrats on the win. I'll have to watch some recaps tonight.

Did I understand football? Not really, but I had zero complaints about watching him kill it on the field. His reply came almost instantly.

> Thanks :) I'll have to see if I can find some footage of your show and get a good look at that pretty face, I miss already.

> Thanks. You didn't look too bad yourself tonight.

> You should see me without a shirt then. For fake research purposes, obviously.

> I'll take that under advisement.

> Please do.

I smirked and hearted the message. Warmth bloomed low in my stomach before I could talk myself out of it.

Fake, fake, fake.

I chanted in my head over and over. He was flirting to make it easier to pretend in public.

I peeled off my stage outfit, and I was halfway through swapping it for sweats when another text buzzed in.

> Since you're playing in Vegas next week, why don't we get together? I'll be close by.

> Did you look up my schedule?

Gotta know where my girl's at.

You'll be in Arizona. That's a long drive for only a few hours together.

Oh, did you look up my schedule?

And I've done worse things for a good cheeseburger. This would be for PR. We haven't exactly given the public much to chew on yet.

He wasn't wrong. The fake dating thing only worked if people actually, you know… saw us together.

We can grab dinner or something? Something casual?

Deal. Casual. Totally casual. Just you, me, and a few dozen paparazzi.

You're really selling the romance here.

You haven't seen anything yet, baby girl.

I rolled my eyes, smiling like an idiot. My thumb hovered over the keyboard for a second longer than necessary.

Can't wait.

A few hours later, I was holed up in the hotel room, with Rachel sprawled on the bed beside mine, both of us knee-deep in room service and halfway through a classic true crime doc.

"What a week," she said, tossing a piece of popcorn in the air and catching it in her mouth.

"I don't think I've actually sat down since Monday."

She gave me a look. "How was everything with Sawyer's family? Weren't you in…what was it? Woodchuck Falls?"

"Woodstone Falls," I said, laughing. "Surprisingly, it was really nice. I thought I'd be anxious, but it was…oddly peaceful."

The family dinner wasn't anything I could have expected. No flashing cameras, no prying eyes, just a house full of people who treated me like I belonged. Dotty's bluntness somehow felt like a secret handshake, and Noah's kindness was the kind that settled into your chest and made you breathe easier. Lilah and I found ourselves quietly swapping glances over the chaos, both of us newcomers trying to figure out where we fit. His brothers joked and laughed like this was just another Sunday night, and his dad's warmth—equal parts teasing and tender— was the glue of it all.

But it was Sawyer's niece, with her unstoppable energy and wide-eyed awe, who reminded me why this felt less like a performance and more like home.

I'd always been used to just my parents and me. Seeing a whole family come together like that was new for me, but it felt surprisingly nice, like watching pieces click into place in a way I hadn't expected.

Then, there was Sawyer.

Whenever I was around him, I felt safe in a way that defied explanation. I could say anything, and he wouldn't just listen. He'd somehow sense exactly what I needed, whether it was silence, advice, or validation. With him, I could finally let my guard down and be myself.

Rachel tilted her head. "You're thinking about him, aren't you?"

I shook my head. "No, not him. His family…and how the visit went."

"You enjoying big, cozy family vibes? Who are you and what have you done with my best friend?"

I grinned. "I know. Growth, right? But seriously, it was easy. I kept waiting for something to feel off, and it never did. Everyone actually seemed happy to be together."

She reached for a fry. "So, when are you going back?"

"No clue. Schedule's insane now that the tour's back on, but he wants to meet up after one of the shows next week."

Her eyes lit up. "Wait, he's coming to you?"

"Apparently."

"Ellie, that man definitely likes you."

"No, he doesn't. It's fake. We're fake, remember?"

But fake isn't calling me Ellie baby in that voice that could melt steel.

Or winking like he invented the gesture.

Or opening my door when no one's watching.

"Bullshit," she said. "A man doesn't fake date a pop star and bring her to a family dinner in the middle of nowhere for good press."

I tried to roll my eyes, but a smile tugged at my mouth anyway. "It was to convince his family."

Rachel narrowed her eyes. "You like him too."

"I don't know." My voice betrayed me. "I mean…I barely know the guy. I like being around him. He's kind—and not pretend kind, actual kind. And with him, I don't feel that weird, icky static, like someone's only talking to me because of who I am. I feel…stupid giddy. Like a teenager with a crush."

My voice dropped. "But after Harold…I don't know if I can ever fully love someone again."

"That's fair. You thought he was your forever."

She was right. I wrote songs that practically signed a blood oath to that belief, but Harold loved the Ellie everyone else saw, the version of me with perfect hair and a million-dollar smile. In reality, I was quieter, goofier, and a little chaotic at times. He never cared to see the me who burned dinner wearing old sweatpants or stayed up way too late writing lyrics.

"It just…sucks," I whispered, leaning my head back against the pillows. "Maybe I'm meant to be the girl with the guitar and a broken heart, destined to sing about love but never actually get the real thing."

She peered over at me. "You're so much more than that, El. I believe with everything in me that someone's out there who would move mountains just to see you smile."

And I was afraid I already knew who that someone might be.

"But maybe the real question isn't whether Sawyer likes you. Maybe it's whether you're ready to let someone in again."

Her words landed like a stone to my chest.

"Yeah…maybe."

I was pretty sure no one could ever want the person I was once the curtain closed—not even someone as ridiculous and big-hearted as Sawyer.

THIRTEEN

Sawyer

THE LOCKER ROOM SMELLED LIKE SWEAT, ADRENALINE, AND whatever protein powder had exploded in West's bag. Again.

"I swear to God," Bronx muttered, grimacing and peeling off his hoodie. "You should be banned from bringing anything Fruity Pebbles flavored within ten yards of this place."

"It's plant-based," West said, as if that was supposed to make it better. He grinned, already half-dressed in his gear, his pads askew and his brown hair doing whatever the hell it wanted. "Organic pea protein. Great for muscle recovery and shit."

"And terrible for nostrils everywhere," I said.

"Yeah, peas shouldn't smell like fucking feet," Bronx said flatly.

I laughed, tugging on my compression shirt. "Just be grateful he's not on another liver cleanse. Last time, he looked like he was on the brink of death."

"Jealousy." West threw a towel at my head. "That's what I'm hearing."

"You hearing voices again?"

I chucked the towel back at him, and he caught it midair.

"Might be time to lay off the pre-workout," I said.

"No pre-workout. That shit's full of nasty chemicals."

Bronx and I gave him a look.

He shrugged. "Sorry, I care about what goes into my body."

Bronx cracked a rare smile, tapping his fingers on the top of his locker like a drummer warming up. "So anyways. Tell us about Ellie."

I groaned, already bracing myself.

"Oh, now you don't wanna talk about her." West's eyes lit up. "As if you didn't call me last week screaming, '*Ellie came home with me. She's so pretty and so smart. I think she might actually like me.*'"

"She's dating you, dumbass." Bronx glanced at me. "Of course she likes you."

I glanced down at the jersey in my hands. I trusted my

guys, but when it came to Ellie, I wasn't ready to put it all out there yet. From the outside, it was real—like maybe I was finally the guy who actually got the girl, even if the world didn't know the whole story.

"Come on," West said. "You can't just announce to the world that you're dating her and then give us the silent treatment."

"We're just…spending time together when we can. Getting to know each other."

West scowled. "Wow, lamest answer possible."

Bronx leaned a shoulder against his locker, his arms folded. "But you like her."

"Of course I like her." I shoved my pads into place. "She's smart and funny. She actually listens when I talk—and not just about football. When I say something dumb, she doesn't make me feel dumb. She rolls with it. Makes me feel…" I trailed off.

"Less dumb?" West offered.

I pointed at him. "Exactly."

"She's cool," I said, my voice softer. "It's easy being around her."

Bronx gave a thoughtful nod. He always caught the stuff beneath the surface. "Is she coming to the game?"

"She's got a show in Vegas tomorrow." I pulled my jersey off. "I'm heading out there to see her after we win today."

"Did you at least ask her to come for the game?" West asked.

I shrugged.

West winced. "Damn, and here I was gonna tell you she's out of your league. Now I'm thinking she realized it herself."

I flipped him off and sat down to lace up my cleats. "Get fucked."

Bronx studied me as if he were reading a play that hadn't been called yet. He knew. Or at least, he knew there was more I wasn't saying.

Even if this whole thing started as a way to spin a story and shift a headline, I wasn't sure what to think of it anymore. Not when we stayed up too late texting, or when she laughed at my dumb jokes and looked at me like maybe she saw something good.

West clapped a hand on my back as he walked by. "Well, I'm happy for you. You know, assuming she doesn't dump your ass."

"Appreciate the vote of confidence."

"Let's win this one. I want to look good in the highlights."

Bronx cracked his knuckles. "Let's give her something worth watching."

I stood up, rolled out my neck, and shook out the nerves.

FOURTEEN

Ellie

MY SCHEDULE WAS PACKED STRAIGHT THROUGH CHRISTMAS. I had a show tomorrow night, and my voice was already on partial vocal rest on my off days—no more interviews, no singing in the shower, just ginger tea and silence.

When Rachel saw Sawyer's team was playing a few hours from Vegas, it suddenly became a strategic PR opportunity. Her words. Not mine.

Still…I didn't say no.

Maybe it was dumb not to tell him. The whole thing made me feel like a teenager sneaking into her crush's Friday night football game instead of a grown woman with platinum records and a private jet waiting on standby. But it felt…fun. A little reckless. For some reason, I wanted to be a little reckless with him. It was easier to let go when he was around.

Would he be weirded out if I showed up without telling him? Was that crossing some invisible line? I wasn't his girlfriend—not technically, not actually.

Fake dating was more complicated than I thought.

And Rachel, being the miracle worker she was, managed to pull last-minute suite tickets for us. I sipped a cocktail that cost more than I cared to think about and sank into the leather seat while the stadium hummed with energy.

What is my life?

I used to sit on the couch next to my parents, watching the news on a secondhand TV that flickered every time the fridge kicked on. I lived in a two-bedroom house with a roof that leaked when it rained and had a dad who worked nights just to keep the lights on. And now, I was here, in a luxury suite at an NFL game, wearing Sawyer's jersey, pretending to date a man who made my heart beat faster than it had any business doing.

"So," Rachel said, dropping into the seat beside me, "how are we feeling about tonight?"

"Good. We haven't really been seen together since the article dropped, so this will help keep the narrative going."

She gave me a flat look. "Nope. That's the press release answer. I already know that one."

I groaned and slouched back into the seat. "Fine. I'm excited, okay? Which is stupid, because this is all a ruse, but…I like being around him."

She smiled like she'd been waiting for me to admit that. "That's not stupid, El."

"It's dangerous," I murmured, tipping the glass in my hand so the ice clinked against the sides. "Getting too close. Forgetting where the lines are."

"Does it feel fake?"

On paper, yes. We weren't dating. This wasn't forever. It was a strategy, a patch-up job for both our public images. He wasn't mine. I wasn't his.

But then, I'd think about how Sawyer didn't make me feel like I had to shrink to fit the way Harold always did.

"I'll let you know when I figure that out," I muttered.

We both turned as the lights shifted, and the crowd cheered.

The players ran out onto the field, and there he was: Sawyer leading the charge, helmet in one hand, that trademark grin stretched across his face. My breath caught before I could stop it. That stupid twist in my chest came again, equally hopeful and terrifying.

"Well," Rachel said, nudging me with her elbow, "I'll let you finish eye-fucking your boyfriend. I have to pee. Need anything?"

I smirked. "No, I'm good. Thanks."

She laughed as she stood.

"What?" I asked.

"You didn't deny he's your boyfriend."

"Ugh, shush."

"Love you," she sing-songed, strutting away.

I was grateful for the time alone—to watch him without trying to act casual or unaffected, even though Rachel knew the truth more than anyone.

He didn't see me. Of course, he didn't. He was one of fifty-something players under the lights, with thousands of fans in every direction. Still, I couldn't take my eyes off him. He was warming up with the rest of the team, tossing the ball back and forth, running drills, stretching—completely locked in and focused.

I'd seen him flirt, joke, and charm everyone in a ten-foot radius, but this was Sawyer in his element. He had all the confidence he typically carried, but he moved like someone who belonged exactly where he was. Tall, powerful, all sharp lines and fluid motion.

He was bigger than most of the guys around him. Broader. Stronger. There was a kind of grace to the way he moved, as if the game wasn't something he played—it was something he understood at a cellular level.

And watching him like this?

Yeah. It did something to me.

Ugh, why couldn't I have decided to have a pretend relationship with someone I would never be interested in?

Rachel came back eventually but sank into her seat, eyes glued to her phone. "Need to catch up on emails real quick."

Fine by me. I was too far gone in my own world anyway.

A sharp whistle cut through the air, signaling the end of warmups. The announcer's voice boomed over the speakers, echoing across the stadium as the players gathered on their respective sidelines. I leaned forward without thinking, my drink completely forgotten. Rachel glanced over and smiled—just a little smug.

The lights dimmed. The music hit with heavy beats, pulsing bass loud enough that the floor shook under my feet. Spotlights danced across the field as the starting lineup was announced. The whole stadium became one giant, electric performance.

I was used to stages and hearing my name screamed by crowds, but nothing compared to this. This was his stage, and I was in the audience.

And God help me, I didn't want to look away.

Halfway through the game, the Rebels were on fire. They were up by fourteen, and the momentum was all theirs. I was on my feet cheering, the stadium doing the same alongside me.

Then, suddenly, the big screen lit up right on me. I wasn't surprised. In fact, I was shocked it didn't happen earlier. My face filled the screen, my name echoing across the stadium speakers.

"Ladies and gentlemen, platinum-selling, award-winning artist, Ellie Miles!"

The crowd roared like I was center stage at one of my own shows. As if that wasn't surreal enough, they started playing one of my songs.

My face flushed as Sawyer's head snapped to the screen. He squinted into the lights, scanning the suite level until he found me. And the smile that spread across his face? Yeah, that would've made my knees weak if I weren't already sitting down.

Rachel giggled and leaned in, cupping a hand over her mouth. "I think he might be a little smitten with you."

I groaned under my breath, trying to keep my expression neutral. "Must you say that when my face is up there for thousands of people to see?"

"Of course."

The music faded, and the players moved into position. I didn't know much about football other than the basics. All I could see was that Sawyer was back on the field, all huge and focused.

He was like a damn boulder that had somehow

sprouted legs and said, *You know what? Maybe I'll try the NFL.*

They froze for a beat, and the stadium was weirdly quiet. Then, the ball snapped. Everything exploded into motion.

I had no clue what was happening.

There was yelling. Crashing. Bodies slamming into each other like a choreographed demolition derby. Then, someone dropped the ball. I was pretty sure that wasn't supposed to happen.

One of the announcers bellowed over the loudspeakers. "Ball's live! Ball's on the ground!"

A collective gasp rippled through the crowd.

Players scrambled. People shouted. My heart launched into my throat.

And then, Sawyer grabbed the ball. Just…picked up the ball and ran.

Wait. He was running.

With the ball?

The announcer's voice cracked with disbelief. "And it's —number seventy-one, Sawyer James? The left tackle has the ball! It's a live ball, and he's running with it!"

I was on my feet before I realized it.

"Go, go, go!" I yelled, as if he could actually hear me over thousands of people screaming.

He bulldozed through one guy and twisted past another. It wasn't graceful. It was wild, messy, and border-line impossible, but he kept going.

Twenty yards. Ten.

And—he was in the end zone.

Touchdown.

The entire stadium erupted. Fans were jumping, spilling drinks, and losing their collective minds. Team-mates tackled him in celebration.

And me?

I was frozen.

Sawyer pulled off his helmet, chest heaving, sweat-slicked and grinning like a kid on Christmas morning. He did a silly little dance, and then he looked up right at me.

He blew me a kiss once again, as if we were the only two people in the entire stadium. Heat erupted over my entire face, down my neck, and Rachel clutched my arm.

"I swear, if you don't marry that man…"

I couldn't respond. Because even if part of me wanted to believe we could be real, I wasn't sure it ever would ever be possible.

FIFTEEN

Sawyer

"HELL OF A GAME, BOYS," COACH CALLED OUT ONCE WE WERE back in the locker room.

A chorus of cheers and fist bumps broke out as I stripped off my pads and tossed them into my locker. My jersey hit the bench in a sweaty heap. After a few post-game interviews, I was grateful to finally be done and on my way out of there.

"Nice touchdown, James," Bronx said, slapping my shoulder on his way to the showers. "Didn't know you had little ballerina feet under all that bulk."

I grinned. "Don't get jealous just 'cause I'm pretty."

He snorted. "Hey, defense held the line. We made that win possible."

"Team effort," I said, and I meant it.

"Yo, what about me?" West piped up from across the room, already halfway out of his pads. "Golden boy needs some love too."

"You're lucky I caught that fumble, man." I pointed at him and smirked. "Having a live ball. Let me get that touchdown too."

"I gave you a Christmas gift early." He grinned, smug as hell. "You're welcome."

I laughed, shook my head, and grabbed a towel. "Appreciate the assist, sweetheart."

Talking shit with these guys was second nature, but underneath it, my pulse hadn't slowed since the second I saw her pretty face on the big screen.

She was all lit up and radiant, wearing my jersey like it belonged on her. I think it did. My heart damn near tripped over itself. When I found her up in that suite—smiling, eyes locked on me as if I was the main event instead of just the guy who caught a lucky break?

Forget the touchdown. That was the best part of my night.

I rushed through my shower faster than ever, scrubbing off the game sweat like a man with a mission.

I needed to see her and for her to know that touchdown wasn't just for the fans, the score, or even the highlight reel.

It was for her.

I stepped back into the locker room, tugging my hoodie over my head, still drying my hair.

West raised a brow. "You heading out already?"

"Yup."

He grinned. "That girl got you sprinting to her, huh?"

"Sure does," I said without missing a beat.

He clapped a hand on my back. "Go get your girl."

My girl.

I broke into a full-blown grin I didn't even try to hide. "That's the plan."

I didn't know if she'd still be here or what I was going to say if she was, but I knew one thing for sure.

If she was waiting, I was running.

Just as I hit the tunnel, Coach's voice cut through the post-game noise. "James. Got a sec?"

I hesitated. My hand was already pushing the door open. "Uh…yeah. Of course."

He nodded toward his office with a tight smile. "Don't worry. I'll make it quick. Gotta get you back to Ellie, right?"

"Yes, sir," I said, trying not to bounce on my heels.

He stepped inside, leaving the door open, and I followed. The office still smelled like turf and sweat, the way it always did after a win.

"Hell of a game tonight." He leaned against his desk. "That fumble recovery? Great job."

"Thank you. Right place, right time."

He gave me a look. "That wasn't luck, James. That was you seeing the play before it happened. Don't downplay it."

"Thank you, sir."

"Still sure you want to hang up your helmet after this season? We'd love to keep you on."

"I'm sure. It's time for me to settle down."

"I can't say I'm not disappointed, but I understand. We will be losing a hell of a player, but you deserve it." He crossed his arms, tone shifting slightly. "Gotta say…whatever this thing is between you and Ellie, it's been good for the team. The press can't stop talking about it. Whether it's real or not, I don't care. Good job."

He gave me a knowing smirk, and I tried not to flinch.

"Yeah, appreciate that, Coach," I said carefully.

"Keep your head straight. Don't let it mess with your focus. You've always been the guy I could count on to do his job and keep the locker room solid. That matters more than the media."

"Yes, sir. I won't let it get to me."

He gave me a nod like that was the right answer. "Good. Now, go. I know you're waiting to see her."

I didn't even try to deny it. Yeah, he was right.

The game was over, but my heart was still in the stands—or wherever the hell she was.

SIXTEEN

Ellie

My security team led Rachel and me through the stadium's lower levels: concrete walls, flickering fluorescents, and the distant echo of the crowd. We moved past the security checkpoint outside the locker room. I could hear voices from inside—celebratory chatter, bursts of laughter, the occasional cheer.

Some of the players had already wandered by with pads slung over their shoulders and wet hair. A few of them did a double-take when they saw me, offered small smiles, and kept moving.

The door opened again. Sawyer—gorgeous, disheveled, and stupidly handsome in a way that should have been illegal—had his head down, thumbs flying over his phone, completely unaware.

My phone buzzed in my pocket, and I pulled it out.

Hey. You still here?

I grinned and typed back.

Look up.

When he did, his whole face changed.

"Ellie," he breathed.

And then, he launched.

Six-foot-five of pure muscle and post-game adrenaline barreled straight toward me. Before I could react, he scooped me up and spun me in a full circle, my feet swinging midair.

I shrieked out a startled laugh. "Sawyer! What are you doing? No one's even watching."

"Don't care." He grinned like a lunatic as he set me down, brushing back a piece of my hair. "You're here."

"Oh my God," Rachel said. "I think I just fell in love."

Sawyer turned toward her with mock seriousness, pointing at me. "Hey, this one's taken."

Rachel stuck out a hand and smiled. "Rachel Thomas, Ellie's PR wrangler slash therapist slash emotional support human."

"Sawyer James." He gave her a firm shake. "So you're the legendary Rachel."

"And you're the golden retriever she won't shut up about."

I elbowed her. Hard.

Sawyer puffed his chest. "If she's talking about me, I must be doing something right."

"As long as I still get her for wine nights, you can have her on weekends."

"Deal." Sawyer's eyes snapped back to mine, soft and full of something dangerous.

"I'm literally right here," I muttered, trying not to blush. "Why does this feel like a bizarre custody battle?"

He leaned in, voice low and rough in my ear. "If it were up to me, you'd be a full-time arrangement."

My breath caught. No. Absolutely not. He had no right sounding like that: deep, gravelly, and full of promises he hadn't even made yet.

"Careful," I whispered. "Someone might think you actually like me."

"Isn't that the point?" He pulled back enough to flash that grin, the one that made my knees question their entire structural integrity. "And I do like you, Ellie Miles. That's exactly the problem."

Rachel groaned. "Okay, I'm definitely in love."

Sawyer laced his fingers through mine as if it was nothing. "You sure you're not just jealous?"

"Please. Men exhaust me. Plus, I've witnessed enough late-night brooding over you to last a lifetime. I'll keep living vicariously through El."

"Rachel," I hissed.

Sawyer's face lit up like I'd just handed him a Super Bowl ring. "You brooded over me?"

"I'm revoking your best friend status," I muttered.

He leaned down and brushed his lips against my temple. "Too late."

And just like that, I was toast. Floaty, flushed, and utterly undone.

"Want to grab food?" he asked, casual and likely completely unaware of the cardiac episode I was having.

"Yeah," I somehow managed to say. "That'd be nice."

Rachel squeezed my arm. "I'm heading back to the hotel. We've got an early flight to Vegas, so try not to let your lover boy keep you out too late."

"I'll have her back by ten," Sawyer said, tugging me close.

"You better, or I'm suing for full custody," she chirped.

"You guys coming?" he asked Ben.

"Yes, sir. We have the car ready outside."

"All right. Let's roll."

"Wait," Rachel called. "Where are you going? I can leak a location, get some coverage."

I groaned. "Do we have to?"

She shot me a look. "The cameras are the whole point, remember?"

"Yeah, yeah."

"I'll text you the spot," he said. "It's close."

"Okay. Love you, El. Be safe."

"Always. Love you."

Sawyer slipped his arm around my shoulders as we left the tunnel, his body still warm from the game. Adrenaline wafted off him, his smile contagious.

"I didn't think I'd see you until tomorrow," he said.

I glanced up at him, the corners of my mouth tugging up. "Surprise. I thought it'd be fun to show up. Are you mad?"

He looked down at me, brows raised. "Mad? Ellie, you showing up at the rare game I get to score a touchdown? That's basically my dream scenario."

We passed through the security checkpoint with Ben and another member of my team beside us, scanning the surroundings.

Sawyer nodded at the exit. "You ready for the circus out there?"

"I've seen worse." I leaned into his side. "Besides, I've got you."

That earned me a soft laugh. "Damn right you do."

The second we stepped outside, the mayhem hit: camera shutters clicking, reporters yelling our names, fans shouting.

"There she is! Ellie, over here!"

"Sawyer! Big win tonight—what's next?"

Flashes sparked from every angle. I kept my head

down and stayed close to him, one hand on his chest as we moved through the crowd. He didn't flinch or slow down, keeping one hand on my back and guiding us through.

Ben was already at the curb, yanking open the back door of the SUV. "Straight in," he said, eyes never leaving the crowd.

Sawyer helped me first before sliding in beside me. The door slammed shut behind us. Inside, it was quiet, just the hum of the engine and the low rumble of voices from outside.

I exhaled slowly, leaning back into the leather seat. "That was fun."

"You okay?" he asked, already turning toward me.

"Yeah." I nodded, stealing a glance at him. "You?"

He shrugged, eyes still on me. "I am now."

For a beat, we just sat there, breathing the same air, shoulders almost touching.

"I didn't have a plan," I said finally. "I just wanted to see you, and I thought it would be good for the media."

"You could've just said you missed me," he teased.

"And inflate your ego? I'll pass."

I bit my bottom lip as I eyed him up and down. His hair had grown longer since we first met, the dark strands curling at the edges. I found myself staring at those curls, imagining how they'd feel wrapped around my fingers, how his breath would hitch if I tugged just hard enough.

His brown eyes held a familiar softness, but something darker flickered when he caught my lingering stare. My gaze drifted down to his mouth and back up to find him watching me with an intensity that made my pulse jump. The space between us suddenly was too wide and too narrow all at once. I wanted to step closer to see if his skin was as warm as it looked, to find out what sound he'd make if I pressed my lips to that spot where his jaw met his neck.

He shifted, and I caught the way his gaze dropped to my mouth before snapping back up. My breath came a little quicker.

"Hungry?" he asked lowly.

"Starving." The word came out breathier than I intended. I let my gaze drop to his mouth for a moment before meeting his eyes.

He smirked, but I caught the way his jaw ticked. "Good. I know a spot. And I scored tonight, so I'm off my training diet for the evening."

His hand moved to rest in the space between us, inches from my thigh. I shifted in my seat, letting my knee brush against his as I angled toward him. My hand found the edge of the seat, fingertips grazing his knuckles on what could have been accident.

Oopsie.

The SUV pulled away from the curb and into the night, the stadium falling behind us in a blur of lights. The city was quieter out here, like it was letting us catch our breath.

"Where to?" Ben asked from the front seat.

Sawyer rattled off a couple of cross streets and pulled out his phone. "Just texted Rachel. Told her to call in the crazies."

I raised an eyebrow. "You say that like it's something to look forward to."

His grin widened. "With you, everything is something to look forward to, Ellie baby."

I didn't answer, mostly because his hand was resting on my leg, just above my knee. His thumb brushed aimlessly in slow, small circles against my jeans.

And he called me Ellie baby. *Again.*

When the car took a sharp turn, I let myself sway into

him, my shoulder pressing against his arm, my hair brushing his neck. I felt him go perfectly still beside me.

I cleared my throat, grasping at something, *anything* else to focus on. "Nice game, by the way."

He glanced over. "Thanks. I gotta say, you look damn good in my jersey."

I arched a brow. "Oh, this old thing? Just pulled it out of my closet this morning."

"You're lying."

"You're right. I bought it at the merch stand before the game."

He chuckled, that low, sexy laugh I liked way too much. "Well then, I'm getting you more. You've got the blue now, but we still need to get you gold, white, dark blue...maybe even a throwback."

"That many?" I teased. "Seems excessive."

"Probably. Don't care. Nothing but the best for my girl."

Before I could answer, Ben spoke. "We're here, ma'am."

I turned toward the window and blinked in surprise. We were parked on a small side street in a historic part of the city. Brick sidewalk lined the streets with cute iron balconies and strings of lights. Nestled between two boutique shops was a small Italian restaurant, its windows glowing warm against the cool night.

"What is this place?" I asked.

"Little hole in the wall spot I found years ago. I come here every time I'm in town. Kind of a tradition now."

I smiled. "Sounds perfect."

He glanced at me—not with the cocky grin or the flirty smirk, but something softer. "Is this okay? I know we didn't really make a plan."

"It's great. Honestly, I love not having to make a decision for once."

Ben stepped out and rounded the car with Sawyer on his heels. Before Ben went to open my door, Sawyer said something to him that I couldn't make out from inside the car. Ben gave a slight nod and stepped back.

Sawyer opened my door.

I peered up at him, eyes catching his.

"Ready?" he asked, offering his hand.

I nodded and stepped out, and his hand found the small of my back as we walked toward the entrance. The street wasn't packed, but there were a few paparazzi scattered around, snapping pictures. A couple of shouted questions flew our way as we walked inside.

Sawyer didn't flinch as he leaned in and whispered in my ear. "Almost there."

I fought the shiver that rolled down my spine.

The moment we stepped inside, the energy shifted. The noise melted away, replaced with low conversation, the gentle clink of silverware, and soft jazz playing through the space. The lights were dim, golden, dreamy.

It smelled incredible—garlic, fresh basil, and something baking in a wood-fired oven. My stomach gave an embarrassing growl.

Sawyer's hand slid from my back to my waist, guiding me around a corner as a petite woman in her sixties burst through a swinging door from the kitchen. She wore a black apron, her gray hair piled into a bun.

"Sawyer James," she shouted in an Italian accent, her face lighting up. She threw her arms open for him. "My boy! Look at you!"

He let go of me long enough to pull her into a hug. "Miss Isabella. You're still the boss around here, huh?"

"Always." She kissed both his cheeks with loud smacks. "You haven't been here in forever. I was starting to think you forgot me."

"Never," he said, smiling big and boyish.

She turned, eyes narrowing, studying me. "And who is this beauty?"

"This is Ellie," he said, sliding an arm back around my waist. "My girlfriend."

My heart did a not-so-casual somersault. I glanced up at Isabella, who watched me with a knowing look, her eyes twinkling. "Oh, this is your girl, huh?"

Sawyer looked entirely too pleased with himself. "Yes, ma'am."

"Well, she's a pretty little thing. Keep her, will ya?"

"That's the plan."

I laughed, warm all over. "I'll try to make it worth his while."

"Oh, I like her," Isabella said, patting my cheek. "Smart mouth. That's what this boy needs."

"I'm right here," Sawyer muttered, but he was grinning.

She waved a hand. "Good. You need someone who doesn't fall for that 'I'm so tall and charming' act. He's actually a big softie inside. Sit, sit. I'll bring wine. You want the usual?"

He turned to me. "What do you like?"

"I'm not picky."

He looked back at Isabella. "The usual would be great."

She disappeared back into the kitchen, and Sawyer pulled out my chair, sitting across from me. The table was tucked into a corner with a view of the whole cozy dining room, a tiny candle flickering between us. Luckily, there weren't many people around. A few seemed to recognize us but respected our privacy.

"This place is adorable." I glanced around at the exposed brick and twinkle lights strung over the bar.

"She's been running it since before I was in the league.

Found it years ago. I came in for takeout, and she fed me four courses and made me promise to call my dad and tell him I love him."

"And you've been loyal ever since?"

"I'm a simple man. Feed me pasta, insult me a little, and I'll never leave."

I grinned, folding my arms on the table. "Good to know."

Isabella returned with two glasses of red wine and a basket of garlic knots that smelled like heaven. "Start with this. I'll bring you something good."

"You're a saint," Sawyer said, grabbing a knot.

"I'm underpaid is what I am." She winked at me. "Don't let him forget that."

Once she was gone again, Sawyer tore a piece of bread and popped it in his mouth. "So, did you enjoy the game?"

"You want honesty?" I said, taking a sip of wine.

"Always."

"You look good out there."

He nearly choked. "That's what you noticed?"

"Well that, and the fact you apparently launched yourself over someone to get the ball and ran it into the end zone."

"Hey, it worked."

"You show off. You're crazy."

"And you liked it?"

I bit my lip. "Maybe."

Sawyer leaned back, smug and relaxed, looking at me like I was already his favorite part of the night.

SEVENTEEN

Sawyer

I was so screwed it wasn't even funny. Astronomically, catastrophically, write-my-obituary-now levels of screwed.

The jersey hung her like a dress, which was doing absolutely nothing for my ability to form coherent thoughts. My name stretched across her back in bold letters, advertising exactly who she belonged to, and my caveman brain was having a complete meltdown about it.

Her hair was wild and messy from the wind, and her cheeks were flushed pink from the wine. Don't get me started on her lips. Fuck, they were stained a deep berry color that made me want to do some very unprofessional things that involved that mouth. Maybe while wearing nothing but my jersey.

Jesus. Focus.

I was a grown man who could handle seeing an attractive woman in his jersey without having a complete psychological breakdown, but lying to myself was probably a bad sign.

I dragged in a breath, planting my elbows on the table

and willing my brain toward safer terrain. Mystery. Ghosts. Old diaries tucked under floorboards. As if that was any safer.

"So." I cleared my throat. "Did you fall down the true crime rabbit hole after you left Woodstone?"

She set her glass down and tucked a strand of hair behind her ear. "The journal? Yeah, I probably spent way too many hours online looking into it. Found a marriage record for a Patrick and Lauren Hutchinson at your address. They were married for seven years."

"So Lauren is L then?"

"Looks like it. Her husband was the son of a congressman, but there's not much information on him either. No obituary for her, so she's probably still out there somewhere." Her brow furrowed. "She just...disappeared."

I shrugged. "Seems like if she is still alive, she turned into a recluse. Maybe there wouldn't be an obituary for her anywhere."

"That's possible. There's no knowing exactly what happened to her, it seems."

"I asked around town a little, but no one knew anything."

The candle between us flickered, and I found myself memorizing the way the light caught in her eyes. Outside, rain began pattering against the windows.

"When do we read the next entry?" I wanted her back in Woodstone, in my house, in my life.

Her lips curved into a small smile. "Trying to lure me back with the journal?"

"Absolutely."

"I mean, you're the one who made the rule about reading them together, in your house."

I shrugged. "Very official rule. Cannot be broken under any circumstance."

"I don't know. We didn't sign a contract."

I shifted forward, close enough that our knees almost touched under the table. "What does your schedule look like?"

She toyed with her wine glass, her nail tracing a pattern on the stem. "Says the guy who Googles my tour dates." She laughed. "I have a break after tomorrow's show. I'll be off until after the New Year."

I hesitated for a second, and the words tumbled out of my mouth. "Come with me to Woodstone for Christmas. I don't have a game until a few days after, and I'm headed there on Christmas Eve."

"Uh…" She went completely still, the glass halfway to her mouth.

"Sorry, you probably already have plans with your folks."

"No, actually, I don't." She set her glass down carefully. "They've been traveling a lot lately and are going on a cruise for Christmas. I told them I'd be fine, since I'm so busy with touring anyway."

"What were your plans then?"

"Rachel invited me to her family's house." She scrunched her face. "But honestly? I was thinking about staying home, ordering way too much takeout, and having a movie marathon. My family's more of a birthday family anyway. I haven't put up a tree or lights in years."

I opened my mouth, closed it, and ran a hand through my hair. "You shouldn't be alone for Christmas."

"I'm perfectly capable of entertaining myself."

"I know you are, but…" I leaned forward. "Come with me. We could read another diary entry, stay in, light a fire."

I paused then added with a grin, "I'll make you cookies. From scratch."

Her expression was unreadable. Not hesitant exactly, but…careful.

"It will be nice," I murmured. "To get away from all the noise. Just for a bit."

Ellie studied me for what felt like forever, her fingers absently tracing the rim of her wine glass. "Are you sure?"

"Completely sure."

She held my gaze for another beat and slowly nodded. "Okay."

"Okay?"

"I have a hard time saying no to you apparently."

Something in my chest eased. "Okay. It's settled, but can I still come to your show tomorrow?"

"Of course. You're already on the VIP list." She winced. "Fair warning—my parents will be there. They don't make every show, but they try to come when they can. Hopefully, that won't make it weird."

"Not weird at all."

She gave me a look. "Even though we're not actually dating and they think we are? You realize they're going to have questions, right?"

I couldn't help but laugh. "I think I can survive pretending to be your adoring fake boyfriend for one night. I've been practicing."

She snorted. "Yeah, but this time, you'll be under full parental interrogation."

"I'll be on my best behavior. Scout's honor."

She cocked her head, eyes narrowing suspiciously. "Were you actually a Boy Scout?"

"Absolutely not." I held up three fingers anyway. "But I look trustworthy when I do this, right? Plus, I'm great with parents. Moms adore me. Dads usually ask for fantasy football tips and try to act intimidating. I'll be a good boy, I promise."

She shook her head, laughing. "You're something else."

"And yet you're still agreeing to spend Christmas with me." I leaned back, too pleased with myself. "So really, who's winning here?"

She shook her head. "Don't make me regret this."

"Wouldn't dream of it."

EIGHTEEN

Ellie

"Okay, don't forget: we changed the order of the first few songs, and the outfit change halfway through is happening later now. Oh, and—"

"Fireworks are going off right before the last song," I said. "I know, Rach."

She gave a big, dramatic sigh. "I know you do. That's why you're the superstar. You'll do great."

I smiled faintly, settling into the vanity chair as the low hum of the opening act came through the walls.

Rachel hovered for a second longer. "I'll go check on things out there. Sawyer's out in the tent, all heart-eyed, waiting for you. Love you."

"Love you too."

The door clicked shut behind her. My fingers found the familiar weight of silver at my earlobes, adjusting what didn't need adjusting. The woman in the mirror wore my face but someone else's composure—steady gaze, shoulders squared, the practiced stillness of repetition. Someone who had done this a hundred times before.

The door opened again. At first, I thought Rachel had

come back, but no. Instead, it was the last person I ever wanted to see.

Harold.

He stepped inside with that same cocky stride I'd once mistaken for confidence and that too-familiar face that now made my skin crawl.

I shot to my feet. "How the hell did you get back here?"

He dangled a lanyard between his fingers, displaying his tour badge.

"Still works, apparently," he said in a clipped tone.

I moved toward the door. "You need to leave. Now."

His jaw worked slowly. "Ellie, come on. It doesn't have to be like this."

My stomach lurched, but I forced steel into my voice. "Actually, it does. Leave."

"Try to look at it from my point of view." He gestured helplessly before his hands fell to his sides. "I was trying to save what was left of us. You were drowning, pulling me down with you. I thought…" He ran his hand through his hair. "I thought if I gave you space, you'd realize how good we are for each other. Come on; everyone thinks so."

The audacity of this fucking man.

"You're delusional if you think we're getting back together after that pathetic speech. You've been dragging me through the press for weeks, and now you break into my dressing room to tell me we're good together?"

"I was there every single time you fell apart." His voice cracked. "That counts for something. You need me."

"No." The word came out with a bitter laugh. "I used to think I did, but you liked it that way, didn't you?"

Something flickered across his face—guilt, maybe? Or just annoyance at being caught. "That's not how it was."

"Oh, then tell me how it was." I stepped closer. "Because

from where I'm standing, you never loved me. You loved the access, the spotlight, the version of me you could parade around. The story you could sell to the highest bidder."

"That's not…" He reached for me then caught himself, his hands trembling before he buried them in his pockets. "Ellie."

The door swung open, and Rachel appeared, phone already in hand.

"What the hell are you doing in here?" she barked. "Security's on their way."

Harold's gaze flicked between us. "Come on, Rachel. Give us a minute."

"Minute's up," she said flatly.

His voice turned pleading, desperate, as he looked back at me. "Please. I know I screwed up, but we can—"

Sawyer filled the doorway like a storm front moving in. No words. No warning. Just steady, terrifying calm. His eyes locked on Harold, and every hair on my body stood on end.

"I think it's time for you to go," Sawyer said, his voice low.

Harold straightened. "This is none of your business."

Sawyer didn't even blink. He placed himself between Harold and me, blocking his access to me completely.

"It became my business the second you opened your mouth to *my* girlfriend. Go. Now."

"Or what?" Harold seethed.

Sawyer smiled, but it didn't reach his eyes. "Or I'll make sure you understand why that's not a smart question to ask."

Harold looked past Sawyer to me. "Is this about him? Seriously? You think he'll still think you're perfect when the honeymoon phase dies, and he sees what I had to deal with? I gave you everything. You'll come crawling back. You always do."

Rachel groaned. "Oh, shut up already."

Harold's gaze shifted back to Sawyer. "This won't last. She's too much of a fucking mess for anyone to handle."

Sawyer let out a bitter laugh. "That's weird. She's been exactly what I needed."

Harold's mouth opened like he was going to argue, but when Sawyer stepped toward him, he shut up.

Harold backed up. Once. Twice. His shoulder hit the doorframe.

"Don't forget to turn in that badge on your way out," Rachel called after him.

The door slammed. My hands shook as Rachel whispered something to security. "Are you okay?" she asked.

"Yeah," I muttered.

"I need to make sure they escort him out. You got her?" she asked Sawyer.

"I got her," he said.

She slipped out, leaving us alone. He turned to me and opened his arms. I stepped into him without thinking twice.

"Ellie baby," he said against my hair. The cold, hard edge he had with Harold melted in an instant.

I gripped his shirt and pressed my face to his chest. The steady thump of his heartbeat slowly pulled mine back from the edge. He didn't say anything, simply running his hand up and down my back until the trembling stopped. When I finally pulled away, his thumb brushed under my eye.

"You okay?"

Yeah," I said, letting out a breath. "I'm fine."

"Bullshit's optional here."

My laugh came out broken.

"You can cancel the show if you need the night to breathe."

"Sawyer, I can't just… The fans. My parents. Everyone's waiting on me."

"*You*, El." His voice was quiet but steady. "We're talking about you. I need *you* to be okay."

I looked away.

He tipped my chin back and met my gaze. "I'll support you either way. I'll take you back to your hotel. I'll stand backstage the entire time if you need me to. Hell, I'll stand on stage with you. It's your call."

"Everything feels…" I searched for the words. "Fuck, I don't want him to have power over me. I need a minute. I can't let him win by cancelling the show."

I stared down at our joined hands as his thumb traced small circles on my knuckles.

"Harold's an asshole who doesn't know the first thing about you."

"But what if he's right?" I whispered, gripping his hands tighter. "What if I'm a manufactured pop star who is nothing but a mess?"

"You write your own songs?"

"Yes."

"You play guitar?"

"Since I could walk basically."

"You sang in dive bars before anyone knew your name?"

I nodded.

"Then you're not manufactured, El. You're successful."

"What if I go out there and freeze up?"

"Then I'll come get you."

I swallowed. "If I forget the words?"

"I have no doubt you could sing every song in your sleep."

"If I'm terrible?"

He smiled. "Impossible."

"Why?" The word barely made it past my lips.

"Why what?"

"Why do you care this much?"

He stared at me like the answer should've been obvious. "Because you matter to me. Not the singer. Not the public image. Not even the fake girlfriend I can't stop thinking about. Just you. I care. A lot."

I took a shaky breath. "Okay. I can do it."

"Are you sure? You don't have to."

"Yeah," I said, firmer. "I want to."

The dressing room door flew open, and Rachel rushed in, her eyes darting between us.

"We stalled the opening act—gave them a couple more songs," she blurted. "We've got flexibility. We can push your set. Cancel, delay, whatever you need. Say the word."

I leaned into Sawyer for half a second longer. Then, I stood taller. "Give me ten minutes?"

Rachel cocked her head. "You sure?"

Sawyer slid his hand into mine, steady and warm. "Give her twenty, just to be safe."

Rachel nodded. "You got it."

NINETEEN

Sawyer

ELLIE OWNED THE STAGE. EVERY NOTE CAME OUT STEADY AND sure, and the crowd roared it right back at her. I didn't even know if she'd walk out there tonight, but she did—with her shoulders squared, chin up, holding nothing back.

I'd seen her perform before and thought I was impressed then. This was different. Maybe because now, I knew what it cost her—how much she had to push through to get here, to be this version of herself under all the pressure.

The past few weeks had given me a front-row seat to the real Ellie—the one who laughed at my nonsense, stayed up too late, kept her favorite people close, and still wondered if she was enough. Seeing her now, it all came together.

When I watched her perform, I wasn't just in awe of her talent. I was in awe of *her*—her strength, her courage, and especially the way she made people feel like they mattered, like they were seen.

I knew she said she wasn't sure if she still wanted this

dream the way she once had, but whether she stayed in the spotlight or walked away tomorrow, one thing was clear.

She didn't get here by accident.

She got here because she was extraordinary.

"She's something else, huh?" Clay, Ellie's dad, leaned toward me as we stood near the edge of the VIP tent. His broad shoulders and square jaw made him look like he could've stepped off a ranch or a football field, but his eyes held the same humble pride I'd seen in Ellie when she smiled.

Meeting her parents had me shakier than walking into my first NFL game, but it went better than I expected. They clearly adored their daughter, and I understood that. She was impossible not to be proud of.

"She definitely is," I said, unable to stop the smile pulling at my lips.

Allison, Ellie's mom, had her hands clasped over her chest. Her brown hair caught the stage lights, and her blue eyes shimmered as they watched Ellie singing a soft, sad ballad about losing someone you loved.

"I'm just glad the world gets to see my girl shine," she said. "I'm so proud of her."

"You should be," I said. "She's amazing."

Allison wiped her eyes and turned to me with a look that made me feel like I was a teenager about to get grilled before prom. "So, tell me, love. What's going on between you and my Ellie?"

I gave her a respectful smile. "Well, ma'am, we're dating."

She laughed and gave my shoulder a little swat. "I know that, silly."

I blinked. "Then what do you mean?"

Before she could answer, the song ended, and the stage

went dark, shifting to the next set. Applause thundered through the tent.

"I mean," she said casually, "do you love her?"

"Allison." Clay's brows rose. "You can't ask him that."

"Well, I did," she replied, not even looking at him. "So? Do you?"

I opened my mouth, then shut it again. The truth was… complicated. We hadn't been together long—if we were really together at all. But it wasn't a yes or no kind of answer.

I'd never told a woman I loved her. Hell, I wasn't sure I knew how to say it without sounding like a sarcastic asshole, throwing out lines to appease someone.

Now, I was standing in front of Allison Miles, trying to figure out how to explain what Ellie did to me—the way she cracked through my walls and pulled out something I didn't know was there.

I took a breath, pushed the doubt aside, and gave her the only honest answer I could.

"We haven't been together long," I said, my voice low but steady. "But if I keep spending time with her…yeah. I think I'm gonna have no choice but to fall for your daughter completely."

Allison's eyes softened. Her lips curled into something that looked a little like understanding, maybe even approval.

As I looked back toward the stage, Ellie was getting ready for the next song.

This wasn't love, not yet, but it was close enough to feel dangerous. I'd made a habit of being easy to like—light-hearted, quick with a joke, the kind of guy people kept around until they didn't It was safe that way. Keep things on the surface, and they couldn't hurt you when they left.

This thing with her? It wasn't staying on the surface.

The closer she got, the more I wondered what would happen when she saw the parts of me that weren't easy.

Still, I wanted her.

Maybe that was how love started—not with perfect timing or even a real relationship, but by agreeing to something temporary and realizing you were scared shitless because you already wished it wasn't.

TWENTY

Sawyer

Goodnight, fake girlfriend. I'll be imagining you next to me.

That's presumptuous.

You're right. I should probably ask first...
Can I imagine you next to me?

I suppose I will allow it.

Good, because I was going to anyway.
See you tomorrow.

"YOU EXCITED TO BE BACK HERE?" I GLANCED SIDEWAYS AT Ellie as we drove the winding two-lane road toward my house.

She had her legs curled up on the seat, her sleeves tugged over her hands, and her cheek pressed to the window. The sweater—the very one I'd convinced her to wear after a full-on negotiation—was covered in glittery gingerbread men and topped off with an aggressively festive candy cane collar. It should've been ridiculous. On her, it was unfair. She was so fucking adorable.

"Yeah," she whispered. "It's nice here. I've always been a big city girl, so this kind of quiet feels like a vacation for my brain."

I smiled and tapped the steering wheel. "Well, don't get too comfortable. I've got big plans."

She tilted her head toward me, suspicious. "Big plans?"

"Hot cocoa taste test, drive-by Christmas lights judging, maybe a snowball fight if you're feeling brave."

She smirked. "Should I be scared?"

I glanced at her, then back at the road. "Terrified. I take holiday spirit very seriously."

"I'm not much of a holiday person."

"I plan to change your mind in the next two days."

I stole another glance at her—cheeks pink from the cold and lips you write poetry about even if you're terrible at it. Which I was, but fuck, she was that beautiful.

And yeah, this was fake. Technically. Contractually, even. But wanting her back at my house? That wasn't pretend. Neither was the picture stuck in my head of her curled up in my bed, tangled up in my sheets.

"There's been some work done on the place." I turned onto my driveway and pulled under the big willow tree. "So it should look a little better than the last time you were here. Still not perfect, but it's getting there."

She tilted her head toward me. "I already love it."

I shifted into park. "I have a little surprise, though. Close your eyes."

Ellie raised a brow. "What kind of surprise?"

"The good kind. I hope."

"That's not very reassuring."

"Just trust me."

She raised a brow. "Is this when I get murdered?"

"I mean," I said with a slow grin, "I wouldn't complain about tying you up in some Christmas lights."

She flushed pink, and my brain started doing that thing it shouldn't: picturing her daring me back and calling my bluff. I gave a lazy wink, yanked the door open, and jogged for the porch.

I plugged in the Christmas lights, and the house exploded into a blinding, ridiculous glow. Then, I ducked inside to switch on the tree full of new ornaments, warm white lights, and ribbon Dotty claimed was tastefully rustic.

Had I gone too far setting this up for a house I was only crashing in for a few days? Maybe. But when Ellie told me she hadn't put up a tree in years, something in me cracked.

I wasn't sure the kind of man Harold was, and I didn't need to know. Any guy who didn't give this woman the most over-the-top Christmas magic possible wasn't man enough for her.

Dotty had overseen most of the renovations while I was out of town. The whole place was cleaned, and the bedrooms were finished. Even the kitchen was stocked with three kinds of hot cocoa.

Yeah, I was that guy now.

When I came back out, Ellie was still in the truck, eyes dutifully closed, hands clasped in her lap. It seemed as if she was trying really hard not to smile, her lips jumping up at the corners.

I opened her door and leaned in. "Still closed?"

"Yes, sir," she said, voice all soft and devastating all at once.

"Good girl."

That devilish little smile of hers made my dick twitch. I cleared my throat and took her hand. I helped her out of the car and stepped behind her, covering her eyes.

"Okay. Walk straight. You trust me?"

"God help me, but I think I do."

I led her up the walkway and stopped at the porch. The house was glowing, the tree sparkling through the window like a damn snow-globe come to life.

"You can open them now." I eased my hands from her eyes and stepped to the side to watch her take it in.

She blinked, lips parting, and turned to me. "You did all this?"

I shrugged. Suddenly, I was twelve years old, trying to impress the pretty girl at school. "Dotty helped, but the tree was all me."

She looked at it and back at me. "I haven't had a Christmas like this in years. It's… Wow…"

I had to bite back a grin.

"Wait till you see my dad's place," I said, shoving my hands in my pockets to keep from reaching for her. "He finally got around to putting up the rest of his decorations last weekend. It's basically a Clark Griswold fever dream."

She laughed, and something warm unfurled in my stomach at the sound. "Your family is kind of ridiculous, you know that?"

"I've been told. Frequently."

"But like…in a very endearing way." She scrunched her nose, and fuck if that wasn't the cutest thing I'd seen all week.

I couldn't help myself. I brushed a loose strand of hair from her cheek, my thumb lingering against her soft skin. She didn't pull away.

"Stick around, Ellie baby. I've got more where that came from."

Her smile spread across her face. "You trying to make me fall in love with Christmas again?"

Or me.

I held the door open and ushered her in. "Let's go inside. It's cold out here."

If I didn't get her inside soon, I was going to do something stupid—like kiss her senseless and forget this was fake for her.

The house smelled like pine and cinnamon. I headed straight for the stack of kindling and grabbed a few pieces, dropped them in, and struck a match. The flames caught quickly. Ellie settled onto the couch, and I slid in beside her as the fire started to crackle, casting a flickering glow over the room.

She noticed the journal sitting on the coffee table between us. "Finally decided to take it out of the floor?"

"Yeah," I said. "Had to. Can't have you losing a finger to a spider."

She gave me a skeptical look. "How do I know you didn't peek?"

I raised my hands in surrender. "I'm a man of my word," I smirked. "Tonight's research night—whatever you want to dig into. But tomorrow? You spend Christmas with me. No sleuthing allowed. Deal?"

"Deal."

I nudged the journal gently toward her. "Ready?"

Her eyes met mine. "God, yes. I've been waiting for this. My mind keeps spinning, trying to guess what she might've written next."

Letting out a breath, she picked up the journal and started reading aloud.

He asked me again whose eyes he has.

I told him mine, but that's not true. Not entirely. He doesn't look like him. He never has.

When he was born, I remember feeling terror under-

neath the joy. I prayed no one would see it, that time would blur the lines, but time hasn't helped. If anything, it's made everything worse.

I see him watching us. Quiet, calculating.

He said something yesterday: I'm not a fool, you know. Just that. Nothing more. But it chilled me to the bone.

Some days, this house feels like a cage I built for myself. I breathe borrowed air. I speak borrowed lines.

I wish someone could tell me what to do.

Ellie stared down at the journal in her lap, her fingers still pressed to the edge of the page as if she was afraid to let go of it.

"So, what's first?" I asked.

Ellie opened her phone and started scrolling. "Okay, I looked up L. Lauren. From this, we definitely know her son wasn't her husband's. Let's see if we can find anything about her. Old social media, friends, news articles, maybe high school stuff. We need to find her to find him. Maybe there's something that can give us a clue. Whoever he is, I'm guessing he's the key."

I folded my arms. "How old was she when all this went down?"

"Mid-thirties, I think," she said without missing a beat, still searching, "based on records I found."

"So probably a little older than me." I lifted an eyebrow.

Ellie looked up with a smirk. "Wait, how old are you?

"Thirty-three."

"Wow, you're ancient."

"Hey, I'm still young enough to keep up with you."

"Yeah, cause twenty-five is so young."

I laughed. "When I was twenty-five, my knees didn't

sound like an old, creaky floor every time I moved. Alright, smart ass. So, on the agenda, we need to find this mystery guy and see if Lauren's still around."

"Yup. There are no obituaries for her, no death certificates. She's probably alive." She swiped to a new note on her phone. "I'll keep checking public records, old news reports from that time, and cross-reference anything about the husband. Something has to show up."

I raised a brow. "An interesting way to spend Christmas Eve."

She grinned. "Think of it as the coziest cold case in history."

I reached for the blanket draped over the back of the couch and tossed it over both of us. "Fine, but first, we need hot cocoa and cookies. And you're not allowed to get murder-board crazy until next time."

She scooted closer, her knee bumping mine as she turned the screen toward me. For a second, I forgot about everything else—forgot about the story, the journal, the tragedy of what had happened in this house. I was just watching her get excited, lighting up like the Christmas lights I'd strung on the porch.

She was beautiful when she was curious.

"Let's start at the beginning," she said, eyes scanning the screen. "This is the article from six years ago. A domestic incident on Maplewood Lane."

Four-year-old boy dead in Domestic Dispute Tragedy.

We sat there, and then Ellie turned toward me, her features softer now, a little more tentative.

"I know you didn't buy this house because of what happened here," she murmured. "But maybe...there's a reason it ended up in your hands."

"I don't know if I believe in fate." *But I believe in you.*

"But I'm on your side, and if this is something you want to figure out, I'm in."

Her lips parted as if she might say something, but instead, she bumped her shoulder against mine. "Thanks, fake boyfriend."

I grinned. "You're welcome, fake girlfriend."

We spent hours combing through everything we could find online—old news articles, public records, social media scraps, anything that might give us a sliver of a clue about the Hutchinson family and what really happened that night. We found out that Lauren's father had worked for her husband's father for years, and the two of them were married young.

After a few hours, Ellie broke the silence and turned her phone toward me. "Hey, look at this."

On the screen was a social media profile for someone named Lauren Boone. Private account. No profile picture. But there were a couple of public posts in local groups. The most recent one was a giveaway—free furniture and kitchen stuff, left out on the curb with an address on the outskirts of Shadow Ridge from a few months back.

I sat up straighter. "Lauren Boone?"

"Her maiden name was Boone, according to public records. She probably changed it back after everything."

"You think this is her? Still living nearby?"

"There's no picture of her, but maybe. It's worth checking out. It could be interesting."

"You want to go to this house, don't you?"

She gave a weary smile. "I mean…"

"Not tomorrow," I said, "but maybe the day after?"

"Okay."

I tilted my head at her. "You think she'll actually talk to us?"

Ellie shrugged. "Probably not, but we won't know unless we try."

We worked through the night until I abandoned all pretense of helping. Instead, I studied her—the way she chewed her thumbnail when she was stuck on something, how her whole face lit up when she thought she'd cracked a code.

When her phone died around midnight, we moved to the floor by the fire. We reread the first three entries together and stopped there—that was the deal. She kept pushing for one more, but I needed her to have a reason to come back. Honestly? I hoped we'd never run out of mysteries.

She ended up using my shoulder as a pillow. Every small movement, every hum when she was thinking, made the world shrink until it was only the two of us, the fire, and those old pages.

There was something in that moment, something impossible to fake. We weren't just reading a tragic story— we were marking the start of our own.

Not a bad Christmas Eve, all things considered.

Sitting there with her against me, watching the firelight catch her face while she got lost in someone else's words, I realized I was already hooked to something else entirely.

And I knew she wouldn't be something I could easily walk away from.

TWENTY-ONE

Ellie

"Ellie, baby," someone murmured, tugging me out of sleep.

His voice was all gravel and warmth, brushing along my skin.

I groaned and buried my face deeper into the pillow. "Yes?"

"Merry Christmas," Sawyer whispered, brushing a strand of hair off my face. "Time to rise and shine. Can't sleep through Christmas morning."

I cracked one eye open and immediately jolted upright. "Sawyer. What are you wearing?"

He grinned and pulled at the front of his sweater like he was presenting a masterpiece. "Gracie got it for me."

"Why the hell does that have my face on it?"

It was bright red, decked out in sequins, cartoon presents, and, because humiliation apparently had no limits, my face. Giant. Grinning. Right across the chest.

He beamed, clearly delighted by my horror. "Because you're my girlfriend."

I sat up straighter. "We are not actually dating, remember?"

"Tragic." He sighed dramatically, hand to his heart like he was wounded. "But today, we're faking it extra hard. Besides, once we get to my dad's, we're gonna have to change into our matching pajamas anyway."

I blinked. "Matching what now?"

"Pajamas," he said, like I was the unreasonable one. "It's a family tradition. We all wear them every year. It's a whole thing, pictures and everything."

I stared at him. "I don't recall agreeing to coordinated outfits."

"It's in the fine print," he said. "You fake date a guy for Christmas, you wear the jammies."

Despite myself, I let out a laugh and leaned back on my elbows. "Fine, but I need coffee first, and if there's not enough creamer, I'm calling off this entire charade."

"Don't be so dramatic, love." His grin turned smug in a way that made something twist low in my stomach. "Already made it. You just gotta add your poison of choice. I got four different creamers—including peppermint mocha. You're welcome."

I rubbed my eyes and blinked at him. "Okay, I'll get ready and be out in a few."

He smiled before walking out of the room and shutting the door behind him. I rolled out of bed, my feet hitting the cool floor, and dug through my suitcase for something cozy: leggings, an oversized sweater, and thick socks with little red hearts on them that I refused to admit I packed on purpose.

I peered out the window to see snow had coated every surface outside overnight. Somewhere between waking up to his voice and hearing Christmas music drifting in from the living room, my usual holiday indifference started to melt away.

I padded over to the bathroom. The mirror was foggy from Sawyer's earlier shower, complete with a little heart he had drawn with his finger. I chuckled and turned on the fan.

Woodstone Falls should have felt foreign and temporary—a brief stop in a town I'd never planned to notice. But standing in this town for the second time, I felt something I'd hadn't dared dream of in years—the pull of a quiet life I could never have.

San Francisco had always been enough. More than enough—it was everything. I'd grown up with music spilling from every doorway, fog rolling in like clockwork each afternoon, steep hills that burned my calves and built my character. The city was woven into my DNA; its restless energy matched my own. I could find dim sum at dawn or tacos at midnight, could lose myself in a crowd of thousands or find solitude on a hidden rooftop. It was home in every sense that mattered. It was why I never left for bigger and better cities for a music career.

But this small town was doing something to me I hadn't expected. In just two visits, it had started settling into my thoughts, making me imagine mornings without sirens, evenings when I could actually hear myself think. I felt myself wanting it, but I knew it was impossible. Some people weren't built for small towns, and some dreams weren't meant for people like me.

My parents and I used to fill winter breaks with performances, back-to-back rehearsals, and promo shoots. For us, Christmas was nothing more than a brief pause between cities. We had a tree sometimes, but mostly, the holiday was marked by late-night sound checks and my mom's birthday cakes instead of sugar cookies.

Being here with him was like a reset, as if that five-year-old version of me, the one who used to sit cross-legged on the carpet circling every dollhouse in the Christmas catalog with a red crayon, had started clawing her way back to the surface.

After brushing my teeth and touching up my makeup, I stepped into the hallway. Sawyer was singing in the living room—badly, loudly, with all the confidence in the world.

I leaned against the doorframe, taking him in. He was cross-legged on the floor, surrounded by a mess of wrapping paper, a roll of tape stuck to his hand.

He didn't seem to notice me, so I watched.

His biceps flexed with each careful, focused movement, folding the edges with more care than I would have expected from a giant football player. I couldn't help but smile at how completely absorbed he was.

It hit me as if I'd been personally victimized by my own feelings—how much I actually wanted him. Yeah, there was definitely the kind of wanting that involved significantly fewer clothes and far heavier breathing. This was more than that too. I wanted someone who would wrap Christmas presents while singing off-key, who found joy in the smallest, silliest moments, and made me desperate to be part of that world.

I started singing along softly, matching the harmony. His head snapped up, and then his face lit up.

I dropped down next to him on the floor, still singing as I helped fold the flaps of a glittery pink gift box. He blushed, but he didn't stop. He kept singing like this was the most normal thing in the world.

Our voices were imperfect and unpracticed, tangled in a surreal way. Goosebumps prickled along my arms when he hit a high note and glanced at me with a pleased little smile.

I wasn't performing. I was just…singing. For fun. For joy.

This. This was why I fell in love with music in the first place.

Not the applause, the charts, or the carefully planned PR stunts.

It was this. Singing without an audience, without perfection, feeling the moment. Letting the lyrics speak when words couldn't. Letting your body remember how to feel before your brain catches up.

I'd lost that feeling somewhere along the way. Music had become a business and a brand. Singing on that floor, surrounded by wrapping paper, next to a man who made me want to be myself—here, I remembered what it felt like.

Sawyer taped the final package and turned to me, palm outstretched. "C'mon."

I took his hand, and he pulled me up. Instead of letting me go, he tugged me closer, his arms slipping around my waist. We were swaying, slow and unhurried, barefoot in a sea of discarded bows and paper.

"Sawyer…"

"Don't stop singing," he whispered.

So, I didn't.

I rested my cheek against his chest, and the notes carried me. We moved slowly, the Christmas lights dancing across his face. The speaker rolled into the next song and then another, and we didn't stop. Didn't speak. Just held on.

I started to say something, and he shushed me. "We're pretending. Practicing for later."

We danced through four more songs, the world shrinking until it was him, me, and the music. Every time I felt myself slipping more into the moment, I let it happen.

His hand moved along my back, nudging me closer. I

let out a breath as his lips brushed my temple. My body ached to tilt my face up to his, to see what would happen if I finally did.

When his phone buzzed on the counter, he threaded his fingers into my hair and pressed a kiss against my forehead. He pulled back enough to reach for his phone.

I knew the moment would pass, but this feeling wouldn't. Whatever was between us wouldn't last, and I wasn't naive enough to pretend otherwise. Still, I couldn't silence the small, reckless voice that whispered *what if.*

TWENTY-TWO

Sawyer

I SHIFTED THE TRUCK INTO PARK. "LAST CHANCE TO FAKE A flat tire."

Ellie gave me a sideways glance. "And have you miss out on the holiday you love so much? No way."

I reached for her hand without thinking—not for the fake dating thing, but because I wanted to. We walked up to the ranch house, and the front door swung open before we got to the porch. Dotty appeared, wearing plaid pajamas and the expression of a woman who had been up since five, fueled entirely by Christmas spirit.

"There you are." She launched a bag at my head. "Get your ass inside and change. Pajamas. Now."

"I love the festive hostile energy," I said, catching the bag walking inside.

Gracie came flying down the hallway like a caffeinated elf on a sugar high. "Uncle Sawyer!"

I barely got my arms out in time to catch her. "Hey, Trouble!"

"I missed you!"

"Missed you more, G."

Behind her, Noah and Dorian appeared, both looking cozy and calm. Ellie gave them a small wave, and they nodded back. I could already feel Colt mentally cataloguing every single interaction we had, as if he was storing data for later.

Which, fair.

Trent yelled something from the kitchen that ended in, "No one touch the bacon!"

Dotty just rolled her eyes.

"Merry Christmas," Ellie said softly beside me.

"Only the merriest," I muttered, nodding upstairs.

"Your room is good for you two to change in, yeah?" Dotty asked.

"Um, yeah. Sure." She gave me a cheeky, knowing smile and walked off.

We trudged up the same old, creaky stairs I knew by heart, every squeak and weak spot memorized. Teenage me had been a menace. My old bedroom still had the same posters from my high school football days and the same bed that was technically too small for me, even back then. Ellie walked in behind me and looked around as if she was seeing inside my brain.

"This is where the legend began, huh?"

"Yep." I dropped the pajama bag on the bed. "Where I first mastered eating six Pop-Tarts in a row and never once did laundry."

She stepped closer, grabbing the bag of pajamas. "I still can't believe I let you talk me into this."

I smirked. "I'm very persuasive."

"Um, is there a bathroom I can use?"

I hesitated, my voice low. "Yeah, but I've got a feeling this is a test."

"A test?" Her eyebrow lifted.

"Colt's figured us out, and I think Dotty's got her suspicions about us not actually being a real couple. Forcing us to change in here? It's definitely a test."

She laughed softly. "Alright then…turn around."

I lifted an eyebrow. "What if I don't want to?"

"Sawyer," she said, stern but playful.

I let out a dramatic sigh and obeyed, facing the wall. I smiled when I noticed the mirror beside me, and since Ellie didn't say *no peeking*, I selfishly looked. She bent down to grab her PJs and slid her jeans down with agonizing slowness.

And fuck—her legs were endless, smooth curves that made my fingers physically ache to trace them. The perfect little curve of her ass was practically begging for my hands, and I had to grip the dresser edge to keep from reaching out.

I forced myself to look away, but the damage was done. The image was burned into my retinas for years to come.

"Are you peeking?" her voice teased from behind me.

"No."

She spun around, catching my reflection in the mirror. "Liar." Her lips curved in a smile that was pure trouble.

My heart hammered. "Maybe."

"Well, then you might as well watch."

I turned around as she peeled off her shirt, her eyes locked on mine the entire time. Her bra was pretty and pink, and I nearly groaned. My pulse went haywire. How could something so simple make me want to lose every shred of control I had left?

She bit her bottom lip. "Like what you see?"

"You know I do."

Once she was dressed, she had the gall to look innocent, but her chest was rising and falling rapidly still. "Your turn."

"Enjoy the show." I shrugged off my sweater with one hand.

"Not looking," she said, turning away.

"You should." I let my sweater hit the floor and reached for the hem of my shirt, pulling it off.

She turned back around and eyed me up and down.

I watched as her eyes tracked every inch of exposed skin as I changed into the pajama pants. The air felt tighter in the room, like we'd sucked all the oxygen out of it.

"You good?" I asked.

"I'm fine," she whispered, but her voice cracked. "Why wouldn't I be?"

"No reason," I murmured, moving closer as I tugged the pajama top over my head. "Just checking."

We stood there, fully dressed, pretending not to look at each other. Except we totally were. Every shift, every breath, was an excuse to steal a glance.

"We should…" she said.

I took another step closer. "Should what?"

Her eyes flicked up, meeting mine with a wild, desperate edge I hadn't seen before.

"Go back down," she finished weakly.

"Should we?" I tucked a strand of hair behind her ear, and my fingertips barely grazed her skin, but she shivered anyway.

"Yeah," she breathed, but she didn't move.

Neither did I.

"Before I do something stupid," I murmured, my thumb tracing her jawline.

Her gaze dropped to my mouth then flicked back up. "Like what?"

"You really want to know?"

She nodded, barely a movement.

I leaned in until my lips almost brushed her ear. "Like kiss you until you forget your own name."

Her breath hitched. "That would be stupid?"

"The stupidest thing I could do."

"Uncle Sawyer!" Gracie's war cry rang through the house.

I stepped back and dragged a hair through my hand. Ellie sighed and, without another word, we walked back downstairs.

Gracie bolted toward the front door, already decked out in a puffy green coat and snow boots that lit up. "You're on my team!" she said to me, handing me a green armband.

"Go team green!" I shouted.

"Wait, what are we doing?" Ellie asked, trailing behind me.

"Snowball fight," Dotty said, tossing her a thick red coat with tiny reindeer antlers sewn onto the hood. "You're team red with me, Colt, and Trent."

Ellie stared at the coat and slowly looked up. "Why does it have...ears?"

"Because we're a festive family," Dotty said flatly. "Now, put it on."

"I get both kids and the detective?" I grinned as I zipped up my own coat. "Hell yeah."

Lilah arched a brow. "You do realize your brother is a detective too, right?"

"Yeah." I shrugged. "But you're more badass."

Lilah smirked.

"My mom's badass!" Caleb echoed proudly.

"Oopsie," I muttered, shooting Lilah a look.

She narrowed her eyes. "You're lucky you're on my team, or I'd make you eat snow."

"What about you guys?" I asked, nodding toward

Dorian and Noah—who were both lounging near the fireplace like the cozy, warm-blooded betrayers they were.

"Papa's making pancakes," Gracie said with a serious nod. "And Daddy's still healing. Noah says she wants to cuddle him on the fireplace."

"By the fireplace, G," Dotty said. "If they were on the fireplace, we might have a bigger problem."

"Aw, the cute little couple," Trent teased, slinging an arm around Dotty's shoulder.

"They want to cuddle *by* the fireplace," Gracie repeated, proud of herself.

"Good job, G," Noah called from the couch. "Have fun!"

"Be careful," Dorian added softly, his gaze flicking to Gracie as we headed out.

Dotty passed out colored armbands like we were heading into a gladiator arena. "Okay," she said as we trudged into the snowy yard. "Team green, you're west near the trees. Team red, east by the shed. We count down, and then all bets are off. No crying, no timeouts, and no mercy."

Ellie glanced around like she'd been dropped into a different dimension. "Do I get a say in any of this?"

"Nope," Colt said, clapping her on the back. "Welcome to hell."

"I thought it was Christmas."

"Same thing," Colt muttered darkly, tugging on his gloves. He leaned closer and gave her a once-over. "How are you at sports?"

Ellie looked mildly horrified. "Um…bad?"

"She can dance around a stage for hours without losing her breath," I said. "She's got stamina for days."

Colt grunted. "We'll take it. Let's destroy them."

Dotty's countdown started. "Three."

I crouched behind a bush and grabbed a handful of snow, already forming the perfect compact sphere.

"Two."

Ellie still looked dazed, her antlers flopping slightly in the wind.

"One."

"War!" Gracie screamed at full volume.

All hell broke loose.

I got nailed in the ribs within the first ten seconds. Ellie ducked behind a tree and popped out like an assassin, pelting me with precision. I doubled over, laughing as snow exploded against my chest.

Gracie tagged Colt in the shin and threw her arms up. "I did it!"

Colt growled and dramatically limped in circles. I spotted Trent mid-sprint and launched a snowball straight at his face. It splattered across his beard.

"Hey! No face shots!"

"That wasn't in the rules!" I shouted, already diving behind a tree.

Ellie emerged from the trees and hit me again right in the chest. Again.

"You trying to impress me?" I asked.

She shrugged, wearing a cheeky grin. "Is it working?"

Always yes.

My dad appeared, wearing slippers and his Christmas pajamas, silently cradling a snowball as if it were a sacred offering. He handed it off to Ellie. She didn't say a word, just turned.

"Thanks, David!" she chirped.

And she nailed me in the sternum with the kind of force that made me question my entire athletic career.

"You traitor!" I gasped, staggering backward.

"Oh, you better run," I said to Ellie before running after her.

She took off for the trees, boots crunching through the snow. That wild laugh of hers spilled from in front of me. I took off after her, cold air burning my chest as we dodged trees. She was fast but not fast enough.

I caught her at the edge of the trees and grabbed her around the waist. We went down together, crashing into the snow. I ended up on top of her, and we laughed, cackling like idiots. The laughter slowly died into breathless pants before a stretch of silence passed.

Her chest rose and fell beneath mine. Those cheeks flushed red, hair tangled and powdered in snow, lips parted slightly. Our eyes locked—and something unspoken pulled taut between us.

I could feel her heartbeat under my hands. Or maybe it was mine. Hell if I knew. Her gaze dipped to my mouth then back to my eyes, and I swore the temperature dropped and spiked all at once. Her hips bucked under me, and my body reacted before my brain could catch up. A jolt of lust, of fucking need for this woman, slammed through me.

I barely bit back a groan as she bucked her hips. "Fuck," I muttered.

"I think there's a rock under my ass," she said, breathless. "Sorry."

"Are you?"

Her smile was nothing short of wicked. Then, she did it again. "Maybe I like having something hard pressed against me."

"Ellie baby." Her name slipped out, half warning, half promise. One more shift beneath me, and I'd forget it was Christmas morning. I'd toss her over my shoulder, drag her back to my place, and pin her down for real.

"Sorry, *Sawyer love,*" she murmured, eyes sparkling.

Her gloved hand hovered near my face. I wanted her touch on my jaw, my cheek, maybe my mouth. I didn't care. The distance was setting me on fire, and I needed her hands on me.

The world shrank to that fragile inch between us. Every muscle tensed, aching for her to touch. If she leaned in, I knew I'd break.

And then—*thwack.*

A fistful of snow slammed into my temple, thrown by her other hand.

Ellie busted out laughing, rolling out from under me.

"You play dirty, Ellie," I said, shaking the snow from my face.

Her grin? Pure sin. "So do you."

"Get her, Uncle Sawyer," Gracie shouted from behind a tree.

"I got him," Caleb hollered, throwing another one that exploded next to my hip.

"Nice shot, buddy," Lilah shouted across the yard.

"Hey," I yelled. "We're on the same team!"

Caleb grinned. "Oopsie."

I groaned, hauled myself to my feet, and held out a hand. "C'mon, you traitor."

Ellie took it, and I brushed snow off her shoulders, her back, her hips—maybe a little more than necessary.

She looked up at me. "Pretty sure your team is losing."

I leaned in and whispered in her ear, "Nah. I got exactly what I wanted."

The rest of the morning passed in a blur. There was wrapping paper everywhere. Gracie had screamed over some glittery pink karaoke machine Dotty and Trent apparently thought she needed, and Caleb parked himself next to his mom and later curled in Colt's lap. Noah and Dorian were arguing over which pancake toppings were superior, and my dad kept hollering like a man who'd won the lottery with every gift he got—even a three-pack of thermal socks that, according to him, might as well have been gold.

It was…perfect.

I'd always loved the holidays. My mom had made them feel like magic—she was the kind of woman who started playing Christmas music in October and cried during every holiday movie. She loved hard, big, and loud. One minute, she was wrapping gifts in the living room, making pancakes on the weekends, always coming to every one of my football games. The next, she was gone. No warning, just an ordinary day that broke our world wide open.

When she passed, that magic cracked, but somehow, my dad held us together. With trembling hands and tired eyes, he found a way to keep the traditions alive, and it showed on days like today. Christmas was a piece of her, and he knew we needed that.

That time in my life marked a turning point. I became the comic relief, the one who made people laugh, who kept it light, who deflected before the silence got too heavy. It started as survival, and then it stuck. For a long time, I thought that was all I was—the funny guy, the human distraction.

But sitting here now, coffee warming my hands and Ellie curled against me on the couch, I realized I wanted to be more than that. This morning wasn't perfect because I loved my family, or even because Ellie fit in so seamlessly. It was perfect because it reminded me of what Christmas always meant to me and what I wanted it to mean again.

I'd watched my siblings fall headfirst into love. Real love. You could feel it just by being in the same room. It was the same love my parents had before my mom passed.

And fuck, I wanted it too.

I wanted the woman who made me smile so hard, my cheeks hurt, who smelled like something better than freshly baked cookies and had shown up in my life and made me want things I never thought I'd deserve.

I didn't know if this whole fake dating thing had made a dent in her the way it already had with me, didn't know if she'd ever want something real with me.

But I think she made *me* want it.

TWENTY-THREE

Sawyer

WE SPENT THE DAY AFTER CHRISTMAS DOING ABSOLUTELY nothing. No plans, just the two of us in my house, wrapped in blankets, surrounded by snack wrappers, taking turns forcing terrible movie picks on each other.

There wasn't anyone around to pretend for, but Ellie curled into my side all day.

After movie number four, she stole the last of the popcorn and then had the audacity to deny it to my face.

I let her, obviously. She smiled every time I fake-glared at her, and I wasn't about to trade that for popcorn.

Around four in the evening, she grew restless beside me. Not dramatically, but enough that I knew she was getting antsy. I knew exactly what she was waiting for. A part of me was stalling. I wanted to spend time with her, and I didn't want to run off the day after Christmas chasing some maybe-lead to some maybe-Lauren.

I had told Ellie we should wait until later in the day— not just for logistics, but because if it was the right Lauren, she deserved at least a scrap of holiday peace. But I knew Ellie had been waiting all day for this.

"You ready to go?" I asked.

She nodded, brushing popcorn crumbs off her hoodie. I grabbed the keys to my grandpa's old pickup—not my usual ride, but it felt right for the occasion.

Ellie climbed into the passenger seat. The sky had gone pale and cloudy, with leftover snow softening the world around us. She pulled her sleeves over her hands, and I pretended not to notice how adorable she was.

We didn't talk much on the drive. She stared out the window, her fingers twitching against her thigh like they wanted something to hold on to. I kept one hand on the wheel and let the other rest near the gearshift—close enough that if she reached out, I could be there in a second.

It took about twenty minutes to reach the edge of town, where the paved roads got rougher. The address led us to a small neighborhood tucked behind a run-down gas station. Rows of manufactured homes lined the narrow road, most with patchy lawns or broken fences, a few decorated with old holiday lights.

The home we were looking for was at the very end, with faded yellow siding and a porch light barely hanging on. There was one sad folding chair out front, next to a recycling bin that had clearly lost a fight with the wind and never recovered.

"This is it," I said as I parked a few houses down.

Ellie squinted at the home. "Do normal people do this? Just casually show up at some stranger's house after FBI-level cyberstalking them to ask if they had journaled their trauma in their last home?"

"Definitely not, but we're not exactly normal."

Ellie chuckled and climbed out of the truck. Gravel crunched under our feet as we walked up. She bumped my shoulder like this was some kind of field trip and not a potential felony in progress.

"If someone comes out with a shotgun, you're taking the hit," she said.

"As your emotionally codependent partner in crime, I accept this."

The porch steps creaked as we walked up. Ellie looked at me with her brows raised, trying very hard not to laugh.

"This is ridiculous," she whispered.

"Deeply."

She gestured grandly toward the door. "After you, brave sir."

"Why me?"

"I don't know. You look less serial killer-y."

"That's a lie."

She rolled her eyes but knocked anyway, lightly at first. Then again, louder.

Nothing.

I leaned in, listening. "Either she's not home, or this place is abandoned."

She stepped back, scanning the windows like she had X-ray vision.

"Hey," I said gently, nudging her hand with mine. "If no one's here, we'll come back."

"I just... I thought maybe this would be it."

"It still could be," I said. "Just not tonight."

She nodded, but the spark was dimmer.

"C'mon. Let's get you back to the safety of my couch."

Then—thump.

We froze.

"Did you hear that?" she asked, her eyes wide.

"I heard something."

"A ghost?"

"A cat with anger issues?"

"A killer clown organizing their bookshelf?"

I opened my mouth to answer, but she was already turning the doorknob. Unlocked. It creaked open.

I stared at her. "Ellie."

"Yes?"

"You're about to break and enter."

She shrugged. "Technically just enter."

"That's not better."

"Come on. Maybe there's a clue, a picture, a clue in a picture. I don't know. I've seen enough crime dramas for this to be a logical step."

With a deeply concerning amount of confidence, she slipped inside.

I hesitated for exactly three seconds, sighed, and muttered, "You're actually insane. This is highly illegal."

But I followed her anyway. I was starting to realize something stupid and heart-wrenchingly obvious.

I would follow her anywhere.

She grinned over her shoulder. "Live a little."

TWENTY-FOUR

Ellie

"ELLIE, THIS IS A BAD IDEA," SAWYER SAID, TRAILING behind me.

The house felt suspended in time—clean but almost forgotten. I couldn't tell if someone still lived here or not. Maybe I was crazy for crossing this threshold uninvited, but recklessness had taken hold of me.

Following cryptic journal entries and breaking into someone's home should have felt insane. It probably *was* insane, but I wanted answers.

The front door had been unlocked, after all. That had to mean something. Was it an invitation? Or at least justifiable if anyone asked questions.

That was what I kept telling myself.

The living room was normal enough—decent furniture, just a little dated. In the kitchen, I found what I was looking for. There it was, sitting on the windowsill above the sink: a picture of Sawyer's house and the willow tree. I glanced at Sawyer, who sighed and walked toward me.

"Shit," I muttered. "It's her. Where is she, though?"

His brow furrowed. "No idea."

A car pulled up, tires crunching over gravel.

My heart stopped. "Oh my gosh."

"Fuck," Sawyer said.

"What do we do? We can't just talk to her when we're inside her home!"

"I don't know! This was your idea!"

"Let's run out the back," I hissed, pointing to the door like it was some brilliant plan I'd invented.

Sawyer didn't argue. He grabbed my hand and pulled me toward the door. We were halfway there when a voice snapped from behind us.

"What the hell!"

We bolted.

I stumbled down the back steps, adrenaline thrumming so loud, I could barely hear myself think. The backyard was muddy and uneven. I was absolutely not built for speed. Sawyer, of course, was annoyingly fast. His long legs cleared the yard in seconds.

"Seriously, Ellie?" he called, already a dozen paces ahead before doubling back.

"I'm trying! It's not my fault you have eight inches on me!"

He flashed that cocky grin even while running. "I got more than eight inches you haven't discovered yet."

"Oh my God. Did you seriously just—" I stumbled, caught between laughing and wanting to smack him. "Now is not the time for jokes!"

But I tripped over something—a root or a pipe or maybe just my own bad decisions, and before I could hit the ground, Sawyer was there. He scooped me up like I weighed nothing, one arm under my knees, the other cradling my back as he took off running again.

"You crazy, reckless, beautiful fucking girl," he muttered, not even winded.

I busted out laughing. I couldn't help it. It was half hysteria, half joy, all tangled up in the thrill of being in his arms as he ran. By the time we reached his truck, my heart was thundering. He yanked the passenger door open with one hand and practically threw me inside.

"Sorry!" he shouted as I landed on the seat with a bounce. He slammed the door, sprinted around the front of the truck, and dove into the driver's side.

Behind us, the woman rounded the corner, fury in every step. "What the hell were you doing in my house?"

Sawyer didn't wait to answer. The engine coughed once and roared to life. In a spray of gravel and tire smoke, we peeled out of the trailer park.

We were silent for a few seconds, both of us breathing hard, the truck rattling as it sped down the uneven road. I turned around and watched the woman disappear.

Sawyer let out this sharp, choked sound—somewhere between a breath and a laugh. And I cracked.

A laugh escaped me, then another, and I was gone, completely lost to it. I pressed my palm to my forehead and smiled.

"What the actual hell just happened?" I gasped.

"You—" he started, pointing at me, eyes wide. "You walked into that house like it was yours. Like, no hesitation."

"The door was open!"

"That doesn't mean break and enter, you lunatic!"

"Oh, please. You followed me."

"I had to!"

I smacked his arm. "You did not!"

"You're not going into some random person's house alone. Bodyguard duties are part of the deal, remember? I'd think randomly walking into someone's home qualifies for that need!"

I wiped at my eyes, grinning so hard, my cheeks hurt. "Okay, maybe I got a little carried away."

He shook his head, laughing as he turned onto the main road. "A little?"

There was a long beat of silence as the laughter finally settled. The wind still whipped through the tiny crack in the window. My chest ached in that good, breathless way.

"Jesus," he murmured. "We could've gotten arrested."

I opened my mouth, but then came the lights. Red and blue lit up the back window like the damn Fourth of July.

Fuck.

TWENTY-FIVE

Sawyer

I GROANED. "COPS."

Ellie turned, spotted the cop, and immediately doubled over laughing. "You're kidding."

"Do I look like I'm kidding?"

She was still laughing uncontrollably. "I can't breathe—oh my gosh. Is this karma?"

I pulled over. The old truck shuddered like it wasn't thrilled about the sudden stop. Me fucking either.

Ellie smoothed her hair down, which was hilarious, given we'd just sprinted out of someone's backyard like teenagers skipping class.

"Do we lie?" she whispered.

"Lie about what? That we broke into a stranger's house to chase down the ghost of a woman from a seven-year-old closed case?"

"Okay, when you say it like that, it sounds bad."

"Because it *is* bad, El!"

She giggled again, and I could feel my soul leaving my body. The truth was, I couldn't be mad. She was radiant—bare-faced in a hoodie, her cheeks pink from the cold.

A cop approached the car, early thirties with a serious expression and a name tag I couldn't make out. He tapped on the driver's side window, and I rolled it down.

"Evening," he said, glancing between us. "I'm Officer Lynch."

I gave him my friendliest *please don't arrest me in front of my fake girlfriend* smile. "Evening, Officer."

"I got a call about a break-in out on Delmont." He tapped on the top of the truck. "Two suspects were seen leaving the property in a vehicle matching this one."

I looked down at my hands on the steering wheel, as if maybe I could pretend I wasn't here.

"Break-in?" Ellie asked sweetly. "That's such a strong word." She pouted her lips.

The cop narrowed his eyes.

I jumped in. "Look, totally a misunderstanding. No harm done. The door was open, and we thought the house was empty."

He did not look amused. "So you admit to entering a home that doesn't belong to you?"

"I mean…technically, yes."

"But like, respectfully," Ellie added.

"Respectfully trespassing?" the officer repeated.

I tried to salvage it. "Listen, this is Ellie Miles."

He blinked. "Is that supposed to mean something to me?"

I gestured toward her like *ta-da!* "Ellie Miles. As in *the* Ellie Miles. Big star. Real famous. You gotta know her, right?"

His face remained blank. I started singing one of her biggest hits, and he frowned.

"Please stop," he said, watching us both, totally unimpressed.

No dice.

I glance over to Ellie, who raised her eyebrows and mouthed *rude* at me.

I tried again. "Okay, okay, if she's not ringing any bells…" I pointed two thumbs at my chest. "I'm Sawyer James."

Nothing.

"You know, offensive lineman for San Francisco?"

Still nothing.

"Local kid," I said, hoping to give him something. "From Woodstone. Made it to the NFL. I'm kind of a big deal."

The cop blinked. "Are you trying to name-drop your way out of a misdemeanor?"

"Yes," we said in unison.

There was a long pause.

Ellie leaned across me toward the window. "You got any daughters? Wives? I'm currently on tour. I'll get them tickets to whatever show they want. VIP tent and everything."

"Ma'am." He sighed like we were his tenth annoyance of the day. "Let me see your IDs."

She leaned in and whispered, "Should we run for it?"

I shook my head at her. She whined sarcastically and pulled out her ID, vibrating beside me as if trying not to laugh.

I grabbed my wallet, pulling out my ID then handing it over.

"Stay here," he said, walking back to his car.

"You know," Ellie whispered, "if we end up in a small-town jail cell tonight, the headlines will be nuts."

"I'm never going to live this down once my brothers catch wind," I muttered.

"Which one?" she asked, trying to stifle a laugh.

"Both of them."

The officer came back, making me jump. "You two always break into homes for fun?"

"Only when we're bonding," Ellie said.

"It's kind of our thing now," I added.

She nodded. "It's romantic, really."

He stared as if he was deciding whether to handcuff us or call Animal Control and have us tranquilized. He stepped back and thumbed his radio.

"Nope," Ellie whispered, eyes locked on him through the side mirror. "No, no, no. He's not—"

He was.

"Dispatch, this is 4-7," he said calmly into the mic. "I've got two cooperative subjects for trespassing on Delmont. Transporting to the station for questioning."

Ellie turned to me, panic climbing up her throat. "Questioning? Sawyer! I can't go in for questioning!"

"I told you we should've left!" I said, already regretting every decision I'd made, including being born.

"No, I told you we should run. You said this would be chill."

"No. No. I said, *Let's not break into a house, Ellie.* You're the one who walked in like a ghost hunter on a mission. I followed *you*!"

"You didn't have to carry me like I was your bride escaping a haunted wedding."

"That was a heroic exit!"

"Both of you—out. You're not under arrest, but you are coming with me."

"Can I ask a question?" Ellie said, climbing out.

"No," he replied without missing a beat.

"Copy that," she muttered.

He popped open the cruiser's back door so casually, as if this wasn't the kind of moment that would haunt me for the rest of my life. As if he wasn't about to load a lineman and a literal celebrity into the backseat the same way he'd handle a couple of drunk teens caught toilet-papering someone's house.

"Is this necessary?" I asked, climbing in.

"You're lucky I'm not cuffing you."

Ellie slid in next to me, biting her bottom lip like she was trying not to laugh once again. The door shut with a little thunk that felt both final and extremely humiliating.

We were in the back of a goddamn cop car, staring at each other. There wasn't enough room to breathe, let alone think straight. The plexiglass partition made it feel even smaller, like we were trapped in a bubble of our own terrible decisions.

Ellie giggled. "Holy shit."

"This is not funny."

"This is so funny."

"We're in the back of a cop car, Ellie."

She gave me a mock little pout. "Would've been hotter if he cuffed you."

I dropped my head back against the seat, trying not to smile. "Please, stop."

"I mean, come on." She leaned closer. "Tell me this isn't the weirdest, most exciting non-date you've ever been on."

I turned my head slowly toward her. "This is definitely a date, and you're definitely deranged."

The cruiser rumbled to life and started down the road. Outside, the trees blurred past in the dark. Inside, all I could feel was the warmth of her next to me and the ridiculous pounding of my pulse, as if I was sixteen and getting caught sneaking beer into a party.

She was smiling. Not the practiced one—the real one, loose and full and just a little reckless. The kind of smile you never want to stop chasing.

We were silent for a few beats. Then, Ellie whispered, "Hey."

I looked at her. "What?"

"Wanna make out?"

I choked on my breath. "Ellie."

"What?" she said innocently. "You've got nothing but time."

"We are literally in the back of a police car."

She shrugged. "That's been covered already. What's more convincing than a little backseat chemistry?"

"Backseat felonies aren't hot," I said, laughing despite myself.

She tilted her head. "Never know if we don't try."

"Ellie."

"Yes?"

"You're the most unhinged I've ever seen you."

"Yeah, I think you make me a little crazy," she muttered.

"I think true crime makes you a little crazy."

"True."

I was sitting there with her, shoulder to shoulder, knees touching, while we rolled down a country back road toward the world's sleepiest police station. I'd do it all over again if she asked.

She giggled, head tilted back against the seat, and I'd never seen anything so reckless and beautiful in my life. There was mud on her boots, her hair was a mess, and her laugh etched its way onto my heart.

God, I was in trouble.

"I haven't had that much fun in a long time," she murmured once the laughter faded into something softer.

Something tugged at the corner of my chest. "We could still get arrested."

"You enjoyed it."

I smiled. "Maybe."

"You don't hate me, right?"

"Never, Ellie baby."

She met my gaze, all trace of sarcasm gone. It was just her. Just this beautiful, chaotic woman who didn't flinch at sirens or scandal or the stupid, dangerous thing growing between us.

And that—*that*—was when it hit me.

I was already falling for her.

What started as a harmless crush had been blown out of the water the second I let myself see her, and I couldn't stop.

It wasn't the version the world saw, not the red-carpet woman with the rehearsed charm. I was falling for this version of her: barefaced and untamed, laughing in the back of that cop car. The version who broke rules like they were suggestions, who looked at me like maybe I was more than the golden boy façade I'd been polishing my whole life.

And the worst part? I knew how this would end.

Not the whole almost-getting-arrested part—though that was to be determined too—but us. *This*. Whatever this was.

I knew the deal going in. There was an end date. Come March, she'd move on. The fake relationship would fade out. She'd go back to her world, and I'd go back to mine, pretending I hadn't memorized every bit of her laugh or catalogued the way her fingers tugged at her sleeves when she was nervous.

She'd walk away with the spotlight, and I'd be the idiot letting her leave with half my heart stuffed in her pocket.

TWENTY-SIX

Sawyer

WE PULLED UP TO THE WOODSTONE COUNTY POLICE Department in the dark. Luckily, there were no cuffs and no mugshots, but we still got walked in like a couple of teenagers caught drinking behind the bleachers.

They stuck us in a windowless room with nothing but a scratched metal table and three chairs. No one said much. The adrenaline had faded, replaced by a cold, creeping dread in my gut. I leaned back in my chair, rubbing a hand over my face.

I wasn't worried about myself, not really. Worst case, I'd survive whatever charge they threw at me. I was retiring after this season anyway. Hell of a way to go out, but it was what it was.

Ellie, though?

She had everything on the line.

She'd worked so damn hard to keep the headlines positive, hence the whole fake dating thing in the first place. A misdemeanor charge wasn't exactly the headline she'd been aiming for.

After what felt like forever, the door opened—and

Henry Reynolds walked in, followed by his partner, Matt Rogers. I sat up straighter. Henry didn't look at me right away. He scanned the room quickly while Matt had a clipboard tucked under one arm and a cup of coffee in the other.

"Evening," Matt said with a practiced, cheerful tone. "Figured we'd handle intake. We're stretched thin with the holiday. Just need to get your details down before the detective takes over."

Henry finally looked at me. "Appreciate you two being cooperative."

He pulled out a pen and sat across from us, flipping open the clipboard. Henry stood nearby, leaning against the wall, arms crossed.

"Alright," Matt said. "Full legal names?"

"Really?" I asked.

"Yes, really."

"Ellie Miles," Ellie said, fidgeting with the drawstring of her hoodie.

"Sawyer Eugene James."

Matt jotted it down with neat, efficient strokes. "DOBs, current address, phone numbers…"

We rattled off the info, and he scribbled like he was filling out a census.

"Why were you digging around someone's private residence?" Matt asked.

I opened my mouth.

Henry cut in lightly, "We're not filing full statements, just basic context for intake. You'll go over the incident with the detective, but anything you'd like to share now might help smooth things out."

"Uh…would you believe me if I said we were house-sitting? Just forgot to tell the owners?"

"No, I would not."

"Okay, okay…it was a surprise party," Ellie said. "For them. Totally planned."

I cleared my throat. "We weren't trying to dig into anything private. The door was open. We knocked. Waited. No answer. We thought the place might've been empty."

"You often walk into houses that might be empty?" Henry asked.

"Only the ones with major unresolved trauma attached to them," Ellie muttered, dry as ever.

Matt choked on a sip of coffee, coughing into his elbow. Even Henry's lip twitched for a second before going flat again.

I sighed. "Look, we found a journal in my house. On Maplewood. It didn't line up with the public record on the Hutchinson case."

Ellie added quickly, "We think it belonged to Lauren. And we think the woman at that house tonight might have been her."

Matt blinked. "You think the old case from years ago is connected to this…journal?"

"We were just trying to find answers," Ellie whispered.

The door opened again, and Lilah walked in.

"Thank you, officers." She nodded once.

Matt stood. "Need anything else from us?"

"Nope," Lilah said, stepping aside. "I've got it from here."

She walked over to the table and dropped a folder on the table before she sat down and crossed her arms. Cool. Controlled. Scary as hell.

"Care to tell me what the hell is going on here?" she asked, pushing her red hair over her shoulder.

"Not particularly," Ellie muttered.

Lilah raised an eyebrow. "Cute. Try again."

There was something behind her eyes, though, a flicker of concern under that badge and attitude.

Lilah turned to me. "Sawyer."

"I'm surprised you're here and not Colt."

"Oh, he wanted to be, trust me, but I told him this was my case today. If you'd prefer the Colt James experience, though, I can always bring him in."

"No thanks," I said quickly.

She flipped the folder open and stared us down like we were a pair of misbehaving preschoolers.

"I usually play bad cop," she said. "But how about instead, we start with the obvious. Why the hell did you break into someone's house?"

I scratched the back of my neck. "Well, long story short, I bought that old house on Maplewood a couple of months ago."

Lilah hummed.

"You see…we found this journal in the floorboards. It had some stuff in it—stuff that didn't line up with the official story of the Hutchinson case."

She tapped her finger on the table. "And you two geniuses decided to do what? Launch your own investigation?"

"We got curious. That's all."

"He's lying," Ellie said, her voice low.

I turned to her. "What?"

She glanced at me then back at Lilah. "He didn't care about the journal. I'm the one who pushed it. I dragged him into it. He just…went along with it."

Lilah blinked then leaned forward, resting her forearms on the table. "Look. I don't give a shit about who instigated it. I care that the two of you were inside a stranger's home without permission. That's not curiosity. That's trespassing."

"We weren't trying to steal anything," I said. "We were just looking for answers."

"About what?"

"We think the journal belonged to Lauren," Ellie said. "And we think the woman living there now is her."

Lilah sat back, exhaling through her nose. She flipped open the folder and scanned whatever notes were in there. Her mouth pulled into a tight line.

"I'll be right back," she said and walked out without another word.

"You know, I think we should've run." Ellie brushed a strand of hair from her face.

I narrowed my eyes, a grin tugging at the corners despite everything. "I think we probably should not have entered in the first place."

"Yeah…" She shrugged. "Probably."

"Probably? *Probably*?" I threw my hands up, laughing despite myself. "Just probably? Ellie, we literally just—"

"Okay, okay, definitely." She held up her hands in mock surrender. "We definitely shouldn't have entered. Happy now?"

"Oh, now you're being reasonable." I shook my head. "What did it? Getting in the backseat of a cop car?"

She gestured vaguely at me. "Actually, it was when you started doing that thing with your face."

"What thing with my face?"

"You know, that panicked-but-trying-to-look-cool thing. Your left eye twitches when you do it."

I touched my eye reflexively. "My eye does not twitch."

"It's twitching right now."

"That's not a twitch, that's…strategic blinking."

The door creaked open, and Lilah stepped back into the room, a new file tucked under her arm and something unreadable on her face. She closed the door behind her with a soft click and scanned both of us, as if weighing what version of herself to bring into the room—friend, officer, or something in between. She rubbed the back of her neck and finally dropped the file on the table.

"You were right," she said. "Lauren Hutchinson, now Lauren Boone, used to live at Sawyer's address."

Ellie's head snapped up, and Lilah nodded once. Ellie tensed beside me.

"She's not pressing charges," Lilah said. "But there's a condition."

Ellie finally spoke, her voice barely above a whisper. "What kind of condition?"

"That you leave her alone."

Ellie flinched and straightened her spine.

"She said she didn't want to cause trouble," Lilah continued. "She asked the department to let it go, but she made it clear she doesn't want to be contacted again."

Ellie nodded slowly. "I understand."

I could see the truth written all over her face. The questions that wouldn't get answers. The war still playing out behind her eyes. She wanted more. A name. A reason. A crack in the silence that hadn't broken in years. Something.

Lilah finally sat down across from us, folding her hands on the table.

"I know you meant well," she said, softer. "But this woman has been through hell. She's not hiding, she's healing. There's a difference."

Ellie looked down at her hands. "We weren't trying to hurt her."

"I know." Lilah's expression shifted. "But even good intentions can leave bruises."

Sawyer cleared his throat. "So...what now?"

"You're free to go," Lilah said, standing. "No charges.

No paperwork. Just…don't make me have this conversation with you again."

Ellie gave a small nod. Lilah made it halfway to the door before pausing. Her hand rested on the knob, fingers tense, as she glanced back over her shoulder.

"Whatever you found in that journal? Leave it there. Let it go. Trust me. Chasing answers doesn't always set you free." And then, she was gone.

The door shut, and just like that, the stillness swallowed the room whole. We sat in it for a while, not speaking.

Ellie leaned back in her chair and stared at the ceiling. Her voice was almost too quiet to hear. "We found her."

"Yeah."

"But it didn't help."

I didn't have an answer, because it was true. I stood and reached for her hand. She hesitated for half a second before lacing her fingers with mine and rising to her feet. We walked toward the door in silence.

"You okay?" I asked as we stepped out.

She turned to me. "Why did you do that?"

"Do what?"

"Try to take the fall for me."

I shrugged. "I wasn't. I told them we're both idiots. I just happen to be the idiot with less to lose."

Her brows pulled together. "What does that mean?"

"I don't need to keep up some squeaky-clean reputation. My career's already coming to an end. You, on the other hand, already have enough bad media on your plate."

"You're not responsible for me."

"No, but I wasn't gonna let you crash and burn alone." I gave her hand a quick squeeze.

She dropped her gaze to the floor. "Still stupid to break in."

"Incredibly stupid." I grinned and came to a stop, tipping her chin up. "But you…you looked happy. Really happy. Lighter than I've ever seen you. You carry so much all the time, El. You deserve that—even if it's for something reckless."

"Even if it was illegal?"

"Maybe next time, we keep it slightly less illegal."

I chuckled, but there was a knot in my throat. No matter what, I knew one thing for sure.

I'd do it again.

I'd follow her into every bad idea, every unlocked door, every piece of chaos, because I was already in it. Not just the mystery. Not the adrenaline.

Her.

I was all the way in.

TWENTY-SEVEN

Sawyer

COLT DIDN'T OFFER TO DRIVE US HOME OUT OF THE GOODNESS of his heart. Nope. He stood there, eyes narrowed as if I'd personally insulted his entire existence.

"Get in the car," he snapped, like he'd already regretted agreeing to be our designated taxi.

Ellie and I slid into the backseat without a word.

The truck rolled forward. Colt grumbled, muttering about idiots and regretting every single life decision that landed him here. I tuned him out, watching Ellie instead for the entire drive.

He pulled into my driveway, throwing the car in park so hard I half expected the damn thing to explode.

"You're on your own for getting the truck back," he said, killing the engine.

"Noted," I said, my voice flat.

"Try not to get into any more trouble. Please, for my sake."

Ellie leaned forward, close enough that I caught a hint of her shampoo—something light and clean that made my head spin. "Thanks for the ride, Colt. We owe you."

"Of course," he mumbled, then drove off once we slipped out.

Inside, Ellie kicked off her boots and peeled off the hoodie, stretching like she had no idea the effect she had on me. Christmas lights made her skin glow. She moved, the hem of her shirt riding up a little, and I had to look away before I did something really stupid.

She curled up on the couch and pulled a blanket around herself. I dropped at the other end, pretending three feet was a safe distance. Which was a joke, because nowhere felt safe when she was close.

"So… what now?" she asked.

I was hypnotized by the way her lips moved through each word.

I dragged my gaze away from her mouth. "Stick to the plan. Read the journals. No more field trips. Definitely no more police stations."

"Agreed. I don't need that hitting the news. Plus, Lauren's been through enough without us getting involved."

I nodded. "I'll make sure Colt keeps everyone quiet at the station."

My eyes tried to betray me, drifting toward the way the lights hit her collarbone.

She tilted her head. "Do you think we've lost our minds?"

"About what?"

"All of it. The fake dating, the mystery hunting…" She bit her lower lip.

Oh, I've definitely lost my mind—less about the journal, more the fake dating the woman I want to do unspeakable things to.

Aloud, I said, "Yeah. I've thought about it."

"And?"

I leaned back, trying to put more space between us even as every instinct screamed to close it. "Still don't care."

I cleared my throat. "There's a New Year's Eve gala next week. Charity thing my buddy Zimmerman throws every year. I'm expected to be there. Press will be there too. Figured it might be good if you went as my plus one. You know, keep up the bit."

"Oh, yeah, good idea. What charity is it for?"

"The Level the Field Foundation."

"I've been donating to them for years." She gave me a shy smile. "I've just never been able to make it to one of their events. It'd be good for me to finally show up."

"Oh, sounds good. I'll send you all the details for it."

Her eyes dropped to my mouth and lingered there. When she looked up again, her pupils were dilated, and her breathing was slightly uneven.

She clutched the blanket. "Okay. I should probably… go to bed."

"Yeah," I said, rougher than I intended. "Probably should."

We stayed frozen for a moment until she finally stood. The blanket slid off her, and she placed it neatly on the couch before walking down the hall.

Just before she disappeared, she glanced back. "Goodnight, Sawyer."

I swallowed, hands tight on my knees. "Night, Ellie."

She vanished into the hallway. I sat there in the golden glow of the Christmas lights, every inch of my skin on fire, knowing that if she walked back into that room, rules be damned—I'd be lost.

TWENTY-EIGHT

Ellie

I'D BEEN LYING IN BED AT SAWYER'S HOUSE FOR HOURS, staring at the ceiling, too wired to sleep. Music had been playing in my ears since the moment I'd crawled under these covers, but even that hadn't been enough to quiet my mind. When I finally pulled out my headphones and blinked into the silence, the house was almost too peaceful.

Every time I closed my eyes, I was back in his arms as he carried me away from the woman we were tracking down. Then, the memory would change, and he was pinning me beneath him in the snow, that low, broken groan spilling from his lips. The sound shouldn't still be echoing in my head, but there it was, making my skin burn and my thighs press together.

In my defense, there really had been a rock digging into my ass. I was just trying to survive two hundred-some-thing pounds of football player crushing me into the frozen ground. That was survival instinct, nothing more.

So why had I thrown snow in his face instead of kissing him?

I don't fucking know. Brilliant move, Ellie. Really brilliant.

I should've kissed him, or at least crawled into his lap and begged him to make good on the promise in his eyes.

We'd been faking this relationship for weeks, but something had shifted. My heart was caught somewhere between wild hope and free fall, and I was achingly aware he was just down the hall, probably shirtless and asleep—or maybe wanting me as much as I wanted him.

The restlessness finally won. I needed to move, to do something other than replay every moment on an endless loop. A trip to the bathroom seemed harmless enough—maybe cold water would shock some sense back into me.

I walked down the hall. The bathroom door was shut, but I figured Sawyer had already passed out. Just in case, I knocked lightly.

No answer.

I pushed the door open and froze, my jaw dropping wide open. Sawyer was next to the shower, completely naked.

Moonlight spilled over his back from the small window, tracing the muscles in a way that felt almost deliberate. It was almost as if the universe itself had conspired to spotlight him in this moment. He had one hand braced against the windowsill, the other wrapped tightly around his cock.

I knew I should've turned around—vanished, pretended this never happened. Instead, I stood there, wide-eyed, heart thudding in my chest like it was trying to escape. His back flexed with every movement, his biceps tightening.

God, he was breathtaking. Masculine, undone, and unashamed. It was intimate—so intimate, it stole the breath from my lungs.

It took him a second to realize I was there, but when he did, he didn't flinch or cover himself.

He turned slowly toward me, and I gasped when we made eye contact.

"Oh my gosh, I'm so sorry." I spun around, heat rushing to my cheeks, embarrassment crashing over me.

"Stop."

The single word halted me. I obeyed, my back still to him, pulse pounding in my ears.

"Turn around, Ellie."

I should've said no. I should've left.

But I still couldn't.

It wasn't just the way he said my name. It was the quiet command in his voice, the way it wrapped around me like a tether, pulling me toward him.

So, I turned, and our eyes met once again. There was heat in his gaze. Dark, liquid heat poured into me and made my knees unsteady. My skin buzzed, awareness zipping down my spine like a live wire.

"Stay," he murmured, his hand sliding back into motion.

"I—" My voice cracked. "I don't think I should."

"You definitely should, Ellie baby."

He licked his lips slowly, his gaze dropping to my mouth like it was something he'd already tasted in his dreams. My breath caught.

"Okay," I whispered.

"Yeah?" He smirked.

I nodded. "Yeah."

My feet didn't move. My hands didn't fidget. I was frozen, rooted to the floor and completely transfixed. He moaned, low and deep, and it vibrated straight through me. I couldn't look away. Every stroke of his hand, every flex of his body was hypnotic.

I let my eyes roam over him—broad shoulders, carved abs, the thick line of his thigh muscles, the way his hand moved around himself. I bit my lip, my thighs pressing together on instinct.

"You like watching me, baby?"

I couldn't find my voice, so I just nodded.

His mouth curved into something feral. "I think I like it too."

Heat rushed to my cheeks, but I didn't look away.

"Be a good girl and put those pretty fingers in your panties for me. Let me watch you too."

My breath hitched. "Sawyer, I don't know if I—"

"You can." His voice was silk and smoke.

My eyes dropped to the floor.

"Hey, eyes on me."

The command lit something low in my belly. My gaze snapped back to him.

"Touch yourself, El," he said, slower this time. "Let me see you. Let me see what I do to you."

Unable to resist him any longer, I slipped my fingers beneath the waistband of my sleep shorts. The fabric brushed over my hypersensitive skin as I pressed my palm between my legs. Sawyer's eyes tracked every movement —heavy-lidded and hungry.

"Take them off," he said, voice deeper now, almost hoarse.

"I'm not..." My voice came out small, breathless.

"Ellie, are you trying to tell me if I walked over there right now and stuck my hand down your shorts, I'd find you bare?"

I nodded, and his jaw clenched.

"Fuck. Parading around my house like that?" He shook his head. "Take them off and let me see you."

My breath hitched as I hooked my thumbs into the

waistband of my sleep shorts and slowly eased them down.

Sawyer's gaze dropped as the fabric pooled at my feet. "Fuck, baby."

My body trembled under the weight of his stare. I was aching in a way that made my whole body flush, and he hadn't even touched me. My hand moved without thinking, tentative at first, the lightest touch against my swollen, aching clit enough to make my knees threaten to buckle.

I gasped, and my eyes fluttered shut.

"Keep looking at me," he said, voice fraying at the edges.

My gaze snapped to him again.

"Touch yourself how you like it," he murmured. "I want to know everything that makes you feel good. I want to burn it into my memory."

His words were reverent, almost broken. My fingers circled, slipping lower and finding the exact rhythm that made pleasure thrum through me. I bit my lip to hold back a moan.

Sawyer groaned again, but this time, it was low and drawn out. His hand moved in slow strokes, each one matching the pace of mine, as if we were tethered—connected.

I couldn't believe I wasn't stopping this. I especially couldn't believe how much I didn't want to.

"Fuck, you're beautiful," he said. "You have no idea what you do to me."

My fingers moved faster, more confidently. I couldn't stop watching him and imagining that it was him touching my skin.

He was starting to unravel in front of me. The moonlight slid across his skin, catching the sweat on his chest, the flex of his muscles, the fierce concentration in his eyes.

Every breath was too loud. Every nerve in my body was too alert. I shook, not from fear, but from the intensity of being wanted like that—looked at like that.

Dripping with need and breathless desire, my thighs trembled and my lips parted. I didn't try to muffle the moan that slipped free this time.

Sawyer's grip tightened. "That sound—fuck, Ellie. I need more of it. Don't hold back."

I couldn't even if I wanted to. Something about him made me unable to restrain myself. I let out a soft and desperate moan as I moved faster. My whole body trembled, and I leaned against the wall for support.

He was watching every second. His strokes sped up, more ragged now.

"I want you so fucking bad," he said, his voice wrecked. "I want my hands on you. You have no idea."

"I think I do," I whispered. My hips jerked forward, chasing the pressure. "Sawyer."

"You gonna come for me, baby?" he asked, eyes locked on mine like he needed the answer to breathe.

I whimpered, unable to form words.

"Say yes."

My head lolled back, my fingers frantic. "Yes," I gasped.

"Let me hear you," he growled. "Please. Don't hide it. Not from me."

That commanding voice pushed me over the edge. I shattered in front of him, his voice wrapped around me. A groan escaped his lips as he said my name and found his own release.

He shuddered, chest rising and falling until his movements slowed. The quiet that followed wasn't heavy or uncomfortable. It was just charged. After grabbing a towel and wrapping it around himself, he stepped toward me slowly. Bending down, he tugged my shorts back up, his fingers lingering at my hips. He slid his arms around my waist and pulled me against him, holding me like he didn't want to let go.

His embrace was gentle and sweet in a way that didn't match the rawness of what had just passed between us. That made it all the more disarming.

He leaned in, kissed my forehead, and murmured, "Good girl."

With a playful swat to my ass, he walked out as if he hadn't completely ruined me.

I stood there for a beat, dazed, and still catching my breath.

TWENTY-NINE

Sawyer

I'm an idiot. A complete, absolute moron with the emotional intelligence of a brick wall and the impulse control of a toddler. Not only did I just watch my very fake girlfriend come apart in front of me, but I decided the best follow-up move was to toss out a *good girl* like some kind of caveman and walk away.

Real smooth, jackass. Real fucking smooth.

Seriously, what kind of masochistic lunatic sees a woman looking at him like he shattered her entire worldview and thinks, *Yeah, this is the perfect moment to make it weird and disappear?*

I didn't think. That was the problem—I never thought when it came to her. I saw her standing there in my doorway, and every functioning brain cell I had left evaporated into thin air. Gone. Bye-bye.

I was so catastrophically screwed.

Because seeing her like that? The way she looked at me, the way my name fell from her lips? Yeah, if I was teetering on the edge of this fake relationship before, I took a swan dive straight into down bad territory. No parachute, no safety net, just me free-falling into feelings I had no business having.

When she burst through the door, I was still fumbling with my sweatpants—because apparently, I also lost all motor function when she was involved.

We stared at each other for what felt like an eternity. Her cheeks were still flushed that perfect shade of pink, her hair a beautiful disaster, and all I could think about was how gorgeous she looked and how desperately I wanted to mess her hair up even more.

I cocked my head, forcing what I hoped looked like a smug grin instead of the lovesick grimace it probably was. "Yes, Ellie baby?"

Play it cool, you disaster. Act normal. Definitely don't think about the little whimpers she made or how much you'd like to make it happen again. And again. And maybe once more just to be sure.

She scoffed, and even that sounded beautiful. Fuck, I need help.

"*'Ellie baby.'*" She tried to mimic my voice, dropping it low and gravelly. "Don't *'Ellie baby'* me. What the hell was that?"

"I think that was one consenting adult coming in front of another consenting adult." I shrugged, desperately trying to pretend like my heart wasn't attempting to break free from my chest and throw itself at her feet.

"*That.*" She waved toward the bathroom. "Cannot happen again. This whole thing between us? It's not real, remember?"

Not real. Right. The fake relationship. The one that stopped feeling fake approximately thirty seconds after she walked into my life.

But sure, El. Let's pretend.

"I mean...it sounded pretty real when you were moaning my name."

She groaned and buried her face in her hands. God, even when she spiraled, she was incredible.

"You're not helping." Her complaint came out muffled.

I crossed my arms—maybe flexed my biceps a little—and caught the way her eyes tracked the movement before snapping back up to my face.

"Sorry, just trying to understand the situation here," I started. "Are you, uh, mad it happened, or are you mad you liked it?"

She threw her hands up. "I'm mad...I don't know! I'm mad I came out here ready to tear you a new one for making everything weird, and now you're standing there being all smug and shirtless and completely unrepentant, which somehow makes everything infinitely worse."

I stepped closer because, well, I was apparently incapable of making good decisions where she was concerned. "Yeah, because I'm not sorry. Not even a little bit."

She shot me a smile so sarcastically sweet, it could have given me diabetes.

"Great. Fantastic." She pointed a finger in my direction. "You're not sorry." Her hand flew to her chest. "I'm losing my mind. I'm great. Everything is great." She flung both arms in the air.

"Ellie."

"*What?*"

"Why'd you come back?"

"I'm trying to figure out what the hell happened," she said, but her voice lacked conviction.

"You already know what happened." I closed the distance between us, my pulse hammering in my throat. "The real question is, what are we going to do about it?"

"Nothing." She poked my chest, hard, right over my

heart like she was trying to restart it. "We're doing absolutely nothing. This changes nothing. We're still faking this relationship."

My eyes drifted down to her bare legs, those perfect, endless legs, then slowly back up to her face. She was breathing hard, and I wanted to push her against the wall and make her fall apart again, this time with my hands, my mouth—hell, I didn't care what I used, as long as I got to watch her come.

"So fake," I murmured, sliding my hands to her waist and pulling her against me, marveling at how perfectly she fit.

Her breath hitched, and that tiny sound went straight to my dick.

"Don't." Her words were a warning, but her hands betrayed her, resting flat against my chest.

"I'm just agreeing with you, baby."

My hand found the small of her back, fingers splaying wide, and I leaned down until our faces were inches apart. She tilted her chin up slightly—barely, almost unconsciously—and I thought I might actually lose what was left of my mind.

"You're being annoying," she whispered, but her voice was breathless and shaky.

"You love it when I'm annoying." I forced my hands to release her before I stepped back.

"Go, El," I said, flexing my hands. "Before I really mess up this whole fake thing we've got going."

Or before I admit I've been pretending to pretend for weeks now, before I completely lose what's left of my self-control and kiss you until neither of us can think straight.

THIRTY

Sawyer

LAST WEEK HAD BEEN A MESS. A FULL-ON, STATIC IN MY skull, can't hear my own thoughts kind of mess. We won the game, which should've had me riding high heading into the playoffs, but all I could think about was the ice-cold silence from Ellie.

My phone vibrated on the counter. I looked at it to see she finally replied to my text.

> We still on for tonight at 9? I sent you the details.

> Of course. I can have Ben swing by your place to grab you?

> Aren't I supposed to be the one picking you up?

> Security detail and all. Complicates things 😬

> Alright, alright. See you soon.

Can't wait.

Can't wait? She moaned my name like it was the only word she knew, went quiet for a whole week, and now that was what she sends me?

Can't wait.

She was definitely shaken that night and made it clear it couldn't happen again. I'd been reeling ever since.

I forced myself into the tux I kept tucked away for special occasions, even though I was crawling out of my skin. Then, I pulled out my phone and called the only other person who knew the full story.

Colt answered after a few rings with a grunt that somehow managed to sound both exhausted and judgmental.

"Well, good to hear from you too," I muttered.

"What do you want?"

I started pacing the living room. "I know emotional expression isn't your thing, but could you pretend to be a decent brother for, like, two minutes?"

"I am a decent brother. You're just a pain in the ass. What's going on?"

"I'm spiraling over here."

"Ellie?"

"Ellie." I dragged a hand down my face.

"What happened?" He was quiet for a beat, and then his voice uncharacteristically softened. "You fucked her, didn't you?"

"Well…"

"Sawyer," he scolded.

"We didn't sleep together, but something happened."

"Define something."

"She might have walked in on me…doing, um, manly

things. And then she stayed and did…uh, womanly things?"

Colt let out a low, rough laugh. "Jesus fucking Christ. You stroked one out, and she watched? You serious?"

I groaned. "Yeah, and then she went silent for a week. Total radio silence."

"Sounds about right," Colt replied, his voice dry as ever.

"I think I freaked her out." I winced.

"No shit."

I ran a hand through my hair. "I didn't mean for it to happen."

"No one means to jerk off in front of their fake girl-friend, Sawyer," he deadpanned.

"I didn't know she was gonna walk in." My voice rose slightly. "Then I just kinda asked her to stay, and she did!"

Colt grunted. "You need help."

"I'm seriously trying here, man. I like her. Like, not fake dating like her. *Like her*, like her."

I could hear the faint sound of him shifting around, probably leaning back somewhere with that permanent scowl of his. "So talk to her. You've got that gala tonight, don't you?"

"Yeah."

"That's your window," he said. "Be honest."

"Be honest?"

"Yeah, dumbass. Drop the golden boy shit for five minutes and tell her how you feel."

I blinked at the wall. "I should do that?"

"Um, yeah. You should." I could practically hear him shaking his head at me.

"Oh…okay. That was almost useful."

"Don't get used to it," Colt muttered, ending the call.

A couple of hours later, Ellie called. She was on her way and wanted to stop in to use the bathroom before we left. When the knock came, I opened the door—and every coherent thought I had cleared out.

She was… Fuck. She was stunning. Black dress. Red lips. Hair that looked like it had been touched by actual angels. My hand shot out to the doorframe to steady myself when my knees literally went weak.

"Ellie," I said, my breath catching. "Wow. You look beautiful."

I could see her mask in place, pushing down everything that had happened last week at Christmas, and I wasn't sure if I was grateful for that or not.

Her gaze dragged slowly down my frame and back up. "Not too bad yourself, handsome."

My face went hot. "Thanks. Come in."

Ben, who stood a respectable distance away, cleared his throat. "I'll be right here when you're ready."

"Appreciate it," I said, not taking my eyes off her.

"Thanks, Ben." She stepped inside, her heels clicking softly, and scanned the place. "Thanks for letting me run up. I was so busy getting ready, I forgot to pee, and as soon as I got in the car, I went into crisis mode."

"All good." I gestured to the hallway. "First door on the left."

She gave me a grateful nod and disappeared down the hall, her dress swaying behind her in a way that made me want to sink to my knees and repent between her pretty thighs.

I forced myself to breathe, to keep my thoughts in check, but the longer she stayed away, the harder it got. I couldn't stop imagining what it would be like to help her out of that dress. No matter how hard I fought it, my mind played out every detail against my will.

After a few minutes, her voice floated out. "Um, Sawyer?"

I straightened. "Yeah?"

"Can you help me?"

There was a beat. "Uh...help you pee?" I asked cautiously.

"No," she said, trying to hold back a laugh. "The zipper. I can't get it down."

"Oh. Yeah." I swallowed hard and walked toward the hallway. "Of course."

She stood in the doorway now, framed by light, holding her hair up with one hand. Her eyes met mine, and she dropped her hair back down.

"Hi," she murmured.

"Hey."

I stepped forward and pulled her into me, my arms going around her without permission. I breathed her in. "I missed you, El."

"Yeah," she said against my chest. "Me too."

I pulled back slower than I needed to. "Okay. Zipper?"

She turned around slowly, sweeping her hair over one shoulder and exposing the delicate line of her spine. The low back of her dress dipped just enough to make my mouth go dry.

I stepped in close enough to smell her perfume. My fingers lifted without thinking, brushing the nape of her neck where a single curl had fallen loose. She shivered under my touch, breath catching.

My hand followed the path of her spine, barely touching, just enough to feel goosebumps rise on her skin. I found the zipper and curled my fingers around it, her body stiffening ever so slightly.

Then, I started to pull.

Every inch the zipper gave way, my pulse ticked up another beat. Her bare back was revealed slowly, teasingly, like the universe was daring me to keep going. I stopped just shy of the curve at the small of her back, and my hand stayed there a second too long. Maybe two. I think her breathing had changed. Mine definitely had.

Neither of us said a word. I could've pressed my mouth to her shoulder, buried my face in her neck, and told her all the things I've been dying to say. Instead, I stepped back, forcing air into my lungs like it wasn't suddenly heavy with the weight of wanting her.

"Okay," I said, my voice hoarse. "You're unzipped."

She spun around fast, cheeks pink. "Thanks. I'm gonna…do the actual bathroom part now."

"Right. Of course." I backed away, half-stumbling into the kitchen, fleeing temptation.

I poured a glass of water and stared out the window at the city, trying to regain my control. A few minutes later, she stepped out of the bathroom, holding her dress up with both hands.

"Think I can trouble you into zipping me back up?" A crooked little smile tugged at her lips.

Trouble? I was already in it.

I held out my hand. "Turn around."

I zipped her back up, careful to keep my hands steady, my gaze somewhere safe—anywhere but the curve of her neck or the way her shoulder blades shifted. I tried not to get caught up in the Ellie haze once again.

Except I was sure I'd always be under her spell.

I tapped her once she was zipped back up, and she turned to face me.

I cleared my throat. "How are you feeling about this?"

She tilted her head, catching my gaze. "The gala?"

"Yeah."

"I'm fine. Great. I've done stuff like this a thousand times. I'm used to it."

"But not with me," I said, attempting to shake off all the tension.

She smirked, slow and teasing, but there was something softer beneath it. "No, that part is new."

I stepped back and swept into a dramatic little bow. "Then allow me to make my gala debut as your boyfriend."

She rolled her eyes, but her lips curved. "Fake boyfriend. You forgot the fake part."

"Did I?"

THIRTY-ONE

Ellie

WE HADN'T SAID A WORD SINCE WE LEFT THE HOUSE—NOT because there was nothing to say, but because there was too much. Too many words I wasn't sure I was ready to face yet, feelings I didn't trust myself to name.

I kept my eyes on the blur of city lights outside the car window, doing everything I could to ignore how aware I was of him beside me. He hadn't touched me since we left his place, but his presence didn't ask for permission. It filled the space anyway.

Downtown San Francisco pulsed with energy. People in sequins and tuxedos flooded the sidewalks. Some fireworks went off in the distance, too early for midnight but loud enough to crack the silence between us.

Having a week to stew over everything that happened at Christmas hadn't helped like I thought it would. If anything, it felt like being caught in a shifting maze with no map, no markers—just walls that moved when I wasn't looking and paths that led nowhere but back to the same questions I'd already asked.

I had no distractions. The tour was on pause for the

holidays, so there were no late-night flights, no screaming crowds, no rush of adrenaline to keep me busy.

There was only stillness that pointed back to Sawyer and the way he looked at me like he saw through all my careful armor and didn't mind the mess underneath.

To distract myself, I'd buried my head in research most days—anything I could find about Sawyer's house and the journal. Every lead had come up empty. There was still no sign of who the mystery man could be, and even that distraction couldn't hold my attention the way it had before Christmas.

I was stuck in a blurry, weightless space between faux labels and rules, and it was driving me insane. I hadn't told Rachel what happened—not because I was ashamed or afraid of her unfiltered advice, which I probably needed. I wasn't ready to hear what it meant. Not from her and definitely not from myself.

From the start, nothing about Sawyer had felt fake. Not the smiles for the cameras, not the staged moments or interviews. Even when we leaned into the act, it felt real, trying to breathe under the mask of a lie.

We wrapped it in flirtation and called it harmless, tucked behind the safety net of an expiration date. That was the contract—easy out, no strings attached, no risk of wanting too much.

But we crossed the line, and there was no script to follow, no clean exit waiting at the end. I didn't know what we were anymore, only what we couldn't be.

We were never built for the long haul. His future was rooted in Woodstone, in something steady, and mine was already mapped out on the road—another album to finish, another tour to chase. I'd keep moving, keep trying to prove I deserved the life I'd built, while he'd go back home and settle down.

There we were, headed to a fancy-ass venue, surrounded by flashing cameras and enough velvet ropes to make it feel like a celebrity zoo—except this one would probably have champagne towers, countdown clocks, and a dance floor that would, in a few hours, become a sea of strangers kissing at midnight.

Sawyer let out a slow breath beside me. "So...about tonight."

I cut him off with a smirk, deflecting all the messy feelings with the flirtatious humor we both knew too well. "What about it?"

"Everyone thinks we are together."

"Well aware. Are you worried I can't act the part anymore?" I tilted my head, making sure to slip my *I'm fine, everything's fine* mask into place.

"No, no. Not at all. I'm just... Fuck, Ellie. We haven't talked about anything that happened."

"Don't worry," I murmured, a smile teasing the corner of my mouth. "If anything, knowing what you look like when you come probably makes me more qualified to be your fake girlfriend."

Sawyer nearly choked on his breath then cleared his throat like he was trying to play it cool. "Yeah? That so?"

"Mhm."

He turned to face me, his eyes narrowing into a familiar blend of playful and dangerous that always made my heart kick up a notch.

Ben pulled the SUV into the circular drive, headlights sweeping over the stone fountain, the velvet ropes, and the wall of photographers already jostling for the best shots. Gold streamers framed the entryway.

"You good?" Sawyer asked, his voice low and rough.

I smoothed the front of my dress calmly, as if I wasn't shaking from the inside out. "Why wouldn't I be? Just a little black-tie fundraiser, a red carpet, and three separate tabloids waiting to catch me tripping in heels I can't feel my toes in."

He arched a brow. "So...super chill night."

"Exactly."

Ben stopped the SUV and stepped out to scope the scene. Sawyer circled the car, opened my door, and held out his hand. I hesitated for a flicker of a second and slipped my fingers into his.

The moment my feet hit the pavement, the world exploded around us. Flashes lit up the night, blinding, relentless.

Sawyer glanced at Ben and said, "I've got her tonight."

I nodded to Ben, giving him my approval.

"Yes, sir," he replied.

Sawyer's hand settled on my back.

"Smile," he murmured.

"I *am* smiling," I snapped, my attention fixed past the photographers.

We moved up the steps. I let myself lean into him—not because I wanted the press of his palm or the heat radiating from his body, but because it was part of the show.

Inside, I blinked past the aftermath of camera flashes and took in the room. High ceilings dripped with chandeliers, every inch polished to remind you how small you actually were. The crowd was a river of faces, all pretending not to watch us, as if we were another couple of guests.

Sawyer's elbow brushed mine.

"Coach incoming," he murmured, his breath ghosting near my ear as he tilted his head toward him.

My stomach dropped. This was the man behind the charade, the reason Sawyer needed me on his arm tonight to play the role of devoted girlfriend. No pressure.

I slid my hand around Sawyer's waist, stepping into him before I could overthink it. His body tensed for half a second and then melted into the touch—or maybe I imagined the hesitation. His heat bled through his shirt, and I told myself the flutter in my chest was nerves.

"Well, if it isn't Sawyer James." Anderson Martinez had the kind of voice that commanded locker rooms—deep, authoritative, with an edge of amusement.

"Coach." Sawyer's smile was easy. "Good to see you."

Anderson turned to me. He extended his hand, and I took it. "Anderson Martinez. Pleasure to meet you."

"Ellie Miles." I let my hand drift to Sawyer's chest as I spoke. "Likewise."

His gaze dropped to me, head tilting slightly. Something flickered in his eyes—surprise? Warning? I couldn't tell, but the look made my skin prickle.

"I see you're keeping this guy in check tonight," Anderson said.

"Doing my best." I gave him a smile and turned to Sawyer, letting my expression soften, hoping my eyes conveyed what they were supposed to—affection, devotion, the kind of look that made strangers believe in love at first sight. "He's something else."

Sawyer's jaw tightened almost imperceptibly, and his hand found the small of my back, his thumb tracing a slow, absent circle that felt far too natural.

Anderson laughed. "Well, if anyone can tame him, I'd bet money on you."

"Hilarious," Sawyer deadpanned, and his fingers pressed a fraction firmer against my spine.

"Surprised you could make it with your tour schedule."

"The things you do for love." The words came out breathy—too breathy—as I rose to my toes and pressed my lips to Sawyer's cheek. His skin was warm, smooth, with the faintest hint of stubble.

He went rigid. I caught the flash of confusion in his eyes before he smoothed it away, his arm tightening around me. "She's incredible, isn't she?"

"Seems like it." Anderson clapped Sawyer's shoulder. "I'll leave you two to it. Nice meeting you, Ellie."

"You too."

The moment Anderson's back turned, I stepped back—or tried to. Sawyer's hand lingered on my waist for a beat too long before falling away.

His voice was low. "What the hell was that?"

"What? I was selling it." I crossed my arms, defensive. "You know, the whole fake relationship thing we agreed to?"

"Ellie." He dragged a hand through his hair, messing the careful styling. "He knows."

My stomach plummeted. "Knows what?"

"That we're faking." He leaned in, close enough that I could count the gold flecks in his brown eyes. "I'm almost certain Anderson knows this whole thing is bullshit."

Heat flooded my cheeks. "And you just—you let me throw myself at you like that?"

"Let you?" His laugh was sharp, disbelieving. "You went rogue. That was all your improv, baby girl."

I shoved his chest with both hands, probably harder than necessary. He barely moved, but his grin widened, infuriating and boyish. He caught my wrists, his thumbs grazing my pulse points. The touch sent electricity racing up my arms, and from the way his eyes darkened, he felt it too.

Sawyer muttered, "West," as a man approached us with teeth so white, they practically glowed.

"Ellie Miles," the man said, taking my hand and lifting

it to his mouth. "I'm Adam West. So nice to meet the woman who's got this guy going crazy." He kissed the back of my hand and turned to Sawyer. "You clean up nice."

"Don't sound so surprised," Sawyer shot back, a smirk tugging at his mouth.

Another man appeared, younger, radiating easy confidence and expensive cologne.

"Oh, great," West muttered. "Trouble's here."

"If anyone's trouble, it's you," he fired back before turning his gaze to me. "Nice to meet you," he said, extending his hand. "I'm Jaden Bronx."

"Ellie," I replied, shaking it.

Sawyer's hand never left my back. If anything, it pressed a little harder. "These are my teammates. Shit-stirrers, every last one. Don't believe a word they say."

West rolled his eyes. "How's the new house?"

"It's good," Sawyer said. "Renovations are going well. We stayed there for Christmas. Still a few things to fix up over the next couple of weeks, but it's shaping up to be a solid spot to settle down."

I smirked. "Full of stories too."

West's eyes went wide for a moment before he cleared his throat. "What kind of stories?"

Sawyer shot me a mock-annoyed glance. "Yeah, it's got a...history."

West leaned in way too close, voice dropping to mock-serious whisper. "Come on, spill it. What kind of history? Murder? UFO sightings? A family of raccoons running the place?"

Bronx blinked at him. "Something is wrong with you."

Sawyer shrugged with a grin. "Something went down there a few years back. Ellie and I found a journal from the woman who lived there. Now, she's acting like a full-on detective trying to figure it out."

I caught Sawyer's eye and grinned.

West shifted his weight. "Man, you guys live in a real-life thriller." He cleared his throat. "I'm going to make sure everything's running smoothly. It was lovely to meet you, Ellie," West said, turning to Bronx. "Coming with me?"

"If I have to."

"You do," he muttered.

We continued to weave through the crowd, the room full of murmurs and clinking glasses. Glittering NYE centerpieces sparkled on every table—crystal clocks and white orchids. Everyone seemed eager to talk to us: Sawyer's old friends and teammates, some curious strangers. His hand hovered at my waist, sometimes slipping to my hip, sometimes guiding me with a touch so subtle, it should have barely registered—except I felt every second of it.

A woman in pearls caught my eye and launched into a gush about our undeniable chemistry, her voice dripping with admiration and a hint of envy. Before I could brush it off with a laugh or a joke, Sawyer leaned in, pressing a quick kiss to my cheek. My skin tingled, but I kept my smile wide and steady, playing the part even as a slow, unmistakable unraveling began beneath it all like it did every time he was close.

When it was time to sit, we found our table near the front with West and Bronx. Sawyer pulled out my chair and slid in beside me.

We traded small talk—sports, food, travel, even the damn weather. Sawyer's eyes never quite settled anywhere for long. Except maybe my mouth. I ignored it.

His hand rested on my thigh and stayed there like a silent claim only the two of us could see.

After a few minutes, a woman in an emerald silk dress stepped onto the stage.

"Good evening, everyone," she began with a warm smile. "Happy New Year's Eve. Thank you so much for being here tonight to support the Level the Field Foundation. Thanks to your generosity, we've brought after-school sports programs to more than forty schools this year, and we're just getting started."

Applause rippled through the room.

"We're here tonight to celebrate coaches, athletes, donors—everyone who believes in building access and opportunity, one field, one game, one kid at a time."

The lights dimmed, and a video started playing—kids running drills in gyms, lacing up cleats, hugging their coaches over inspiring music. Voices of parents played in the background, sharing what the program meant to their families. A few tables back, I caught the sound of someone quietly sniffing.

The lights rose, and after a few more announcements, plated dinners were set before us. Throughout the meal, Sawyer's grip on my leg never loosened—not once.

People stopped by to say hi. I smiled and posed for photos, and his hand shifted from my leg to my side or my arm—always touching, never intrusive, just...there and impossible to block out.

The night floated around us as a soft jazz trio playing a slowed-down version of *Auld Lang Syne* somewhere off to the side. My glass was never empty—Sawyer's silent promise in every refill.

Then, the lights dimmed again, and a voice rang out across the ballroom. "Before we move into our auction and headline entertainment," came the smooth announcement from the stage. "please welcome our event chair, Adam West."

Sawyer groaned softly. West strolled onstage with a drink in hand, as if he'd been waiting for his entrance cue in a Broadway production.

"Evening, everyone," he said, grinning. It seemed like the spotlight was his home. "I'll keep this brief so we can get to the part where we raise lots of money and maybe get a little competitive about it."

The crowd laughed.

"On this fine New Year's Eve, we're auctioning off some once-in-a-lifetime experiences all for a great cause—private chef dinners, signed memorabilia, suite tickets... And for those of you looking for something really exclusive..." He paused, letting the anticipation build. "A dinner date with some of your favorite San Francisco Rebels. That's right. One-on-one, real conversation, decent food, and if you play your cards right, maybe a post-dinner game of catch and release."

More laughter, this time laced with a few ooos and ahhs.

Sawyer stiffened. "Uh oh."

West gave a bow, as if delivering the final punchline of a set he'd been practicing in the mirror. "We'll start the auction off with Jaden Bronx, me, and our very own Sawyer James, who have all graciously agreed to auction themselves off for a good cause."

Sawyer turned to me, stunned. "I didn't agree to shit."

I smirked. "Apparently, you did."

"I'm going to murder him."

The applause was too loud to interrupt. Bronx stood, groaning, and headed toward the stage with a resigned smile.

"First up," the auctioneer announced, "Jaden Bronx!"

The bidding climbed faster than I expected. A woman in a navy gown raised her hand, then an older woman with a thick diamond bracelet. A third bidder, calm and disinterested, said a number so casually, you'd think she was ordering lunch and not dropping over a grand for dinner with a man half her age. I leaned back, sipping my drink. Cool on the outside, spinning like a storm drain on the inside.

Bronx went for a respectable number. Cheers and polite applause followed. Then, West stepped back into the spotlight.

"Oh God," Sawyer muttered.

West milked every second of it, tossing in a few winks at the bidders. The numbers jumped even higher, the crowd eating it up.

Next to me, Sawyer didn't react, but I caught the tick in his jaw.

"And finally," the auctioneer announced, drawing the syllables out like they meant something, "a private dinner with none other than Sawyer James."

When Sawyer didn't move, West took the hint.

"He's a little shy to come on stage tonight, it looks like. Sawyer, raise your hand and let everyone know where you are!"

All polite chatter stopped. Sawyer froze for a moment before waving his hand in the air. I adjusted my dress, crossing my legs, the silky fabric whispering against my skin.

"Let the bidding begin."

A woman in a blue dress raised her hand with effortless confidence. "Twenty-five hundred."

A beat later, a sleek blonde lifted her fingers. "Four."

The blue dress arched a brow. "Five."

The crowd quieted, the rhythm of bidding falling into a tense, poised dance.

"Six thousand."

"Sixty-five."

I knew where this was going. And God, I didn't want her going out with him—didn't want her laughing at his jokes, letting him pay for dinner, maybe letting him walk her home. It made no sense, but it felt like a betrayal of the thing we weren't even calling real.

My fingers curled around the stem of my champagne flute. This was insane. I was insane. We weren't together. I'd made it clear this was temporary, surface-level, an arrangement with an expiration date.

The thought of him sitting across from someone else, giving them that lazy half-smile he'd given me a thousand times—

My stomach twisted.

Sawyer's hand flexed slightly on my thigh. He was calm, still, but not relaxed. I could feel the tension radiating through his palm, the way his jaw had gone tight. He wasn't looking at me, hadn't looked at me since the bidding started.

"Six-five, going once…"

The woman in the blue dress leaned back, confident, giving me a smug little smirk, as if she'd already won.

And something in me snapped.

Maybe it was the champagne or the way she looked at him like he was already hers. Maybe it was the realization I cared—more than I should—and I was so tired of pretending I didn't.

He was no one's but *mine* to claim.

"Twenty thousand." The bid slipped out of me, smooth, sure, and loud enough to cut through the silence.

The auctioneer blinked. "I—excuse me?"

I didn't flinch. "Twenty thousand," I said again, louder this time.

Heads swiveled. Conversations died mid-sentence. The

entire room turned to me—West, Bronx, the blonde, the woman in the blue dress. Everyone stared. Sawyer went perfectly, entirely still.

"What the hell are you doing?" he whispered, low and strained.

"Being generous," I said lightly. "It's for a good cause."

"Ellie…"

The auctioneer recovered. "Twenty thousand going once…"

I smiled, serene and dangerous.

"Going twice…"

Sawyer's grip on my leg tightened again.

"Sold, to Ellie Miles at table three."

A wave of polite applause scattered across the room, but I barely heard it. I took a slow sip of champagne and finally turned to him.

Sawyer stared at me, disbelief flickering in his eyes, like I'd rewritten the rules we were supposed to be following.

"What?" I tilted my head, giving him a fake pout. "I didn't want to share."

"You are unbelievable," he murmured.

I leaned in until my lips brushed the shell of his ear. "That's why you like me."

He stood abruptly, took my hand, and tugged me out of my seat. The next auction item was already being announced, but I barely registered it. He walked us out of the ballroom as if he couldn't breathe there anymore.

And I followed—heart racing, heels clicking, champagne still fizzing on my tongue—without a single second of hesitation.

THIRTY-TWO

Sawyer

ELLIE TRAILED BEHIND ME, AS IF SHE HADN'T DROPPED TWENTY grand in front of everyone to stake a claim she swore wasn't real. Maybe she didn't think it mattered, but my skin still hummed from the fallout.

I pushed open the door to the hallway, the muffled noise of the auction fading as it clicked shut behind us.

Once we were in the empty corridor, I spun around. "What the hell was that?"

Her heels clicked once more on the tile as she stopped a few feet away, chin lifted in the stubborn way that made me want to either shake her or kiss her.

"I think that was one consenting adult bidding on another, maybe slightly less consenting, adult for a dinner date."

"Don't do that," I snapped. "Don't joke."

"What did you expect me to do?" She stepped closer. "Let some stranger buy you for a night and pretend I'm fine with it? I'm your girlfriend."

My heart slammed into my ribs. "Oh, are you now?"

She scrunched her face. "Well…pretend girlfriend."

"Yeah." I let out a bitter laugh. "We seem to be really fucking good at pretending, huh?"

Her lips parted, the sharpness slipping from her expression. Then, she reached out slowly and brushed her fingers across my cheek.

"Yeah," she whispered. "I think we are."

I closed my eyes, forehead falling to hers as if my body had finally found gravity. Her chest fell and rose quickly, just like mine. Every breath we shared made me want to drop to my knees for this woman.

As I pulled her closer, my hands slid to her waist, and I wished they were finding bare skin instead of her dress. I didn't know how to exist with any space between us.

A light flashed through the darkness behind my closed eyes, and I snapped my head toward the hallway.

"Oh, shit." A girl stood mid-step, holding up her phone. "That wasn't—shit, I'm so sorry. I didn't mean to." She stumbled over her words, backing away.

I groaned under my breath and dragged a hand down my face. I looked back at Ellie, not giving a damn if the girl stayed or went. I scanned her features, trying to get even a glimpse of what was going on inside her beautiful, tortured mind.

"Ellie," I warned. I caught her wrist, pressing her palm flat against my face. "I need you to back up."

"Why?"

"Because I really want to kiss you right now, and if you don't back away, I'm not sure I will be able to *not* do just that."

Her breath hitched, but she didn't pull away. "Sawyer—"

"Tell me to back away. Tell me, and I will." I stepped closer, pinning her against the wall.

Her eyes darted to my mouth then back up. "Does it matter?"

"Yes, it matters." My free hand found the wall beside her head. "Do you want me to kiss you?"

She swallowed hard. "It doesn't matter what I want."

"Bullshit. It's the only thing that does." I leaned in until our foreheads were almost touching again.

"It'll make everything more complicated."

"Everything's already complicated, baby." I traced my thumb along her jaw. "Tell me to stop."

"Sawyer…"

"Say the words. Tell me this is all pretend, and I'll walk away right now," I echoed.

She didn't respond.

"I can't," she whispered.

I backed away anyway, but she pulled me right back to her.

"Fuck it," she breathed.

She crashed her lips against mine.

Not politely. Not carefully.

It wasn't a gentle question. It was a claim, a long overdue surrender wrapped in desperation. My hand slid up the back of her neck, fisting gently in her hair as I angled her mouth to mine.

I pressed her harder against the wall, one hand tangling in her hair, the other gripping her waist, as if she might disappear if I didn't hold tight enough. She kissed me back with a kind of reckless abandon that made my head spin.

Her mouth opened on a soft, aching sound that nearly undid me.

And when her tongue brushed mine?

I moaned—full-bodied, from deep in my chest, moaned.

It didn't feel new or awkward the way it should have.

There was no uncertainty, no tentative learning curve. It was familiar in a way that defied logic—as if our bodies had already memorized each other in another lifetime spent doing exactly this, and it was just now crashing through us, full force.

Her hands slid up, one wrapping around the back of my neck, the other framing my jaw. Her touch was greedy. She kissed me like she didn't know if she'd ever get to again, and I kissed her like I'd never let her stop.

Her mouth was so warm, so soft, and so fucking responsive. When I bit her bottom lip and tugged, her hips jerked, pressing harder into mine.

I slid one hand down to her waist and hiked my knee up between her legs. She gasped, and then she kissed me harder. Sloppier. Hungrier.

But even still, I needed her closer. If I didn't hold her, she'd vanish and take whatever this was with her.

"This is fake, right?" she murmured against my lips. "Tell me this is us pretending."

I pulled back just enough to meet her eyes.

"Wish I could," I said. "Turns out, I'm fucking terrible at pretending."

Then, I kissed her again, and I forgot how to focus on anything else. She was everywhere all at once, stealing my breath and whatever sanity I had left. And fuck, maybe I didn't want to breathe if it meant letting her go.

"God," I whispered against her lips. "Ellie…"

I pushed my knee up again as my hands shot to her ass. Her moan was instant, muffled by my mouth. Fuck, I felt it everywhere.

"Ellie baby…"

"I need—" she started, breathless, before kissing me again. "I can't. Sawyer, I need more."

"Tell me to stop."

She kissed me.

"Tell me to back away."

Her nails dug into my shoulder, her mouth trailing down my neck, open and wet and desperate.

"Say the word, Ellie. I swear—"

"Don't you dare," she whispered, wrecked and breathless and mine. "Please, just…don't stop."

I groaned, hands everywhere: spanning the dip of her back, splaying across her ribs, tracing her spine like I was relearning a body I somehow already knew.

Another flash in the distance.

Another reminder we were in public.

I didn't give a single fuck. All I could think about now was getting her alone.

THIRTY-THREE

Sawyer

AFTER THE GALA, BEN DROVE US BACK IN SILENCE—EYES forward, hands on the wheel, pretending he didn't know what had happened.

But he knew. It was his job to know everything. Why else would we be leaving a New Year's gala before midnight?

I kept my hand on her leg during the drive, drawing slow circles over her dress, letting my fingers climb higher each time. She shifted, squeezing her thighs together. I gripped tighter—just enough to let her know I noticed.

By the time we pulled up to my place, I was hanging on by a thread.

I unlocked the front door and held it open. Ellie walked in slowly and stopped just inside, arms crossed, mouth pulled into a frown. I could practically hear her freaking out.

I slipped off my jacket, tossed it on the counter, and turned to face her.

"Ellie."

"Yeah?"

I leaned against the island. "Get out of your head."

"I'm not in my head."

"Yes, you are."

She rubbed her temples. "Alright, genius. What am I thinking?"

"You're panicking, convincing yourself you didn't mean to kiss me like that. That you don't want to do it again. You think crossing this line is going to screw everything up."

Her jaw tightened. "I don't know what this is anymore."

I laced my hands behind my head. "Neither do I. But I like you. Not pretend, not for show, not for a single fucking headline. I like you. And I really like kissing you."

"Sawyer…" Her voice cracked on my name, and that tiny fracture hit me square in the chest. She looked down. "You can't say things like that."

"Too late."

Her eyes fluttered shut. "I don't know if I can do anything real right now."

There it was.

I could've pushed, could've told her how badly I wanted her to feel something real. But I didn't.

I sat down on the barstool. "That's fine." I nodded for her to join me, hoping she would. "You set the pace."

She hesitated. Then, she moved—slow, unsure—but she came to me.

When she stopped in front of me, I slid my hands to her hips.

"Is this fake?" she asked.

I pulled her to me until her stomach pressed against my dick. "Does this feel fake to you?"

She shook her head.

I caught her chin, forced her to look at me. "Good. Because we don't have to be real for you to use me."

Her lips parted. "What?"

"Use me." I pushed my knee between her legs and felt her breath catch. "Take whatever you want. Real or not. Pretend or don't."

Her hands found my neck, pulling us closer.

"I don't care." I tilted her chin up, our mouths inches apart. "Use me however you'll have me."

She was breathing harder, eyes darting between my mouth and my eyes. "And then what? When this ends, we just stop? That simple?"

I leaned in, my mouth brushing her cheek. "It ends when you want it to." I let my lips trail past her jaw.

Her breath caught. "One night. Just one. We get it out of our system then go back to normal."

"Whatever you say, baby."

My hand slid up her spine. Not rushed, not gentle. Just enough to make her inhale sharply and sway into me.

"Tell me what you want, Ellie."

She didn't respond, so I let my hand drop, giving her space even though every part of me was screaming for more.

"We don't have to do anything," I said. "I can drive you home."

She stayed there, motionless.

Then, her hands moved to my shoulders and pushed me back. "No."

I lifted my eyebrows. "Okay?"

"Okay."

"We stop the second you say. No questions, no pressure. You're in control here." I leaned back so I could look her straight on. "So, tell me, Ellie. What do you want?"

She didn't answer with words. She climbed into my lap instead, straddling me on the stool.

"Say it, El."

"You already know," she breathed.

I shook my head. "Not touching you again until you say it."

On the outside, I could tell she was still holding back, but her pupils were blown wide, giving her away.

"I want you to touch me." The words came out so quietly, I almost missed them.

"Yeah?" I muttered, dragging my hands up her sides because I couldn't fucking help it.

She nodded, lip between her teeth.

I ran one hand along the back of her thigh and the other up the back of her neck, tugging slightly at the roots of her hair until her face tilted up. Her mouth parted on a breath I wanted to swallow.

"You want my hands on you, baby?"

A soft sound escaped her throat. "Yes."

"Where?"

She went still.

I leaned in, my lips brushing her ear. "Come on. Use me, remember? Be greedy. Be fucking selfish with me. Where do you want me to touch you?"

Her hands slid up my chest, tentative at first, then with purpose. "Everywhere."

Fuck. That did it. That single word burned. I took a breath and stood with her legs wrapping around my waist.

"I need this fucking dress off you," I said, striding toward my bedroom.

Once inside, I set her down on her feet beside the bed. We stayed close, eyes locked, breathing the same air. Then, fireworks covered the room in bright colors.

Midnight.

I didn't wait. My mouth crashed to hers with everything I had—no softness, no hesitation. Her hands wrapped around my waist, and her lips gave way beneath mine.

I gripped her chin, needing proof she wasn't a figment of my screwed-up imagination. She moved one hand up to my neck while the other trailed down to grip my shirt.

The kiss broke, just enough to catch our breath, before I dipped my head, trailing kisses along her jawline and back up to her ear.

"Turn around," I whispered.

I gripped her waist as she spun around so her back pressed against me.

"May I?" My fingers brushed the spot I'd zipped up just hours ago.

"Please," she breathed.

I slid two fingers beneath the fabric and eased it down, one hand trailing her spine, slow enough to watch the goosebumps rise.

She turned to face me, and those fucking pretty hooded blues locked on mine. I exhaled a curse and let my mouth drag down her throat.

"You've been driving me fucking insane since the second you walked into my house tonight," I said, my lips brushing her skin. "Looking like a fucking angel I'm not supposed to touch."

"You did, though," she whispered, extending her neck toward me.

I straightened, breathing hard, eyes dragging over her, desperate to memorize every inch of her. "Not nearly enough."

She whimpered when my hands found the edge of her dress. I pushed it down slowly, savoring the moment. And then, she was there, standing in front of me in black lace so delicate, it looked painted on.

Holy. Fucking. Hell.

Lace across her chest, thin straps biting into her shoulders, tiny bows I wanted to sink my teeth into. The panties matched—barely there, all tease and sin.

"Baby."

Her eyes lifted to mine. "Mmm?"

"You're mine tonight. Every gasp, every moan—I want to be the reason for all of them."

I moved to the floor without thinking, my knees hitting the carpet. She stood there, watching me like she owned me—and fuck, maybe she did.

"Step out," I said.

She did, one foot at a time, getting rid of her dress. Then, she backed up and sat on the edge of my bed like it was her throne.

She lifted one foot, resting it against my chest. The heel was thin and strappy, making her legs look miles long. I met her gaze.

"Take it off for me?" She cocked her head.

My hands curled around her ankle, and my thumb dragged along her skin. "Anything for you."

I unclasped the tiny strap and slid the heel off slowly, pressing a kiss to her bare ankle. Then, I reached for the other. Starting at her knee, my hand glided down to her shin, all the way to her ankle. "Fuck, El. You're sitting there like you were made to be worshipped, and I'm about to prove my devotion."

I set her foot down and lifted onto my knees. Her hands landed on my chest, that lace bra doing absolutely nothing to hide how hard her nipples were. My mouth brushed the edge of one before trailing down the line of her ribs. My palms slid up her thighs, under her ass, lifting her just enough to scoot her back on the bed. I followed, bracing a knee on the mattress as she leaned onto her elbows, watching me, hair wild and cheeks flushed.

"You said everywhere." My fingers ghosting along her waistband. "So, you tell me—what's first?"

"I want your mouth."

"On your lips or between your legs?"

Her breath stuttered, and she shrugged.

I was going to fucking lose it. "Say it."

"Put your damn mouth on me, Sawyer."

I grinned against the inside of her thigh. "That's my girl, telling me what you want and how you want to use me."

My hands slid up her thighs slowly until I reached the edge of her underwear. With one knuckle, I traced along the lace seam, back and forth, teasing her until she was trembling. Then, I bent forward and dragged them down with my teeth, letting them fall to the floor before I tucked them in my pocket.

"Fuck." Her head fell back.

"Don't look away, Ellie," I murmured, lips brushing her skin. "Eyes on me. I want you to watch exactly how I make you come."

I licked up her center slowly, just to hear that breathy little moan again. When she tried to squirm away, I pressed a hand to her stomach and held her down. I dragged my tongue through her, rougher this time, until she gave me that sound—all needy and undone.

My cock was impossibly hard, straining against my pants as I noted every little reaction. I slid one finger inside her and had to bite back a curse at how she felt around me. She rocked her hips against my mouth, chasing it, and I gave her what she wanted. No teasing. No games. Just the steady rhythm of my mouth and the curl of my finger inside her.

Every flick of my tongue, every pass over her clit, every moan she tried and failed to hold in just pushed me closer to the edge. I was barely hanging on. I pressed my hips into the mattress, grinding down like I could feed off the pressure building in me.

"Fuck, baby—Sawyer." She panted. "Don't stop. Please, please don't stop."

She was falling apart. I felt it in her thighs, the way they tensed against my shoulders, the way her fingers twisted in the sheets. Getting her off like this—watching her unravel because of me—was pushing me closer to the edge.

"Come for me," I said, my voice low and urgent. "Now. Give it to me, Ellie baby."

Her body shattered beneath me. Moans spilled freely from her lips, and her hands tangled in my hair, pulling me closer and arching hard into me.

That sound, her surrender, destroyed what was left of my control. Every shudder, every desperate whimper, pushed me straight into oblivion. I came in my fucking pants from the sounds of her alone. My hips jerked uncontrollably, heat crashing through my body all at once. My forehead dropped to her thigh, breath ragged.

"Fuck," I whispered, trembling.

Her laugh was soft, warm, still tangled in the aftershocks. "Wait, did you just…"

"Yup. Couldn't help it. Came just from the taste of you," I growled, my teeth dragging along her thigh.

THIRTY-FOUR

Ellie

THE FIREWORKS HAD STOPPED HOURS AGO, AND GRAY morning light filtered through the room. I lay twisted in Sawyer's bed, one leg caught in the sheets. My skin hummed with phantom touches, lips tender, my mind replaying the sounds he made.

Sawyer slept beside me, sprawled on his stomach. His short hair was a tousled mess, one arm stretched across the mattress. Even in sleep, he was trying not to let me go. I turned away, staring up at the ceiling as if it might have answers I wasn't ready to face.

One night.

That's what I'd told myself. One night to lose control. One night that wouldn't mean anything.

I didn't know what I wanted anymore. This wasn't meaningless. It was real—too fucking real. It terrified me that the edges were blurred and I couldn't tell where I stopped and Sawyer began.

I sat up, reached for his shirt draped over the chair, and slid it on. It was warm, smelled like him, and I hated how much comfort that gave me.

I padded down the hall. The kitchen was still and dark except for the pale light slanting through the blinds. I opened the cabinet as quietly as I could, grabbed a glass, and filled it from the fridge. The door creaked behind me, but I didn't turn. I held the glass in both hands, bracing for what came next.

"Hey." Sawyer's voice was scratchy from sleep.

I swallowed. "Hey."

He stopped a few feet behind me. "You okay?"

I nodded, but I wasn't sure it was true. "Sorry. Wasn't trying to wake you. Just needed water."

He hesitated. "I can't tell if you're about to bolt or spiral."

I let out a short, bitter laugh. "Little of both, probably."

The silence between us stretched on. He didn't rush to fill it or push me.

Slowly, I turned around. His jaw was shadowed with a few days of stubble, and his eyes were softer than I could handle. He looked so effortlessly sexy, I wanted to scream.

I gave him a tight, bitter smile. "Horny pop star. Stupidly sexy football player. One-night agreement in the middle of a fake relationship. Feels textbook, right?"

His eyes didn't leave mine. "Last night didn't feel textbook."

I set the glass down on the counter and crossed my arms. "Sawyer…we can't do this again."

He raised an eyebrow. "Because it was bad?"

"No." I shook my head, biting back the ache in my throat. "Because it was good. Too good. One night. That's what we said. We have an end date, and this—whatever it is—can't go on after that."

His face cracked for the briefest moment, something vulnerable and raw showing through—a glimpse of the man beneath the bravado. I wanted to reach out and catch him, but I kept my hands clenched at my sides.

"We had an agreement," I whispered. "This ends in the spring. It was supposed to be manageable, something I could walk away from."

"And now?"

"Now, I'm standing here in your kitchen, wearing your shirt, and honestly? My whole body still feels wrecked. Like…in a good way, but also like I got hit by a truck." I ran a hand through my hair, trying to sound normal. "I thought I could handle it, but I really need us to be just friends."

He drew in a breath, as if he was going to speak, but he didn't.

"We had out one night," I said. "Now, we just need to go back to just friends."

"What does that mean?"

"No more late-night dates. Only PDA in public if we need to. No more crossing lines. We act normal when it's just us. Friends."

"You want normal?" he asked, his voice low.

"It's what we agreed to."

He nodded once, hands shoved deep in his pockets. "Okay. Friends it is, Miles."

Just like that, he gave me what I needed—the out, the boundary, no questions asked.

I studied him for a long moment. "I should get dressed."

He didn't move. "I'll make coffee then drive you home."

"Ben can come get me."

"I'll drive you home, El."

"Fine." I slipped down the hall, my heart heavy. I already missed the weight of his hands on my skin.

THIRTY-FIVE

Sawyer

THE LOCKER ROOM REEKED OF SWEAT AND VICTORY. HELMETS clanged against lockers, music blasted from the sound system someone had cranked way too loud, and a few guys were shouting like we'd just won the Super Bowl.

We hadn't. At least, not yet.

It was just the first round of playoffs, but we were still in it. Usually, this was the kind of night that lit a fire under me—something that made the fatigue and pain worth it. I used to crave it.

Tonight, I felt nothing.

I sat on the bench, elbows resting on my knees as I stared into the cracked paint of my locker door. My phone lay face down beside me. It hadn't lit up in hours, but I kept checking anyway, like waiting would change the silence.

Bronx dropped down next to me, still in full gear, sweat dripping off his brow. "You gonna celebrate or sit there lookin' like your damn dog died?"

"Not really my thing." I pulled my shirt over my head without looking at him.

"What? Winning?"

"Celebrating."

West flopped onto the bench on my other side, peeling off his gloves with a snap. "Bullshit. You're usually the first one dancing around like a lunatic after a win."

I grunted and crouched to untie my cleats. "Maybe I'm evolving."

Bronx raised an eyebrow. "You sure you're good?"

"I'm fine." But it came out flat. I knew it didn't land.

Bronx didn't let it go. "This about Ellie?"

My jaw twitched before I could stop it. I didn't want to talk about her. Hell, it had been a couple of weeks, and even now, I was still doing everything I could to not think about her—and failing spectacularly.

I couldn't even escape her in my own home. She wasn't there, not physically, but she was still everywhere. One night in my house was enough to make me want to keep her there, no matter how stupid that was. My shirt still held her scent. The sheets did too. Even now, I could taste her on my tongue, as if she'd never left.

"You two have a fight?" Bronx asked.

"Nah, we're good," I said, trying to sound steady.

It wasn't a lie. We hadn't fought. She'd walked out of my kitchen and told me we needed to stay friends.

But friends don't do what we did.

West nodded toward the tunnel. "She didn't come tonight?"

"She's still on tour," I muttered, standing and slamming my locker shut harder than I meant.

I pulled out my phone again, thumb hovering over the screen, but there was nothing. Just silence. So, I went back to the messages she'd sent earlier.

Good luck today

You too

That was it. No emojis. Not even a damn exclamation point. Just a few words that could've come from a stranger. I knew she had a show tonight and couldn't be here for my game, but I looked for her anyway, scanning the stands like a damn fool.

I should've ended this whole contract the night she stood in my kitchen wearing my shirt, regret written all over her face when she said we would have to keep pretending. That would've been the smart move—pull the pin, let it explode before it swallowed me whole.

I was never the one people fell in love with. I was the funny, uncomplicated guy, the one who made people laugh and didn't ask for much.

With her, it never felt like she saw me that way.

Not once.

Now, I understood the truth she never said aloud—that maybe she never wanted the real me. Maybe all I ever was to her was the role I played. And that was fine. That was the deal, after all.

West clapped me on the shoulder as he stood. "Come on, man. At least grab some food with us. You can't go home to an empty house after a win like this."

"I'm good." I slung my bag over my shoulder.

"Sawyer—"

"I said I'm good."

My phone buzzed. For one stupid second, my heart jumped, but it was just Dorian, texting congratulations with about fifteen emojis, which I know was Gracie's doing. I stared at the screen, my thumb hovering over Ellie's contact.

I pocketed the phone and left.

As I headed home to a house still haunted by the memory of her, I realized the problem wasn't that she'd walked away. It was that I was still here, hoping for more.

THIRTY-SIX

Ellie

THE DOORBELL CUT THROUGH THE STILLNESS OF MY apartment. I glanced up from the mess on the kitchen table —tour schedules, scribbled lyrics, half-finished song ideas, all scattered like a roadmap I wasn't sure I wanted to follow anymore.

"Come in," I called.

The door opened, and just like that, the tension in my shoulders eased. My parents stepped inside, bringing that quiet, familiar comfort I didn't realize I'd been missing. Mom's smile was soft but steady, and Dad's eyes searched mine like he was trying to read me.

"It's so good to see you, sweetie." Mom placed a small bouquet of wildflowers on the counter.

I managed a smile and pulled her into a hug. "Thanks. It's great to see you."

"How are you holding up?" Dad asked as he stepped inside.

"I'm good. Busy. How are you guys?"

"Oh, you know," he said, waving a hand. "Your mother's got us chasing down her travel bucket list before we get too old to enjoy it. I'm just along for the ride."

Mom gestured toward the scattered papers on the table. "You've been writing a lot lately?"

"Yeah," I said with a small shrug. "Here and there."

I always wrote—songs, scraps of melodies, half-finished verses tucked into voice memos or scribbled in the margins of old notebooks. It was how I made sense of things, how I processed feelings, but writing didn't always mean I created something worth sharing. Sometimes, it was just noise. Sometimes, it stayed unfinished on purpose. Not every thought needed a spotlight. Not every emotion wanted to be turned into a chorus.

Still, with everything going on lately, it felt like my head was full of little songs—none of them finished but all of them trying to be heard.

Mom took a seat across from me. "How's the tour going? Not too much longer now, right?"

"It's good," I said automatically. "I've been going full speed for almost a year, so I think I'm ready for a break."

"You deserve one," she murmured.

Mom tucked one leg under the other, and Dad settled back on the couch, his arms crossed and gaze steady. It was the kind of look that made you feel like he was listening even when you hadn't started talking yet.

"I watched your acoustic set from Atlanta," Mom said after a quiet moment. "You looked different. Calmer. Like you were really there."

The set right after Christmas.

I smiled faintly. "Yeah. That one felt good."

It was one of the rare nights lately when I wasn't just performing—I was feeling. The music hadn't felt like a job, a brand, or a blur of expectations. It had felt like mine.

Dad tilted his head. "You've always had that. When it's real, people feel it."

Mom, never one to tiptoe when she saw something, added, "But you haven't been like that as much lately."

The smile slipped from my face. I dropped my gaze to the mess of papers on the table—all the evidence of effort with no clear direction.

"I know," I whispered.

"What's going on, El?"

My throat tightened without warning. I blinked fast, willing the sting behind my eyes to back off.

Dad leaned forward, his voice gentle but grounded. "It's okay, Ellie. Talk to us."

I hesitated then exhaled. "It's just...a lot."

"Start there," Mom said.

I ran a hand through my hair. "I'm doing everything I ever dreamed of. I have everything I thought I wanted."

"But?"

"I should be happy. I should be soaking it in, loving every second."

"But you're not," Dad said, his tone calm.

I shook my head. "No. Not the way I used to."

Mom didn't rush me. She just held my gaze.

"I don't know what's going on," I said. "It's probably just the schedule, the pressure, or whatever. I've worked too hard to start questioning it now. I...I keep wondering if I should be doing more or pushing harder. Like if I ease up, I'll lose everything I've built. I just want to make you guys proud."

Mom reached across the table and took my hand, her thumb brushing over my knuckles. "You have already made us proud, over and over again."

I swallowed. "But you sacrificed so much. You dropped everything for me. Drove me to every tiny venue, probably maxed out credit cards so I could get new equipment. You put your lives on hold so I could have a shot."

"And we'd do it again," my dad said. "A hundred times over."

"But I don't want to throw it away. I don't want to walk away from something this big because it's hard or because I'm tired. There are people who need what I do, who look up to me."

Dad nodded. "They do, but the people who really see you? They want what's best for you too, not the version of you on that stage."

I looked down. "Some days, the touring, the spotlight—it feels heavier than it should. And every time I think about slowing down, I feel like I'm disappointing people, like I owe it to everyone to keep going."

Mom squeezed my hand. "You've climbed a mountain most people only dream of. You've built something out of nothing. You're allowed to want peace. It's okay to change your mind. That's not failure."

I looked between them, my voice barely above a whisper. "You wouldn't be disappointed in me?"

Dad's answer was immediate. "We could never be disappointed in you."

Mom nodded, her eyes full of something fierce and unwavering. "You're not here to live anyone else's dream, not even ours. You've already made us proud. The rest? Those are just details."

"What about that football player you're dating?" Dad asked. "Does that play into this at all?"

I groaned. "Seriously?"

He shrugged. "Curious father. Sue me."

I bit back a groan. Of course, he brought that up. That football player was tangled up in more parts of my life than I liked to admit, but I'd wanted distance. Boundaries.

Something clean and controlled I could walk away from when the time came.

Nothing about Sawyer was easy.

He made me think about things I didn't want to want and feel things I didn't trust. He made me question the way I measured success, why I kept people at arm's length, and how I'd turned independence into a wall instead of a choice. Somehow, he chipped away at all of it without even trying.

"I don't know," I said finally, picking at the edge of a page. "He complicates it."

Mom tilted her head slightly. "Because you like him more than you meant to."

It wasn't a question.

I hesitated before admitting, "I do."

Dad let out a quiet chuckle. "Well, I'll be honest, I was surprised to find out my daughter was dating someone I'd never met, but after seeing you two at your concert a few weeks ago…"

"What?" I asked.

"I recognized that look," he said, his voice softer. "The way he watched you when you weren't looking. It's the same way I used to look at your mom."

I glanced away—not because I didn't want to believe him, but because I did, and that terrified me. "Dad—"

My mom thankfully interrupted. "But you're afraid?"

"I don't know," I murmured. "It just…doesn't make sense. He's retiring after the season. He's going back to Oregon. My whole life is here. My career, my people, everything I've worked for. I don't see how any of it adds up long-term."

Mom reached across the table, her hand warm and steady over mine. "Ellie, I say this with love—but Harold? He was a boy, and he never saw you for who you are. I didn't say anything then because I didn't want to meddle, but from the one time we met Sawyer…I knew. That man cares about you in a way Harold never even came close to. Don't walk away from that just because you're unsure where it'll lead."

Dad nodded. "You've been chasing this dream with tunnel vision for a long time. It's okay to widen your view or for the dream to change altogether."

The words lingered long after he'd said them. I did want something real—Sawyer and a life that didn't keep carving me into smaller, shinier pieces. Wanting that and believing I could have it—those were two different things.

THIRTY-SEVEN

Ellie

After my parents left, I told myself I'd clean up the kitchen table, sort through the stack of half-finished lyrics, maybe answer some emails or revise set lists.

Instead, I drifted from room to room, like a stranger in a house that didn't quite feel like mine anymore. We were on a short break before the last leg of the tour, and for once, I had a few days at home. My real home, the one I'd fought for, decorated, poured pieces of myself into over the years. I'd always loved San Francisco, but now, the silence here echoed.

I was curled up on the couch in leggings and an over-sized hoodie, halfway through a true crime doc I'd already seen twice, when my phone dinged.

RACHEL

What are you doing tonight?

Couch. Blanket. Possibly a murder show. You?

> Change of plans. You're going out
> with me.

> No, I'm not.

> Yes, you are. You need a night out. You're
> starting to sound like a grandma.

> I've got us into a new bar downtown. It's
> supposed to be hot. Like, rooftop views
> and tattooed bartenders hot.

> Girl, my social battery is in the negative

> Pretty please? For me?

> Ugh, fine.

> Hehe, good. I'm on the way to your house.

> I'll be there in ten.

I stared at the phone for a second, then tossed it onto the cushion beside me and sighed.

When I wasn't traveling or performing, I spent the last couple of weeks in my own head—spinning circles around my career, my feelings, and that damn journal I couldn't stop researching, even when I came up empty every time. When I wasn't obsessing over the journal, I was obsessing over the man who owned the house it came from, with his stupid big muscles and that stupid, annoyingly handsome face.

Shit.

Maybe I needed a night out away from my thoughts.

I texted my security team and made my way to the closet. If I was going out, I might as well commit.

The rooftop bar was alive with bougie lighting, strings of lights that blended into the city skyline, and too many people to count. Everyone around us looked like they either owned a yacht or wanted you to think they did. This should have been my scene, but I wasn't one for going out. Usually, I preferred quieter corners and nights that didn't feel like a performance. With three drinks in me and a fourth on the way, I didn't give a fuck anymore.

Ben and a few members of my security team lingered nearby, keeping watch.

Rachel shoved a pink cocktail in my hand. Something was floating in it—maybe fruit, maybe potpourri. Who was to say?

"It's called...something French. I don't remember," she said, squinting. "The hot bartender told me it was good. I trusted his biceps."

"You're drunk."

"I'm hydrated," she slurred, raising her glass like a toast.

"That's not water, babe."

She held up her cucumber garnish like a trophy. "It has produce. It counts."

We stumbled toward a half-lounge, half-dance-floor situation and collapsed onto a velvet bench. I immediately kicked off my heels. Feet, dead. Brain, soup. Dignity, gone.

Rachel curled her legs under her and gave me the look, the one that meant she was about to dig into something I definitely didn't want to talk about.

"So..." she said, drawing the word out, "how's the sexy football player?"

I stared into my drink like it might save me.

"Oh, there's a story there," she sang. "Tell me, tell me! Are we entering not-so-fake territory now?"

"I'm not talking about him. This is a Sawyer-free zone. Tonight is about being unbothered and relaxed."

"Relaxed, huh? So…did he not help you relax?"

I groaned and dropped my head back against the booth. "He's fine. It's fine. Everything's fine."

Rachel sipped her drink and smirked. "You know you say that a lot, right?"

I glared at her. "Don't make me throw your cucumber at you."

She grinned. "Okay, but spill. Have you just been window shopping, or did you buy the whole damn place?"

I rolled my eyes. "What in the world is wrong with you?"

"Daddy issues." She shrugged like it was the most obvious thing in the world. "But hey, that's beside the point."

"Nothing happened," I slurred, heat rushing to my cheeks.

Rachel's grin was wicked. "Liar! You definitely took that guy for a spin."

I groaned.

"Oh, you so did." She wagged a finger. "I see that post-orgasm glow."

I covered my face with both hands, trying to disappear. "We didn't have sex, okay?"

She gasped as if I'd told her I ran off to join a fucking circus. "Wait, wait—so you had full access and didn't even go for a joyride? Not even a little test drive?"

"We didn't…" I tried to protest, but it was a lost cause. The words came out halfhearted.

"Enough about what you didn't do. What *did* you do? Tell me everything. Is he big? You take one look at that man and know he's good in bed. Tell me."

I took a huge sip of my drink to avoid speaking.

Rachel's jaw dropped. "Oh my fucking God. He's dirty, isn't he?"

"I'm not talking about this."

"You have to. I need to know if he does that thing with his hands. I *know* he does that thing with his hands."

"He does a lot of things with his hands," I muttered before realizing it had escaped aloud.

Rachel shrieked. "Ellie! You're in love with the football player."

"I am *not*."

"Holy fuck," she breathed, eyes wide. "You're going to marry him. I can feel it."

"Please stop. I'm already having an identity crisis."

"Bitch, you're spiraling in a sparkly dress. This is exactly what your twenties are for."

"Why did I agree to come out again?"

"Because you love me, duh! You should text him."

"Absolutely not."

"Why the fuck not?" she asked.

"Because we…did stuff. And then I was like, 'Hey, let's maybe not do stuff anymore?' And now it's—ugh, weird and awkward and I hate everything."

"Jesus," she groaned. "Just text him. Say hi. You don't have to propose."

I narrowed my eyes. "Do I have to?"

"I'll leave you alone about publicist things for a whole month."

"A full month?"

"Well, like…three weeks. Ish. I'll try really hard."

"Fine."

I pulled out my phone and sent him a quick message.

Hi

I turned the screen so she could see it then chucked it back in my bag.

"Hi? Hi! That's it?" Rachel gaped. "You had full creative freedom, and you went with 'hi'? Not even a 'hey, big man, can't stop thinking about your cock'?"

"You told me to say hi. And I didn't even see his dick this time!"

Her jaw dropped. "What? This time? There was another?"

"*No.*"

"Ellie, when did you see his dick the first time?"

"Well, back at Christmas…"

"Oh my God." She gasped. "What did you do?"

"I kinda walked in on him…" I winced, "doing some self-care."

"So why didn't you see his dick the second time? What the fuck did you do then?"

I shrugged. "We made out. He, um…went down on me then came in his pants, and we passed out."

Rachel slapped her leg. "No fucking way."

"It wasn't, like, bad," I rushed out, letting out a little whine. "It was so hot, Rach. He was just—into it. Like, dangerously into it."

Her eyes were huge. "So, you're telling me he got off just from—"

"Yeah." I nodded.

She leaned back, shaking her head like I'd told her I met Jesus. "Girl. I hate you, and I love you, and I'm living vicariously through you. Say more words immediately."

"What did you expect me to do? He's over there all," I mimicked his voice, "'Ellie baby, use me. Take what you want from me.' How the fuck could I resist that?"

Her jaw fell open. "He calls you Ellie baby? He said that?"

I whined. "I know, right?"

She grabbed my bag and pulled out my phone. "Oh, look, he texted back!"

I glanced at the screen.

SAWYER

Hey, what's up?

"Oh! Text him where we're at!"

"Why the hell would I do that?" I shot back.

She narrowed her eyes at me. "So he can come rescue you, obviously."

"Last I checked, you wanted me out with you, not to ghost you."

"Yeah, but honestly? I'm way more invested in hearing the play-by-play later." She grinned, nodding at my phone. "Mind if I...?"

I rolled my eyes but handed it over. "Fine."

She typed out a message, then showed it to me.

Oh nothing. Just getting a little tipsy with Rach. We're at that new nightclub. Was thinking of you 😉

"You sent him a fucking winky face?" I shouted.

"The winky face is elite. It's flirty, mysterious, and says, 'I might blow you later, but I also might not.' Perfectly balanced."

"I can't with you."

Just as Rachel opened her mouth to make it worse, a male voice cut through the music.

"Ellie Miles?"

We both turned. A guy stood there, probably in his late twenties, cute-ish, in a very LA way. Designer sneakers. Sculpted facial hair. Eyes just drunk enough to be brave.

"Uh, yeah," I slurred, trying to sound cooler than I felt. "That's me."

He grinned. "I'm Jake. Big fan. I know, random. But hey, figured I'd shoot my shot. I mean, how often do you run into Ellie Miles?"

"Often, really," Rachel said.

He laughed. "So what's a superstar like you doing in a dive like this?"

"You know I have a boyfriend, right?"

"Doesn't bother me," Jake said, his eyes twinkling.

Rachel narrowed her eyes and typed on my phone again. "Well, it should, Jake."

"What are you doing?" I asked her.

"Oh, just texting your boyfriend about how this Jake dude is hitting on you."

I snatched my phone from her.

Oh yeah? :)

Mhm, now some guy named Jake is trying to hit on me and you aren't here to save me :(

"Are you fucking insane?" I asked.

Rachel kicked her feet up, triumphant. "God, I hope he shows up. I want to witness that man's jealousy in real time."

Jake was still standing there, just…watching.

"You're dismissed," Rachel told him sweetly. "Thanks for playing."

He blinked. "Seriously?"

"She's in love, Jake," Rachel said with faux sadness. "You never stood a chance."

He muttered something and walked away. I slumped back into the booth, half-drunk, half-dead inside.

Rachel raised her glass with a grin. "To bad decisions, unresolved sexual tension, and your future as Mrs. Sawyer James."

I clinked mine against hers. "To blackout-level mistakes!"

"Cheers, bitch."

THIRTY-EIGHT

Sawyer

Mhm. And now some guy named Jake is trying to hit on me and you aren't here to save me :(

Where are you?

Sorry, Rachel stole my phone. That wasn't me.

Ellie. Where are you?

I'm out

Out where?

Ellie, don't play with me.

Why? You jealous?

You're my girlfriend. Of course I'm jealous if some dude named Jake is trying to hit on you.

You know, I might consider dropping the fake part for tonight

You won't be able to unless you tell me where the fuck you are.

Fine. We're at Nova's, new little nightclub downtown

I'm coming.

I SHOULDN'T HAVE COME.

I'd told myself that twice in the car, once more while I sat in the parking lot gripping the steering wheel so hard, my knuckles burned, and then again in the elevator, breathing through the kind of jealousy that didn't simmer —it fucking boiled.

I pushed through a sea of sweaty finance bros and girls covered in rhinestones to find my girl. Neon lights pulsed overhead. Someone bumped into me and muttered something—didn't hear it, didn't give a single fuck. Nothing existed except the singular, brutal need to find her. My eyes were locked on the table near the back, where Ellie sat like a goddamn flame in a room full of moths.

She was curled up with her legs tucked beneath her, drink in one hand, phone in the other. She was glowing like a goddamn spotlight in a short black dress that clung to her curves as if it had been stitched in place—bare shoulders, too much leg, not nearly enough sense.

Rachel was next to her, equally loud, equally drunk. I got closer and slowed. She hadn't seen me yet, so I stood there, watching her talk to some dickhead with a mustache, leaning way too close for a girl with a boyfriend.

He wasn't touching her, not yet, but he was close enough, whispering something that made her laugh.

I didn't know if I wanted to fight him or fuck her. Maybe both.

Definitely both.

Rachel spotted me first. "Oh shit," she cackled, tapping Ellie's thigh. "Daddy's here."

Ellie blinked up at me like I'd crawled out of a hallucination. "Sawyer?"

I kept my tone even.

"Ellie baby," I said, the nickname sliding off my tongue.

Rachel grinned. "I think he came to claim what's his."

Damn right, I had.

My jaw clenched as I scanned the guys around her. "Which one of you fuckers is Jake?"

Ellie blinked. "Who?"

"Jake," I repeated. "The one who tried to hit on you. Where is he?"

Some idiot raised his hand. "Uh…I think all of us tried, my dude. I mean, look at her."

Wrong fucking answer.

"You've got three seconds to leave before I knock your teeth in."

"Whoa, chill, man."

"Three."

"Shit, okay, okay."

"Two."

They scattered like roaches.

Ellie shrugged, unbothered. "What are you doing here?" She laughed—fucking laughed—like I was the ridiculous one. It only made the jealousy twist deeper. "I'm just having fun. I don't even know who Jake is."

"Don't care. He looked at you."

She raised an eyebrow. "I'm not yours, Sawyer."

"Could've fooled me."

Rachel choked on a laugh.

Ellie smirked lazily. "Didn't realize I needed your permission to exist in public."

I hovered over her, caging her in with my hands on either side of her head. "You didn't need to text me either, but you did."

Her smirk flickered, and she slouched back into the chair, swirling the melting ice in her glass. "I was drunk."

"Still are, by the looks of it, baby girl."

Rachel held up her hands. "Love this energy. Just go home with him. He looks like he's one second from throwing a chair."

Ellie lifted her drink defiantly. "I'm not going anywhere. I'm having fun."

"You're infuriating," I said.

She licked her lips. "Maybe I like making you mad."

That was it. I didn't think. I bent down, grabbed her waist, and tossed her over my shoulder.

I nodded over to where I saw Ben on watch nearby. "I got her tonight, sir."

He nodded in response.

"Sawyer!" she shrieked, kicking heels against my chest. "Put me down!"

"Nope," I grunted, pushing through the crowd. "You've had enough fun."

Heads turned. Phones were out. I didn't care. Let them watch.

Rachel howled behind us. "If you don't bang him tonight, I will!"

"Rach!" Ellie yelled.

"You're welcome, big man!" Rachel shouted as we made our way out.

Without looking back, I waved at Rachel but kept walking. I didn't stop until we reached the elevator.

Inside, I set her down, my hands lingering on her waist longer than necessary. She swayed, drunk and flushed and so goddamn gorgeous, I couldn't breathe.

She rounded on me with her pink cheeks and wild eyes. "What the fuck was that?"

I flexed my hands, trying to breathe through my frustration. "This is fun? Being wrapped up in a crowd of guys who want to fuck you?"

She lifted her chin. "Maybe I like the attention. Besides…you're no different."

"You know? You're right, Ellie," I snarled, pressing her against the wall. "Maybe I am no better than those guys, but they don't want you the way I do. They want a story they can brag about over bourbon at their next goddamn tee time."

I dipped my head, lips grazing the shell of her ear.

"But me?" My hand slid down her waist, fingers flexing just enough to coax a gasp from her lips. "I want you. All of you." I dragged my mouth down her jaw as I spoke. "I don't want the version they fantasize about—the pretty, untouchable image they've made up in their heads. I want Ellie. Not the fantasy. Not the image. *You*. The woman who's scared shitless to let anyone in. The one who's so real, I lose my damn mind."

"Oh," she whispered.

I inched back and tilted her chin toward me. "I want the part of you that stops pretending you don't feel this. The part that wants me just as bad."

Our breaths tangled in the space between us, hers shaky, mine already uneven.

"So maybe I'm just like them, because yeah, I do want to fuck you. God, I really want to fuck you, but not for a story."

"I hate you," she said.

"No, you don't."

"You're just jealous," she rasped.

"Damn right I am," I growled. "I show up after you text me and find you laughing with some guy like he had a fucking chance—"

"He didn't," she snapped. "You think I want some fanboy with a spray tan? I don't!"

I stepped back. "Then what do you want?"

She blinked up at me, breathless and off-balance, gorgeous in all the ways that undid me.

"You."

That word hit me harder than any tackle I'd ever taken. "You literally just told me you hated me."

"Ugh, shut up. You're so hot, and you're so nice, and I don't want to think right now." Her hands pressed to my chest, sliding up slowly. Her eyes dropped to my mouth, voice low. "Stop thinking, just for a second."

Her lips hovered over mine, and fuck, I wanted to give in. Every inch of me ached to take her, to drown in her. Instead, I gripped the back of her neck, gently but firmly, holding her in place.

Because she'd already pushed me away twice.

"You're drunk," I whispered. "You don't know what you're asking for."

"I'm fine," she breathed, desperation creeping into her voice. "I know what I want."

I shook my head slowly, forehead resting against hers. "No, you think you do, but you don't. You're tipsy, pissed off, and trying not to feel again."

Her expression faltered. "I won't."

I cupped her cheek as my thumb brushed across her mouth. "You want me?" I murmured. "Then want me sober. Want me when you remember exactly what you're asking for."

Her eyes searched mine.

The elevator dinged. The doors slid open, and she stepped out, heels clicking on the pavement, her head held high. I stood there, choking down the yes I so desperately wanted to give her.

THIRTY-NINE

Sawyer

THE COOL NIGHT AIR HIT US AS WE STEPPED INTO THE PARKING garage, Ellie stumbling beside me.

"I'm fine, you know." She swatted at my arm when I reached for her. "You don't have to baby me."

"I'm not," I muttered, steadying her anyway. I couldn't help but touch her. "Just making sure you don't crack your skull open."

She glared at me, wobbling in heels that had no business being worn outside of a photo shoot. "You walk like you're trying to leave me behind."

"Maybe I should, with all that fucking attitude."

"Asshole," she grumbled, but her voice was soft around the edges. "Ugh, I don't even know why I'm following you."

Because I'd burn down the world before I let anyone else have you tonight. Because I couldn't fucking help myself.

"Because I'm taking you home."

She stopped walking, planting her feet, stubborn as hell. "Where's Ben? He was supposed to take me."

I kept walking. Looking at her too long was dangerous. "You were right there when I told him I've got you."

She narrowed her eyes, her stare sharp enough to cut. "You can't tell him what to do. You're not his boss."

"No," I said quietly, "but you're mine." Her lips parted, and I raised a brow. "I don't think either of us wants you navigating downtown in those heels with half a bottle of vodka in your system."

"You're not my dad."

"Thank God for that," I muttered.

"You're the worst."

"So you've said."

She took a step and tripped again, and that was it. I did what I'd done back at the club, scooping her up and tossing her over my shoulder.

"Oh my God," she shrieked, pounding weakly at my back. "Are you serious? Again?"

"Can't have my fake girlfriend breaking her ankle mid-tour, can I?"

"I don't need saving," she groaned, still kicking.

"Didn't say you did. I'm just making sure you don't face-plant on the concrete before I get to see you perform live again."

I reached the car, juggled my keys out with one hand, and unlocked it. Once I set her down gently on her feet, I opened the door for her. Her cheeks were flushed, her eyes blazing like she was ready to start another fight. She slid into the passenger seat with a dramatic huff and crossed her arms.

I rounded the hood and climbed in, but I didn't start the car. I stared straight ahead, jaw clenched, trying to breathe past the storm inside me.

But the words broke loose anyway.

"What the hell are we doing, El?"

She blinked, mascara smudged under her eyes, looking like sin and softness all at once. "What?"

"This." I gestured between us, trying to keep my voice steady. "You texted me to come save you. You flirt. You kiss me then avoid me. Then, you act like none of it means anything." My voice cracked on the last words.

She looked away.

I kept going, because now that I'd started, I couldn't stop. "I'm not mad," I whispered. "I'm confused. I like you, Ellie. That's not new information, but I can't keep getting yanked back and forth. I'm not built like that."

Silence.

Then, slowly, she reached across the console and laced her fingers through mine. Her touch burned.

"I know." Her thumb brushed over my knuckles. "I know, and I'm sorry. I just..." She swallowed, her voice small. "I'm scared, Sawyer. I don't know what I'm doing most of the time. But when I'm around you, I want...more. I just don't know if I'm ready for more or if I even know how without being too much."

I let her words sink in—let myself feel every damn inch of them. I squeezed her hand.

"I'm not asking for everything," I said, my voice rough from the pure fucking weight of wanting her. "I just need to know if this," I lifted her hand, pressing it to my chest, right over the thundering heart, "is real, or if I'm a fool for thinking it could be."

Her fingers curled against me.

"It's real," she breathed—and then she climbed into my lap.

"Ellie."

Her finger pressed to my mouth, silencing me. "Shh."

"You're drunk," I rasped.

"I know exactly what I'm doing."

"You don't," I bit out, fighting every instinct inside me. "You think you do, but you don't."

"Tell me what I know again." She leaned in, kissing a line along my jaw—soft, sweet, devastating.

"Ellie," I warned, my voice shaking.

"No." She smiled against my skin. "Say it. Ellie baby. Call me Ellie baby."

I gritted my teeth, hating how fast I caved.

"Ellie baby," I groaned.

She moaned softly, a sound that damn near broke me, and I leaned in to capture her mouth. My eyes rolled back in my head at the feel of her lips against mine again, and fuck, I wanted more.

But I pulled back.

"I'm not touching you," I said through clenched teeth.

She pouted. "Why not?"

"Because you told me twice this couldn't happen again." My hands fisted against the seat beneath her, desperate to hold on. "And I'm not stupid enough to fall for it a third time."

Her eyes gleamed, lips hovering near mine. "So what happens now?"

My chest burned. My body screamed for her.

"If you need something tonight?" My voice was strained. "Fine. Use me. Ride me. Do whatever it takes to forget the world for a few hours. But I'm not laying a single hand on you until you're sober, looking me in the eye, and asking for it."

She trembled in my lap. "And your words?" she asked. "Can I still have those?"

Fuck. I nodded once.

"You sure you can handle that?" I rasped.

"Try me."

Her hips rolled once, slow and devastating. A taunt. A threat. A fucking promise. I groaned; the sound ripped straight from my chest.

"Tell me what you'd be doing to me if your hands weren't staying put," she said.

I closed my eyes for a beat, forcing every muscle in my body not to betray me.

"You sure you want that?"

She leaned in, lips brushing mine without kissing. "Yes."

Her breath hitched, hips rocking harder. My exhale came rough, ragged. I clenched my jaw, trying to hold on.

Then, I gave in. I leaned up and put my mouth right at her ear.

"You want me to be your boyfriend tonight?" My voice was rough. "Want me whispering every filthy thing I've dreamed of while you ride me like you already fucking belong to me?"

Her breath hitched. "God, yes."

She rocked down on me again. The heat of her pressed right against my cock, searing through every damn layer like it wasn't even there.

She bucked forward again, slow, dragging herself over me with just enough pressure to make me hiss through my teeth.

"You feel that?" My voice broke apart, low and raw. "Feel how fucking hard I am for you? God, Ellie—please— don't stop. Don't fucking stop."

She whimpered, grinding harder, rubbing herself over me with a need that shattered something inside me. My hands dug into the seat, desperate not to grab her. If I did, I wouldn't let go.

"Fuck, Ellie." My head tipped back, breath totally gone. "You're making me lose my goddamn mind."

She leaned in, her nails scraping along the back of my neck, dragging tiny shocks across my skin. Her touch was barely there, but it lit me up like a fuse.

"More," she whispered shakily, voice shaky. "I need your words."

I almost groaned from how much I needed her to fucking need them.

"Keep grinding like that," I rasped. "Rub that sweet, soaking cunt all over me. Ruin my fucking jeans. Let me feel how wet you are. Please, baby, give it to me. Give it all to me."

Her moan punched straight through my chest. She rolled her hips harder. The heat between us was brutal, pure torture, and I wanted every second of it.

"That's it," I growled, breathless. "Just like that, baby. Get it. Take what you need."

Her breath stuttered as her hips jerked. "God, Sawyer—"

"Yeah, that's it." My voice darkened. "You're so fucking wet for me, aren't you? Couldn't even wait. Had to crawl into my lap and use me. That what you're doing, Ellie baby? Using me to get off?"

She whimpered, and her forehead dropped to mine.

"Fuck," I groaned, dizzy from her. "I want to bend you over this seat, push that little dress up, and rip your panties off."

Her breath caught, her hips grinding faster, reckless now.

"More," she gasped, her voice breaking apart. "Tell me what you'd do."

"I'd tease you with just the tip. Just enough to make you beg. Then, I'd push in so goddamn slow, El. So slow, you'd feel every inch of me stretching you."

She let out a strangled sound as her hips moved faster, chasing it.

"You'd beg me to go deeper." I kept going, the words half a snarl. "Beg me to fill you up until you couldn't think. And I'd give it to you. Right here. In this car. I'd fuck you so hard, you wouldn't be able to walk tomorrow. You want that, baby?"

"Yes—fuck, yes—please," she gasped, all wild and desperate.

I was shaking, fucked up from the sight of her head thrown back, body grinding in my lap, falling apart because of me.

"I wouldn't stop." I groaned. "Not until my cum dripped down your thighs. Until you were crying my name loud enough to wake the whole goddamn city."

"Yes," she sobbed. "Yes. Please, please—"

"Don't stop," I begged. "Please, baby. Make yourself come. Be my good girl and take what you need. Show me what I do to you."

She rocked harder, shameless. I could feel her unraveling, the tension building with her movements growing erratic.

"Come on, baby," I murmured, my lips brushing her ear. "Let go. Show me how beautiful you are when you fall apart."

And boy, did she. She let out a broken cry, biting her lip as her body shuddered against me. She kept moving, riding it out, trembling with every wave crashing through her with breathless whimpers and desperate little gasps.

I didn't move, even when every part of me begged to.

Her forehead dropped to my shoulder, her breath hot and uneven, chest heaving against mine.

God, I wanted to hold her and never let her go.

But I kept my promise. I only brought my mouth to her ear again.

"You're fucking perfect when you fall apart for me, Ellie baby."

She whimpered something between my name and a prayer.

And I stayed right there, letting her come down, still aching for her.

FORTY

Ellie

A SPLITTING, MERCILESS POUNDING STARTED AT MY TEMPLES and radiated through every inch of my body. I groaned, cracked one eye open, and immediately regretted it. Too unfamiliar. Too quiet. Too…not my bed.

I sat up too fast, which was a rookie mistake, instantly making me wince as the room spun around me. I scanned the space until my eyes found the clock on the nightstand: 5:03 a.m. And then, I looked down.

His T-shirt.

His bed.

Oh, fuck.

My heart slammed in my chest as I took in the rest of the room and the neatly placed ibuprofen and glass of water waiting on the nightstand.

Everything flooded back—the club with Rachel, too many drinks, and then Sawyer. God, the car. I remembered every second of sliding onto his lap, every desperate grind of my body against his.

Now, here I was, drowning in his bed, forced to face what I'd been running from. I liked it, and I liked him.

Sawyer was dangerous in a way no one else had ever been before. With him, I wanted to forget everything— every carefully built wall, every calculated move. I wanted to feel something real for once.

I was tired of fighting the pull I felt whenever he looked at me as if I wasn't some carefully packaged product but something worth wanting.

Maybe it was reckless and stupid, considering it was definitely destined to end badly—we both knew that. Whatever mess waited for me on the other side, I'd deal with it later, probably in an overpriced therapy session. Future me's problem.

Today, I was done pretending. If we were going to crash and burn anyway, why not enjoy the fall?

Still swimming in his T-shirt, I wandered into the living room, and there he was: asleep, bare chested, and stretched out on the couch like a cruel temptation.

I didn't think, sitting on the floor beside him and resting my head on the cushion near his arm. He stirred almost immediately, shifting toward me with a sleepy sound. His hand moved through my hair like it was instinctive. Without opening his eyes, he grabbed me, wrapped his strong arms around me, and pulled me straight onto the couch as if it was the most natural thing in the world.

I chuckled and curled into him, pressing my face against his chest. He made a low sound that sent heat straight through me, and our legs intertwined without thought. The way I fit against him should have been impossible, but it was as if his body had been built with the exact dips and angles to hold me.

Which, obviously, meant I had no choice but to kiss him. It was just a soft, barely there press of my lips to the curve of his throat.

"Ellie baby," he rasped, his voice laced with sleep.

"Hi," I whispered and kissed him there again, lingering long enough to feel the shiver that went through him.

His hand slid down, settling possessively at my waist. "What are you doing?"

I hummed, not bothering to answer as I kept my lips against his skin, too drunk on him to stop. He shifted under me to look down, dragging his gaze over me.

"What are you doing, El?" he asked again, a whisper this time.

I tilted my chin up, my mouth brushing the edge of his jaw. "Not pretending for once."

That earned the smallest smile curling at the corner of his mouth. "Not pretending to pretend?"

"Exactly."

His eyes stayed on mine, dark and steady, his hand still lazily resting on my waist.

Neither of us moved.

"Ellie." His voice was all low and raspy. "You're making it really hard to think straight."

I didn't even blink. "I'm not here to think."

His lips twitched. "You're aware I'm in no shape to stop you right now? You're sober now, and I'm barely half awake."

"Good."

Another soft breath of a laugh from him. He shifted under me, his fingers flexing against my waist.

"I'm serious." He tilted his head slightly, enough that his breath ghosted across my cheek. "Tell me what this is."

I felt his words as much as I heard them. Each one caught on my skin, sinking in, making it impossible to remember why I ever tried to resist him.

"This is me," I whispered, my lips hovering near his

jaw, "finally shutting off the part of my brain that over-thinks everything and telling you I want you."

His hand stilled. His chest lifted in slow, uneven breaths, like he was hanging on by a thread and I was the one holding the scissors.

"You're sure?" he asked. "Because if you start this…you don't get to act surprised when I listen."

I held his gaze, letting every reckless, terrifying part of me rise to the surface.

"Then listen," I whispered.

I didn't wait for him to take the lead. I was already leaning in, closing the space between us and pressing my mouth to his. It was soft at first, a barely there touch, tasting him.

He let me continue with my lazy movements for about two seconds, and all that careful restraint he was clinging to snapped.

His hands locked around my waist, moving me to straddle his lap in one pull without breaking the kiss. Suddenly, there was no patience, only heat and something feral clawing out of us both.

The kiss deepened quickly, open-mouthed and desperate. My head spun, as if I'd been pulled into some alternate reality where NFL players actually kissed emotionally damaged pop stars who came with more baggage than an airport carousel.

His hands were everywhere—gripping, dragging, anchoring me to him like he couldn't bear the thought of even an inch between us. He wasn't gentle. He was rough and greedy, and it only made me want him more.

I matched him—every bite, every tug, every frantic grind. There wasn't enough air in the room, but I didn't care. I didn't think. I moved with him, chasing every dizzying drag of friction between us, shamelessly aching for more. His abs were hard beneath me, and I rocked against him without a single ounce of hesitation.

"Ellie," he gasped, like my name was being ripped out of him. His hands locked down on my hips, guiding me, pulling me exactly where he wanted me. Where *I* wanted to be. "Fuck—don't stop. Please, don't you dare stop."

I wasn't planning on it. Every ridge gave me exactly what I was chasing. I ground down harder, the friction hitting just right through the thin layers of fabric between us.

Sawyer's breath stuttered. "Shit, baby—yeah, that's it."

God, he sounded wrecked, and it made me wild. I bite down on his bottom lip, swallowing the needy noises he kept making—deep, broken groans.

His hands moved like he couldn't decide where to start —skimming up my back, slipping under my shirt, tracing the curve of my ribs. His thumbs dragged across bare skin, rough in a way that made every inch feel new. One hand slid higher, fingers brushing over my nipple, and I rocked against him, catching the sound of his breath stalling against my mouth.

"God, this is so much fucking better when I can touch you." His eyes were wild when he pulled back to look at me. "Keep going. You're doing so good, El."

He wasn't even trying to keep it together anymore. He buried his face in my neck, hands gripping my ass tight enough to bruise as he guided me down on him.

We were fully clothed, and somehow, that made it worse.

"Ellie baby, please. I need more. Please, baby."

"Yes, more." My voice came out as a breathless whisper. "Please, more."

He sat up, dragging me with him, his hands gripping my waist. My legs hooked around him as he stood, lifting me. I barely registered him carrying me down the hallway until my back hit the mattress.

"You want this?" he asked, standing over me at the foot of the bed.

"Yes."

His eyes narrowed on me, and he knelt. "No, Ellie." His hand wrapped around my jaw. "Don't say it just because you're caught up in it. Don't say it if you're gonna wake up tomorrow acting like it was a mistake."

I blinked up at him, breathing hard.

"I need you to mean it," he said. "I need you to want this. Want me."

"I don't know what this is, but I do. I want you."

He didn't move.

I started to say, "If that's not enough—"

His mouth crashed to mine, fierce and claiming in a deep, raw kiss that left no space for doubt or hesitation.

"I'd take the fucking crumbs you left me," he murmured between kisses.

Sawyer didn't kiss like he was testing the waters. He kissed like he'd already drowned and had no plans to come up for air.

"Again." His breath hitched as rough hands slid under my shirt. "Say it again."

I dragged my nails down his spine, and that small touch made him curse under his breath.

"I want this. I want you," I said against his mouth.

He pulled away, and my shirt was gone before I finished exhaling.

"You're killing me." He groaned. "Swear to God, you're gonna fucking kill me—"

"Shh. You like it."

My words died on a moan when he sank his teeth into my skin, making me arch into him.

"You have no fucking clue what you do to me," he mumbled against my skin.

His mouth dragged lower, every breath hot and uneven against my skin. He didn't rush. He just kept going, slow and steady, until my stomach tensed beneath him. Then, he hooked his fingers into my underwear and tugged them down in one pull. Before I could so much as inhale, he flipped me on top of him.

"Come here." He tapped his chest. "Sit on my face, Ellie baby. Ride me till you come. Please. I need it. I need you."

I giggled. "Such a dirty, good boy you are, Sawyer love, begging for me."

I crawled up his body to position my knees on either side of his head.

He wasted no time putting his mouth between my thighs. There was no teasing, no slow build-up. He dove in, tongue flicking once, twice, before he locked his arms around my thighs, holding me down. I had a feeling he wasn't letting me go until he got exactly what he wanted.

He was taking in every second, taking note of everything—every inch, every sound I made, touched with that mix of care and hunger. His eyes never left mine, and when they darkened, the goofy, joking Sawyer I knew vanished. His hands clamped down on my hips, pulling me closer. Every movement stole my breath until the rest of the world didn't exist—it was only him and the way my body wanted more.

"Fuck." His voice vibrated against me between frantic strokes of his tongue. "Just as good as I remember."

Every time I rocked down on him, every broken sound I made, he moaned like it only drove him higher. When he pushed two fingers inside me, curling them as if he knew exactly what I needed, I gasped, and my hand flew to the headboard for balance.

My legs were shaking, and my fingers gripped the headboard tighter. He kept me right there, holding me down through every sound.

"God, you're perfect like this," he murmured against my skin. "You gonna come for me, baby?"

I nodded, unable to make any sounds but whimpers and moans.

"Come on, El. Let go for me."

A ragged cry slipped past my lips as my body went tight around the flood of sensation. Release tore through me in waves, each one stealing my breath until I was left trembling on top of him.

"Ride it out, El," he said, easing his grip.

I was still shaking when I moved down his body and lay next to him. We were both sweat-slicked and flushed, but I wasn't anywhere near done. I slid down his body, dragging my nails over the ridges of his abs. His abs flexed again, and his hand shot to my shoulders.

"El," he said, still breathing hard. "You don't have to—"

"I know." I was already working his sweats down his hips. "I want to."

His cock sprang free, and my jaw dropped as I took him in.

"You're not even pretending not to stare." He let out a raspy chuckle.

"As if you're complaining," I shot back, wrapping a hand around him.

He twitched in my palm, and I dragged my thumb through the bead of precum at the tip and smeared it down, teasing the head. His hips jerked up.

"Fuck," he bit out.

I took him into my mouth slowly, heavy and hot against my tongue. The taste of him was perfect. He was thick, stretching my lips, and I didn't even care. I wanted to make him fall apart and see how he reacted to me.

His hands tangled in the sheets. "El... Jesus—fuck—stop for a sec."

I pulled off, dragging my tongue over the tip, just to be a menace. "What?"

"If you keep going, I'm gonna come," he said, breathing hard. "I want to be inside you. I need it. I need you. *Please.*"

I crawled back up his body and straddled him.

"You could've just said that," I said, pushing my hair over my shoulder.

His eyes were blown wide as I reached down and dragged his cock through my center.

"Please, baby. Please. I need you. Don't play right now."

"I'm not." But I kept doing it anyway, watching his jaw clench, the way his abs locked up under the pressure.

"Condom?" he asked.

"I'm clear. Birth control. You?"

He nodded. Then, I sank onto him without another word. His head fell back, a low sound tearing out of him.

"Holy shit," he gasped. "You feel—God, baby, you feel so fucking good."

I paused halfway down, panting, already shaking from the stretch. "You're uh..."

"Big?" He let out a choked laugh. "Yeah, and you're tight. Stop stating facts and ride me. You can take it."

I tried to take more, but my thighs still trembled.

"Relax, baby. I got you," he whispered, his voice somehow gentle and desperate at once. "Let me help."

He sat up, one arm braced around my back, the other sliding down to circle my clit with steady pressure. I melted under his touch. My body eased finally, and he slid all the way in. I cried out—part in shock, part from the stretch, part in pure fucking bliss.

"That's it," he muttered, his lips dragging over my jaw.

I whimpered and started to move—slow, deep grinds, rolling my hips just to watch him unravel. Sawyer's grip tightened.

"Look at you, taking all of me." He lifted his hips to meet me once. "Riding me like you were made for my cock."

I smiled through my haze. His chest rose and fell like he couldn't catch his breath.

"Ellie," he said. "You've got no idea what you're doing to me right now."

I leaned forward, bracing my hands on his chest, and rolled my hips down again, deliberately tight, slow, dragging every inch of him.

"Try to last longer than last time," I teased.

That was when he snapped. His hands grabbed my ass, flipping me under him so fast, I gasped.

"Oh, you wanna tease me?" he growled, standing. "Two can play that game. Hands and knees. Now."

I obeyed, flipping over and crawling to the edge of the bed. Behind me, I heard the rustle of movements. His hands gripped my hips, and I leaned down on my elbows.

He lined himself up and drove into me with one hard, deep thrust. I gasped, my fingers clawing at the sheets as he pulled back and slammed into me again.

Every stroke knocked the air from my lungs, every sound he made bringing me closer to the edge. Again. And I gave it to him. Every inch, every sound, every part of me he wanted.

My back bowed as he thrust into me, one arm wrapped around my stomach, hauling me closer while the other caught my wrists and pinned them behind my back.

"You're unreal." He panted. "You were made for me. Say it."

I couldn't speak, just gasps and whimpers.

"*Say it*, El," he demanded. "Tell me I'm the only one who gets you like this."

"You are," I choked out. "You. Sawyer, don't stop.

His rhythm faltered, and he pulled out.

I whined in response. "Sawyer."

"Oh, you don't like me teasing you?" he asked, sliding his cock over my center. He slapped it up, earning a gasp from me. "I thought you wanted to tease? Huh, Ellie baby?"

"Please, Sawyer. Please."

"Hmmm. You sound pretty when you beg for me too."

Then, he pushed back inside, moving in long, languid strokes.

"Ellie, I'm close." He dropped his mouth to my shoulder. "Fuck, I can't—you're too good."

His hand slid between us, rubbing tight circles over my clit, and I shattered. My back arched, body shaking as the orgasm tore through me. He didn't stop. He fucked me through it, holding me down while I came apart underneath him.

"Good girl," he whispered into my neck. "That's it. Fucking perfect."

He went still, a raw, guttural groan ripping from his chest as he came, grinding deep. His whole body tensed, like he was trying to drag it out. He cursed again, breath broken, hips twitching as he emptied inside me.

When he finally collapsed next to me, I couldn't feel my legs. My body was Jello, shaking in the best way.

His hand stayed curled around mine, thumb brushing back and forth over my skin as our breathing slowed.

Then, finally, barely audible, almost ashamed, he whispered, "Still would've taken the crumbs."

I turned to him, caught that messy, real smile, and let my eyes fall shut.

FORTY-ONE

Sawyer

I DIDN'T KNOW WHERE HER HEAD WAS AT. HELL, I WASN'T even sure where mine was.

So, I soaked it up and let myself have this—her—while I still could and hoped I wouldn't hate myself when she inevitably walked away.

She was sprawled across my chest, asleep, hair sticking to her skin, still warm and flushed. It was just after nine in the morning now, but neither of us had moved much since we fell asleep a few hours ago.

I brushed her back lazily and leaned in.

"Hey," I murmured.

She groaned, her eyes still shut. "Sleep."

I grinned. "What if I told you I brought the journal?"

Her eyes snapped open. "You didn't."

I shrugged. "Figured after almost getting arrested, it wouldn't hurt to bend the rules. It's safer here. No chance of us breaking and entering again."

She sat up, the sheet slipping dangerously low. "You could've mentioned that earlier."

I smirked. "What, when you were too drunk to

remember your own name? Or maybe when you were too busy riding my t—"

She slapped a hand over my mouth, her cheeks flushed. "Sawyer."

I laughed under her palm, and she pulled it away. "Suddenly shy, are you?"

"Asshole," she muttered.

I got up, grabbed the journal from my drawer, and held it just out of reach.

"One page," I warned.

She looked up, her eyes bright. "Yes, sir."

"Careful, El." My voice came out rougher than I meant it. "Or I'll occupy you in other ways."

But I gave her the journal anyway, because I already knew I wouldn't say no to her. She smiled at me and flipped it open.

I can't stop noticing him. The way he moves through the kitchen. The way the drawer slams when he's angry, like it's meant to remind me I'm not safe.

Sometimes, he doesn't even look at me when he speaks, but I flinch anyway. I've done things I shouldn't have. Things that would make this worse if he ever realized.

I keep my son close. I whisper nonsense to him, sing a silly song, make him laugh, anything to keep him from noticing. He shouldn't see it. He can't.

I try to tell myself it's nothing, that I'm just tired, but it isn't nothing. Every step I take feels like it matters too much. Every pause, every glance, every snap of a cupboard handle makes me feel small and pinned.

I stay quiet. I smile when I have to. I do what I need to. But the fear is getting heavier, like the walls are closing in, and I don't know how much longer I can keep breathing.

She was quiet for a beat then nodded and went back to the pages. "He was definitely suspicious."

"Yeah." I rubbed a hand down my face.

"Maybe…" Her fingers curled tighter around the journal. "That's what pushed him over the edge. This definitely wasn't an accident. Why didn't the real father come back? And who is he?"

I sat up straighter. "I don't know. Maybe he got scared too. She said before that he needed more time."

Ellie's thumb rubbed the corner of a page, thoughtful. "You think the real dad's still alive?"

"I mean, even back then, he could be anyone between, what? Twenty and maybe forty, realistically. We don't know anything about him. It's possible he's still out there somewhere."

I watched her reread a line again and again, like she was trying to memorize it.

"You okay?" I asked.

She exhaled, slow and uneven. "I don't know. It's just… She kept it all inside, as if the second she told the truth, it'd get her killed. Except it wasn't her who died."

I nodded.

"This whole time, we've been treating it like a mystery," she went on, her voice quieter. "Like a puzzle to solve. But this wasn't just clues in a journal. She was begging someone to hear her."

I leaned forward, elbows on my knees. "You want to stop?"

"No," she said quickly. "I want to keep going. I just…" She closed the journal and held it against her chest. "For once, I'm ready to put this down for a moment instead of wishing we could read another page."

"Yeah…I've got to start getting ready soon anyway."

She blinked, like the shift in topic caught her off guard. "Right. The game."

"Yup. NFC Championship today."

She sat back a little, as if she was recalibrating. "Is this the furthest you've ever gotten?"

"Yeah."

She squeezed my arm. "How are you feeling?"

"Excited, mostly." I let out a breath. "We've made it this far before, but we've never pulled it off. This is my last shot."

"You've got this." She leaned in to press a quick kiss to my cheek.

But I wasn't in the mood for quick. I caught the back of her neck and pulled her closer. Her lips met mine, and her hand pressed into my chest. She leaned in without hesitation, and for a moment, it was just her, me, and the way we fit together.

The game, the noise, everything else—it didn't matter. Not with her here, letting me take a little more. For a second, I let myself imagine I could have both: her and the win.

But I knew I wasn't that lucky.

I eased back, though it took more effort than I cared to admit.

"My family's coming today," I said. "They've got an extra ticket. You should come."

She blinked. "Wait, really?"

"Yeah. I would've asked you before, but I figured you wanted a little space."

She nodded with a shy smile. "You want me to come through?"

"Why wouldn't I?"

"They're not gonna think it's weird?"

"Ellie, they already think we're dating. Plus, they love you."

"Well…" Her mouth pulled into the start of a smile. "I don't have a show until the day after tomorrow."

"See? Meant to be."

Her smile grew. "Okay. I'm in."

An hour later, Ellie was in my passenger seat, looking like the cutest fucking thing I had ever seen, all decked out in my jersey. The wind tangled her hair as she flicked through my phone, skipping songs like she had a personal vendetta against every single one of them.

After another abrupt skip, I shot her a look. "You know, most people pick a song and stick with it."

Her eyes stayed glued to the screen. "Most people don't have to survive your playlists."

That pulled a laugh out of me.

"Survive?" I shook my head, easing the car around the curve. "Baby, you were singing every word five minutes ago."

She finally looked over. Her eyes sparkled with a smug tilt of her lips that I could feel in my damn chest.

"Desperate times," she said. "Your playlists are either me or a man crying about his truck and the girl who dumped him."

"Nothing wrong with that."

She flicked through another song, and I glanced over, giving her a look.

Her tone went sweet—too sweet. "Eyes on the road, Sawyer."

I obeyed but not before catching the glint in her eye.

"Good boy."

Dammit, I already wanted to fuck her again.

Eventually, she finally settled on *Anywhere but Here* by Ruby Lynn Hayes. The road stretched out ahead of us, and her foot bounced in time with the beat.

She caught me staring and smirked, like she knew exactly what she was doing to me. "Don't look at me like that."

"Like what?" I asked, even though we both knew.

"Like you're about to pull this truck over and make us late."

I dragged my gaze back to the road. "Not my fault you look like that."

She laughed, low and throaty, before kicking her feet up on the dash.

"God, you're shameless," she muttered. "We both know you really, really wanted me to wear this."

"What I really want is to fuck you wearing only that."

She hummed, a teasing little sound that ran straight down to my dick. "I could be down for that."

Fuck. She was just sitting there, wearing my name on her back and smiling as if she was unaware of the storm she'd caused in my heart.

"At least you don't have to go out there and fake being my girlfriend now," I said, my voice low and rough.

Her grin grew wider. "Oh yeah?"

My fingers curled around the wheel, holding steady because every other part of me wasn't. "Mhm."

She bit her lip, barely holding back a laugh. She kept her eyes on me, chin tilted just enough to make it impossible to look away.

I swallowed hard, eyes dragging over her that smug look she got when she knew she'd won.

She did. She already fucking did.

FORTY-TWO

Ellie

Sawyer's entire family had packed into the front-row sideline section all decked out in Rebels gear.

Dotty claimed the seat beside mine and immediately started trash-talking the other team like it was her full-time job. Gracie proudly held up a homemade sign that read: *#71 is My Uncle and He's Better Than Yours*, made with glitter glue that had already attached itself to my jacket. Trent bounced between seats, yelling at players who definitely couldn't hear him. Dorian and Noah were curled up together two seats down, laughing at something on her phone. Colt and David were next to them, arms crossed, eyes fixed on the field.

It was loud and slightly freezing, but it was perfect. I wasn't entirely sure if I could full-send a relationship with Sawyer, but I was warming up to the idea of trying.

The game started off with the opposing team scoring first. The Rebels tied it up on a clean throw from West on the next turnover. The score went back and forth from there. In the second quarter, they pulled ahead by three points with a field goal. The others were glued to the scoreboard, but…

I was too focused on Sawyer.

The way he moved on the field, head down, laser-focused, in constant communication with his teammates. It was clear why he was here—why he was a starter. He didn't just know the game. He was part of it.

Even with all the noise and bodies packed around me, he was the only thing I saw. The air had turned colder after halftime. January in San Francisco wasn't snow-level cold, but it was enough to make me tuck my hands beneath my thighs to keep them warm. I watched him jog out with his helmet tucked under one arm. He looked up once and smiled at me, and I gave him a little wink before he ran back out for the next play.

Dolly leaned in, bumping my shoulder with hers. "You doing okay?"

"Yeah. I'm good." I gave her a quick smile, but my eyes never left the field.

"You sure?" She gave me a once-over. "You've barely said a word."

"I'm just taking it all in."

"You mean you're swooning all over him."

I bit back a smile. "I am not."

"You are," Gracie chirped. "You got all wobbly when Uncle Sawyer looked over here!"

"He plays better when you're in the crowd, you know," Dotty said.

I scoffed. "You're just saying that."

She squinted, like she was trying to decide if I was clinically insane. "Last time you were at a game, he got a touchdown."

"And the time before that, he got a concussion."

She shrugged. "Eh, doesn't count."

A whistle blew, and her head snapped back to the field.

"Third and long," Dorian said.

The section fell silent as the crowd dialed entirely to the game.

Trent leaned forward. "He's gonna take that poor guy for a ride."

I followed to where everyone else was looking. Sawyer crouched low on the line, his fingers brushing the turf, that massive frame waiting. He rolled his shoulders and dropped into position. I tried not to catalogue how good he looked doing literally anything, but my brain was a traitor with a damn zoom function solely focused on him.

The ball snapped, and everything happened fast.

Sawyer surged forward with so much force, I gasped. The guy across from him met him head-on. It lasted half a second, maybe less. Then, he was driven backward like he weighed nothing at all. I stood without thinking as everyone else did the same.

Sawyer didn't stop. He kept going, cleared the lane like he'd planned the whole thing two plays ago. The ball was gone before I even realized it left West's hands.

A clean pass. A clean catch.

Touchdown.

The stadium lost its mind.

Gracie shrieked, her glitter sign shaking in the air. Trent jumped up, yelling something unintelligible. David didn't move, but there was a quiet sort of pride in the way he nodded.

Sawyer pulled off his helmet, a victorious grin already spreading across his face, and suddenly, he was moving. Not walking, not jogging—running straight toward me as if I were the only person in that packed stadium.

"Is he—?" I started but couldn't finish the thought.

Dotty whooped. "Oh yeah, he's coming for you."

"He wouldn't."

"He absolutely would."

And he did, right over the barrier as if it were nothing, as if the crowd and cameras and security had ceased to exist. Still breathing hard from the game, hair damp with sweat, he stopped directly in front of me with an expression that made my heart stutter.

His hands found my face before I could process anything, and when he kissed me, the rest of the world dissolved.

The cheering crowd, the blazing lights, the thundering music—all of it melted away until nothing remained but us and this overwhelming feeling that rewrote everything I thought I knew about wanting someone.

"Had to celebrate with my girl," he said with a wink.

He pressed his forehead to mine and then gave it a quick kiss before hopping down, not acknowledging his family other than a quick wave as he jogged backward.

Dotty let out a breath like she'd been holding it the whole time. "Okay. So that happened."

"That happened," Gracie shouted with her sign, now completely upside down. "He kissed her!"

I dropped into my seat before my knees decided to do it for me. Everything inside me was scrambled—my pulse, my brain, my entire sense of reality.

Colt didn't say a word, but I felt him watching me.

The rest of the game played out in pieces. I clapped when they clapped, stood when everyone else did, but my eyes stayed locked on Sawyer.

The Rebels had a six-point lead after a late field goal in the fourth, but the other team had possession and thirty yards to the end zone. Enough time to ruin everything.

There was another down, another huddle. I mouthed numbers along with the play clock, hoping I could hex the other team.

Snap.

The pass never left the quarterback's hand when he was sacked. At least, that's what Dotty told me happened.

Clock: 0:05.

The stadium erupted with noise. Only five seconds, and the other team had no time-outs. Victory was practically printed and laminated. Still, I didn't exhale until the scoreboard's last red digit flipped to zero.

Final. Rebels 27, Wildcats 24.

The buzzer went off and helmets flew, bodies collided in celebration, and somewhere in the madness, #71 tore off toward the sideline, searching.

For me.

We'd won. *He'd* won. And judging by the way his smile bulldozed every rational thought in my head, I was about to too.

Sawyer spotted me and broke into a sprint, cutting through the sidelines like nothing else mattered. I barely had time to react before his arms wrapped around my waist, lifting me clear off the ground.

"Ellie, baby." His voice was low as he placed me back down.

Before I could answer, his family started shouting and laughing, pulling him away in a mix of congratulations and back slaps.

I stepped to the side, trying to catch my breath. Sawyer gave me a little smile, then started talking to everyone.

I stepped back, letting the noise pass over me and

giving Sawyer a moment. Colt approached me a few seconds later.

"Ellie," he greeted.

"Hey."

He didn't look at me right away. His gaze stayed on Sawyer, who was grinning as he said something to Dorian and Trent, completely wrapped up in the moment. The joy radiated off him, his brother standing next to me with his normal unreadable look.

"I don't really know you," Colt said finally. "But I know him. Better than anyone."

I said nothing.

"He's given up more than most people realize. For football, for this team, for our family. You're the first thing I've seen that makes him light up like this."

He didn't sound mad or even emotional. Just factual, like he was laying down the truth and leaving it there.

"But if you're not all in, you need to let him go." He glanced at me. "You've got your own world. Big stage. Big future. And that's fine, but if he's not a part of that future, don't keep him hoping. Because he will."

I still didn't answer.

He gave a small nod, as if that was all he came to say, before he disappeared into the crowd.

I stood there for a while, eyes back on Sawyer. He hadn't stopped smiling, and I didn't know what the hell I was supposed to do with any of it anymore.

FORTY-THREE

Sawyer

THIS WAS THE DREAM. I WAS GOING TO THE SUPER BOWL FOR my last season, but it didn't feel the way I always imagined.

Something was wrong. Ellie hadn't said anything, but she didn't need to. I could sense it. She was fine after the game for a minute. Then, I saw it—Colt pulling her aside, saying something he probably thought no one else would notice. But I saw the way her face changed, that tight nod, the way she didn't look at him again.

She hadn't been herself since.

My family came back to my place to celebrate. There were music, drinks, and way too many people in my small condo. And Ellie barely said two words the whole time.

Now, the place had cleared out, leaving just the two of us. She was curled into the corner of my couch, shoulders tense, picking at her fingernails. Her smile flicked up when I walked over, but it didn't reach her eyes. I dropped to my knees and took her hands, coaxing her fingers to still.

"Ellie." I pressed a quick kiss to her knuckles.

She let out a breath that shook and gave me another version of that fake smile.

"What's going on?" I asked.

She shrugged, but it was mechanical. "Nothing. I'm good."

"What did he say to you?"

Her brows pulled in. "Who?"

"Colt."

Her eyes flicked away before they snapped back. "What…what do you mean?"

"I saw him talking to you after the game. Something changed. You've been off since then."

She tugged her hands from mine and folded them into her lap. "I know."

"El." I kept my voice steady. "Tell me."

"You're coming off a win. Everything's good right now. Let's talk tomorrow."

"No. We're doing this now."

She stood, brushed past me, and rubbed her hands over her jeans. "I should go home."

"Ellie."

She stopped but didn't turn around.

"What did he say?"

"He didn't tell me anything I didn't already know."

"Like what?"

She spun to face me. "That I should walk away if I'm not in this."

I swore under my breath. Of course he did. My silent, passive-aggressive brother waited until one of the biggest days of my career to say something that would screw everything up.

I stood. "And are you not in it?"

"I don't know." Her voice cracked, and she rubbed her

temples like it might help her brain catch up. "I don't fucking know. It's too real."

"It's not too real. It's just real."

She started pacing. "It is! It is real, and that's exactly the issue. I thought for a second it would be fine, but then your brother comes in and tells me to walk away, and now, I don't know anymore."

She stopped at the kitchen counter, both palms braced against it, facing me, but her eyes were glued to the floor.

"I think it's better if we start pulling back now." Her voice cracked, and she gripped the counter tighter. "Before it gets…harder."

I was across the room, but it felt like miles. Every instinct screamed at me to go to her, to pry her hands from that counter and make her look at me, really look at me. Instead, I stayed frozen in place.

"Harder for who?" The question came out harsher than I meant, desperation bleeding through the edges. "You think I can just turn this off because a date on the calendar says so?"

For a second, I thought she might bolt—I could see it in the way her weight shifted, ready to flee. But she stayed, rooted to that spot, still refusing to meet my eyes.

"I don't know what this is anymore, Sawyer." Her voice was barely above a whisper. "I don't know what we are. Maybe it's nothing. Maybe it was never anything but convenient."

The words hit me like a physical blow. My jaw clenched so tight, I had to take a breath to steady myself.

"No," I snapped. "Don't do that. Don't minimize this. Don't act like this was convenient. You want to know what we are?"

"Sawyer, I can't…."

Finally, *finally*, she looked up at me through her lashes.

Those eyes—God, those eyes—swam with unshed tears, wide, terrified, and so fucking beautiful, it made my chest ache. Her lower lip trembled, just once, before she caught it between her teeth.

The sight of her broken like that shattered something inside me. I rounded the counter, closing the remaining distance and bracing my hands on the counter on either side of her, caging her in. She sucked in a sharp breath but didn't face me.

"We're real," I whispered into her ear. "Maybe we started as something fake, but we crossed that line so fast, I didn't even see it happen."

She turned to face me. "I just...I don't know where I stand with you anymore. I don't know what this is."

I leaned closer, close enough that my forehead almost touched hers. "You're not on the outside or even beside me. You're not a question mark or a placeholder or some PR stunt I tolerated. You're the center of this." My voice broke on the words. "You're where I land. You're where I begin. You're not standing beside me or behind me—you *are* the place I'm standing. Everything else moves around that."

Her breath hitched, and a single tear slipped free, tracking down her cheek. Without thinking, I reached up to brush it away with my thumb, and she leaned into my touch.

Her composure finally cracked completely. Her face crumpled, and she pressed her hands flat against my chest, fingers curling into my shirt.

"Sawyer," she breathed, and it sounded like a prayer and a plea all at once.

I couldn't hold back anymore. My hands found her face, thumbs brushing away the tears, and then, my lips were on hers. She kissed me back desperately, like she was drowning and I was air. Her hands fisted in my shirt, pulling me closer.

For a moment, everything else disappeared—Colt's words, the uncertainty, the fear. There was just us, just this.

When we broke apart, we were both breathing hard. Her forehead rested against mine, eyes still closed.

"This is what I'm afraid of," she whispered against my lips. "This feeling. How much I need it. Need you."

I pulled back enough to look at her. "Why is that so scary?"

She wiggled her way out of my reach and leaned against the opposite counter.

"Because I'm standing at the edge of this cliff, and the only way is down or back." Her eyes welled up again, and her hands flew to her sides. "If I go back, I get the life I know. The one I built that's safe and easy." She pointed at her chest. "I can keep pretending I'm fine, keep performing and proving to myself, to my parents, that everything we did to get here was worth something. Or…or I jump, but I don't know what's down there. And I'm not sure I'm brave enough to find out. If I let myself have this—have you— then I'm giving everything else up. I'm letting everyone down. My team, my label, the tour. The version of me I worked so hard to create. I'd be walking away from Ellie Miles."

I moved toward her. One step. She flinched, so I stopped.

"You wouldn't be walking away from anything," I said. "Not for me. I'll never ask you to give anything up for me."

"I know." Her voice caught. "But I want to. That's the problem. I want to walk away from all of it. I want this… with you." She laughed, but there wasn't any humor in it. "I don't want the spotlight. I don't want to be a brand. I just want to write songs that matter to me and share them when I feel like it. Or not at all. I want to wake up and not feel like I'm pretending."

"Then do it."

"I can't." She shook her head. "This was supposed to be an easy arrangement, remember? A plan. A clean start and a clean end. We were supposed to help each other, solve a couple of problems, and move on. I didn't plan for this. I didn't plan to feel like this and to question everything more than I already was."

I ran a hand through my hair and let out a breath.

"Ellie, it's okay for your plans, your dreams, to change."

She scoffed. "Why do you even care? Why do you care about someone like me?"

That pulled a dry laugh from me. "You're kidding, right?"

She didn't respond.

"You really don't get it, do you?" I whispered.

"No, I don't. I don't get why someone like you would want someone who's such a mess and whose entire life is under a microscope."

"Ellie, I love you. I'm *in* love with you. Not the version of yourself you think everyone needs to see, but you—the real you—"

She shook her head. "You can't love me. You don't really know me."

"I know you. I know you get completely lost in a story because it grabs hold of something deep inside you and won't let go. I know you like to laugh in the back of a cop car after we broke into someone's house like it's the most natural thing in the world."

She blinked back tears, and I stepped closer.

"Sawyer…"

"I know the woman who shows up to my games, even though football might as well be a foreign language to you. I know the goofy, ridiculous Ellie who dances with me on Christmas morning and ambushes me with snowballs when I least expect it. I *know* exactly who you are, Ellie. I *love* exactly who you are." I closed the distance and cupped her cheek. "I love every part of you. The person you are on stage, the one you are off it."

Her breath hitched, and I took a small step back.

"You say that now," she said, her voice shaking. "But what happens when the novelty wears off? When I'm not a project to figure out anymore?"

"Ellie, you aren't just some project to me. I can't breathe when you're around. It's like my body can't keep up with how much I need you. And when you're not?" I shook my head. "Fuck, it's worse. It's as if I forget I'm running on empty until you're back."

She pressed a hand to her chest and searched my face. "Don't..."

"You were the woman I crushed on for years, and I thought maybe it was just that—some silly thing I'd eventually grow out of. But you're not who I thought you were. You're so much more. This isn't a phase or some fake relationship. It's you. I mean, fuck, I've built my days around the chance to see you or hear your voice. I've taken whatever you've been willing to give, hoping and waiting for you to feel the same."

She took a step back. "You can't say things like that." Her voice was barely above a whisper, and she wrapped her arms around herself. "This was supposed to be simple."

"Guess I'm not built for simple. I've been the funny guy, the steady one, the guy who laughs things off so nobody actually sees me. Then, you walked in, and now, I can't pretend that's all I am."

Her expression softened, and she looked up at me through her lashes.

"I see you," she whispered, her voice cracking. "I've always seen you."

"Just tell me the truth." I pinched the bridge of my nose. "Because I can't do the back-and-forth anymore."

She wrapped her arms around herself. "You want the truth? The truth is, you terrify me. Not because of who you are, but because of what you make me want. What you make me feel."

She turned away, running her hands through her hair in that frustrated way that made my chest ache.

She continued, her voice low but steady. "I've spent years keeping pieces of myself locked away. Not just because it feels safer, but because every time I let someone close, it backfired. They got a look at the mess underneath and decided it wasn't worth sticking around. So, I learned to play the part. If I stop, if I admit I don't want this constant grind anymore, I'll let everyone down."

Her arms tightened around herself. "You…you're the exception I never planned for. You slipped past all the defenses I swore I'd never let down. And that scares me more than anything, because I don't know how to keep being the version of me the world wants and the version of me you see. I don't even know if that version is worth loving."

"You are worth it, El."

"Be realistic for a second. You're going back to Wood-stone. Our lives don't make sense together. We'll be in different places. Different lives. You'll be with your family I'll be on tour. We'll be—"

"I'd be wherever you are."

That stopped her cold. Something shifted in her expression—surprise, hope, and terror all at once.

"I'd follow you anywhere, Ellie. I can be there for them and still choose you. This doesn't have to be one or the other."

She stared at me like I'd offered her something she'd never dared to dream of. Her lips parted, but no words came out at first.

"You don't understand," she finally managed to say. "I'm not good at this. At letting people stay. At believing they want to."

"Then let me prove it to you."

She closed her eyes, pressing her palms against them like she could push back the tears. When she opened them again, they were red-rimmed but determined.

"I...I need time. I need to think about it."

I ran a hand over my face, jaw tight. "Okay."

She started to step back. "I'll go home."

"I'll take you," I said, moving closer.

"Sawyer...no." Her eyes flashed, and she shook her head, but her hands lingered near mine, as if she couldn't quite pull away.

"Fine." I moved on instinct, reaching for the last thing I had that connected me to her. I grabbed the journal and held it out.

"Here. Take this with you."

She hesitated. "I...I can't."

"Yes, you can." My voice was steadier than I felt. "And you will."

She took it without another word. Then, she walked out, and, like I knew she would, she took a piece of my heart in her pocket.

FORTY-FOUR

Ellie

I SPENT THE NEXT TWO WEEKS UNAPOLOGETICALLY WALLOWING in self-pity. As I sat in my top-of-the-line hotel suite in New York City, I let myself go through all the emotions.

When I wasn't traveling or performing, it wasn't the productive kind of wallowing either. Every free moment, I spent with no makeup, no pants on. I didn't half-ass my wallowing. I let myself spiral the way I only ever allowed approximately once a year, and it was overdue.

Between cities, I spent my nights watching true crime docs back-to-back and ordering every form of carbs and cheese DoorDash had to offer. I turned off my phone, ignored everyone's texts. I knew Rachel and my parents meant well, but I didn't want comfort, advice, or someone reminding me I was supposed to be fine.

I wanted to sit in my feelings, with the ache in my chest I couldn't explain.

I'd built this life piece by piece, spent my childhood shaping it into something that looked like success. I gave up so much to get here, even when it made me feel small—even when it never quite felt like mine. And now, I stood at the edge of something real for probably the first time in my life, something I hadn't let myself want in years, and I didn't know if I was supposed to jump or walk away.

The rational part of me knew the truth. I didn't have to choose one or the other. I could keep going, keep building, with him beside me. But that kind of love, the kind Sawyer offered, wasn't something you could half-choose.

And a part of me wanted to jump, even if I didn't know where I'd land. Whether it was San Francisco or Woodstone didn't matter half as much as who would be waiting on the other side.

But I wasn't sure I was brave enough.

I stared at the ceiling long enough to memorize every dip and curve of the plaster. The life I'd built was pressing in from all sides, and I was shrinking under the weight of it.

The notebook came out almost without thought; it was the only thing that made sense when everything threatened to pull me under. I sank to the floor, my knees drawn up, and let the pencil move across the page.

Sawyer saw through the walls I had built so carefully, through all the parts of me I tried to keep hidden, even from myself, and it terrified me to want something that may never fit inside the life I had always believed I was meant to live. And yet, maybe that life was already behind me, fading into something I no longer recognized.

The words poured out before I could stop them, before I could question or weigh them. For the first time in a long time, I let them. Everything I had held back spilled onto the page until there was nothing left but the truth.

The stage lights dimmed, and a ripple of anticipation swept through the crowd. My heart raced as I crossed the stage. One of the backup dancers handed me my guitar, and I slung the strap over my shoulder.

I stepped up to the mic and drew in a slow breath.

"So…I'm doing something a little different tonight."

A wave of cheers, loud and eager, filtered through the crowd. I smiled softly, not quite ready to meet their energy.

"I've been writing a lot recently," I said, my voice echoing through the arena, "but not necessarily for an album. Not even for anyone to hear, really. It started off as lines I didn't know what to do with. Thoughts. Pieces of things I couldn't say aloud."

The crowd quieted again, their stillness stretching out in support. I exhaled.

"This one wasn't planned. It's raw and unfiltered and probably not perfect, but it feels honest. And after some thought, I think it deserves its moment."

A few screams rose up again from the front rows, and I chuckled. I adjusted the mic slightly and looked down at my hands as I started to strum, the opening chords humming through the speakers.

"I haven't played this for anyone," I said, glancing up, meeting the lights. "But this is Unscripted."

> I'm standing on the edge of all I know
> A cliff so high, I'm scared to let go
> Behind me lies the life I thought I wanted
> Ahead's a choice that leaves me haunted
>
> You came like lightning, sudden and bright
> Breaking through the walls I built so tight
> Now I'm suspended between the sky and
>   ground

Hoping solid footing can be found

I'm halfway here, between the fall and
    the fear
The risk feels close, but I can't make it clear
My heart's spinning fast, I don't know where
    to land
I'm scared to jump, though I want to take
    your hand
I'm halfway there, and it's all unscripted
Wild and unknown, and I'm not sure I'll
    risk it

The life behind me's a story carved in stone
But it's heavier now, and I feel alone
If I let go, will I fly or break?
Or will your hands be there when I wake?

You came like a storm I couldn't foresee
Pulling at the pieces I thought were only me
I'm hanging here, between doubt and desire
Feeling the spark that could set me on fire

We built it on make believe, lights and lies
But I saw forever when I met your eyes
We had a script, but you tore it in two
Nothing fake ever felt this true
I don't know what this is or how it came
    to be
But whatever it is, it's wildly, beautifully
    unscripted

I'm halfway here, caught between the fall and
    the fear

You're the risk I want, though I can't make it
    clear
My heart's in overdrive, and I don't know
    the plan
I'm scared to jump, but I want to, hand
    in hand
I'm halfway there, and it's all unscripted
Wild and unknown, but I don't want to
    miss it

The last note faded, and the crowd erupted much louder than I anticipated. I stood there for a moment, letting the noise wash over me, raw in a way I hadn't dared to be in years.

I was still Ellie Miles. Still me.

For a long time, it felt like I could never fully reconcile the two sides. Now, no matter what came next, I knew I could.

I lifted the guitar from my shoulder and smiled, a real one this time.

"Thank you," I said, my voice shaking. "That song… it's everything I couldn't say before. It's about standing on the edge of who you are and who you want to be. Sometimes, the hardest part isn't jumping. It's deciding you want to."

The crowd cheered again.

After the encore, I finally left the stage.

Backstage was a blur of voices, lights, and the rush of adrenaline. I sank down on the edge of the dressing room couch.

Rachel opened the door, coming crashing in

"Ellie!" She ran over to sit next to me and gave me a hug. "I'm so fucking proud of you. That was beautiful."

"Thanks. Sorry, I went…a little off script there."

"It's okay. The crowd loved it, and I could tell you did too."

"I did."

And I wonder if Sawyer would too.

After I got back to the hotel, I showered, pulled on an old shirt, and climbed into bed. Then, I called my mom. She picked up right away.

"Hey, sweetie," she said.

"Hi."

"It's late there, yeah?" she asked.

I glanced at my phone. "One in the morning."

"Can't sleep?"

"You could say that."

"What's going on?" she asked.

I hesitated. "Sawyer."

She paused. "Oh no. What did you do?"

"Why do you assume it was me?"

She let out a laugh. "Because I saw that boy's face during your show. He had hearts in his eyes watching you, and I know you."

"Wow. Thanks?"

"Call it a mother's instinct. Tell me what's going on."

"Okay…well, I have a confession."

"Oh, no," she mumbled.

"Sawyer and I…it wasn't real. Not at first."

"What do you mean?"

"We were fake dating. To clean up the Harold mess in the press."

"Well…that's news to me."

"Yeah, but—"

"He caught feelings."

I let out a breath. "Yeah."

"And now you don't know what to do with that."

"Yeah, because I think I did too."

She didn't sound surprised. "I know."

"You do?"

"El, that song? The one you played tonight?"

I winced. "You saw that?"

"Of course. Someone always live-streams your shows, and your dad and I always watch, even when we're traveling."

"Where are you now?"

"Fiji. Don't change the subject. That song was about him, wasn't it?"

"Yes…"

"What's holding you back?"

"Ellie Miles," I stated.

She laughed. "Sorry, sweetheart, but I don't follow."

"The person I've been building since I was little. I don't know how to walk away from her."

She went quiet for a second before speaking. "No one's asking you to. You don't owe your past self anything."

"I don't want to let anyone down."

"You won't."

"I don't want to let you down either."

"El…"

"I'm tired. I'm so tired, Mom. I used to want this more than anything. Now, I don't even know what this is."

"You've done enough. You've given more than enough. You can't keep chasing a dream you don't believe in. It doesn't mean any of it wasn't worth it. That doesn't stop being true just because the dream looks different now."

"Then why do I feel like I'm failing?"

She chuckled. "Because it's the only life you've ever

known, but letting go doesn't erase it. It makes room for something new, something that makes you happy."

"And how do I know what that is?"

"Well, something tells me it's a very handsome football player."

I smiled, even though it hurt. "Yeah…maybe it is."

Maybe I wasn't ready to jump. Maybe I never would be. But maybe I didn't have to be perfect to take a step forward.

Because, for the first time, I wasn't alone on that cliff.

After we spoke for a while longer, she caught me up on their travels, and we hung up. The hotel room was too quiet without her murmured words of assurance, and my mind was spinning, so I got up and pulled the old journal out of my suitcase.

The one I'd been avoiding since the moment he handed it to me. I wasn't sure I was ready to read the last few pages, but I missed him. And this, the mystery, the mess, the truth, was the only part of him I still had.

So, I turned the page.

I found the drawer empty this morning. It was a small thing, a photo I kept folded in the back beneath old bills and receipts. I shouldn't have kept it. It was foolish. Dangerous. But it was the only proof I had of a time when I felt like myself.

Now, it's gone, and he hasn't said a word. Not at breakfast, not over supper, not in the way his hands rested too still on the table.

The silence is worse than any accusation. It's a door waiting to slam.

I've thought about running, but there's nowhere to go where he wouldn't follow.

My eyes burned as I read her words. I blinked hard and turned the page, finding the final entry but quickly closing the journal. I was unsure if it was a weird loyalty, but it felt wrong enough to read it without him, let alone break our other rule of only one at a time.

Instead, I opened it back up and stared at the page I had just read. I read it again. Then again. Then, I went back and read all of them. My thoughts scattered in a hundred directions. None of it made sense.

I sat there for hours, flipping back and forth through the pages and retracing Lauren's words like they might lead me somewhere new for once. The longer I reread, the more questions began to rise.

Who was the real father? Why hadn't she named him? And why did it all still feel unfinished—like a door half-open, waiting for someone to step through it?

I didn't know what I was looking for, but when I typed her name into the search bar for the thousandth time, I knew this wasn't about a little mystery anymore. It was about the boy. The one who never got to grow up. The one who still didn't have a voice.

And the woman who still had one.

FORTY-FIVE

Sawyer

Sweat dripped into my eyes, but I didn't stop. The ground blurred in front of me. The pounding of my feet against the track was easier to deal with than everything else.

Practice had ended over an hour ago, and Bronx and West stuck around without asking why. They didn't need the details. They could sense I was upset and needed to work out all this shit from my body.

Ellie walked away.

She said she needed time, and I told her I understood. Meant it too. It had still hurt like hell, even if I saw it coming.

That was two weeks ago, and I hadn't heard a word since. I knew she was busy touring, but fuck, if my heart didn't long for a single text from her.

I've been avoiding the headlines, the concert recaps, and even the damn livestreams of her performances I always tried to watch.

I sneaked a few glimpses here and there, but I instantly

regretted it when my heart was suddenly a lead fucking weight.

After too many laps to count, Bronx finally bent at the waist, panting. "Are you trying to kill us? It's been two weeks of this fucking broody bullshit and you going ham in training. I'm dead."

West slowed, shaking out his arms. "You're a professional athlete. You'll survive."

"I'm defense," Bronx said. "I stop people, not chase them."

West let out a laugh and glanced over at me. "You good?"

"Super Bowl's coming up. Gotta be game ready."

"Nah, that's not it."

"Agreed. What's going on?" Bronx asked.

We walked the curve of the track, and Bronx let out a breath.

"It's Ellie, isn't it?" West asked.

I didn't respond.

"Okay, so it is. What happened?"

West gave me a look. "You two break up?"

"No. Maybe. I don't know." I let out a long exhale.

"You're down so fucking bad for her," Bronx said. "It's written all over your face."

"Fuck off," I replied.

Bronx waited a beat, still breathing hard. "You love her, don't you?"

I ran a hand through my hair. "Yeah. I do."

West blinked. "Damn."

"I really fucking do, but I don't know where her head's at. Fuck, I love her—I mean, I almost got arrested for her."

Bronx looked up. "What the fuck?"

"Yeah, that house I bought had a journal hidden under

the floorboards, and we started digging into an old case that happened there. Took it a little too far."

"What does that mean?"

"Broke into a place. Nobody pressed charges, though. Kept it out of the press."

West shook his head. "That's not normal."

"Nope, but fuck. She was all 'Hey, let's do this', and I was like 'Whatever you say, Ellie baby. Sure, why not?'"

We reached the straightaway, and I kicked a rock off the track.

Neither of them spoke. Bronx nodded once.

"She said she needed space," I said. "So, I'm giving her that."

West grabbed his water bottle from the grass and took a sip. "She'll figure it out."

"I hope so."

A few hours later, after I'd finally gotten home, I paced my kitchen enough times that I swore the tile would fucking give out. So, I decided to call Dorian. Colt was definitely off the table after the stunt he pulled at the game, and I needed someone who had been through this crazy love shit before.

He picked up after a few rings.

"Hey, man," he said.

"Hey." I sank onto the couch, elbow on my knee, phone pressed to my ear.

"You good?"

"No."

There was a beat of silence before he said, "This sounds familiar."

I frowned. "What do you mean?"

"Remember when I called you freaking out about Noah?"

"Uh, yeah…" I shifted, rubbing the back of my neck.

"Well, now it's your turn." He laughed, but there was a shift in his tone when he continued speaking. "Alright, what's going on?"

"Can I trust you?"

"I'm your brother. If you can't trust me, this family's way more fucked up than I thought."

I groaned.

"Tell me."

I exhaled slowly then said it before I could overthink it. "Ellie and I…might've had a fake relationship."

After a pause, Dorian shouted, "Noah! You owe me twenty bucks!"

I sat up straighter. "What the hell?"

"I knew it," he said smugly. "Noah was convinced it was real. I told her it was fake as hell."

"You knew?"

"Come on, man. I think everyone at least suspected."

"Mother fuck."

"Well, what's going on now?"

I scrubbed a hand down my face. "Now I think I went and fell in love with her."

"Noah! Make it forty!"

"You're fucking kidding me."

"I bet her you'd fall before the Super Bowl. She swore you weren't there yet. Guess I was more observant."

"I officially hate you both."

Noah's voice called out faintly in the background. "Hey, I was on your side!"

"Sure you were," I muttered.

Dorian chuckled. "So, what happened?"

"What the fuck did you do when you were in love with

Noah but convinced you weren't, and she was also totally not in love with you except obviously was?"

"I tried not to be a disaster," he said. "Did Ellie pull away?"

"Yeah. She said she needed space, time to process everything."

"Then give it to her."

"And just…what? Sit here hoping she comes back?" I leaned forward, elbows on my knees again. "How do I know when it's been long enough? How do I not screw it up by doing too much or not enough?"

"With Noah, when everything was going down with John, I stayed close. I didn't push. I showed up, but I didn't demand anything. I let her get there on her own, even if I was doing the same. She had a fucking lot going on with him, and I was working through my own issues, but us… It just took some time."

"You're glad you did?"

"Glad?" he asked. "Noah is the love of my life, and I would be nothing without her. Of course I'm glad."

"Even if you got a broken leg out of it?"

"Even then."

I chewed the inside of my cheek.

"She probably needs that from you too," Dorian said. "This whole thing started on your terms. She's still catching up."

"What do you mean?"

"You've had a thing for her since forever. Yeah, I'm sure that's only grown since you've gotten to know her, but you still had this idea of Ellie in your head before you actually had her. You started on the fifty-yard line, man. She's still back at the twenty. Give her time to run the play. Give her time to catch up."

I pressed my thumb to my temple. "And if she doesn't want to?"

"I don't think that's your problem."

"How the fuck do you know that?"

"Have you seen the video from her show the other night?" he asked.

"No, dumbass. She asked for space. Normally, I watch every show or catch the highlights. But…not right now. It's too hard."

"Well," he murmured, "I think you should check it out. Might change how you're feeling."

"How do you know more about what's going on with Ellie than I do?"

"Did you forget I live with your niece?" he shot back right as a crashing sound came through the speaker. "Shit, sorry, gotta go. Gracie's redecorating with glitter. But seriously. Watch the video."

"Yeah, yeah. Sure."

I hung up and typed her name into the search bar without thinking. The first result said it all.

Ellie Miles Debuts Unreleased Song in New York

I skipped past the fluff, ignored the gossip, and hit play on the embedded video.

"I haven't played this for anyone, but this is 'Unscripted'."

Her voice hit me like a punch to the ribs—same as it always did. Only this time, it cracked. Not off-key, not broken: raw. Shaky in a way that felt…real.

And then, she started singing about us.

About standing at the edge of something and not knowing if it was worth the fall. About me. About everything we almost had, maybe still had, depending on what the hell this was supposed to mean.

By the time she reached the end, I wasn't sitting anymore. I was up, pacing, hands in my hair, chest burning, trying to make sense of what the hell she was trying to say.

> I'm halfway here, caught between the fall and
>   the fear
> You're the risk I want, though I can't make it
>   clear
> My heart's in overdrive, and I don't know
>   the plan
> I'm scared to jump, but I want to, hand
>   in hand
> I'm halfway there, and it's all unscripted
> Wild and unknown, but I don't want to
>   miss it

God. Was that her way of saying she still wanted me? Not just me—us. She threw it out there like a song for the whole damn world, but every word landed as if she'd carved it straight into my chest.

And I was halfway across the country, trying to figure out if I was already too late to give her the ending she left blank.

FORTY-SIX

Ellie

BEN DIDN'T SAY MUCH ON THE DRIVE FROM THE AIRPORT TO MY house, and I was grateful for the quiet. My nerves were loud enough on their own.

The city blurred past the windows, familiar streets soaked in memories. I performed that song last night and hadn't heard from him. I tried not to overthink it, but I definitely wasn't doing so hot.

Once we arrived, Ben and I parted ways, and I went to the one thing I knew would distract me.

I opened the journal to the next page and started reading.

I can't stop hearing him. Even when he's quiet, the house is full of him—his footsteps, his breathing, the way he leans on walls like the world owes him something. I can feel it in my chest, tightening with every second

I've packed a bag. I told him we might visit family. He smiled and nodded. I couldn't tell him the truth. Not yet.

I don't know how much longer I can keep this up.

Every room feels smaller. Every silence presses down on me. I know I can't let him see me scared, but inside, I am.

I'll do whatever I have to. I don't know what I'll do, but I won't let him take him.

I love him. I always have. He is the only thing that ties me to the real man I love and the only thing keeping me from breaking entirely. If I need to stand in the dark and face everything, I will. I have to.

My eyes welled up. I knew what happened there—at least the final result. All her fears of losing her son were valid because, in the end, that was what happened.

I needed answers. Maybe the real dad showed up when it happened. Maybe he was interviewed, or there was information about who he was in the file. I pulled out my phone and hit the number I probably wasn't supposed to use for this purpose.

She answered on the second ring. "Detective Dodge."

"Lilah, it's Ellie."

"Should I be worried?"

I groaned. "Probably."

"What's going on?"

"I need a favor."

"Ellie..." she said knowingly. "You're not supposed to be digging. I told you to let it go."

"I know. I just... I found something in the journal, and I need to know what really happened. I think someone must have shown up on the day of the incident. I was thinking maybe...maybe you could..."

She sighed. "Spit it out."

"There was the shooting, but I need to know who responded. If anyone else was there or showed up, anything else you can give me."

"Ellie…no."

"I know, I know. I promise, if it's nothing, I will let it go. There's nothing left to read. But I need some kind of closure, even if it just ends up being an accident like the article says."

"This isn't easy shit to look at. That file will tell the cold, hard truth of how that little boy and his father died. You may not want to see all of that."

"I need to," I whispered. "I need the details so I can move on."

"On one condition."

"Anything. Name it."

"You truly let it go after this. Don't let it haunt you forever," she said, and it seemed like she wasn't just giving advice—she knew what it cost to hold on.

"Okay," I sighed.

"I'll look and send you the information, but I didn't do this for you. This will not trace back to me, understood?"

"Yes, ma'am."

She hung up, and an hour later, my phone dinged with an email notification. I swiped it open, the subject line blinking back at me.

From: Lilah Dodge
     Subject: Case Report — Hutchinson Incident

Ellie,
     Here you go. It's not everything, but it's enough.
Now let it go.
     Lilah

My fingers trembled as I stared at the attachment, my

heart thudding in my chest like a warning drum. It was a folder full of cold, official documents—pages stamped and signed, marked with dates I knew too well.

I landed on the section I'd been dreading—the cause of death.

Patrick Hutchinson. Gunshot wound to the chest.

Lower on the page, the boy's details caught my eye.

Cause of death: strangulation.

I blinked, rereading the words like they might rearrange themselves into something less brutal, but no.

Strangulation. The word was a blow to the stomach. I whispered it aloud, as if saying it might make it less real, but it didn't. It echoed in the empty room.

It made no sense. The boy accidentally fired the gun. It was a tragic accident born from fear.

But strangulation? That wasn't an accident. It was deliberate.

The questions came rushing in, too fast to catch. If the boy had been strangled, who did it? Did the husband do it before he was shot? Did he manage to get the gun in an attempt to save himself?

Or was there something deeper buried in this silence?

My chest tightened as I sank back onto the couch. My mind spun in a thousand directions, piecing together fragments that no longer fit.

I scanned through the report further, but half of it was missing—there were notes about the scene, the paramedics' statements, and police observations, but no mention of a child fumbling with a gun.

Just cold, unemotional facts that clashed violently with the story the article painted.

I swallowed hard and closed my laptop. The room was too quiet, too small. The story I'd been told unraveled beneath me, and I was standing on the edge of something darker than I'd imagined. The truth was still out there, hiding in plain sight.

And I was nowhere close to finding it. Even as I said it all aloud, none of it made sense.

My phone buzzed on the counter, and I walked over to grab it.

SAWYER

Hey, are you still planning to come tomorrow? I got your ticket if you do.

I'll be there.

Okay, see you there.

FORTY-SEVEN

Ellie

I DIDN'T WAKE UP BUZZING WITH ENERGY OR PLAYING OUT some fantasy of what this day could mean like Sawyer probably was. I wasn't in a glam chair or surrounded by a team of stylists prepping me for cameras.

I wanted it to be me, especially since I was unsure where Sawyer and I stood and still hoping that showing up might mean something to him. Maybe it would be a step in the right direction toward whatever the hell we were doing.

He hadn't texted or said anything about the song, and that had me on edge in a way I didn't want to admit.

I pulled on jeans and a blue sweater and layered a puffy coat over them. I twisted my hair back into something that could pass for intentional. Mascara, a little color in my cheeks—just enough to feel like myself.

My phone buzzed against the kitchen counter.

BEN

Pulling up.

I stepped onto the sidewalk, and Ben stood beside the back door of the SUV, steady as always.

"Ellie," he said with a nod.

"Hey, Ben." I climbed in, grateful for the familiar ritual of it.

The door shut with a soft click. We pulled away from my house, and my neighborhood disappeared through the tinted windows. The hum of tires filled the silence.

"You doing okay?" he asked, glancing at me in the rear-view mirror.

"Yeah," I said then paused. We both knew that wasn't entirely true. "Just nervous, I guess."

He nodded once. No follow-up, no small talk, just acknowledgment, which was exactly what I needed.

I turned my attention to the window. San Francisco was alive in a way that made my chest tight. Sunlight pushed through the clouds, and everywhere I looked, people wore blue jerseys. The closer we got to the stadium, the more electric it felt: flags waving from balconies, horns honking in a chaotic symphony, strangers high-fiving at crosswalks. Today, they were family.

I pressed my hand to my stomach. Maybe it was adrenaline, or that all I'd had since yesterday was leftover takeout and a bottle of water—my nerves had apparently decided food was optional.

Ben cleared his throat. "Security's tight today. Too much foot traffic at the public gate, so we're going in through the service side. Quieter. No press."

"Good. Thanks."

"Of course."

A few turns later, we slipped off the main road. I didn't think much of it at first. Detours happened, especially on big days like this. The city had probably shut down half the streets just to manage the chaos.

But then another left. Then another.

The farther we got from the crowd, the quieter it became.

I leaned forward, my eyes on the window. These streets didn't look familiar. There were no signs pointing toward the stadium, no vendors selling overpriced hot dogs. Just gray walls and chain link fences and the kind of industrial corners most people drove past without a second glance.

"You said this was a security reroute?" I asked, trying to keep my voice casual.

Ben didn't flinch. "Yeah. Stadium ops confirmed it this morning. We're bypassing the main gates and heading straight to the lower-level entrance."

He was calm, two hands on the wheel, everything about him screaming professional competence.

But outside, the city was gone, replaced with concrete buildings that looked the same and a silence that felt wrong.

I sat back. We were close. We'd round a corner any second, and there it would be.

"We're almost there," Ben said, eyes on the road. "Don't worry."

I nodded even though he wasn't looking.

The SUV slowed as we approached a fenced-off lot. In the middle of it sat a warehouse. No markings. No security guards. No sign of anything at all, really.

Definitely not the stadium.

"Ben?" I asked, and I could hear the shift in my voice.

He didn't answer.

The tires crunched over gravel, the sound too loud in the sudden quiet. The lot stretched empty in every direction, not another car in sight, not another person. Just us and a building that looked like it had been forgotten by the world.

I sat forward. "Where are we?"

Ben put the vehicle in park and turned off the engine.

Then, slowly, he twisted around in his seat.

His sunglasses stayed on. His expression didn't change. But something in the air shifted, and I realized with a clarity that made my stomach drop that I'd been reading this all wrong.

The door creaked open beside me.

Before I could register what was happening, before I could even think to be afraid, someone grabbed my arm and yanked me out of the car.

A sharp blow landed against my head.

"You've been asking the wrong questions, Ellie."

Then, everything slipped into darkness.

FORTY-EIGHT

Sawyer

WHEN I WAS A KID, I USED TO LIE AWAKE AT NIGHT REPLAYING this exact moment in my head like a movie. Super Bowl. Packed stadium. National anthem playing. Me on the field, wearing some random number that felt impossibly cool at the time. I didn't know what team I'd be on or what city I'd represent; I just knew I wanted to be there one day.

Back then, it was simple. Win the game, make people proud. Easy-peasy.

Now, it was loud, bright, blindingly massive, and somehow still not the thing I was thinking about.

The second the anthem started, I looked up at the suite where Ellie was supposed to be. Everything else, every cheer, every flashing light, every ounce of childhood wonder I'd stored up for this day, went quiet.

She wasn't there. My family was; I spotted them instantly. Everyone except Colt, who couldn't get the time off a case to come. They were all up there to support me, but Ellie's absence left a hole in my stomach.

Was she late? Stuck somewhere? Had she just…decided not to come?

I didn't know, and I didn't have time to spiral, not with the whole damn world watching.

I turned back to the field, helmet in hand, heart nowhere it was supposed to be, and told myself the same thing I'd said a thousand times since I started playing this game.

Show up. Play hard. Don't screw it up.

The other team won the coin toss. I was grateful for those extra minutes before our offense took the field. I needed a moment to clear my head and remind myself why I was here: to play the game, not to think about anything else.

Even as I focused on the field, my mind kept drifting.

Bronx was out there like a damn tank, holding the line. The other team wasn't making it easy. Every time they pushed forward, they came that much closer to breaking through. A couple of quick passes slipped past our defense, but we got it back. Turnover after turnover, the tension in the stadium was intense.

When it was finally my turn to take the field, I tried to slip into the zone. Coach's voice echoed in my head—the plays, the assignments, every muscle memory I'd drilled in over the years. I knew what to do. I was ready.

But West wasn't himself, and I wasn't either. The first few throws were rough: balls too wide, too far, pockets collapsing faster than usual. You could see the frustration building in his jaw, the tightness in his shoulders.

We fought our way down, grinding inch by inch, and finally got close enough for the field goal. Three points. Not enough, but points, nonetheless.

Back on the sidelines, I kept stealing glances toward the suite. My family was loud and alive, but there was still no Ellie.

It felt off, but I didn't have my phone. I had no way to

check if she'd tried to reach me, so I shoved the worry down deep. No distractions, not now.

The next quarter moved in a haze of hits and blocks, every yard a battle. I was on autopilot on the field, blocking, pushing, protecting West as best I could. The scoreboard flicked back and forth, neither side pulling far ahead.

When halftime came, the three-point deficit felt heavier than the numbers said. Once we were back in the locker room, it felt so much different than being behind at halftime during any other game. It was silent except for heavy breaths and the low murmur of the guys trying to regroup.

West ran a hand through his hair, muttering curses under his breath.

Bronx came up beside him, steady as ever. "You good?"

"Yeah." West sighed. "I just can't seem to get a clean pass. Feels like I'm throwing bricks out there."

"We're only down three," I said. "There's time."

Music from the halftime show seeped in through the walls.

Bronx looked over at me next. "You okay? You're playing well, but you seem…off."

I shook my head. "All good."

He didn't buy it, narrowing his eyes like he could see right through me. "Sure?"

I nodded, even though I definitely wasn't sure.

"Ellie here?" West finally asked.

"No. Not that I've seen."

Bronx frowned. "What? Why not?"

"I thought she'd be in the box with my family. She's not."

"Have you called her?" West asked.

"Haven't had my phone."

"Well, go get it," Bronx said. "Call her."

"I don't want to get distracted."

"Dude, just check your phone." Bronx scoffed.

I sighed, grabbed my phone from my locker, and stared at the screen—no missed calls, no messages. I tapped her name and called.

Straight to voicemail.

"Guess she decided not to come," I said, hanging up.

"Shit, man," West said. "I'm sorry."

"It's cool. I'll talk to her later."

"Listen up." Coach's voice rang out, and all heads snapped to him. "We worked damn hard to get here. This is the biggest stage there is, but nobody's handing out rings for luck or half assed effort. We don't take home that ring by making bad passes, missing assignments, or giving up free yards on defense. West, you've gotta keep your head in the game, make the smart plays—the ones we've practiced a thousand times. Defense, tighten up. Stop giving them room to breathe. We're down by three, but that means nothing if we don't come out and own the second half. Every play matters. We're gonna win this game because we want it more than they do. So, get your heads right. Let's finish this."

I nodded along as Coach spoke, every word hitting hard. No bullshit. No room for doubt.

West let out a breath, and I caught his glance, giving him a quick nod—a silent promise I'd have his back.

My hands clenched at my sides. The noise from the stadium seeped through the walls, a reminder that the whole world was watching.

No mistakes. Every play counted. I took a deep breath and shook off the knot tightening in my gut. This wasn't just another game. This was it.

I was ready.

We took the field to start the second half. Coach's

speech was still in my head, keeping me steady. The stadium felt louder.

I glanced at the suite again before we lined up, just to be sure.

Still no Ellie.

West called the play—three receivers to the right, no one in the backfield, a clear pass play meant to open things up and get us going. The snap came fast. I stepped into the defender, got my hands under his pads, and held the pocket. West threw a clean pass, and we gained fifteen yards. First down.

We were moving.

The next few plays were a battle. We fought for every yard, doing whatever it took to keep the ball moving. No flashy plays, just hard work. By the end of the third quarter, we'd managed to tie the game.

The fourth quarter started, and just like that, they were ahead again. They got the ball back and ran it all the way to our twenty-yard line, kicking another field goal.

West slammed his helmet onto the bench. "We can't keep trading threes."

"No one's trying to," Bronx said, already standing.

Coach pulled us in. "You know what works. Clean football. You stay focused, you stay smart, you win."

On the next offensive play, West fired a perfect pass—forty yards downfield to our wide receiver. The guy caught it right on the sideline, stayed in bounds, and we scored. Touchdown.

We were up by four.

I looked up, and there was still no Ellie.

Cameras swept the stands. Celebrities, families, random crowd shots. No sign of her. No big-screen moment. Nothing.

I couldn't let my mind dwell on it.

The other team got the ball with four minutes left. They threw a couple of long passes; one was almost intercepted, but they continued to move the ball down close to our end zone. On third down with six yards to go, their quarterback ran for the first down himself.

West was pacing. "Come on," he muttered. "One stop. Just one."

They lined up like it was a run then faked it. Quarterback rolled right, but our linebacker read him and came running.

We sacked their quarterback on third down. Now, it was fourth and thirteen. They had no choice but to go for it. The ball snapped, the quarterback scrambled, looking for an open man, but threw it too low.

Incomplete pass.

The crowd went wild. West threw his arms around one of the coaches, nearly knocking over the water table. Everyone was yelling and celebrating, but I couldn't stop glancing at the suite.

Still empty.

One-twenty left on the clock. They had timeouts. We had the ball. The defense made a huge stop, and now, it was on us.

Coach grabbed West's shoulder. "Finish it. Ball security. Kill the clock. Win the damn thing."

We jogged onto the field. I was locked in and ready.

First down—the running back hit the gap for four yards. Nice and steady.

Second down—same play. He spun through the tackle and kept the chains moving. First down.

Timeout.

I took a deep breath. Less than a minute to pull this off.

West wiped the sweat off his face and looked over to me. "We got this."

We ran down the clock with smart plays and quick throws. West kept his cool, and I kept anyone from crashing the pocket. When it came down to the last play, he found the guy in the end zone like it was nothing.

Touchdown. Game over.

Super Bowl champions.

Confetti fell like it was snowing fucking paper. Bronx ran from the sidelines and launched himself at West. Reporters swarmed. Someone shoved a Gatorade jug. I hugged whoever was closest and let it hit me.

And still, I looked.

After a few minutes, people flooded the field. I saw Dotty first, pushing her way forward like a linebacker. Trent followed behind her, holding Gracie's hand, trying not to get trampled. My dad shouted my name.

"You did it!" Dotty grabbed my helmet and hugged me hard.

"Where's Ellie?" I asked.

She pulled back, frowning. "She didn't show."

Trent caught up. "Congrats, man!"

"Uncle Sawyer!" Gracie said, hugging my legs.

I took off my helmet and picked her up.

"You did it! You won!"

"I did, didn't I?" I said. "Hey, can you…call Ellie? See if she's okay?"

"Maybe something came up?" Dotty said.

"Congrats, son," my dad said, patting my back. "Proud of you."

"Thanks, Dad." I smiled. "Noah and Dorian still up there?"

"Yeah, hard to make it down here with one working leg." He chuckled. "He said he'd congratulate you after."

I set Gracie down as Bronx came barreling toward me, yelling something in my ear about rings and glory and maybe immortality, I couldn't tell. West was already mid-interview, gesturing like a cartoon character, helmet swinging from his hand.

A reporter shoved a mic at my chest. "Sawyer James—how does it feel?"

I blinked. "Uh…incredible. Really proud of the guys. Team effort."

Did I sound like a coach? That felt coach-y. Whatever. I smiled for the camera. Gave a couple of high fives. Took a photo with my family. Gave another quote that made no sense. Someone sprayed champagne in the air, and I accidentally caught it with my eyeball.

It was chaos. Beautiful, loud, head-spinning chaos. Everything I'd dreamed this would be.

Except something was missing.

No matter how many people were on the field, I couldn't stop looking for one face. Just one. I scanned the sidelines, the tunnel, the stands. Nothing. No flash of Ellie's hair, no goofy smile. Not even a grainy jumbotron shot.

If she'd made it, I would've known. Someone would've seen her. I wouldn't still be searching.

Bronx was the first to notice the shift.

"Everything okay?" He dragged a towel across the back of his neck, breathing as if he'd arm-wrestled a god.

"Yeah. Yeah, totally. Just…gimme a sec." I turned to walk off casually, like I wasn't about to spiral.

"Wait—what for?" Bronx called after me.

"I just wanna check something."

West jogged over, half-laughing, still soaked in Gatorade. "Dude, we just won the Super Bowl. Are you seriously gonna be the guy who checks his texts during the celebration?"

"I need to check on Ellie. I think something's wrong."

I really fucking hoped I was wrong.

Bronx stepped in front of me, blocking my path like he was a damn security gate. "James."

"I need to check."

He sighed. "Alright, fine. But if you're not back in ten minutes, I'm telling the media you sobbed and tried to call your dog."

"Joke's on you," I muttered, already moving. "I don't have a dog."

The tunnel was quiet, dim, and cold in a way the field wasn't. There was just the thud of my cleats on concrete and the leftover smell of adrenaline and victory. I passed a couple of staffers cleaning up, nodded once, and didn't stop.

The locker room was mostly empty. A few trainers spoke in low voices. Equipment was getting packed up. But it was like a different world in here. No music. No celebration. Just me and the nagging, itchy feeling in my chest.

I grabbed my phone from my locker and flipped it over.

Four missed calls.

All from Rachel.

Shit.

I tapped Ellie's name first, but it went straight to voicemail. Then, I called Rachel, walking toward the far end of the room, where I could hopefully hear myself fucking think.

She answered on the first ring. "Sawyer?"

Something was off. Her voice was tight. Clipped. Not panicked, but close.

"What's going on?" I asked. "Where's Ellie?"

She hesitated. "I was hoping you'd tell me."

"What?"

"I thought it was weird. Usually, they show her on the screen, but I've been watching since kickoff and...nothing.

Not even once. I figured maybe she was late or didn't want the attention, but I kept checking. And—"

"She's not here," I said. "She never made it."

There was a beat of silence.

"She texted me," Rachel said. "Right when she left her place. Said she was on her way."

"She was coming? I thought maybe she changed her mind."

"Of course she was coming."

"Rachel…" My voice dropped. "She didn't come. I don't know what happened, but she's not here."

"…she never made it."

FORTY-NINE

Ellie

THE BACK OF MY SKULL THROBBED AS I FORCED MY EYES OPEN. Panic rose like smoke, curling around my chest, but I held it down—swallowed it whole until it sat heavy in my stomach.

Something rough pressed between my teeth, the sour taste of cloth filling my mouth. I tried to spit it out, but the knot at the back of my head held it tight, forcing me to breathe through my nose.

I blinked, taking in my surroundings. The warehouse stretched out around me. Concrete ran in every direction, scarred with cracks that spider-webbed toward the walls. Grime streaked down from broken windows high above, and debris lay scattered everywhere—broken pallets, cardboard boxes, and twisted metal that caught the harsh light from a single bulb swaying overhead.

My ankles were tied to the chair legs with duct tape that bit into my skin. Rope circled my wrists so tight, I could feel each pulse throb against it. Every shift only made it cut deeper.

Maybe six feet away, sitting on an overturned crate as if

it were a velvet throne, a woman watched me. She hadn't moved when I stirred, hadn't even blinked. Her posture was too relaxed—one leg crossed over the other, hands folded in her lap like she was waiting for afternoon tea instead of holding someone gagged and bound.

But it was what sat beside her that made my blood turn to ice—a red plastic gas can. My muffled sound barely made it past the gag. Her lips curved the slightest bit.

"Good. You're up."

She stood, the scrape of the crate legs echoing in the space. My pulse hammered as she crossed the short distance between us. Without a word, she reached behind my head, fingers brushing my neck as she tugged at the knot. The gag came loose, and I sucked in a shaky breath.

The air smelled like gasoline. My stomach dropped.

For a second, she watched me like she was studying what I'd do with the small mercy she'd given.

Then, I saw it—something in the shape of her mouth. The way her chin tilted just slightly to the right. Features I'd memorized from a grainy newspaper photo, imagining them softened by years of pain.

My mind scrambled to catch up. She looked normal. Clean, brown hair pulled back in a neat ponytail. Properly fitting clothes, no tears or stains. This wasn't the broken woman I'd constructed in my mind from those desperate letters.

"Lauren?" The name felt strange in my mouth, like speaking to a ghost.

A smile unfurled across her face—not warm or pleased, but entertained, like I was a particularly amusing puzzle she'd solved.

"I was worried," she said, examining her nails absently. "Thought maybe I'd hit you too hard. Would've been inconvenient if you'd died before we had our little chat."

She walked back to the crate, picked up the gas can with casual ease, and unscrewed the cap. The chemical smell intensified, and my eyes watered.

"Lauren." My voice cracked, the sound bouncing off the walls.

She tilted the can, and liquid sloshed onto the concrete floor between us. A puddle formed, spreading slowly toward my chair.

"Stop!" The word ripped out of me.

She paused, the can still tilted. "Why? You wanted the truth, didn't you? That's why you kept digging, why you read my journal, broke into my house, and got your hands on the police report." She poured more gas around me. "Well, here we are. Truth time."

Heat rushed to my cheeks. "I thought…" I shook my head, making me dizzy. "The entries. You sounded like you were…"

She laughed, not unkindly, setting the can down with a hollow thunk. "Oh, that damn journal." She took a step closer, her heels clicking against the floor. "I didn't even know I'd left it until it was too late to go back."

The casualness of her tone made my skin crawl. "I don't understand…"

Lauren's smile turned wry. "I meant to burn that damn journal, actually. I was a different woman back when I wrote it."

She crouched, and my heart thudded in my chest.

"So it wasn't a call for help?" I asked, my eyes locked on her hand.

"I mean, at the time, it was, I guess. I needed to get it out somehow. That was the only outlet I had. But I left it," she repeated, her voice sharpening. She stood, wiping her hand on her pants. "And I prayed no one would ever be stupid enough to go looking."

"I thought you were a victim." The words were heavier than I expected.

She nodded like she'd been waiting for them.

"I was a victim. I *am* a victim, but not from the neat, simple version people like to hand out." She folded her hands. "My life wasn't clean. It was messy. Dangerous. And sometimes, messy requires a messy answer. Hence this." She gestured around us. "Can't leave loose ends this time."

I searched her face for the woman from the journal— the mother who wanted to protect her child. Instead, I found a practiced storyteller. The bulb overhead buzzed then steadied.

"Your son…he died."

"Yes." Her voice didn't change. "He did."

"You said you were trying to leave, to protect him."

"I said a lot of things when I was scared." She folded her fingers, glancing down at her hands as if tracing a memory. Then, she picked up the box of matches, shaking it.

My heart slammed against my ribs. "What are you doing?"

"You talk, I light. Pretty simple, actually."

"What changed?" My voice wavered, attempting to stall as long as I could. "You loved him. You wanted to save him."

"Everything."

"Your husband. He found the photo."

"Yes." She pulled out a single match, holding it between her fingers like a cigarette.

"What happened?" I asked again, more stern this time, trying to keep my voice steady despite the match in her hand.

"A lot happened back then."

"What. Happened?"

Her jaw tightened. She struck the match, and the flame caught. "Patrick found out. He confronted me, threatened me."

"So you killed him." I said it flat, matter-of-fact, watching that flame dance.

"He went for the gun first." Her voice rose. "I just got there faster! He ran like a coward, and I chased him outside and—" She stopped herself, chest heaving. The match burned closer to her fingers.

"And you shot him."

"Yes." She glared at me, shaking out the match. "I shot him."

I held her gaze, unblinking, trying to ignore the relief flooding through me. "And your son?"

Something flickered across her face: fear. "That's different."

"He saw it, didn't he? He saw you murder his father."

"He wasn't his real father."

"What did you do to him?"

"He was *screaming*." It exploded out of her. She pulled out another match and struck it hard. "He was on the porch, and he wouldn't stop. He ran inside, I followed, and he kept screaming that I killed his father over and over. I couldn't—I needed him to stop."

"So you stopped him."

"I just wanted him to shut up." Her hands shook, the flame trembling. "I grabbed a pillow, and I just—I put it over his face to make him pass out, to get him quiet for one second, but—" Her voice cracked. "None of this would've been so complicated without him! I could've just left. I could've—"

"But he never woke up," I finished coldly.

A figure stepped out of the shadows—tall, broad-shouldered, unmistakably Ben, but his face looked wrong somehow.

His eyes were wide, horror-struck, fixed on Lauren as if she'd grown a second head. "You told me Patrick killed him."

Lauren turned toward his voice, and for the first time since I'd woken up, she looked genuinely surprised. "Ben…I thought you were checking the perimeter still."

My jaw dropped. "B—Ben…"

"I heard…" His voice came out strangled as he slipped his phone into his pocket. "I heard what you said. About my son. Tell me I misunderstood."

She didn't respond; she just pulled out another match as the other one burnt out.

"Lauren…" Ben's voice broke. "Put the matches down."

"Why?" She struck it, the flame casting dancing shadows across her face. "So she can run to the police? So she can tell everyone what I did? I don't think so."

Ben stepped directly in front of her, and his shoulders shook. "You let me think he died in a struggle," he said, his voice rough as sandpaper.

Her expression didn't change. "Yeah, well, that version served you better."

She waved the match dangerously close to the puddle's edge.

"You used me." His words came out broken.

"I needed you."

"I loved you." The shout bounced off the walls like a physical thing. "And you killed our son! For what?" His voice cracked completely. "Put down the fucking match."

"You wouldn't leave your wife for me. You never loved me," she yelled at him before turning to me. "I loved him. My son. I did. But it was never…easy. Sometimes, I looked at him and saw my mistake staring back at me."

Bile rose in my throat. The rope around my wrists felt like it was cutting off circulation to my hands. The match in her hand burned lower.

Ben's voice dropped to a whisper that somehow carried more weight than his shout. "You said you wanted a future with us."

"I did." She reached toward him with her free hand, but he stepped back like she'd struck him.

The match burned down to her fingers. She dropped it —this time dangerously close to the main puddle. It sizzled out just inches from the gasoline.

Her head tilted to me, and that predatory smile returned. "Have you ever been so trapped, you'd do anything to claw your way out?"

"Yes." The words came from somewhere deep in my chest, somewhere that had been locked away for years. "But I've never murdered a fucking child."

She shook out the match and pulled out another. "You still don't get it."

"No." I met her gaze and didn't look away, even though everything in me wanted to. "I do. You snapped. You killed your son, spun some story to the cops, then lied to the father of your child to make it all seem like a mistake."

"Well, at least you're smarter than you look." She struck the match.

"And you're sicker than I thought."

Ben's hands were shaking visibly, and he kept clenching and unclenching his fists. "How? How did you get away with this?"

Lauren's voice took on an almost dreamy quality. "It's not that hard." She feigned an innocent voice. "I found Patrick killing our son, so I grabbed the gun and shot him in self-defense after he went after me." The match burned.

"The cops ate it up. Traumatized wife, dead child—clear-cut case of domestic violence gone wrong."

She turned back to me, and her smile returned sharper, more focused.

"Except you," she turned to me, holding the match closer, "started to dig a little too deep. You found my journal and somehow got your hands on the fucking police report. You were taking it too far, and I knew you wouldn't let it go."

"How do you know that?" My voice came out smaller than I intended.

"I may have asked Ben to plant a bug on your phone." She shrugged like she was discussing the weather. "I've been listening all along." She waved the match in a small circle, leaving a trail of light in the darkness.

"But...I thought he was my bodyguard?"

"You think that was a coincidence?" She let out a sharp, bitter laugh. "A stupid football player buys that house—my house—and suddenly, he's dating you? I had to do something."

"Ben," I said, staring at him.

"Yup. He worked for my husband's father years ago. That's how I met him. So, when your little boyfriend bought my house, I called him, got him on your team—"

"Because of the journal."

"To make sure no one else found it first." Her voice cracked higher. "I didn't need anyone digging around, finding out about the affair, pointing fingers at me. But you." She jabbed a finger toward me, pulling out another match. "You found it anyway. You couldn't just leave it alone. You had to play detective, break into my house. You wouldn't stop! You just kept digging and digging."

Ben scoffed, stepping forward. "I thought I was helping

you. You told me it was an accident. You told me Patrick killed him. I thought I was helping you protect yourself."

Lauren shot him a look—more disappointed than angry, like a parent whose child had broken something valuable.

"You think you're still the hero?" she said. "You helped me get her here. You loaded her in the car and drove her to this warehouse. You're in this as deep as I am."

Ben's face went white. "I didn't know—"

"You did know. You knew something was wrong, and you came anyway, because some part of you still loved me even after years apart. Even if you never would leave your damn wife."

She held the match higher. "God, I thought someone would get it. If not you, then her!"

She pointed at me with the match, and I flinched despite myself.

"How in the world would I understand you?" I asked, my voice shaking.

"Because you do." She took another step closer, the match still burning, close enough that I could see the fine lines around her eyes and the way her lipstick had started to fade. "You know what it's like to build your whole life around an image. Around being perfect. You know what it's like to sell yourself to survive."

The words hit too close to home, and something cracked open in my chest—raw and painful, something I'd kept buried for years.

"You're right." The admission tore out of me. "I know what it's like to feel trapped. To build everything around an image that isn't real. I've spent my whole life performing, trying to prove I was worth something."

Lauren's eyes lit up. She lowered the match.

"I thought if I worked hard enough, sang loud enough,

stayed on every headline and tour and red carpet, maybe I'd matter. That I'd prove to everyone that I was enough." My throat tightened, but I kept going, the words spilling out like blood from a wound.

Lauren's gaze sharpened, predatory. She was waiting—waiting for me to admit she was right, that we were the same, that I understood her choices.

But I didn't.

"I don't want to live that way anymore." The words came out stronger than I felt. "I'm done chasing it, done thinking I need to accomplish more to be worthy. You think we're the same, but we're not. You killed people to protect a lie. I'm choosing to stop living one."

For a moment that stretched like eternity, Lauren didn't speak. Her expression faltered—barely, like a mask slipping—and I saw it. The hollow place where a person used to be. The empty space where empathy, love, and basic human decency should have lived.

She shook out the match once again. The warehouse closed in around me.

"What are you planning to do with me?" I asked.

She tilted her head like I'd asked the most boring question. She picked up the gas can again, this time carrying it around my chair. I couldn't see her anymore; I could only hear the slosh of liquid, smell the intensifying fumes.

"Isn't it obvious?" she said from behind me. Cold liquid splashed against my back, soaking through my shirt. I jerked forward, but the ropes held. "I obviously can't let you walk away from this."

Ben moved forward. "Lauren, don't."

"Stay back!" She came around to my side, and I could see she'd poured gasoline near my feet, creating a trail back to the main puddle. "You don't get to grow a conscience suddenly, not after everything."

She pulled out the entire box of matches, shaking them into her hand.

"Wait—" My voice came out strangled. "Please…"

"You couldn't leave it alone," she hissed, pulling out a match. "I told myself I wouldn't do this. I told myself there had to be another way." She struck it. The flame caught. "But you left me no choice."

She held it up; the small flame reflected in her dead eyes.

"No!" Ben lunged forward.

Time slowed. The match arced through the air toward the gasoline trail. Ben's hands closed around her wrist, yanking it back. The match landed on concrete, three feet from the nearest gasoline, sputtering out harmlessly.

Ben slammed into her, sending them both crashing to the floor. The box of matches scattered, skittering about. He pinned her down, one hand on her wrist, the other grabbing for his phone.

"You will not hurt her," he barked, his voice shaking. "I'm not letting you kill her!"

A sound cut through the warehouse—a distant wail that grew quickly louder. Sirens. Red and blue light flickered through the broken windows.

Lauren's eyes went wide beneath Ben. "You…you called someone," she hissed, disbelief lacing her voice. "You actually called someone!"

"I called 911 the moment I heard you confess," Ben said, his voice steadier than it had been all night.

All her control shattered. She bucked beneath him, shoving him off with surprising strength, and ran. Ben lunged after her, his boots pounding against the concrete.

"Police! Don't move!"

Two officers stood silhouetted in the doorway, weapons raised, their voices cutting through the warehouse.

Lauren made it maybe ten steps before they tackled her. The impact of bodies hitting the floor echoed through the space, followed by the metallic click of handcuffs.

She didn't scream. Didn't cry. Didn't beg or bargain or make excuses. She went still as they cuffed her. That predatory smile was finally completely gone.

More officers flooded in. One rushed to me, working on the ropes behind my back. Blood rushed back to my wrists with a painful tingle.

Another cuffed Ben.

"Are you okay?" Ben asked me.

I nodded, flexing my fingers as feeling returned to them, my shirt still damp with gasoline.

"You're fired," I managed to say, my voice hoarse but steady. "And going to jail. But yeah, I think I'm fine."

Ben turned to look at me as they walked him toward the door. Our eyes met. I saw it—the apology, the regret, the knowledge there was nothing he could say that would make any of this right.

The sirens were louder now, filling the warehouse. Red and blue lights flashed through the broken windows, painting everything in shifting colors. An officer draped a blanket around my shoulders, guiding me toward the door and away from the gasoline, away from the matches still scattered across the floor, away from the woman who'd been willing to burn me alive to protect her secrets.

I was alive.

I was free.

And for the first time in longer than I could remember, it felt like I could finally breathe.

FIFTY

Sawyer

I SHOVED MY HAND THROUGH MY HAIR, MY SKIN DAMP FROM sweat and the sticky champagne someone had sprayed near me. None of that mattered now.

"I'll call my brother," I said into the phone. "He's a detective. We'll figure this out."

"I'll keep looking into it," Rachel said. "Maybe someone knows something. But—Sawyer?"

"Yeah?"

"She wouldn't disappear. She was going to show up for you."

"I know."

I ended the call and tapped Colt's name. He picked up on the first ring.

"Aren't you supposed to be celebrating?" he asked.

"She's gone."

A pause. "What? Who?"

"Ellie. She was supposed to be here. She never showed."

"You sure she didn't change her mind?"

"No. Rachel said she texted her before she left. Said she was on her way. Ben was supposed to bring her in through a private entrance."

Colt was silent for longer this time. I could almost hear him running it over in his mind.

"She wouldn't miss this," I said. "Not without saying something."

"I'm with Lilah. Hold on."

I heard muffled voices.

"Putting you on speaker."

Lilah's voice came through next. "What's going on?"

"Ellie was supposed to be here, but she never showed. She's gone, Lilah. She's gone. What do I do?"

I glanced down at my phone and saw a new text from Rachel.

RACHEL

Confirmed she left. Ben drove her to the stadium, but the GPS lost signal. He's not answering his phone.

"I sent her the police report yesterday," Lilah said.

Colt cut in. "What report?"

"Lauren Hutchinson's," Lilah answered. "The one Ellie asked about. It was sealed, but I managed to get it. Figured it might give her some closure so she could let it go."

"Why the hell would you do that?" Colt asked her.

"I didn't have time to dig through it all. Thought the basics would help Ellie move on. Let me look at what it says."

"I'm freaking out here, guys," I choked.

"Okay, okay," Lilah sighed. "It says the husband was shot, but the cause of death for the child was strangulation…"

"How the hell did that get overlooked? Ellie found out, and someone took her because of it," I whispered.

"Let me pull up the whole report. I didn't send her everything."

"Are you fucking kidding me?" Colt shouted.

"We'll unpack that later," Lilah said. "Okay, Lauren claimed self-defense. She found her husband strangling the boy, so she pulled out the gun and shot him. When EMTs arrived, they were both dead."

I gripped the edge of my locker until my knuckles went white.

"But who?" Lilah asked.

"The dad," I said.

"The dad is dead," Colt said.

"The real dad."

"What do you mean, the real dad?" Lilah asked.

"The letters," I said. "Lauren wrote about having an affair and the kid not being her husband's."

Colt's voice was calm but urgent. "I'm trying to trace Ben and Ellie's number. If they were taken, that's our best lead."

"I'm not waiting around," I said, already moving. "If Ben left with her, he used a vehicle. Get me plates, traffic cams—anything."

"This isn't exactly a missing person case yet, but we'll do what we can."

I was already walking out of the locker room and through the tunnel, past half-dressed guys and equipment carts. My brain buzzed full of grief, fear, adrenaline, all piling up at once.

"I'm going to her place," I said. "Maybe there's something there."

"Wait," Colt said. "We just got something."

I stopped cold at the top of the tunnel steps.

"A 911 call came in an hour ago. Location near a warehouse in Dogpatch. Police found Ben and Lauren."

"What about Ellie?"

"Don't know yet."

I turned back, already rerouting. "Send me the address."

FIFTY-ONE

Ellie

I WAS SITTING ON THE BACK OF AN AMBULANCE, AN ITCHY gray blanket draped around my shoulders, when I saw him.

His car screeched to a stop just beyond the police barricade. The second he stepped out, I let out a relieved breath. I hadn't realized how tense I was, how locked down everything inside me had been, until that moment.

Sawyer's car door slammed shut, and he barreled out of the car before being stopped, getting in an argument with one of the officers. Panic was clear in his eyes, and he was soaked from the rain. His shoulders looked so tight, I could feel the tension from thirty feet away.

I stood, blanket slipping off my shoulders, but an EMT reached out to stop me. "Ma'am, you need to stay seated until we've completed a full—"

"I'm fine," I said, brushing past him without looking back.

I didn't care if I wasn't cleared. It didn't matter that my wrists still burned, that my legs were unsteady. The flashing lights closed in from every direction, but the only thing that mattered was getting to him.

I reached the barricade as one of the officers tried to block Sawyer again.

"He's with me," I said quickly.

"Ma'am—"

"Oh my God, just let him through. He's my boyfriend."

The officer blinked at me and reluctantly stepped aside.

Sawyer didn't wait. He was in front of me in an instant, his arms around me.

"Ellie, baby," he breathed, his voice breaking.

"I'm okay," I whispered, clutching him like it was the only thing keeping me upright. "I'm okay."

He pulled back, his hands framing my face. "Are you—did they—fuck, are you hurt? What happened? Why weren't you at the game? I don't understand. I kept looking for you, and then Rachel called and—" His voice hitched. "God, I was so fucking scared."

"I know," I whispered. "I'm sorry. I didn't have my phone. Everything happened so fast."

He kissed my forehead like it was instinct, like his body had to touch me to confirm I was here.

"I thought maybe..." His voice dropped. "I thought you changed your mind. Didn't want to come. I didn't want to believe it, but I kept wondering if I messed every-thing up."

"No," I blurted out. "God, no. I wanted to be there. I was on my way when everything happened."

He exhaled and looked up at the sky, blinking.

"I need to call Rachel," I said. "She must be freaking out."

"I'll text her."

"What about the game? Did you...win?"

He looked at me like he didn't understand the question. "What?"

"The Super Bowl. Did you win?"

He let out a short laugh. "Yeah. Yeah, we won."

"You won the Super Bowl and you're here with me?"

"Ellie," he said, like my name was a full sentence. "You disappeared. You think I was gonna pop bottles and take selfies while you were missing?"

I swallowed the knot rising in my throat.

"I left the field before the press conference," he added. "Didn't even shower. I probably smell like ass."

"You didn't have to—"

"Yes, I did," he said firmly.

I cupped his jaw, grounding myself in the rough stubble under my palm, the warmth of his skin. My throat tightened with everything I couldn't say—how much it meant that he chose this, chose me, over the one thing he'd worked his entire life for.

"You won the Super Bowl," I whispered, "and you left to find me."

His hand covered mine, pressing it closer to his face. His eyes were dark, intense, like I was the only thing in the world that mattered.

"I'd leave a thousand Super Bowls for you. Do you get it yet?" His voice was rough, raw. "None of it means anything if you're not there."

"I'll throw you a celebration party to make up for it."

He chuckled. "Sounds like a plan."

A long silence settled between us, heavier than the rain that started to fall again. This time, it was a drizzle, and neither of us moved.

"Come sit," he said finally. "You look like you need to stop standing."

I let out a small giggle, and we found a bench under the

awning of an empty building. It smelled like wet pavement and cheap metal, and I'd never been more grateful for a seat in my life.

Then I told him everything.

Ben. Lauren. The letters. How I figured out pieces, which led them to take me here. How close it came to going wrong.

He didn't speak, didn't interrupt, keeping his hand wrapped around mine the whole time. His other hand kept clenching and unclenching.

"They arrested them about half an hour ago," I said. "The police are still collecting evidence, but it's done. It's over."

Sawyer shook his head slowly, like he still couldn't wrap his mind around it. "Jesus."

"Yeah," I said, leaning back against the bench. "It was a lot."

He looked down, nodded once, and went quiet.

"So…" His eyes lifted to meet mine.

"So…"

"I heard your song."

I winced and covered my face with both hands. "God, of course you did."

"Mhm."

I peeked through my fingers. "You did?"

He gently pulled my hands away from my face. "Ellie. I loved it."

"I didn't know if you'd hear it."

"I did. Well, not at first, but then Dorian told me about it."

I smiled, my heart pounding in that way it only ever did around him. "Well. This is embarrassing."

He watched me closely, like he was building up to something. "So…what do you say we ditch the script? You, me, no more fake anything."

"You want to be my real boyfriend?"

"I mean…yeah." He laughed nervously. "If that's something you want."

"I do," I said, the answer rushing out before I thought about it. "I really, really do."

His whole face softened. "Yeah?"

"Yeah. I've been thinking a lot. About the life I've built, the goals I've chased. I'm proud of what I've done, but I've spent a long time chasing stuff I don't even want anymore."

"Okay…"

"I'm tired. Not of the music. Not of the fans. Just…of the pressure. The constant chase. I want to slow down. To write what I want, share it when I want, live without everything being a headline."

"Sounds nice."

"I want to figure out what it looks like to be a whole person again. Not the version of Ellie who sells out arenas —I want to be just me. And I want to do that with you."

He looked stunned. "With…me?"

"Yeah. If you'll have me."

"If I'll have you?" His eyes widened. "I think I've been in love with you since before you even liked me."

I laughed, a little breathless. "I liked you more than I let on."

He smirked. "I knew it."

I rolled my eyes. "Also, I was thinking…maybe I could do that figuring-out-my-life thing in Woodstone. If you'll let me crash at your place."

He blinked. "You're serious?"

"Dead serious."

He looked like he didn't know whether to cry or kiss

me. Instead of doing either, he asked, "Wait, you're really okay? You're not hurt?"

"My wrists are a little sore. That's it."

"Good," he said, standing and pulling me with him.

He picked me up and spun me around, laughing like he'd been given the world. The rain came down harder, soaking us both, but neither of us cared.

When he finally set me down, my cheeks were flushed and my heart was racing.

"Ellie?" he said, his hands still around my waist.

"Yeah?"

"I'm gonna kiss you now."

"As your real girlfriend?"

He grinned. "Hell yeah."

Then, he kissed me, and it was everything. Honest and messy. Soaked in rain and long overdue. But it was ours. Finally, truly, completely ours.

We stayed like that for a while, grinning like idiots, forehead to forehead, letting the rain do whatever it wanted. Then, Sawyer reached back and pulled out something from his wallet.

I squinted at it. "Is that—?"

He held it up between us. "The contract."

Sure enough, it was the stupid napkin we'd scribbled on the day everything started, half-smudged now, a greasy coffee ring bleeding through the corner.

"You've had that in your wallet this whole time?" I asked.

"Obviously. I take all legally binding agreements very seriously." He looked down at it for a second nostalgically and ripped it clean down the middle. "Contract terminated."

I grinned. "Good."

He tucked the torn halves into his pocket and looked back at me. "I think we should renegotiate."

I tilted my head. "Oh yeah?"

"Yeah. New terms. Real dating. Equal partnership. No end date. And you still owe me that dinner date you paid twenty grand for."

I leaned up to kiss him again. "Deal."

FIFTY-TWO

Sawyer

A COUPLE OF WEEKS AFTER EVERYTHING CAME OUT—BEN being the real father, Lauren killing her son, and the discovery that my house had been a murder scene for years—there was still fallout.

But all of that was behind us now.

Ellie was preparing for her final concert. The last one on her tour. The last one…probably for a while.

She didn't call it a retirement. Maybe she'd perform again someday, she'd said—maybe in a smaller venue, maybe at a festival if the mood struck—but definitely not like this. Not with a tour bus and stylists and people shouting in her ear every hour of the day.

She wanted something quieter, and tonight, she was getting her goodbye.

I watched from the VIP tent with her parents by my side, just like I had a few months ago.

Tonight felt different. The energy was heavier. Electric. Final.

The whole arena was going nuts, fans screaming her name, glitter signs bobbing above their heads. They were chanting for her before the countdown started. The floor vibrated beneath my feet. Then the platform rose, the spotlight hit her, and the moment the music dropped, the place went feral.

Fans screamed like crazy. Everyone stood. Phones shot up. The opening chords blasted through the sound system. Ellie came up from beneath the floor into the spotlight like she was born for it.

The moment she started to sing, the crowd joined in, thousands of people shouting every word back to her like they belonged to them too.

It was unreal.

She moved through the first song effortlessly, all energy and presence, as if nothing could touch her up there. When it ended, she pulled her mic closer and took a step back, letting the guitar hang at her side as the music faded.

"Hello, LA!" she called out, voice bright and breathless.

The crowd went ballistic.

She grinned, tucking her hair behind her ear. "As you probably know, this is the final stop of my tour."

A wave of groans and *nooos* rolled through the audience.

"I know, I know," she said, laughing. "I've had the most marvelous few months sharing these nights with you. I'll never stop being grateful that you show up, that you care, that you listen."

The fans screamed louder, and she let it ride out before strumming a soft chord on her guitar.

"But tonight's a little different."

A hush fell over the crowd as people recognized the tone shift.

"I've spent my whole life living through lyrics," she said, quiet but clear. "Pouring myself into songs and chasing the next thing. For the first time…I want to figure out who I am outside all that. Not because I'm walking away from it forever, but because I think I've earned the right to slow down. To be still."

Silence stretched across the room. Not the awkward kind—the reverent kind.

"I'll always write music," she said. "That's never going away. But I don't think I'll be performing like this again. Not for a long time. So tonight, this show…it's kind of a goodbye, at least to this version of me."

Another strum. Another beat of silence. Then, the crowd erupted. Screaming. Crying. Chanting her name.

I blinked hard. Damn it, I was about to fucking cry. I was supposed to be the tough football guy, but watching her say goodbye to this life with that kind of grace—on her own terms, in her own words—hit me in a way I wasn't ready for.

She wasn't walking away from something. She was walking *toward* something. And I got to be part of whatever that was.

She closed her eyes, soaking it all in, then shifted into her next song—her and the guitar, no lights, no backup vocals, nothing flashy. Just Ellie, stripped down and honest.

I leaned against the railing and let the music fill me, let her voice settle in my chest the way it always did—warm, steady, and a little cracked in the places that made it real.

She wasn't pretending anymore. She wasn't performing a version of herself to keep everyone happy.

She was her. And she was enough.

FIFTY-THREE

Ellie

LIFE WAS SETTLING DOWN IN WOODSTONE, THE KIND OF SLOW, quiet rhythm I didn't know I needed until I had it. For so long, I'd measured my days by red carpets and call times. Now, it was the chirp of birds in the morning and the hum of the coffeemaker in his—our—kitchen.

Sawyer had finished the last round of renovations on the house, and every now and then, I caught him standing in the middle of a room, arms crossed, like he couldn't believe it was real. Sometimes, I couldn't either. He brought that place back to its original glory and added a few new elements to enhance it. The exposed beams. The creaky floorboards he refused to replace because they had character. The living room couch we definitely broke in the night it arrived. Everything was coming together perfectly.

I'd called it his house once, and he'd gone full offense about it, acting like I'd insulted him.

"It's our home," he had said, dead serious, holding my face in both hands.

I hadn't called it his since.

For the Super Bowl champion party I'd promised him, I

even made sure the invitations read 'Ellie and Sawyer's house'—just to keep him happy.

Leaving San Francisco was bittersweet, but not a single part of me regretted it. Rachel landed a job faster than I expected, probably thanks to the glowing letter I wrote about how she could organize international chaos in heels. She swore she'd visit soon, and we still texted daily.

My parents were off on their long-overdue retirement trip somewhere in Greece, sending me blurry selfies and photos of every meal they ate. Sawyer had asked me what kind of decorations they liked and then went out of his way to put together a guest room with framed photos of me as a kid, a lavender candle my mom used to burn, and the fluffiest pillows on Earth.

It was all so simple and kind. So…him.

Tonight was the first full James family dinner in a while. I'd ditched my security team a few weeks ago, which had been liberating, and left my safety in the capable, broad hands of my six-foot-five boyfriend.

When we stepped inside the ranch house, Gracie was on a step stool at the counter, flour on her nose, while Dorian and Noah supervised the baking as if it were a science experiment.

Dotty and Trent were curled up on the couch, both in sweats, the kind of comfortable love that made you believe in forever. David was in the kitchen, finishing up dinner with a dish towel slung over his shoulder. Colt was already at the table, spinning his glass slowly between his hands.

He looked up and cleared his throat as we walked in. "Hey, so I have an announcement."

Dotty squinted at him from across the room. "Since when do you make announcements?"

Trent leaned forward from the couch. "Yeah, what'd you do? Knock someone up? Get married?"

Colt went pale. His jaw clenched, lips pressing into a tight line.

Dotty's eyes went wide. "Holy shit, you did."

I kept my mouth shut, not revealing anything I knew from the call I got from Lilah last week.

Trent stood. "No way. Who'd you knock up?"

"I didn't knock anyone up," Colt said, rolling his eyes.

The front door creaked open, and Lilah and Caleb walked in, as if it was perfectly normal to waltz into a room moments after that kind of accusation.

Everyone turned at once.

"No fucking way," Dorian said.

Trent pointed between them. "You knocked Lilah up?"

I turned toward Sawyer, whose eyes were glued to Lilah now, jaw slack.

"Mommy, what's knocked up mean?" Caleb asked, looking up at Lilah.

Lilah froze. "Uh—hello, everyone." She glanced around. "Not knocked up. Just…married." She winced.

Caleb looked around and spotted Gracie at the counter. "I want a cookie!"

Sawyer let out a stunned laugh, rubbing the back of his neck. I wasn't sure if it was disbelief or the chaos unfolding at full volume. Probably both.

Dorian peeked out from the kitchen. "We're still baking, buddy. Only a few more minutes."

Lilah stepped farther inside, slipping a hand into Colt's. His grip tightened around hers.

"So," she said, lifting her chin. "Surprise?"

Dotty flopped back on the couch like she needed a second to reboot. "You're married?"

Lilah smiled, small, a little nervous, but sure. "Yeah. We are."

There was a beat of silence.

Then, Noah shouted, "I knew there was something going on!" from the kitchen, and Dorian pulled a bill from his pocket and slipped it to her.

David clapped a hand over his mouth, shaking his head. Noah gave Gracie a high five.

Sawyer shook his head and muttered, "This family, man."

I looked between Colt and Lilah, my chest softening. Something about the way he stood next to her—not just close, but anchored—made me realize this wasn't sudden. Maybe the news was, but not the bond. Not the choice.

He was in love with that woman. I had no doubt.

"You okay?" I whispered, mostly to Lilah.

She met my gaze and nodded. "Yeah, I'm good."

Sawyer moved behind me, his hands landing gently on my shoulders. He leaned down and murmured in my ear, "You think if I announced something this crazy, it'd go over half this smooth?"

"Depends," I whispered. "Wanna knock me up and see?"

He huffed a laugh, kissed the side of my head, then said, "I could make that happen."

I didn't say anything for a second. I just stepped into him, wrapped my arms around his waist, and pressed my face against his chest.

"I love you," I whispered.

Life was different now. Slower, steadier. For the first time in a long time, it was mine.

And I wasn't living it alone.

Epilogue

SAWYER

A few years later…

There was a baby sleeping on Ellie's chest, a guitar sitting next to her, and grass tangled in her hair, and I swear, I'd never loved her more in my life.

She was lying in the yard behind our house, completely at peace. Just her, the sun, and the tiniest human I'd ever seen, snoozing like he owned me.

Which, technically, he did.

I was barefoot on the porch, holding a glass of lemonade I one hundred percent made from scratch. Like, squeezed the lemons, used the juicer, probably made a huge mess in the kitchen that Ellie would pretend not to notice.

"Hey, hot mama," I called, stepping into the yard. "Brought you something citrusy and possibly too sweet."

She glanced over and smiled—and just like that, I was gone for her all over again. "You really commit to the barefoot husband aesthetic, huh?"

"Babe," I said, making my way across the grass, "I was born for this role."

She patted the blanket beside her, and I dropped down.

Our son, Neo, shifted against her chest, and Ellie soothed him without thinking. She was wearing one of my old hoodies, no makeup on, hair twisted into something messy and soft. She looked more like herself than she ever had.

The breeze kicked up a little, and Ellie shifted closer. Neo made a tiny sighing noise, one hand curled into his mom's hoodie, the other tucked against her cheek.

I traced a fingertip along his sock-covered foot. I still couldn't believe he was real. That *this* was real.

"You know, I used to think football would be it," I said. "Like that'd be the biggest thing I'd ever accomplish."

Ellie didn't say anything right away. She just let me talk.

"But it wasn't the game," I said. "It was this. You. Him. All the other babies you let me knock you up with. And all the quiet things no one claps for. This is it."

She turned her face toward me, her eyes warm. "You're way too good a dad—and a DILF at that—to be made only for a sports ball game."

She laughed.

And I didn't argue. Not anymore. I believed her. That belief, that she saw the parts of me no one else had and stayed anyway, was what made everything different.

Because of her.

She hummed, soft and low, the edges of a song she hadn't written down yet. Then, she kissed Neo's head and closed her eyes.

I lay there beside them, hand tucked behind my head, grass under my feet, the sun warm on my face. A husband. A dad. A man who didn't have to earn love to deserve it.

The three of us stayed there a while, tangled up together.

Ellie smiled, eyes still closed.

Because maybe this was the only spotlight she ever needed.

THE END

Acknowledgments

Woodstone Falls was born in the quiet hours of the night, when my house was silent, and my mind was loud. I started writing these stories because I was drowning in a life that no longer felt like mine. Motherhood changed me in all the most beautiful ways, but somewhere in the chaos of sippy cups and sleepless nights, I lost myself completely. These stories helped me find her again.

Now, as I sit here, late at night per usual, I'm preparing to release my third book into the world. My heart isn't just full—it's breaking open with gratitude, terror, and love.

And none of this would exist without the people who refused to let me give up on myself.

To my love—you've watched me ugly-cry over fictional characters at one in the morning and still told me I was brilliant. When I wanted to delete everything and pretend I never had dreams this big, you wouldn't let me. You've carried this dream when I was too exhausted to hold it myself. You are the reason I believe in love stories worth telling.

To Kiarah—you were the first person to fall head-over-heels for Sawyer and Ellie, but more than that, you were the first person to see something in me worth fighting for. Your *yes* comes before I even finish asking the question. You show up for everyone with your whole heart, but the way you've shown up for me is something I'll be forever grateful for. I'm not just counting down the days until I can pay you properly—I'm counting down the days until the world gets to see what I already know: that you're extraordinary.

To Rachel—my fierce protector, my soft-landing place, my reminder of who I am when I forget. You've been in my corner since day one, celebrating every tiny victory like it was your own. Our friendship is the plot twist I never saw coming and the gift I'll never stop treasuring. I don't know what the next five years will bring, but I know I want you by my side for all of it.

To my beta reader McKenzie—you took my raw, vulnerable words and treated them like precious things. Every note, every gentle suggestion has made this book what it is. Your fingerprints are all over this book, and I'm forever grateful.

To Willa—you've held space for every breakdown, every breakthrough, every moment when I couldn't tell the difference between the two. You've let me be petty, dramatic, and utterly human without flinching. The care you brought to my characters, to my story, and to me is something I can't thank you enough for.

To Elle—thank you for taking my messy, grammatically questionable words and polishing them until they sparkled. You helped make my story better while keeping it authentically mine. Thank you.

To the team at Books & Moods—thank you for giving me my favorite cover in the series, which is saying something because you've absolutely nailed every single one. You somehow manage to pull the exact vision from my head and make it even better than I imagined. You create magic every single time, and I'm so grateful to work with you.

And to my readers—God, you beautiful humans. You've made me believe in magic again. Every single message, every post, every time you grab a friend and say *you HAVE to read this*—you're changing my life. On the days when imposter syndrome whispers that I don't belong here, your voices are louder. You love Woodstone Falls the way I do, and that's the greatest gift a writer could ask for.

There's one more story left in Woodstone Falls, and while my heart is already breaking at the thought of saying goodbye to the James Family, I'm going to soak up every precious moment we have left together.

But don't worry. I'll see you all in **Shadow Ridge** in 2026, where new love stories are waiting to wreck us in the most beautiful ways.

Thank you for letting me do what I love. Thank you for making my dreams come true.

With love,

Anna

Anna has been in love with love for as long as she can remember. From getting swept up in rom-coms on screen to devouring love stories on page, she's always found comfort in a happily ever after. In 2024, she decided to chase a new dream: crafting her own love stories. The Woodstone Falls Series is full of swoon-worthy romance with just enough suspense to keep readers on their toes—all set in her beloved home state of Oregon.

Content Warnings

- Death of a Parent
- Descriptive open-door sex scenes
- Violence on Page
- Death of a child referenced
- Kidnapping
- Discussion of a fatal car accident
- Insinuated or suggested domestic violence
- Vulgar language

9 798991 020961